continued . . .

Morning Light

"This is a story not to be missed. *Morning Light* delivers on all levels, and is a fantastic read that will touch readers at the very core of their being."

—The Romance Readers Connection

Sun Kissed

"This smart, wholesome tale should appeal to any fan of traditional romance." —*Publishers Weekly*

"Another heartwarming chapter in the Coulter family saga is on tap in the always wonderful Anderson's newest release. . . . Anderson is at her best when it comes to telling stories that are deeply emotional and heartfelt."

—*Romantic Times* (4½ Stars)

Summer Breeze

"Anderson understands the inner workings of the human soul so deeply that she's able to put intense emotion within a stunning romance in such a way that you'll believe in miracles. Add to this her beautiful writing style, memorable characters, and a timeless story, and you have an unmatched reading adventure." —*Romantic Times* (4½ Stars)

"The kind of book that will snare you so completely, you'll not want to put it down. It engages the intellect and emotions; it'll make you care. It will also make you smile . . . a lot. And that's a guarantee." —Romance Reviews Today

My Sunshine

"With the author's signature nurturing warmth and emotional depth, this beautifully written romance is a richly rewarding experience for any reader." —*Booklist*

Blue Skies

"Readers may need to wipe away tears . . . since few will be able to resist the power of this beautifully emotional, wonderfully romantic love story." —*Booklist*

"A keeper and a very strong contender for best contemporary romance of the year." —Romance Reviews Today

Bright Eyes

"Offbeat family members and genuine familial love give a special lift to this marvelous story. An Anderson book is a guaranteed great read!"
—*Romantic Times* (4½ Stars, Top Pick)

Only by Your Touch

"Ben Longtree is a marvelous hero whose extraordinary gifts bring a unique and special magic to this warmhearted novel. No one can tug your heartstrings better than Catherine Anderson." —*Romantic Times* (4½ Stars, Top Pick)

Always in My Heart

"Emotionally involving, family centered, and relationship oriented, this story is a rewarding read." —*Library Journal*

"[A] superbly written contemporary romance, which features just the kind of emotionally nourishing, comfortably compassionate type of love story this author is known for creating." —*Booklist*

Sweet Nothings

"Pure reading magic." —*Booklist*

Phantom Waltz

"Anderson departs from traditional romantic stereotypes in this poignant contemporary tale of a love that transcends all boundaries . . . romantic through and through."
—*Publishers Weekly*

Catherine Anderson

Here to Stay

A Harrigan Family Novel

A SIGNET BOOK

SIGNET
Published by New American Library, a division of
Penguin Group (USA) Inc., 375 Hudson Street,
New York, New York 10014, USA
Penguin Group (Canada), 90 Eglinton Avenue East, Suite 700, Toronto,
Ontario M4P 2Y3, Canada (a division of Pearson Penguin Canada Inc.)
Penguin Books Ltd., 80 Strand, London WC2R 0RL, England
Penguin Ireland, 25 St. Stephen's Green, Dublin 2,
Ireland (a division of Penguin Books Ltd.)
Penguin Group (Australia), 250 Camberwell Road, Camberwell, Victoria 3124,
Australia (a division of Pearson Australia Group Pty. Ltd.)
Penguin Books India Pvt. Ltd., 11 Community Centre, Panchsheel Park,
New Delhi - 110 017, India
Penguin Group (NZ), 67 Apollo Drive, Rosedale, North Shore 0632,
New Zealand (a division of Pearson New Zealand Ltd.)
Penguin Books (South Africa) (Pty.) Ltd., 24 Sturdee Avenue,
Rosebank, Johannesburg 2196, South Africa

Penguin Books Ltd., Registered Offices:
80 Strand, London WC2R 0RL, England

First published by Signet, an imprint of New American Library,
a division of Penguin Group (USA) Inc.

ISBN 978-1-61129-314-2

To my husband, Sid, who has always been my rock; and to our wonderful sons, Sidney and John; my daughter-in-law, Mary; and my three grandsons, Joshua, Liam, and Jonas, who always make me smile. I also want to thank Kate Allen, who works so hard to keep my writing day uninterrupted so I can be productive, and my assistant, Julia Stapp, for her unflagging enthusiasm and encouragement.

Acknowledgments

Over the course of this book, I had to pick the brains of different individuals to get my facts straight. I greatly appreciated the knowledge that my son John, my husband, Sid, and Ashley Buck shared with me about horses. Special thanks are also due to Mona Ramoni and her beautiful mini guide horse, Cali, for all the inside information about these fabulous little equines who make such a difference in the lives of the sight impaired; Ann Edie, who helped me temper my passion for the guide horse movement with facts so I could present both sides of the issues; Dolores Arste, who shared information about the guide horse training process; and Renata Di Pietro, a trained guide dog handler who sent me so much information, about both guide dogs and horses. I also want to thank John Newman, who guided me through the legal issues involved when individuals are charged with a crime in Oregon, and also explained what kind of evidence is needed at an arraignment hearing to document the abuse or endangerment of animals.

Prologue

Music blared from the barroom stage where the Bushwhackers, Crystal Falls' top country-western band, pounded out rhythms that kept the dance floor packed. The lead singer, a tall dude in Wranglers, a spangled Western shirt, shiny cowboy boots that had never met up with cow shit, and a Stetson studded around the crown with silver conchos, offered a fervent rendition of John Michael Montgomery's dated hit "Be My Baby Tonight." The fast beat throbbed in the air, inspiring couples to pick up the pace as they executed the intricate heel-and-toe steps of a country line dance on the well-waxed plank floor surrounded by small tables.

Zach Harrigan lounged in a far corner of the room, his chair tipped precariously onto its rear legs and his arms folded loosely over his chest as he studied babes with the ease of long practice. Bronco Bart's was his favorite hunting ground, a popular watering hole that normally attracted a lot of gorgeous women. Problem was, tonight they all looked the same—tall, slender bleached blondes in skintight jeans and figure-hugging knit tops that left little to the imagination. As he took measure of their cookie-cutter bodies, Zack wondered whether a terrorist had spiked the Oregon water reservoirs with a virus that made women want big boobs. A large percentage of the females within his line of sight looked as if they'd gone under the knife. Hell, a lot of the women he'd slept with over the past six months—and that was no small number—had paid thousands for breast augmentation. Some had even suffered nerve damage during surgery. What man in his right mind wanted to suckle a numb tit? In Zach's opinion, a guy could have almost as much fun nibbling on an overfilled water balloon.

Feeling oddly irritated, Zach reached for his bottle of beer. Empty. Zach glared at it with dark suspicion. Maybe he was drinking too much, but what the hell. He lifted an arm and signaled the new waitress. She wasn't hard on the eyes, and getting another beer would give him an excuse for a closer inspection.

She nodded, dealt with another customer, and approached Zach's tiny table. "What's for you, mister?"

Noting automatically that while she had magnificent breasts, she was also wearing a wedding ring, Zach placed his order. She gave him a knowing smile, stepped away from the table, and soon reappeared with a fresh bottle.

Zach snatched it up and took a long pull. Condensation beaded on the glass, wet and icy under his fingers. The ale had a brassy edge that puckered his tongue and left his throat feeling as if he'd just swallowed a piece of chalk. *What the hell's wrong with me?* Zach usually loved beer and women. Okay, he always loved beer and women. That was why he was a steady at Bart's, where the taps ran cold and the babes ran hot. He'd come here to pick out a squeeze, cozy her up in a Texas two-step, and sweet-talk her into bed, preferably at her place. Then he'd scat before two so he could catch a little shut-eye before starting a long day of hard work at his ranch before dawn. As a bachelor, that was his modus operandi. It had worked nicely for years. So why did he suddenly feel bored, disgruntled, and at loose ends?

Maybe, he decided with a vague sense of panic, he was getting too old for this shit. The thought no sooner took root in his mind than he shoved it away. *Old, my ass.* He was only thirty-one. He could still work circles around his hired hands, and the women still went for him. Just why they did, Zach wasn't sure, but they did. Always had. He'd studied himself in a mirror many times, trying to figure it out, and all he saw was a carbon copy of his dad, Frank—trim, well-muscled build, skin that had turned permanently dark from too much sun, black hair, brown eyes, and the Harrigan nose, which was more along the order of a beak. *You sure couldn't call either of us handsome*, he decided. Nevertheless, females seemed to be attracted to the package. So he couldn't be over the hill yet. He was just having an off night.

Just then the dance ended, and a blond sexpot left the floor to undulate between the tables toward him. Zach narrowed his eyes on her face. *Wake-up call.* He knew her. He'd slept with her last Saturday night, an experience he didn't care to repeat. A year ago, some bozo had gotten too rough with her during sex and ruptured her right breast implant, leaving her with serious hang-ups about any kind of pressure on her chest. She didn't want to be hugged. She couldn't lie on her stomach. When Zach bumped accidentally against her breast, she went ballistic. He didn't mind being gentle with his partners. It was the way his dad had raised him to be. But to his way of thinking, sex should be spontaneous and fun, not a lesson on the proper handling of saline sacs.

"Hey," he said, knuckling up the brim of his hat, a cowboy's casual gesture of respect when a lady approached. "How's it going?"

Without an invitation, she perched her world-class ass on a chair across from him, flashed a smile of pearly white overlays, and batted her mascara-coated eyelashes. For the life of him, Zach couldn't recall her name. Mary, Sherry, Terry? Something like that. *Shit.* She'd feel insulted, and rightly so, if he couldn't think of her moniker.

"I'm feeling sad," she said. "The best dancer in the

place is sitting on his duff." The eyelashes did another spider dance. Her baby blues locked on his. "I thought you might at least come over to my table and say hi."

Zach forced his lips into a curve that he hoped would pass for a grin. *Terry.* That was her name. "It's crowded in here. A pretty little gal like you gets lost in the maze of bodies. I didn't see you when I came in."

She pursed her lips in a well-practiced pout. "So I don't stand out in a crowd? Thanks. I had no problem spotting you."

Zach took another swallow of beer, making a mental note to switch brands the next time the barmaid made table rounds. Maybe it was just a bad batch, but the stuff tasted nasty. As he set the bottle back down, he studied Terry's face, then dropped his gaze to her deep cleavage, which was seductively exposed by the low scoop of her cherry pink top. *Not interested.* She could hassle some other poor bastard tonight. He wanted no part of it.

"So . . . are you with someone?" she asked. "I'm pretty much free for the evening."

Probably because every man in the bar had slept with her and knew she was about as much fun as a bad case of the clap. "I'm on hiatus tonight. Hurt my back yesterday picking up a foal."

"Oh, no." She flashed her dental work again. "I'm a fabulous masseuse. Come to my place, and I'll make it all better."

Zach shifted on the chair and pretended to wince. "Give me a week, and maybe I'll take you up on that. Not tonight, though. A pretty little thing like you deserves a cowboy who can deliver, and I'm out of commission."

Her eyes darkened, and Zach knew she saw right through him. He hated hurting someone's feelings. He and Terry hadn't really connected on a personal level last weekend. It had been only about sex, two consenting adults scratching each other's itch, only he had come away from the experience feeling unsatisfied. Not her fault. Some guys probably didn't mind the "don't touch" routine, but for Zach, it had been a turnoff.

He was about to flip on the cowboy charm and convince her that he truly was interested in seconds some other night. He always began that routine by asking for a woman's phone number. But just as he opened his mouth to speak, a ruckus erupted on the opposite side of the room. Ever on guard, Zach zeroed in on the commotion. A thin brunette was arguing heatedly with some rhinestone cowboy, waving her hands and yelling. Behind her stood a lanky redheaded man who wore dark glasses and carried a white cane. *Blind?* Zach had never seen a sight-impaired guy in a place like Bart's, but he guessed there was a first time for everything. And, hello, even the disabled had a right to patronize a bar and listen to a local-yokel band.

The woman turned to take the redheaded man's arm. As she tried to guide him forward, the cowboy dude grinned broadly, stuck out his boot, and deliberately tripped the blind fellow, sending him into a staggering sprawl that ended with what had to be a painful faceplant on the planks. Zach rocked forward on his chair, bringing the front legs down so fast they emitted a loud popping sound.

Zach didn't feel himself move, but he could hear Terry calling out from behind him as he pushed his way through the couples who stood frozen on the dance floor. "Don't interfere, Zach! Someone will call the cops. Let them handle it!"

Yeah, right. Even through the maze of bodies, Zach could see the blind guy regain his feet, right his dark glasses on his bloody nose, and try to step forward again, only to be tripped a second time by that stupid excuse for a cowboy.

"Pardon me," Zach said as he squeezed past a woman. "Sorry," he said to her partner.

When he reached the edge of the dance floor, he

grabbed hold of the blind man's arm to help him stand up. "Hey, man. Are you okay?"

The frames of the guy's dark glasses were now broken, and his bottom lip was streaming blood. Zach's own blood went from hot to boiling. His father had taught him never to start a fistfight. The only exception was when a bully was harming another person or an animal. Zach figured deliberately tripping a blind man was an offense that fell into that gray area his father so often talked about. *Sometimes, son, you got no choice but to man up and kick ass.*

Even so, Zach had no desire to get cuffed and stuffed by Crystal Falls' finest, or to spend a sleepless night in the local hoosegow. He turned to the grinning idiot who'd just tripped a blind man for the hell of it. Nudging back the brim of his hat, Zach squarely met the dumb fuck's gaze and said, "Partner, you're either a little too drunk to be in a public place, or your daddy failed to teach you any manners. Which is it?"

Zach never saw the blow coming. The other man's fist landed like a wrecking ball right between his eyes. Everything went star bright and then pitch-black. Zach felt his body going airborne and his muscles turning limp. Someone screamed. And then he landed on his back, his spine striking something flat and hard. The next instant the surface broke under his weight, and he tumbled to the floor in a splintering pile of wood. A table, he determined as his vision spun blurrily back into focus.

Dumb Fuck stood over Zach, smirking as he sucked his bruised knuckles. Somehow Zach doubted the man's hand was hurting as badly as Zach's face was, but the mean-hearted asshole was about to find out he'd made a hell of a mistake by laying into a Harrigan. When Frank Harrigan read about this fracas in the *Crystal Falls Courier*, Zach wanted him to laugh and say, "That's my boy. He kicks ass first and takes names later."

Zach tried to break free of the debris to sit up. As

he did, he saw Dumb Fuck lean forward with one fist knotted to deliver another blow. Zach fell back onto the pile of wood, knifed up with one knee, and planted his foot dead center on the other man's chest. With one hard shove, he sent the bastard into fast reverse, the other man staggering to keep his balance, flailing with his arms, and then sprawling across a table. Zach scrambled to his feet, swiped at his eyes to clear his vision, and then leaped on the guy. The combined weight of two grown men sent the second table into a joint-shattering meltdown.

Zach didn't have a clear thought in his head after that. Vaguely he realized there was a lot of commotion and screaming, and he felt someone grab his arm from behind. He jerked free and let the creep have it again. His mind came clear only when two other men dragged him off his opponent, saying, "That's enough. He's had enough."

Zach shook his arms free and wiped his mouth with his shirtsleeve. Blood came away on the cuff. No matter. Dumb Fuck lay on the floor in a fetal position, holding his middle and whining that his jaw was broken.

"Police! Break it up! Step aside. Police!"

Shit. Hoosegow, here I come. Zach was a little unsteady on his feet and sidestepped to remain standing. A second later, his balance, or lack thereof, didn't matter. His wrists were cuffed behind him, and a cop held him erect by one arm as he was led from the bar to a waiting police car.

"He hit me first!" Zach protested.

"Tell it to your lawyer, buster. You have the right to remain silent. Anything you say—"

"I know my rights," Zach interrupted. "I've heard them a few times."

"We know, Harrigan," the cop said as he cupped a palm over the top of Zach's head and shoved him down into the backseat of the vehicle. Zach squinted hard to focus. This same guy had taken him in a few months back for jumping in to defend a mistreated bull at the rodeo. He seemed like a decent sort for a cop.

"Wait a minute! Where the hell's my Stetson?" Zach yelled.

The slamming of the door was the only answer he got.

Three hours later, Zach, still minus his hat, sat on the edge of a jail cot, knees spread, his aching head compressed between his swollen hands. Dumb Fuck hadn't been brought in yet. He'd been taken to the ER for some stitches before lockup time. Zach had learned minutes ago that the idiot was filing charges against him for assault with intent to kill, or some damned fool thing like that.

Yeah, right. Zach couldn't believe this. He was in the clink, faced with serious charges, and all he'd done was step in to defend some blind guy he didn't even know.

No real worries, though. Zach had used his one phone call to contact his dad. Frank Harrigan had money and connections. He'd have Zach out on bail in a matter of hours. It was the wait between now and then that had Zach's nerves jangling. He was a little claustrophobic, and being locked up gave him the cold sweats. Of course, he wasn't looking forward to another chewing out from his dad on the subject of his nightlife, either.

Man. He couldn't believe this, just couldn't believe it. Only, when Zach rewound the scene at Bart's and replayed it in his mind, he knew he had no regrets and never would, even if he cooled his jets in this hellhole for a week. Sometimes a man couldn't turn a blind eye. For Zach, the abuse of a disabled person was one of those times. Kick a dog, and Zach was there. Beat a horse, and he came running. No man who called himself a man stood aside with his thumb up his ass while some jerk made sport of an animal or person who couldn't fight back.

Maybe, he decided, he'd reacted so angrily because of the article about guide horses that he'd read at the dentist's office last week. The mini horses being trained to guide the sight impaired were amazing, and as a horse trainer, Zach had found the entire feature fascinating. So fascinating that he'd torn the pages from the magazine for future reference, thinking he might try his hand at training a mini himself. The thought had remained with him for a couple of hours, and then he'd forgotten all about it until now. *Typical.* He was so busy with his horse ranch and barhopping that he had little time for anything else.

Staring blearily at the floor, he decided a hangover would have been preferable to the headache he had right now. At least then he would have had some fun earning his misery. The thought made him wince. *Yeah, right, like my life is fun? I'm so sick of this.* What would next Saturday night bring, another woman like Terry? Another boring round of sweaty sex with him hurrying away before the semen dried on his dick?

There has to be something more than this to look forward to.

His father and a couple of his brothers had found love and happiness, but it hadn't happened for Zach yet. Maybe it never would. So where did that leave him? Was he destined to spend the rest of his time on earth working his ass off by day and taking up space on a bar stool at night? The thought made him feel almost as claustrophobic as the cell bars did. *Okay, fine.* Maybe he wasn't cut out to be a family man. Maybe that simply wasn't in God's plan for him. But surely the old man in the sky had something in mind for him to do that would be meaningful, something that would make a difference.

Zach's thoughts circled back to the article he'd read about guide horses, and the blind man he'd fought to defend in the bar tonight. Was God tapping him on the shoulder? *Maybe.* The blind guy's dilemma in the bar could have been God's way of yanking Zach's chain to remind him of that magazine feature.

Zach straightened from a slump. *Tiny horses?* Oh, man, if he decided to train them, he'd have to keep it under wraps. Zach was renowned for his work with world-class cutting horses, not toy equines that slept in the bedroom and accompanied you to the grocery store. His brothers would laugh themselves sick and never let him hear the end of it.

Besides, Zach knew squat about training a service animal. Hell, he didn't know anything about disabled people, period. Even so, Zach had this weird feeling, way deep inside, that he'd been meant to read that article and that the incident tonight had been a reminder to him that there were better ways to spend his time than having less-than-satisfying sexual encounters with women whose names he couldn't remember.

When his dad got here, and after they went through the familiar bailout crap, and after he'd listened to his dad fulminate about his son wasting his life, Zach was going to go home and find that article. He'd careened through young adulthood thinking mostly about himself. Maybe it was time he gave a little something back. He knew horses. And if they could be trained to guide a blind person, he could learn how to do it.

What did he have to lose by giving it a try? *Nothing*. A mini horse would cost him some money, but Zach had plenty in the bank. His biggest investment in an experiment like that would be time, and at the moment, with the inside of his mouth still bleeding from a barroom brawl, keeping busy with something worthwhile seemed like a plus.

An odd feeling welled within Zach's chest. He realized that he felt excited, really excited, and he couldn't remember the last time that had happened. There had to be more to life than sex and beer, and maybe, just *maybe*, he'd found it—something he could do that would make a real difference in the world.

Chapter One

Two Years Later, February 2009

Mandy Pajeck sat by her brother, Luke, on their battered tweed sofa and balled her hands into fists. She had to talk to him again. She'd been stalling for days because she knew, and dreaded, how he'd react. But she had no choice. His future was at stake.

Pulling in a breath, she surveyed his face, biting her lip as she searched his sightless gaze. Right now, he was focused on music blasting through headphones that pushed his chestnut hair into a rooster tail. His backbone slumped against the worn cushions. His long, slender fingers tapped his knees in time with the rhythm.

Sunlight slanted into the living room through the wood-framed windows, illuminating the scars on his handsome face and emphasizing the opacity of his hazel eyes, once so very like her own. At his feet, candy wrappers peppered the burnt-orange carpet. Mandy kept a wastebasket at his end of the couch, but he still tossed the papers on the floor. She didn't know if he found it difficult to locate the basket or if he was just thoughtless. For her, it was a minor irritation, so she'd never taken him to task for it. She'd learned over the years to choose her battles.

"Luke?" When he didn't acknowledge her, she touched his arm. "Can we talk?"

He jumped with a start. Then, brows snapping together, he jerked off the headphones. "Dang it, Mands, give me some warning. You scared the crap out of me."

"I'm sorry. With the music so loud, you couldn't hear me."

"Next time, jiggle the cushion or something to let me know you're there."

"I'll do that," Mandy assured him. "I just didn't think."

Luke nodded, and his scowl melted into a reluctant grin. "No big. My heart has started beating again. So, what's up?"

Mandy moistened her lips. "It's just—we need to talk."

The stony look that settled over his face told her he knew what the topic would be. "We've had a great day so far, and you're not going to change my mind, so just drop it."

Mandy wished she *could*. It would be lovely to float along, pretending all was well, but experience had taught her that giving in to Luke was a mistake and not what was best for him. "Can't we talk like two adults? You're nineteen, not a little boy anymore."

"That's right—nineteen, old enough to make my own decisions. Just let it go."

"Sweeping problems under the rug doesn't make them go away." She kept her tone nonaccusatory. "It's February. You passed the tests and got your high school diploma last June."

"And all I've done since then is take up space. I've got that part of the speech memorized, okay? You can skip the demoralizing details and get right to the point."

Mandy lifted her hands. "You've got no life! *That's* the point. All you do is sit in this house! I love you. How am I supposed to deal with that?"

"The same way I do, by accepting it." His voice rose in anger. "What do you want from me? It's not as if I can go out and get a job!"

Why can't you? she yearned to ask. Luke's counselors said there was no reason her brother couldn't do everything other blind people did. Unfortunately, as a child, Luke had refused to use a cane and resisted rehabilitation, and when Mandy was awarded custody of him seven years ago, he'd insisted on being home-schooled, an option in Oregon that allowed kids to get a high school diploma through the local education service district. Mandy had gotten Luke textbooks on tape that had been supplied by the state, appropriated everything she could find for him in Braille, and had hired tutors she couldn't afford when her workload interfered with Luke's lessons. Luke had excelled academically, but the seclusion had left him socially inept.

Mandy knew her brother's negative attitude and helplessness were mostly her fault. She'd been barely thirteen when their mother had left their dad and abandoned them. Their father should have hired household help to look after his four-year-old son. But although Tobin Pajeck had been wealthy, he'd also been a tight-wad. He'd found a cheap day-care facility near where they lived, and every day after school, it had fallen to Mandy to walk Luke home, care for him, clean the house, prepare a gourmet supper, tidy the kitchen, do laundry and ironing, find time for her homework, and put Luke to bed.

Traumatized by the loss of his mother, Luke had clung to his sister for reassurance, and Mandy, who'd felt lost herself, hadn't discouraged him. Luke's neediness had worsened; it had grown more pronounced at age six, when he lost his sight.

A burning sensation washed over Mandy's eyes as she recalled that time in their lives. She'd tried so hard, ached to make everything right for him, and still she had made every mistake in the book, doing things for him, giving in when he threw tantrums, and never correcting his behavior. For the next two years, what Luke wanted,

he got. Even after Mandy had their father thrown in jail
for beating her up, and she and Luke became wards of
the court, Mandy had run interference for her brother,
trying to placate their foster parents when Luke mis-
behaved, making excuses for him so he wouldn't be
punished, and enduring frequent moves into different
homes without complaint because she'd been afraid
their caseworker might separate them. When Mandy
had been emancipated at age eighteen, she'd been frantic about leaving Luke behind in foster care and had
petitioned for custody. The judge had turned her down
until she turned twenty-one, saying he couldn't give a
girl her age that much responsibility.

For the next three years after Mandy left foster care,
she and Luke had been apart except for weekly visita-
tions. In a perfect world, the lengthy separation would
have forced Luke to become more independent. Instead
he'd thrown tantrums at home and at his special school,
broken things, and had even struck one of his foster
mothers. Only his blindness had saved him from being
transferred into a juvenile correctional facility. By the
time Mandy could finally assume responsibility for her
brother, he'd become nearly impossible to handle.

Mandy would never truly know why she hadn't insisted that Luke straighten up, but she felt pretty certain
guilt played a major part. Luke was blind and she was
responsible, a circumstance he reminded her of whenever she confronted him. She'd slipped right back into
the same old patterns, protecting and spoiling him. If
only she could turn back the clock, but life didn't come
with a rewind button. Why had she given in so easily?
Had she been *that* weak-willed and spineless? Or had it
been more a case of bad judgment? She knew only that
she'd been sorely ill equipped to deal with a needy, disabled teenager, and now both she and her brother were
paying the price.

She pressed a fingertip to her throbbing temple. "I

don't expect you to get a job right now, Luke. You need some kind of training first."

"Here it comes," he muttered. "The college pitch again."

"You need an education."

"Why? I'm happy the way things are." He switched off the CD player. "Besides, what would I study to become? It takes no training to sell pencils on a street corner."

"Don't be ridiculous. Blind people aren't reduced to that unless they choose to be."

"Are you saying I *choose* to be helpless and live in limbo?"

She wasn't touching that observation with a ten-foot pole. "I'm saying you can have a wonderful, productive life if only you put forth some effort. There are people at the college to help you pick a major. They'd give you aptitude tests to see what you're good at. You could find something that you really love to do."

"And how would I make my way around the campus?"

"You were taught how to navigate with the cane. Your failure to use it doesn't mean you're *incapable* of it. It's in the closet. You could start practicing with it here."

"No way! I might fall. I could get hurt again."

Mandy gritted her teeth in frustration. He'd tripped and sprained an ankle years ago, and ever since, he'd wielded the incident like a club whenever the cane was mentioned. Now Luke wouldn't even move from one room to the next without her help, and he refused to go outdoors alone. One sunny day when Mandy had insisted that he walk around the backyard, using the fence to guide himself, he'd tripped over a shrub and banged his head on a rock. For an instant, Mandy had wondered if he'd fallen on purpose, but she'd quickly pushed the suspicion from her mind. Who would injure himself that badly to make a point? The cut on his scalp had required nine stitches.

"If you use the cane properly, it's very unlikely that you'll fall, Luke. If you'd only practice with it every day, you could be running footraces around here in nothing flat."

"Easy for you to say. You're not blind. You forget to push the chairs back under the table. You kick off your shoes and leave them on the floor. Sometimes you don't put the vacuum attachments back in the closet. The whole place is booby-trapped."

"I don't worry about keeping the traffic paths clear because you never move around the house without help!" Mandy cried. "If you start practicing with the cane, I'll make sure there's never anything left out to trip you."

Luke snorted in derision. "Even if I could use a cane inside the house, finding my way around a campus would be a whole different story. Get real, why don't you?"

"I admit that it might be challenging for you the first few days. Maybe I could attend your classes with you for a while. I'm sure I can get special permission to do that."

"And have everybody think I'm a big baby who needs his sister to hold his hand?"

In truth, Luke *was* a big baby—a spoiled, demanding young man who was frozen in place—and, God help her, she didn't know how to help him reverse that.

"Sometimes," she said carefully, "the things we fear turn out to be no big deal once we force ourselves to face them."

"You're really into pontificating today, aren't you? We should rent you a soapbox."

Pinching the bridge of her nose, Mandy counted to ten and then replied, "Any young man who knows the word 'pontificate' has the brains to do something worthwhile with his life. All you need are some solutions. I know you get upset when I bring it up, but maybe a guide dog is the answer. We could get you on a waiting list and—"

"*No!* We've been over this a hundred times. I'm terrified of dogs."

As a child, Luke had been badly bitten by the family Doberman, and a fear of canines had bedeviled him ever since. "Guide dogs aren't your average, run-of-the-mill animal. They're well trained and trustworthy. Why not at least give it a try?"

"End of subject!" He flipped on the CD player, clearly intending to block her out again. "Not one more word." He pushed the headphone cups firmly over his ears. "Get off my back and leave me alone."

Mandy shot up and grabbed the headset, feeling a stab of satisfaction at her brother's startled expression. He flailed for the headset but she jerked it out of reach. Frustration and fear for Luke's future churned inside her, and she spoke louder than she intended. "What if something happens to me? You have no one else. Mama had no family. Dad's in prison. His rich, snobby parents hung up on me the one time I called them for help. Name one other person you can count on besides me!"

Luke parted his lips but then sank back against the cushions without speaking.

"I'm it, Luke! What if I get hit by a bus or die of cancer? Who'll take care of you? Our grandparents don't give a damn about us. You need to get your head on straight and start acting like an adult instead of a spoiled brat!"

"You haven't seen *brat* yet, and you aren't going to die. You're only nine years older than me. Don't be melodramatic, and give me back my headset."

"I'm not finished! Just because I'm only twenty-eight is no guarantee I'll be around forever. It's not just about a job. It's about your being able to do simple things, like make a sandwich! If something happens to me, what will you do, sit here and starve?"

Luke groped for the headset. "Stop it," she grated. "Will you please listen to me?"

"All I hear is white noise." He made a lucky grab and wrested the headphones away from her. "Leave me alone, I said."

Mandy trembled so violently, her legs almost buckled. Luke put the headphones back on and turned up the volume so far that she feared the mirror behind the sofa might crack. "If you don't stop that, you'll end up deaf!" she yelled, but Luke couldn't hear her. His closed eyes, crossed arms, and hunched shoulders signaled total shutout.

Scalding tears pooled in Mandy's eyes. From dawn until well after midnight, she devoted nearly every minute of her day to Luke—helping him shave and dress, cooking, doing laundry, cleaning, and then working long hours as a medical transcriptionist in the tiny bedroom she'd converted into an office. And this was the gratitude she got?

Whirling away, she cut through the dining room to the adjoining kitchen. When she reached the chipped sink, she curled her fingers over the edge of the counter and stared out the window at the huge backyard, which was fenced and perfect for a dog. Her brother was such a blockhead. She hated to see him wasting his life this way.

Her knuckles throbbed from the force of her grip on the Formica, the ache in her temples had shifted behind her eyes, and her chest felt as if it might explode. *Take deep breaths. Don't let him get to you.* It was easier said than done.

Mandy blinked and took in the view of the yard, which always calmed and soothed her. One of her passions was gardening, and seeing the tidy flower beds under a thick crust of snow filled her with a sense of accomplishment. The peony she'd planted last spring was trimmed close to the ground now. She hoped it would snuggle under the icy white and push up fresh green shoots again next summer.

Central Oregon was experiencing a cold snap, the

temperatures so low that the air sparkled. Condensation blurred the window glass. Her gaze shifted to the tiny pots on the windowsill. Hopefully the cold seeping through the pane wouldn't stunt the growth of her starts: marigolds, pansies, baby's breath, pink carnations, and chrysanthemums. She wanted them to be large and ready to bloom by June, when it would be safe to transplant them into the flower beds and patio planters. It was her dream to get a degree in horticulture and one day own a plant nursery, but for now all she could do was pore over gardening books and pretend she was an expert, yet another frustration in her life.

Before long, it would be Valentine's Day. With a fingertip, she drew a heart in the moisture on the glass, wishing the holiday were today. She could make fudge and applesauce bread. The smell of loaves hot from the oven made her feel festive.

My fault. She always came back to that after a quarrel with her brother. It didn't ease her conscience to remember that she'd been a child herself when she'd been raising Luke and only twenty-one when she'd finally gotten custody. Her brother had been her responsibility, and she'd made countless mistakes, end of story. Now he was a mess, and unless she could get through to him, he would remain a mess.

She wouldn't think about it now. She needed to focus instead on salvaging the rest of the evening. She had no applesauce for bread, but chocolate-chip cookies would fill the house with lovely smells. Even better, Luke would be forced to call a truce if he wanted some. Not that he'd give in that easily. Unlike her, he was a brilliant strategist when it came to cold war.

Each evening before dinner, Mandy treated herself to an hour of television, her program of choice the local five-o'clock news. She wouldn't forgo that today because Luke was in a snit. She made a cup of hot chocolate dotted with marshmallows, filled a dessert plate with cookies, and went to the living room. After lowering the blinds, she snuggled under a throw at her end of the couch. Holding the mug close to her chin, she breathed in the sweet scent, enjoying that almost as much as the drink itself. It gave her a wicked satisfaction to bite into one of the cookies when she knew Luke smelled them. Well, he could either politely ask for some or do without.

Grabbing the remote, she turned on the TV. Luke's sulky expression told her he was still pouting. Tough. This was her only downtime, and she would *not* let him ruin it. A talk show was ending, and the drone of voices soothed her. She waited through several commercials for the news to come on. She didn't care that much about what was happening in her hometown of Crystal Falls. It was the ritual she needed. Vegetating for an hour restored her energy before she started dinner.

Sometimes Luke listened to the news, but today he was bent on maintaining the frigid silence. Good. Attending college was important, and the longer he stewed about it, the better her chance of impressing that upon him. As if he read her mind, Luke wadded a candy wrapper and sent it flying with a flick of his finger. Mandy knew he did it to tick her off. Well, for all she cared, he could throw papers as far as the dining room. She'd just vacuum them up in the morning like she always did.

Another wrapper went flying. This one struck the television, which she knew was accidental. Luke couldn't see to take aim. She tapped a toe on the cushion. He was *such* an ingrate sometimes. As if she didn't have enough work to do?

"I have to use the toilet," he informed her.

Luke had perfect timing; she'd give him that. The news was starting. She hit the record button. No matter what, she would enjoy her hour of TV. If he played the interruption game, he'd get a late dinner. She wasn't hungry yet because she'd eaten cookies. Luke, on the other hand, couldn't even heat up a can of soup to tide him over.

Having that thought made Mandy feel terrible. She had no idea what it was like to be blind. It was wrong for her to have so little sympathy. Still, it was absurd that she had to guide him through this small house to the bathroom.

While Luke went inside to do his business, Mandy remained near the closed door, waiting to lead him back to the sofa. Seconds later when Luke emerged, he said, "I think I missed the bowl when I peed."

His faint smirk announced that he'd done it on purpose. *Fine.* She'd have to clean it up, making dinner even later. Saying nothing, she led him back to the living room, got him situated on the couch, and then went to get rags and disinfectant.

It was twenty after five before she could sit down again. Luke scowled, but she ignored him. He put his headphones back on and cranked up the volume until the sound reached her. She responded by turning up the television.

Setting thoughts of Luke aside, Mandy focused on the screen to see a cowboy leading a tiny palomino horse along a sidewalk in downtown Crystal Falls, only a half mile from her house. He didn't seem thrilled to be caught on camera, but when he tipped his black Stetson low over his eyes and quickened his pace, the news team hurried to keep up. The animal wore a harness with a handle that lifted over its back and a looped leash attached just below the chin. Interest piqued, Mandy curled both hands around the now-cold mug and shifted to get more comfortable.

A slender blonde wearing an expensive-looking gray trench coat announced, "This is Zach Harrigan, a renowned local quarter horse trainer."

Mandy recognized the name. The Harrigans were well-known, not only in Crystal Falls but all across the nation, for breeding and training world-class cutting champions.

"Mr. Harrigan has been spotted here on Main with this tiny horse at about the same time each afternoon for nearly a week," the reporter continued. "That sparked our interest, so we did some investigating. To our delight, we've discovered that he has recently embarked upon an incredible journey: training a guide horse for the blind."

Guide horse? Mandy jerked upright. Shooting a glance at her brother, she snatched the remote, thumbed down the volume, and leaned closer to the set.

"Recently is right." The cowboy, clearly annoyed, just kept walking. "Rosebud's in the early training stages, not yet ready to be in the public eye. Why not wait until she's trained to feature her on the news? The future of guide horses is on the line."

The blonde scurried to keep pace. "Can you tell us about the training process?"

Harrigan tugged his hat lower and declined to comment. The reporter stepped in front of him, leaving him no choice but to halt or cannon into her on-camera.

"Please, Mr. Harrigan. Surely you understand what a novelty this is. People have seen you working with Rosebud. We're curious, not here to catch her making a mistake. We merely hope to educate the public about these wonderful horses, the assistance they offer sight-impaired individuals, and the fact that the Department of Justice and the ADA might ban them as service animals." The reporter smiled into the camera. "For viewers who don't know, ADA is an acronym for the Americans with Disabilities Act, and the Department of Justice is the agency that deals with enforcing it."

"You've done your homework," Harrigan observed.

"Yes, and by running this footage, we may inspire the public to begin writing letters in support of guide horses to the ADA and the Department of Justice."

Tension easing from his shoulders, the cowboy turned toward the camera. Though the brim of his hat shadowed the upper planes of his face, Mandy could see that he had jet-black hair, a sun-burnished complexion, a strong jaw, and a firm but mobile mouth. From his broad shoulders down, he was pure cowboy, trim but well muscled, dressed simply in a blue work shirt, faded jeans, and dusty riding boots. He wore no jacket. Maybe, Mandy decided, working outside so much had made him immune to the cold.

He settled a hand on the little horse's head. "Letters of support for mini guide horses would be much appreciated."

"How many blind people have guide horses?" the reporter asked.

"At present, only a few, but those who do are undoubtedly worried about losing them."

The blonde frowned. "What happens to the minis if their owners can't keep them?"

Harrigan shrugged. "It may be difficult to find good homes for them. Minis are cute, and some people might be willing to adopt one, not comprehending the responsibility they'd be assuming. After the new wears off, the animal often ends up being neglected. Visit some mini-horse rescue sites online. You'll find lots of horror stories."

"Do you believe guide horses might be banned?" the woman asked.

"It's possible." Harrigan looked dead into the camera. "Apparently, when horses were added to the list of service animals, there were no training standards or *enforced* size restrictions. Note that I emphasize the word *enforced*. If restrictions are in place, some people ignore them, and nothing is being done to stop that. That jeopardizes the status of true mini horses as service animals and may even call into question the legitimacy of other assistance animals."

The newswoman pressed the mike closer to Harrigan's face. "Examples?"

"I'm not qualified to make judgments on specific incidents. Check them out online." He flashed a crooked grin that warmed Mandy's skin. He had dark brown eyes that could melt ice. "I'm just here to train a tiny horse, not take on Washington, D.C. I do hope the agencies involved don't impose a blanket ruling against all horses because a handful of people have abused the situation. It would be a huge step in the wrong direction, because mini horses—true minis—can be fabulous assistance animals." He patted the mini's head. "My focus is to train Rosebud to be a bulletproof guide animal. I'll leave the controversy to others."

"If others wish to write letters to the appropriate agencies, is there any advice you might give them?" the newswoman pressed.

Harrigan frowned. "Know the facts and be aware of any abuses of the law. Knowledge is power."

The reporter tipped her head in question. "Despite the controversy, have any prospective buyers been in contact with you about Rosebud yet?"

"Quite a few," Harrigan replied. "I've been in touch with two guide horse trainers, and word travels fast. Judging by all the interest, I'm confident Rosebud will have a prospective home long before her training is over."

Mandy tore her eyes from the screen to flash a glance at Luke. He was still absorbed in his music. For once, she was grateful.

"Do you know what the status of guide horses is right now?" the blonde asked.

"For now, the ADA regulations state that any animal trained to mitigate a disability is recognized as a service animal, so horses are still sanctioned to go anywhere people go." The cowboy gestured with a jerk of his hand. "Let's just hope any amendments to the current status are imposed judiciously by fair-minded individuals."

Mandy wriggled to the edge of the cushion to get closer to the screen. The reporter switched the mike from her right hand to her left. "You've taken on a big challenge. How did you prepare yourself to train Rosebud, Mr. Harrigan?"

"I've been training horses most of my life. I also worked for two years with a guide dog trainer to learn what blind people need a service animal to do."

The reporter settled a solemn gaze on the mini. "It appears you're doing a marvelous job. I saw Rosebud lead you around a planter and signal you to step up at a curb. Watching her is fascinating. She seems as accomplished as any guide dog. What else must she learn?"

"Heaps of things." Harrigan's mouth tipped into a halfhearted grin. "A good guide horse has to be prepared to work in any environment—busy city sidewalks, crowded airports, fancy restaurants, transit buses, and so on. She has a long way to go."

"Crystal Falls is a midsize town. Will you take her to a large city for more sidewalk and street training?"

"Yes. To prepare her for that, the present challenge is teaching her how to deal with stairs. She must be able to board a transit bus or climb the portable stairs into a small aircraft parked on the tarmac. Once in a large city, we'll visit museums, courthouses, and other places with a lot of steps. We're working toward that at home. Stairs intimidate her."

"Will you be able to teach her how to do it?"

"We'll get there. She's very smart and catches on pretty fast."

The reporter nodded. "What inspired you to do this? You're already renowned as a quarter horse trainer. A lot of the Crystal Falls tourist trade comes from people who visit your ranch to buy or breed horses. Can you tell us what led you to purchase Rosebud and embark on this journey?"

"I've done well with cutting horses, but there's more

to life than making money. I wanted to do something more, something that would make a real difference. When I found out about guide horses, I knew I wanted to try my hand at training one. It hasn't been easy to reach this point, but I was determined two years ago, and I still am today."

The reporter glanced down at a black notebook in her hand. "With guide dogs already in use, why is it necessary for horses to be trained to perform the same job?"

"Not all blind people are candidates for a guide dog. Some are allergic to canine dander. Others are prohibited because of religious beliefs. Mini horses are a great alternative. A dog has an average life span of twelve years. A horse can live to be thirty and sometimes even forty, which means they can be of service much longer."

"Was it difficult to find Rosebud?" the reporter asked.

"It was. There are several things to look for in a guide horse—size, temperament, intelligence, good conformation, and health. Rosebud was perfect on every count. For a time, she performed in a circus. Then she went on to become a champion many times over in halter performance and other Division A classes. She's accustomed to large crowds and a lot of noise, yet she's only three, with plenty of years ahead of her."

The camera lens widened to show the newswoman grinning broadly as she leaned forward to pet the animal. Harrigan blocked her reach. "I'm sorry," he said, "but no contact is allowed. Rosebud is very affectionate and enjoys the attention of strangers a little too much. When we're working, she needs to stay focused on her job."

"I see." The reporter withdrew her hand. "She's darling!"

Mandy had to agree. With a stocky golden body and fluffy white mane and tail, the mini was one of the cutest creatures she had ever seen. Rosebud's cowboy sidekick wasn't half-bad, either. He had a deep, rich voice and an easy grin. Even on-screen, he exuded strength and had an air about him that commanded respect.

Glad that Luke couldn't hear, Mandy settled in to watch as the news team followed Harrigan to Gliddon's Pharmacy. As man and horse approached the entrance, Harrigan said, "Hold the mike close." Then, to the mini, he said, "Find the door, Rosebud."

The instant Rosebud pressed her nose against the portal, Mandy heard a clicking sound. Harrigan held up a gadget for the camera, then gave the mini a treat from a pouch on his belt. "Good job, Rosebud," he said softly. "Find the doorknob."

Rosebud touched the lever, was clicked and rewarded, and then Harrigan opened the door. Mandy smiled as she watched the man and tiny horse enter the drugstore. Inside, a handful of shoppers did double takes. So did Mr. Gliddon. He came from behind the counter, adjusted his gold-rimmed glasses, and gaped. Any comment he made was drowned out by a cluster of customers.

"I thought it was a dog!" a woman cried.

"I'll be damned—a tiny horse," a man said.

As people pushed forward to pet Rosebud, Harrigan once again went through his spiel about no contact with strangers being allowed. When all the curious onlookers had backed a respectful distance away, he said, "Find the checkout counter, Rosebud."

The horse came to a stop, clearly bewildered. Harrigan unfastened a short wand from his belt. A yellow tennis ball was attached to its end. He held the ball in front of Rosebud's nose and repeated, "Find the checkout counter." When the horse bumped the ball with her nose, he clicked and gave her another treat. Then, repeating the command, he inched the ball forward, leading the mini behind it. When, under careful direction and verbal cuing, the horse finally touched her nose to the edge of the checkout counter, Harrigan once again clicked and rewarded her.

"What's that noise you're making?" someone asked.

"It's made with this." Harrigan again displayed the small device. "It's used in clicker training, affording a handler the ability to give instant reinforcement for a desired behavior. I also give verbal praise, but it's not as immediate. With the clicker, I'm able to reinforce Rosebud at the exact instant I need to. She knows that she found what I wanted her to find. If I had said, 'Good girl,' she could have been focused on something else by the time I got the words out, and that might have confused her. When I ask her to find the checkout counter, I don't want her to lead me to a candy rack."

Rosebud heard the magic words, *find the checkout counter*, and nudged its edge again. A burst of laughter ensued. Harrigan clicked and gave the horse a treat. "A nice thing about the reward system is that Rosebud is an eager participant in her training."

Someone in the crowd asked, "What's that ball on the stick for?"

"This is Rosebud's target," Harrigan explained. "It can be anything, even one's hand. The target is an important training tool. In the early stages, I got Rosebud to touch the ball with her nose. Even if she touched it accidentally, I'd click and give her a treat. She quickly learned that touching the ball got her a goody, and she began nudging it deliberately. When I'm training her to find something new, I can lead her toward it with her target. When she touched the counter, she got clicked and treated. Soon, she'll find the checkout counter without any cues from me."

When Rosebud heard her handler say "find the checkout counter," she nuzzled its edge again, prompting more laughter. Harrigan clicked and gave the mini a treat. "I was a little slow on the uptake that time," he said with a chuckle.

"I think she's got it down already!" someone said.

Zach Harrigan flashed a grin that made Mandy's

stomach feel as if it flipped and fluttered. Determinedly she returned her gaze to Rosebud. "She's not bullet-proof yet," he said. "We'll have to practice again and again before she'll find the checkout counter without fail every single time. To an onlooker, it may appear that she's already trained, but there are dozens of things she hasn't learned yet. She barely has the basics down pat."

Harrigan glanced directly at the camera. Mandy got butterflies again. His brown eyes twinkled with warmth, yet had a sharp, perceptive edge that made her feel as if he were looking directly at her.

Mandy noticed that the little horse had started to prance a bit, her tiny hooves making a *tat-a-tat* sound on the floor. At just that moment, Rosebud lifted her tail. Mandy watched in startled horror as the mini emptied her bowels on the pharmacy floor. The pile looked runny, as if the animal had loose stool, and as the camera zoomed in on it, Mandy could almost imagine the stench. Mr. Gliddon retreated precipitately.

Someone cried, "Oh, my *God*!" The female reporter wrinkled her nose and stepped back. Zach Harrigan glanced down and said, "Oh, shit." At least, Mandy felt fairly certain that was what he said. Over the air, the second word was bleeped out.

Shoppers left the pharmacy rather quickly. Only the news team and proprietor remained. Mr. Gliddon produced a roll of paper towels and a plastic bag. Harrigan apologized profusely as he cleaned up the mess. "This is totally unprecedented. She's completely housebroken and *never* does this. I heard her prancing. That's how she signals when she has to go. But she waits until we find a place that's appropriate."

"I saw a mini online that had a potty bag attached to her halter somehow," the female reporter observed. "Could Rosebud wear something to prevent accidents?"

"She doesn't *have* accidents, and it's called a relieving bag. It's attached to a relieving harness, a belt just behind the working harness. A handler can take the horse to a Dumpster, attach the bag, tell the horse to go, and then the mess is simple for a blind person to clean up."

"Do you think she might be sick?" the reporter asked.

"It's possible." Harrigan's jaw muscle bunched. "She wouldn't do this if something wasn't wrong." He knotted the plastic bag, and Mr. Gliddon disposed of it. Harrigan scratched behind the mini's ears. "This is why I didn't want her on camera yet. Now people may think all minis have accidents in public places, and that is absolutely, unequivocally *not* true."

The newswoman's expression went taut with concern. "I've researched these horses online, and I can back you up on that. They're wonderful little animals."

After the pharmacy debacle, Harrigan and the mini left the establishment and approached a silver SUV. Harrigan opened the rear passenger door and Rosebud loaded into the vehicle without hesitation. After lowering the car windows to give the mini fresh air, the rancher remained on the sidewalk for a few minutes to answer questions. Mandy was disappointed when the news segment ended.

A guide horse. Glancing at Luke, who was still lost in his music, Mandy set aside her chocolate drink and pushed to her feet. Hurrying to the kitchen, she grabbed the phone book. When she located the Hs, she was disappointed to find no Zach Harrigan listed. She had to get in touch with him. Other people had already contacted him, wanting to buy Rosebud. Until a few minutes ago, Mandy hadn't known guide horses existed, but now she believed an animal like that might be the answer for her brother. She couldn't let someone else beat her to the draw. She'd figure out how to pay for Rosebud later. Somehow.

There was no listing in the Yellow Pages for quarter horses. Next she looked under "Horses." She found several boarders, breeders, and trainers, most of their names displayed as subheadings under different ranches or stables. Her finger stopped on the Crooked H. Under the ranch's name in small, bold italics were the words, *Champion Quarter Horses, Training and Behavioral Correction. Zachary Harrigan, Proprietor.*

Mandy jotted down the number and address, then glanced toward the living room. She couldn't handle another argument with Luke today. She'd wait until she got him down for the night before she called to see about getting a sitter to stay with him while she went out for a while this evening. A hesitant smile touched her mouth. Her brother didn't know it yet, but maybe he'd finally gotten his wish. With a little luck, she might never have to discuss the guide dog issue with him again.

Chapter Two

Zach had just opened a rear door of his SUV for Rose-bud to unload when he heard the spitting of gravel and a blast from the distinctive horn of his brother Clint's pickup. He groaned. Zach had been home less than three minutes, and the Harrigan clan was already descending. *Baby brother messes up again. Now he's playing with toy horses on TV. Let's get over there and uphold the family honor.* Terrific. After the disaster in the pharmacy, Zach was worried about Rosebud being sick, and was in no frame of mind to deal with his family.

Clint's tooled boots had barely touched the ground when another pickup, green this time, careened up the gravel access road at a speed better suited to a free-way. When riled, Parker drove like a maniac. Ignoring the racket, Rosebud stood awaiting her next cue. As Zach's brothers approached, the mini pricked her ears and looked across Zach's north pasture, where a rum-bling sound could be heard. That would be Quincy com-ing over on his battered red ATV. For Zach, one of the drawbacks of owning one-sixth of what had once been a twelve-hundred-acre parcel of Harrigan land was liv-ing so close to all of his family. He didn't mind impulse visits—enjoyed them, in fact—but this evening he was tired and concerned about Rosebud, and he just wanted a cold beer.

Loosely holding the mini's halter grip, Zach knew

without question that his brothers had seen the broadcast. And they must have considered it a major screwup for them to tear over here at dinnertime. It was after six. Clint and Parker both had wives who'd be miffed if they were late to the table and the meal grew cold.

Quincy swung off the ATV, his brown eyes sparking as he shot a scathing look at Rosebud. He didn't mince words. "Do you realize you've just made a laughingstock of the whole Harrigan family? A *mini* horse? What the hell are you *thinking*?"

Clint slammed the door of his truck. "Amen. If you're bent on training that damned thing, don't embarrass us by doing it in town, where everybody and his cousin can see you make an ass of yourself. Just how many times has it crapped in public?"

This was going to be worse than Zach had expected. And they did have a legitimate gripe. They were a tight family, and he hadn't said a word about training Rosebud. If he mucked it up, the less said, the better. Needing to succeed and impress his brothers were hang-ups of his, a result of being the youngest and the black sheep of the family. It had probably been a shock to find out the way they had. "She isn't a damned *thing*, Clint. She's a horse."

Parker strode across the grass-pocked dirt, the heels of his boots kicking up puffs of dust. His red shirt was streaked, a black smudge lined his jaw, and when he tugged off his Stetson to slap it against his leg, Zach saw that his pitch-black hair was as dusty as his boots and flecked with hay.

"*That*," Parker spat, jabbing a rigid finger toward Rosebud, "is not a *horse*. It's a dwarf. I can't believe you took it into a drugstore and let it shit on the floor. Our reputations as trainers are on the line, and our livelihoods as well! Do you get that?"

A lot more was at stake than their reputations as horse trainers, namely the public's perception of minis as service animals, but Zach decided that saying as much would be tantamount to tossing a lighted match into a gas can. His shoulders ached from the long day he'd put in, mucking out stalls before daybreak, spending the morning and early afternoon working with his big horses, and then turning his attention to Rosebud. He was in no mood for this. Facing his brothers when they were pissed off was like looking at three mirrors and seeing his own glowering reflection in all of them. The old man's sperm produced Harrigan carbon copies. Even their sister, Sam, looked like Frank, the family patriarch.

"Here's how it goes," Zach said. "You do your thing; I do mine. I may be the kid brother, but I've been shaving for years and I even go to the can by myself. If I want to train a guide horse, I don't need your permission *or* your approval, so get off my case."

"We bear the same last name," Quincy barked. "We've worked our asses off to build sterling reputations. When one of us makes an ass of himself, it reflects on all of us. People were laughing at you. That sorry excuse for an equine crapped on the floor. Some trainer you are, and people are going to be thinking the same about us."

"Hell, the next thing we know," Parker inserted, "he'll be taking the damned thing into the house! It's just not dignified."

"I've already taken her into the house." Zach felt a surge of malicious glee at his brother's horrified expression. "Guide horses need outdoor time just like big horses, but they also need time indoors with their human companions. They learn to fetch toys for exercise. They eat pellets from a dish and Timothy hay from a bin. In the city, some are even trained to go in a litter box. Rosebud is completely housebroken. She hasn't had an accident in over a month. I don't know what happened with her today."

Zach's brothers gaped at him, and then they started

to laugh, not just chuckles, but the wrenching kind of mirth that made strong men go weak at the knees. Clint braced a hand on the fender of Zach's SUV. Parker hooked an arm over his middle, his shoulders shaking so hard his face went red. Quincy threw back his head and roared.

"Housebroken, hell," Parker said with a gasp when he could speak again. "Ask old man Gliddon at the pharmacy if she's housebroken. Does she sleep in bed with you, too?"

"Fetching toys . . ." Quincy swiped at his streaming eyes and aimed a brotherly poke at Zach's arm. "You should train her to fetch you a cold beer, little brother."

When their mirth subsided, Clint settled his hands at his hips. As the oldest, he'd always been the one Zach looked up to the most. Anger smoldered in his dark eyes as he met Zach's gaze. "Can you even start to explain why you decided to do this?"

Zach guessed they hadn't caught the first part of the news footage. But when he started to speak, Clint cut him short. "You've always been the hellion of the family," he ground out, "a daredevil without a serious thought in your head. We've waited patiently for you to finally grow up, and we've pretty much turned a blind eye to the womanizing and barhopping and bad decisions, even when you ended up in the hoosegow. But, damn it, Zach, this time you've gone too far. This tops stupid and goes beyond crazy."

Zach wondered if his brothers weren't right. Maybe he'd lost his mind. But then he glanced down at Rosebud and remembered why he had embarked on this mission. Rage welled within him, burning low in his belly and crawling up his throat. And part of his rage, he knew, was mixed with guilt, because what they said about him was true.

"Point taken," he retorted. "I've been a flake a lot of times. But did it ever occur to any of you that maybe, just maybe, my decision to do this was a turning point for me?"

Obviously, it hadn't. That comment sent Parker and Quincy off into further spasms of mirth. Only Clint, narrowing his eyes, surveyed Zach's taut features as if he were giving serious consideration to what he'd heard. He rubbed the back of his neck.

"Turning point? What the hell? Are you saying you're going to quit training cutting horses and go for these dwarves full-time?"

Zach shook his head. "Do you want to hear what I've got to say, or do you want to stand around and laugh like hyenas and poke fun at something you don't understand?"

His brothers fell quiet, their expressions a mixture of solemnity and bewilderment.

It was Zach's turn to point the finger, and he did so with a sharp thrust at the air. "You're all so damned sanctimonious. You're looking down your noses at me so much of the time, you can't see what's happening right before your eyes. Two years ago, I finally grew up, but none of you noticed. When I was working with the dog trainer every night, where did you think I was, off screwing women or taking up space on a bar stool? Did you ever once bother to *ask* what I was doing every night? Hell, no. You saw my truck coming in late and figured it was just Zach, up to no good again.

"Well, if that's what you thought, you were dead wrong. I haven't had time for women. I've been too busy earning my bread and butter while trying to do something meaningful with my life. Maybe you're satisfied with breeding and training prize horses, raking in the dough, and living high on the hog, but I want to . . . to contribute."

"Contribute? Contribute what?" Quincy blinked. "You sent in a damn big donation to the Justin Cowboy Crisis Fund last year."

Zach shook his head. "That's not what I mean. I've done well with quarter horses. We all have. I've got no quarrel with that. I love breeding and training the best, and I always will. But I want to do *more*—" Zach broke off and gestured with his free hand. "What's so damned wrong with wanting to make someone else's life a little better?"

Zach's brothers said nothing, just stared at him as if they were waiting for his words to start making sense. At least silence meant he'd snagged their attention. He plowed ahead. "Two years. Two frigging years I worked my ass off, learning everything I could so I might do this. Now you want to flip me shit? Well, you can shove it where it'll never again see daylight. The people these guide horses are going to help will never see daylight again. Ever. Think on that. Blindness isn't fussy, and it strikes every day. People are blind, and service animals make things a little easier for them. Go home to your wives and your cushy little lives and your small-mindedness. I have better things to do than argue with you about my choices."

Quincy rubbed a hand over his face and blinked. "I don't have a wife."

Zach shot him a searing look. "That's all you've got to say, Saint Quincy? When was the last time you slept with a woman?" He turned the burn of his gaze on Clint and Parker. "Neither of you is without sin, either. Married now, and doing everything right, but there was a time when you didn't. Maybe I screwed up longer than you, but that sure as hell doesn't give you a free pass through the pearly gates." He tugged on the halter handle. "Come on, Rosebud. The company around here is starting to stink."

As Zach turned to walk away, Clint spoke. "Hold up there a minute, little brother."

Zach glanced back. "Why? So you can chew my ass some more? Forget it. If you want a piece of me, make like a frog and jump on it. Otherwise get off my land."

Clint jerked off his hat, then plopped it back on his dark head. "Give a man a second, all right? I'm trying to figure out how to apologize."

"That'll be the day," Zach sneered. "You never say you're sorry. You damned near choke on the words."

Clint settled a thoughtful gaze on the tiny palomino. Typically of him, he bypassed saying he was sorry. "A horse is a horse. I don't guess size really matters."

Like Clint, Parker had to fiddle with his hat before speaking. It was a trait of the Harrigan brothers, handed down to them by their father. "Clint's right. It's a horse, and maybe we were out of line to get all fired up. It's just . . ." He looked to Quincy for help.

"We were just shocked to see you on the news, especially when everything went wrong like it did," Quincy said. "Okay, so maybe all of us initially thought you were doing something harebrained again. It's not like this would be the first time. And you sure as hell could have given us a heads-up before you took her out in public."

Zach clenched his teeth. An inability to apologize without flubbing it up was another Harrigan trait that he was not happy to share with his brothers.

"Scratch that," Quincy quickly added. "*Harebrained* wasn't a good choice of words. I meant . . ." He shot a look at Clint. "Your turn, big brother. I'm mangling it."

Clint sighed and kicked halfheartedly at a clump of grass. "Like I'm a slick talker?"

Parker took a second stab at it. "We didn't understand. About this being so important to you, I mean. It's not like none of us has ever messed up with a horse in public. Shit like that happens—no pun intended."

"That's right," Clint agreed. "We've all messed up a time or two. What you're doing makes some sense, now that you've explained. Any man worth his salt has moments when he wants to do something more with his life, something that'll really count."

Quincy nodded. "If you can train that"—he broke

off and swallowed hard—"*horse* to assist a blind person, hats off to you. It really might make a huge difference in someone else's life, and that's a commendable intention."

Zach wanted to cling to his anger, but it dissipated as quickly as it had come, and with it went the stiffness in his body. "It wasn't a momentary urge that came over me. The idea took hold and wouldn't turn loose. Do you think I *enjoyed* cleaning up horse shit in front of a camera? Whatever went wrong with Rosebud in that pharmacy threatens the future of *all* guide horses. What if that footage goes to the syndicates?"

All three of his brothers looked horrified at the prospect.

"Sweet Lord," Quincy said, "let's hope not. The whole world will think we're a bunch of crazy fools."

Parker studied Rosebud, his mouth twitching at one corner as he struggled not to smile. "I gotta say, though, she does kind of grow on you. Rosebud, huh? Once the wife sees her, it'll be all over. You know Rainie. She'll fall madly in love, want one for herself, and I won't have it in me to tell her no."

Zach's heart twisted because he was still stuck on the pharmacy incident and how it might affect public opinion of guide horses overall. "Yeah, well, maybe you can adopt one of the minis that may soon be banned as service animals because I fucked up."

"That won't happen," Parker rebutted. "And if it does? We'll donate to a pot and lobby like hell to get the decision reversed."

Clint nodded. "Count me in. She is cute. Loni will probably want one, too." He rolled his eyes. "First thing we know, we'll have midget horses everywhere."

"The proper term is *miniatures*," Zach said. "They aren't dwarves or midgets. They're a recognized and respected equine breed today. Rosebud is a blue-ribbon champion, and she cost me a pretty penny."

Clint shrugged. "Okay, I got it."

"No more wisecracks, then," Zach warned. "She's a horse, just like every other horse on this ranch, except that she's much smaller and a lot smarter."

"Smarter?" Parker scowled. "Smarter than a *cutting horse*? Bullshit."

Zach sighed. Parker was never going to wrap his mind around this idea. "No bullshit, just fact. I've never seen a horse learn as quickly as she does." Zach bent to stroke Rosebud's fluffy forelock. "In another six months, she'll blow your socks off."

"She scarcely comes up to the tops of my socks," muttered Parker. "But hey, okay. I'm on board."

Zach's brothers ventured forward to pet the mini. Quincy glanced up questioningly before he touched her. "Is it okay? I heard you say on TV that contact isn't allowed."

"Only when she's working," Zach replied. "Go ahead."

Quincy hunkered down to get at Rosebud's eye level. After searching the mini's gaze, he muttered, "I'll be damned. She really is a horse, blind spot and all."

Clint laughed. "A horse is a horse." He went down on one knee to run his hands over the palomino's legs, then leaned back to give her body a long study. "She's got beautiful conformation, perfection in miniature."

Rosebud nuzzled Parker's thigh for petting. Parker laughed and scratched behind her ears. The mini angled her head sideways and leaned into his fingers. "Just like any other horse, a hog for affection." He looked at Zach and extended his right hand. "Are we good? Apologies accepted?"

Zach shook with him, and then said, "Oh, to hell with it," and hooked an arm around his brother's shoulders to give him a hug. "Apologies accepted, you hardheaded ass. Just remember, from now on big horses aren't the only game in town."

"Apparently not," Parker conceded. "Just do us a favor and try not to embarrass us again when cameras are pinned on you." As he drew back, he playfully slapped Zach's shoulder. "Has it really been two years since you've been to bed with a woman?"

Zach laughed. He and his brothers were tight, but Zach's encounters with females, no matter how rare in recent months, needed to remain *private*. "Let's just say sex is no longer my mainstay in life."

Quincy and Parker exchanged skeptical eye rolls, and Clint grinned. "If you're going to train a guide horse, don't do a half-assed job of it. Turn it into another coup for the Harrigan clan."

"I will," Zach promised. "At least, I'm going to try. It's no easy task to teach her some of the things she has to learn."

"Like what?" Quincy asked.

"Leading me around overhead obstacles, for one. She's short, so I have to teach her to watch for stuff I may hit my head on."

Quincy shot the little horse a startled look. "Are you shitting me?"

After his brothers left, Zach couldn't wipe the grin off his face as he led Rosebud toward the house. He felt as if he'd just gone through a rite of passage. Until now, he couldn't remember a single time when his brothers had ever looked at him with respect. Maybe, he decided, he should fire up and tell them to shove it more often.

But no. Clint had been nothing less than honest. Until Zach had decided to do this, he truly had acted like a jughead much of the time. Rosebud, or at least the thought of Rosebud, had turned him onto a different path, and over the last two years he'd grown up, setting aside his swinging-bachelor ways to concentrate on something that really mattered. The longer he was away from the whole bar scene, the less he missed it. He still dropped in for an occasional beer, but not often.

It felt good. He might not have a wife and kids, but he had a purpose, something to drive him. He rested his hand on Rosebud's head as they approached the steps, twelve of them, which led up to the deck of his veranda. Zach drew Rosebud to a stop, wondering why in the hell he'd built a house with a daylight basement. Rosebud hadn't gotten the hang of stairs yet, which was undoubtedly his fault. He was screwing up somehow in his teaching methods. Over and over, he'd watched a video of a trainer teaching a mini how to handle risers, but so far, Rosebud, who caught on to everything fast, wasn't getting it. She'd start out fine, and then she developed four left feet.

As Zach began working with her to climb the steps, he asked himself for at least the hundredth time why he didn't build a ramp. The answer was always the same. With a ramp, Rosebud wouldn't master stairs as quickly, and it was an important skill for her to learn. Rosebud drove that point home by planting a hind foot squarely on his toe.

Luke proved to be difficult about dinner. He didn't want hamburgers. He preferred fish. Mandy put the beef back in the fridge and fixed Luke's favorite, an apple jelly and horseradish salmon recipe, which was surprisingly delicious. When she served the meal, Luke sniffed the air. "Is that salmon?" he asked, making a face. "We had salmon last week. How about some variety?"

Mandy slammed her fork down on the table with such force that Luke jumped. "Luke, you're being impossible! What do you *want* from me?"

She regretted the question immediately. Luke's mouth pulled into the thin line she knew from experience meant trouble for her. Her brother hung his head, as many blind people often did. "I want my eyes," he said flatly. "Give me back my eyes."

Mandy's stomach contracted into a football-size knot

of pain. As she removed the plate of food from in front of him, her hands shook so that she nearly dumped the contents in his lap. It was her fault her brother was blind, but must he remind her of it constantly for the rest of her life?

"If not the salmon, what do you want to eat?" she asked tautly.

He sighed and gestured limply with one hand. "I'll just eat the stinking fish."

For a moment, Mandy had the unholy urge to throw the food at him. But when she glanced at his scarred face, her temper flagged. Luke did make her life difficult on a daily basis, but when she looked at it objectively, how much more difficult had she made his?

She set the plate in front of him again. "I'm sorry it's not what you wanted. Normally you love it."

Her brother groped for his fork. "Yeah, well, same old, same old. I'd just like something different every once in a while."

Here was something different: She was about ready to clobber him. Instead she sat across from him and tried to eat her meal. She couldn't look at Luke, so she stared at the beautiful china plate. Her mother had had that pattern, which was still horrendously expensive if purchased brand-new, and had used it when she set a gorgeous table each evening for her perfectionist husband. Mandy had always loved the dishes and regretted that she'd been forced to leave them behind when she and her brother became wards of the court. She'd bought a few pieces of the china over time, at thrift stores and garage sales. Some of it was chipped, but it gave her a sense of family and tradition. She guessed everyone needed that, even if the family in question had been dysfunctional and her memories of childhood were mostly awful.

Though the salmon was moist, it caught in her throat. Luke cleaned his plate. Mandy felt so miserable she ate only a few bites and put the rest under plastic wrap.

"I want to go to bed," Luke informed her as she started to clean up the kitchen.

"Right this instant?"

"Yes, right this instant. I'm tired."

Mandy looked at the skillet and dishes, which would be difficult to scrub if left to sit. *No matter.* If Luke was tired, she had to settle him in for the night. She could deal with the kitchen later. Besides, she'd be able to call in a sitter and leave the house earlier.

It took nearly a half hour to get Luke into bed. He dawdled, dropped things, wasn't satisfied with the first set of pajamas, and then wanted a drink, his way of getting back at her because she'd dared to argue with him. He said his pillowcase stank, so she changed it. She forgot to put his slippers out, and he complained that she never remembered all the things he needed during the night. He wanted ice in his water. His arm itched, so she rubbed cortisone on the spot. The horseradish in the salmon glaze had given him heartburn, and he asked for antacid tablets. Then, to top it off, he didn't want to listen to a recorded book tonight. He wanted Mandy to read to him.

She opened a John Grisham novel to where she'd left off days before and began to read. Luke appeared to be staring at the ceiling. Mandy could only wish. He was completely, totally blind.

"Mands?" he said softly.

Mandy broke off in the middle of a sentence. "Yes?"

"I'm sorry." He gulped. "I shouldn't have pissed on the wall and said all that stuff. I wanted to tick you off and hurt you, and I probably did. I'm sorry."

With quivering hands, Mandy marked her place and closed the book. When they quarreled, Luke never apologized. This was the first time. "I'm sorry, too. I don't mean to harp; really I don't. I just want so much more for you than this."

"I know." His voice went thick. "I want more, too, but a dog isn't the solution."

Mandy thought of Rosebud, but this wasn't the appropriate moment to broach that subject. Luke needed a couple of days to recharge before she started in on him again.

"I know your fear of the dogs is real," she settled for saying, "and maybe it _isn't_ practical of me to think you can simply get over it."

A surprised expression settled on his face. "Has an alien taken my sister's place?"

Mandy laughed softly. "It's me, the harping sister. I've just been thinking, you know? Maybe a dog isn't the only solution. It's worth checking into. Don't you think?"

Luke took a moment to answer, his surprised expression giving way to wariness. "Sure. Maybe you can get me a potbellied pig. I've heard they're as smart as dogs."

A tingling sensation crawled up the nape of Mandy's neck. Had Luke been listening to the news spot about mini horses, and this was his way of poking fun?

"There's a plan," she settled for saying. "Will you be okay if I bring the sitter in for a while tonight after you're asleep?"

"Why? Where are you going?"

Luke didn't like it when Mandy went out to have fun, and she'd long since forgone the privilege, because something dreadful always happened while she was gone. "I'd like to do some research to see what might be available out there by way of an assistance animal for you." That much was true; Mandy would be checking into another kind of assistance animal. To avoid telling an outright lie, she chose her next words carefully. "The library would be a great place to do that. They don't close until nine."

"Can't you do research online?"

"I could, but I think a librarian might be able to steer me in the right direction, saving me time."

Luke seemed to accept that. "No dog," he reminded her, "even if it's toothless and doesn't have a tail."

Mandy reopened the novel and began to read. When her brother drifted off to sleep, she set the book aside. After drawing the covers beneath Luke's chin, she smoothed his hair and quietly left the room. When she reentered the kitchen, her shoulders sagged. *What a mess*. But it would have to wait until later. She stepped over to the small table where she kept the phone and punched in the number of the sitter, hoping against hope that the older woman was free to come over. Mandy breathed a sigh of relief when the lady said she could be there in less than ten minutes.

Mandy tried not to think about Zach Harrigan's possible reaction when she paid him a surprise evening visit. On TV, he had seemed nice. Hopefully he wouldn't get in a grump when he learned why she was knocking at his door. If he did, oh, well. If she settled for calling him, he might hang up on her. In her experience, it was a lot harder to get rid of someone face-to-face, and there was absolutely no way that she was going to let someone else stake a claim to that little horse if she could secure it for her brother.

It took Zach and Rosebud nearly an hour to get in the house, and by then, Zach was exhausted. He suspected the horse was, too. The first thing Zach did was call his brother-in-law, Tucker Coulter, a renowned vet who specialized in equines. He and Samantha lived on an adjoining parcel of land now known as the Sage Creek Ranch.

Tucker listened while Zach explained his concerns about Rosebud's loose bowels. "Most likely, she ate something that disagreed with her," he told Zach. "It happens. For now, just keep an eye on her. If you see blood or a lot of mucus in the stools, it may be something more serious, but until then, I wouldn't worry."

Zach released a breath. "She never has accidents, and she crapped inside the—"

"Inside the pharmacy, I know," Tucker finished for

him. "I caught the newscast. She's definitely got something going on, but at this point, I wouldn't fly into a panic."

"I'm a novice with minis," Zach confessed. "You know? Give me a large horse, and I'm on solid ground, but my experience with tiny horses is zilch."

"She's still an equine. Would you be this upset if a cutter got the squirts?"

Zach felt better after the call ended. Tucker knew his stuff. If he said there was nothing to worry about, there was probably nothing to worry about.

Rosebud stood by the table and hung her head, the stance of any horse at rest. Zach went to the fridge for a longneck. *Nothing like a cold beer to work out the kinks.* He settled on a kitchen chair, done in walnut and flat black to match the table, and took a long pull from the bottle. Then he went to rifle through his Sub-Zero freezer for a man-size dinner entrée. He settled on Salisbury steak with mashed potatoes and gravy. As he shoved the tray into his microwave, he thought of his brother Quincy, the health nut. He was probably having a green smoothie for dinner. The man could pontificate for hours about how Zach was systematically killing himself with all the crap he ate.

Zach liked crap, thank you very much. He'd never have a love affair with kale and spinach whizzed into green froth with nonfat yogurt, raw eggs, sesame seeds, and every other nauseating thing Quincy could think of. Zach wanted meat, and he wanted carbohydrates, and he wanted fat. He was a man, not a rabbit. One of these days Quincy was going to turn green and grow bunny ears.

Zach's microwave had no sooner pinged than Rosebud started to do a tap dance, her signal that she needed to go outside. "Not *now*. Hello, my dinner is ready."

But the horse continued to put Fred Astaire to shame, looking up at him expectantly. Zach kissed his hot dinner good-bye and haltered her up to go back outside. Just as they reached the door, Rosebud lost control of her bowels and deposited a huge dump on the indoor mat Zach used to wipe his boots. The stench almost took his breath. And Rosebud still tapped her feet, telling him there was more to come.

Zach hooked the mat with the heel of his Tony Lama and slid it away from the door so they could go outside without smearing horseshit everywhere. As they gained the porch, he wondered if he shouldn't resort to putting a kiddie-pool litter box in the laundry room. *Frigging stairs.* He was coming to hate the damned things. It was extremely tempting to just pick Rosebud up and carry her, but if he did that, he would be defeating the whole purpose of not having a ramp.

They made it to the yard just in time. She deposited steaming feces to the left of the steps. Despite the looseness of the stool, Zach praised her and offered a treat, which she declined. Rosebud always loved her rewards, and she never had this many bowel movements in one day. *No worries.* She didn't seem sick otherwise, only a little tired, but so was he.

It took Zach forty-five minutes to get her back into the house. For the first time, he considered putting a potty bag on her for the rest of the evening. But that was cheating. Zach didn't want to insult her by using one. Horses were intelligent, and as a trainer, he knew they had a tendency to measure up to your expectations.

By the time Zach got the harness off the horse, he was too tired to reheat his dinner or even bother eating it. After scraping the manure off the mat into an outdoor trash can and doing a dance in the dark with a stiff garden hose, he hung the mat over a porch rail to dry, poured the now-warm beer down the kitchen drain, and tossed the bottle into the recycle bin. Then he opted to crash on the sofa downstairs in case Rosebud needed to make another emergency trip outdoors. He peeled off his shirt, boots, and socks, rested his head on a sofa pillow, and covered himself with the afghan his stepmother, Dee Dee, had made for him. The mini came to stand near the couch. Zach gave her nose a scratch, closed his eyes, and was promptly out like a light.

Mandy stared through an intimidating blackness at the sign beside Zach Harrigan's front gate, illuminated by the headlights of her previously owned Honda Element. NO TRESPASSING. VIOLATORS WILL BE PROSECUTED. Knotting her hands over the steering wheel, she considered her options. She rolled down the driver's window and tried pushing the intercom button, but no one answered. *Darn it.* If she gave up now and settled for calling Mr. Harrigan, he'd probably hang up on her. For Luke's sake, she had to get inside that gate to talk to him, and she needed a prosecution-proof reason for doing so.

Mandy backed her vehicle out onto the road, nosed it over to the shoulder, and cut the engine. After groping under the front seat for a flashlight, she exited the car, hurried to the rear doors, rummaged through her metal box of emergency tools, and then circled back to lift the front hood. Within seconds, she had one of the battery cables disconnected. She put the tools away, wiped her hands on a rag, and closed the rear doors. *Mission accomplished.* Though Mandy hadn't been around her mom for years, Sharyn Pajeck had still managed to impart tidbits of wisdom to her daughter that had stayed with Mandy into adulthood. *No red-blooded male alive from age fifteen to ninety can turn his back on a woman with car trouble.* Mandy wasn't clueless about automobile mechanics. Taking a car to a shop for simple maintenance cost the earth, so she did a lot of stuff herself. But for tonight, it suited her purposes to play dumb.

She used the anemic beam of her little flashlight to see as she picked her way over the rutted ground to the gate. Mentally haranguing herself for wearing pumps instead of flats, she'd just stepped up onto the third rung and was about to throw her leg over the top rail when another vehicle approached. *Caught in the act.* The glare of the headlights nearly blinded her. Mandy watched in startled amazement as a huge diesel pickup stopped only a few feet away and a stocky, vertically challenged man who definitely wasn't Zach Harrigan climbed out. He strode purposely toward her.

"This land is posted," he informed her in a gravelly voice. "You climb over that gate and you're likely to have an up-close-and-personal experience with Smith and Wesson."

Mandy's father had owned a pistol, but otherwise, she'd never been around weapons very much. She had lived in cattle and horse country all her life, though, and knew Smith & Wesson was the largest manufacturer of handguns in the United States. Thinking quickly, she said, "I'm not looking for trouble, only some help. My car died on me." That was the truth—if she failed to mention the deliberately loosened battery cable. Swinging one hand to encompass the dark landscape, she added, "This is the closest house. I was hoping I might use the phone to call Triple A."

"You don't got a cell phone?" He sounded skeptical, and she didn't blame him. Most people had them nowadays.

"No," Mandy replied, and it wasn't a lie. "I can't afford one."

With the headlights outlining him in brightness, the older man resembled a sidekick character in an old black-and-white Western. The battered brim of his hat hung limply from the misshapen crown. His shoulder-length gray hair bushed out from under it like tufts of bedraggled moss. The cropped legs of his jeans skimmed the tops of worn, dusty riding boots.

"Well, hell. I got me a cell phone, but it's low on juice, and the charger is up in my apartment." He rubbed his jaw, squinting at Mandy through the gloom. "Boss won't like it if I let you in, but he'll like it even less if I leave you stranded out here. Gonna get colder than a well digger's ass tonight."

Mandy climbed down off the gate and jumped with a start when the old fellow wrested the flashlight from her hand. He directed the beam at the ground and snorted with disgust. "I'm good with engines, but I won't be able to see under your hood with this sorry excuse." He gestured toward his truck. "Hop in. I'll take you up to the house. The boss has flashlights. Maybe I can have a look at your engine and figure out what's wrong while you warm up over a cup of coffee."

"Oh, *thank you.*" Mandy wanted to do a victory dance. If this picturesque old ruffian was taking her to the boss's home, she stood a good chance of being introduced to Zach Harrigan. And over a cup of coffee, she might have time to convince him to let her have first dibs on Rosebud when her training period ended. "It *is* cold out here, and I didn't wear a heavy jacket because I planned to be mostly in the car." Mandy failed to add that she'd dressed up to impress the man's boss. "I'd freeze if I had to wait for a passerby to stop. There's not much traffic out here."

As she circled the front fender of the gigantic truck, she heard her rescuer mutter, "*Car?* More like a tin can on wheels if you ask me."

Mandy didn't care what the old guy thought about her vehicle. She was far more concerned about how she meant to get inside his truck. There were no running boards, and the floorboard was as high as her hip. After a bit of groping, she found a hand grip, grabbed hold, and, by wedging one foot on the edge of the door opening, was able to swing up onto the passenger seat.

Her chauffeur didn't bother to fasten his seat belt, which made the warning bell chime after the doors were closed. He thumbed a remote attached to his visor to make the gate swing open. "Boss's name is Zach Harrigan," he told her. "He may be gnarly when he first sees you. Some horses was poisoned a while back at his sister's place, so the whole family has gone nuts with security. Don't cotton to folks comin' around without an invite. Once he understands you've got car trouble, he'll mellow out."

After a rough ride over a rutted road, the old man pulled up in front of a huge house. In the fast wash of headlights, Mandy took in the cedar siding, the steep front steps, and the impressive roof angles, which told her one room in that place was probably as large as her entire home. She refused to let that intimidate her. As a kid, she'd experienced opulent living, and she knew for a fact that riches didn't make the man.

When the ignition was turned off, the diesel truck coughed, sputtered, and lurched as its engine died. "My name's Cookie," the old fellow told her. "I'm the foreman on this spread." He pushed open the driver's door. "And you are?"

"Oh!" Mandy was so nervous about her real reason for being there that her manners had abandoned her. "Miranda Pajeck."

"What're you doin' out here in the back of beyond after dark?" he asked.

Mandy hated to fib, but circumstances gave her no wiggle room. "I was visiting a friend and sort of lost my way back to town. Murphy's Law and all that. Naturally that clunker I call a car chose tonight to conk out."

Cookie seemed to turn that explanation over in his mind. Then he nodded. "Well, don't let the boss rattle ya. His growl is worse than his bite."

Chapter Three

Zach awakened to a strange sound, a cross between thumping and knocking. He jerked, started to roll over, and barely avoided toppling off the sofa cushions. *Living room*, he recalled groggily. After rubbing his eyes, he struggled to see through the moon-washed shadows. He could discern dim outlines of the furniture. But what was making that noise? Someone knocking at the door, he realized. He swung to his feet, rapped his shin on the coffee table, cursed, and then stumbled over his boots, which he'd toed off and left by the sofa.

"Son of a bitch!"

Rubbing his shin, Zach didn't bother to don the Tony Lamas or grab his shirt. Nobody could get onto the property unless they were relatives or employees who knew the gate code. Otherwise, the electric eyes inside the fence lines would trigger an alarm that sounded like a cross between an ocean foghorn and a police siren.

Knuckling his sleep-blurred eyes, Zach staggered into the kitchen. His stomach snarled with hunger as he opened the front door and flipped on the porch light. His foreman, Cookie, stood at the other side of the screen, scratching beside his nose.

"What's up?" Zach asked.

Cookie jabbed a thumb over his shoulder. "This here lady has car trouble. I thought you might warm her up with a mug of coffee whilst I borrow a decent flashlight and have a look under her hood."

Zach squinted to see the female who stood behind his foreman. A mop of hair the color of a fresh-curried sorrel was the first thing he saw. Then, as he blinked to clear his vision, he noticed a blur of big, innocent-looking hazel eyes surrounded by delicate, pale features, including a pert nose that sported a spray of freckles. *Red alert.* Unless a female was twelve years of age or under, Zach didn't buy into the innocent look.

"Cookie, it's after eight. And what the hell are you thinking to bring a stranger into the ranch compound after dark? You know the rules."

Cookie gave Zach a deadpan look. "That's right. I know *all* the rules, and one my mama taught me when I was knee high to a jackrabbit is never to leave a lady out on the shoulder of a road after dark to freeze when the heater of her car don't work. That's where I found her, and her car's deader than hell."

Zach stifled a curse. He slapped a palm against the screen, opening the door just enough that it slapped closed when he released pressure. "Okay, okay. Come in, then. I'll put coffee on." As Zach swung away, he realized, belatedly, that he was half-naked. "Excuse me for a minute while I get decent."

Zach muttered obscenities under his breath as he dragged on his boots and shirt. *A stranded motorist?* If not for bad luck, he'd have none at all, and didn't it figure this would happen when he was so exhausted he could have snored standing up? He barked his shin on the damned coffee table again as he returned to the kitchen.

Little Miss Innocent sat at his table, shivering in a quilted brown jacket—one of those useless things with three-quarter-length sleeves and rounded tails that fell well above the waist. What did his sister Sam call them? *Boleros.* Zach had another name for them that he felt was more applicable: *stupid*. When being fashionable meant you'd freeze to death on a winter night, you should select more practical outerwear.

While Zach showed his back to his unwanted female guest to make a pot of coffee, Cookie rummaged through the two deep junk drawers to find a flashlight with a strong beam. Then the foreman excused himself to go have a look at the car. Zach punched the grind button on the machine and then turned to face the interloper, who sat so tensely on her chair she might have been waiting for a firing squad. He thought he caught a guilty look flicker across her face, but he was too tired to think about it right then. He ran a hand over his eyes and stifled a yawn.

"The coffee will take a few," he said. "My name's Zach Harrigan. Normally, I'm a little more gracious to guests, but you caught me sound asleep. Long day, sick horse. I decided to call it an early night just in case she goes south on me before morning."

"A sick horse? Not Rosebud, I hope."

This was Zach's second red alert since meeting this lady, and it topped the innocent look by a mile. He came wide-awake fast. "As a matter of fact, it is Rosebud. And how do you know her name?"

She batted lush, reddish brown lashes, and splotches of pink flagged her cheeks. "I, um . . ." She tugged the rounded edges of the bolero closed and dipped her head. The mane of sorrel hair fell forward in shimmering curtains to hide her face. "I was—"

Before she could finish her explanation, Zach heard the thumping sound again. He'd heard it earlier when he'd been jerked awake, but then it had been interspersed with sharp raps, and his sleep-deprived brain hadn't recognized that the two noises had been coming from different sources. He sprang away from the counter, his heartbeat picking up speed. "Rosebud?" As he raced toward the archway leading to the living room, he followed that utterance with a breathless curse unfit for mixed company.

"What is it?" his guest cried.

Zach heard the tap of her low-heeled pumps trailing him across the kitchen. As he entered the dark living room, the woman's muted footfalls were drowned out by the sporadic whaps of miniature hooves on the thick carpeting. "Rosebud?" Zach called.

Following the sound, he found the tiny palomino behind his recliner. She wasn't merely tapping her hooves. She was stomping them, and then to Zach's alarm, she stretched her body as if to pee and began pawing at her belly with a hind hoof.

Shit. He promptly forgot all about the woman. Zach had been around horses too long not to know what Rosebud's behavior might mean.

Dropping to his knees, he felt her belly. *Hard as a rock.* Pressing an ear to her barrel, he listened for gut activity. To his surprise, he heard some rumbling. He took her pulse. *Way too fast.* He turned on the floor lamp to peel back her lips and check her gums, praying he'd see healthy pink. Instead, he saw grayish white.

Shit! He shifted on his knees to look at the lady. City shoes and ridiculous jacket aside, he needed her to step up to the plate, and he didn't waste time on politeness.

"I've got to call the vet," he bit out. He jabbed a forefinger at the carpet. "You, right *here*! Keep an arm under her belly. If she starts to go down, hold her up. Got it? And for God's sake, no matter what, don't let her start to roll."

Zach half expected her to retreat, but instead she dropped to her knees beside Rosebud, curled an arm under the little horse's belly, and said, "I've got her. *Go!*"

Lunging upward, Zach raced to the kitchen, slapped on the lights, and shot out a hand for the cell phone he usually left on the table. His fingers closed on air. Spitting out a word that would have made his sister blink, he grabbed the landline portable instead and speed-dialed Sam's house. Tucker answered, his voice scratchy with sleep. As a vet, he kept hours as crazy as Zach's and often went to bed with the chickens.

"Tucker, it's Zach. Get over here! I think Rosebud may have colic."

"ASAP." A vet accustomed to middle-of-the-night emergencies, Tucker suddenly sounded wide-awake. "Be there in five."

Zach tossed the phone and hurried back to the living room, furious that he hadn't realized sooner that something was seriously wrong. He'd known the loose, frequent bowel movements were out of the ordinary, but he hadn't thought for a second of colic. Normally horses' bowels became inactive with colic. *Oh, God.* Colic was one of the leading causes of equine death. *Not Rosebud, please, not Rosebud.*

Zach sank to his knees beside his horse and visitor. Dimly he registered that Miss Bolero was not only doing exactly as he'd instructed, but she was also stroking Rosebud's tummy, as if she understood the pain the mini was in. That earned her a couple of points, even if she had popped up at his ranch for what he suspected were self-serving reasons. Zach shoved her hands aside to palpate the mini's belly, which still felt hard. Judging by the way Rosebud looked at her flank, she was in agony.

An awful thought struck Zach. Tucker would assume Zach would meet him in the arena. He surged to his feet and ran to the kitchen, sliding to a stop when he saw headlights slant across the walls and heard a truck door slam. His brother-in-law had made record time driving over from Sam's place. Tucker hurried in, his dark hair tousled, his rangy body clad in jeans and a ratty leather jacket. A flash of bare chest and a crookedly buttoned shirt offered mute evidence that he had dressed in a hurry. "Where is she?"

"Living room. I was afraid you'd go to the stables."

"News travels fast in this family. I'm aware that Rosebud is an indoor horse." He tossed his bags onto the table. "Move her in here on the slate in case it gets messy."

Zach went to collect his charge, his stomach twisting with anxiety as he gathered her in his arms. Barely aware of the woman who trailed behind him to the kitchen, he realized that he'd fallen in love with this little horse. As Zach set her on the slate floor, Tucker went to work, taking Rosebud's temperature and pulse, then feeling her belly.

"Symptoms?" he barked at Zach.

"Stomping her feet, stretching like she needs to pee, and kicking at her stomach, all classic signs. I could hear intestinal noises, though. With colic, I usually can't."

"Anything else?" Tucker pressed a stethoscope to the mini's side.

"Frequent bowel movements, all loose, more like cow patties than horseshit."

Tucker sat back on a boot heel and arched a brow. "That's unusual with colic."

"I know." Zach raked a hand through his hair and dimly realized that his unwanted guest stood beside him, her pretty, delicately sculpted face taut with concern. "But I think it's colic, Tucker. She's got belly pain. I'm sure of that."

Tucker ran a hand along the mini's neck. "Well, hell." He frowned in thought. Then he shot a sharp glance at Zach. "You still got the shit?"

"The what?" Zach realized he was getting the mother of all headaches.

"The shit," Tucker repeated. "I want a look at it."

"I scraped some of it off the doormat into the outside trash can. Are you kidding?"

"No. Go get it." Tucker pushed to his feet. "Do you have a bucket?"

"Mop bucket, in the laundry room."

Tucker was already heading that way. Zach turned to tell the woman to keep Rosebud on her feet. *Unnecessary*. His guest picked up on things fast, and her concerned expression as she stroked the mini's belly told him he needn't worry about Rosebud rolling while he was gone. Despite her pain, the mini was nosing the woman for comfort, and her ears twitched in response to the soft words of reassurance.

Zach rushed outside. Fishing through trash with a flashlight to retrieve runny manure wasn't a plum assignment, but he finally got a sizable amount scooped into a gallon-size freezer bag. Leave it to Tucker not to specify how much he needed.

When Zach reentered the house, he found Tucker at the sink, filling the mop bucket with water. The woman still knelt beside Rosebud, holding her up with the brace of an arm under her belly and talking softly, as if calming horses in physical distress came naturally to her. As Tucker swung the oversize container to the floor, he motioned Zach forward and jabbed a thumb at the Baggie of shit. "Dump it in," he instructed.

Zach looked at him quizzically. "Do what?"

Tucker grinned. "We're gonna make some horseshit soup, bro. Dump it in."

Zach did as he was told, wondering if Tucker's brain was still half-asleep. He *really* questioned his brother-in-law's sanity when Tucker grabbed a wooden spoon from a caddy near the stove and started stirring the concoction. Rubbing his temple, Zach made a mental note to throw the spoon away later. He glanced at his stranded visitor, expecting her to look a little green. Instead she seemed to be focused on Rosebud, speaking softly and stroking the mini with gentle hands. Rosebud's eyes were nearly closed, and she leaned against the woman as though she couldn't get close enough.

Pretty lady, Zach noted distractedly. Normally he went for blondes, but this gal's hair, glimmering red in the light, was a beautiful color. She didn't appear to be wearing cosmetics, either. *Not possible.* No woman could look that good without makeup.

When the poop and water were mixed, Tucker returned to Rosebud's side, elbowing the woman out of his way. As he soothed the mini with capable hands, he said, "Zach, I don't make house calls for free, and I smell coffee brewing. Get the whiskey. It'll be a while before the soup settles, and I could use some Irish coffee." He opened a bag and pulled out a syringe and bottle of Banamine. After giving the mini an injection, Tucker caressed her with gentle hands. "There you go, girl. That'll ease you up soon."

Zach stepped into the downstairs bathroom to wash and disinfect his hands. Then he collected three mugs from a cupboard. "Call me a dumb cluck, Tucker, but why, exactly, are we making horseshit soup?"

"To see what settles at the bottom." When Zach set a bottle of Jack Daniel's on the table, Tucker poured himself some whiskey. He waved the bottle at the woman, who shook her head hastily and grew even paler. Zach wondered why as he sloshed some coffee into all three cups, then fetched some creamer, sugar, and one spoon.

After mixing his Irish coffee, Tucker settled back on the chair and crossed his feet. "How long you had Rosebud, Zach?"

Zach detached the rein from Rosebud's harness, looped it over the mini's neck, and began walking her around the kitchen. Walking a horse sometimes helped with colic. The woman left the table and went to stand with her hip resting against the countertop. "I finished working with the dog trainer a little over two months ago and then started looking for a mini. It took me three weeks or so to come across Rosebud. I'd say I bought her six weeks ago, give or take."

"You toss her hay on the ground instead of putting it in a feeder or on a mat?"

"Never." Zach turned. "I'm careful my horses don't ingest a lot of dirt. We don't have much sand in our soil, but I'm—" Zach broke off and shot a worried glance at Rosebud. "You think she's got sand colic?"

"Long shot. As you say, our soil isn't that sandy." Tucker took a sip of spiked coffee. "I agree with you, though. Way she's acting, could be colic. Frequent, loose stools aren't symptoms. One exception is when there's sand in the intestines."

"I've never had a horse get sand colic. How serious is it?"

"Like all colic, it can be deadly."

"Oh, no," the woman whispered.

Tucker smiled slightly. "On a bright note, though, it's often easily treatable."

"I'm sure she hasn't eaten any dirt. Not on my watch, anyway." Zach changed directions again. "She loves grass, but I make sure it's thick and tall, not patchy."

"Sand can build up in the intestines over time. If her other owner tossed her hay on the ground, she may have ingested sand, and it could just now be causing her trouble." Tucker checked his watch. "We'll give it an hour and see what settles in the bucket. If we find a lot of sand, we'll go from long shot to probable, and I'll treat her accordingly."

Rosebud flopped down and started to roll. The woman leaped forward, and Zach's heart twisted with fear even as Tucker came to his feet so fast he spilled his drink. "Get her up! *Get her up!*"

Zach didn't have to be told twice. He grabbed the struggling Rosebud and forced her back to her feet. When a colicky horse rolled, the guts could twist in a millisecond, and intestinal death would be swift. Many horses died from that complication, even with immediate surgery.

"Hold her there," Tucker said.

The woman came to kneel near Zach, her slender

hands catching Rosebud under the chin and bracing her head. Zach was so worried about his horse that he no longer cared why the gal was there, only that she seemed to have a way with animals. Rosebud responded to her touch with chuffs and grunts, as if trying to convey in horse-speak that the pain in her tummy was horrible.

Tucker snatched a towel and dabbed at his soaked thigh. "Even if it is sand colic, I think we've caught it in time. If the preliminary treatments don't work and she goes south, I'll open her up and remove the impaction. That can be risky. If the quantity of sand in the gut is large, it can weaken the walls and make them more prone to tearing. But surgery is my specialty. I won't lose her unless something goes horribly wrong. Just make sure to keep her on her feet."

"You don't have to tell me that! This isn't the first time I've dealt with colic." Zach immediately regretted his sharp tone. "Sorry. I don't mean to snap."

"I'm keeping in mind you're plenty upset right now."

Zach released a shaky breath. He loved all his horses, but with Rosebud, he was beyond upset. Maybe it was because of her size, but he felt more protective of her. "What are the preliminary treatments for sand colic?"

Tucker checked his watch. "Let's see what we find before we get in too deep."

Zach took an unhappy sniff of the odor arising from the bucket. The house would smell for days, but it was too cold outside to open a window. Still, it was worth it if they saved Rosebud. For him, the minutes that followed were the longest of his life. Rosebud, relaxed by the Banamine, stopped trying to roll, but even with the medication to ease her pain, Zach could tell she still didn't feel well. He also knew how quickly a horse with colic could die. Sometimes there was absolutely nothing a vet could do.

The woman rose to her feet and started to pace, her stiff, agitated movements mirroring the gigantic knot of anxiety in Zach's stomach. At some point, she introduced herself, but Zach was so distracted that he promptly forgot her last name. *Miranda.* She didn't look like a Miranda. Big name, little gal. The two didn't fit.

Cookie returned to the house, briefly informed the woman that he'd fixed her car, and then demanded to know why Tucker's truck had shot past him at about sixty miles an hour. Zach didn't have to explain after Cookie clapped eyes on Rosebud. Once assured they were doing everything they could, the old foreman turned to the woman and told her that one of her battery cables had been shaken loose. Out in ranch country, where roads were often unpaved and rough, that wasn't uncommon. What Zach did find unusual was that the woman didn't offer to leave when she learned that her vehicle was running again. Instead she hovered near Rosebud, kneeling beside her when there was room, speaking softly in a tone that the mini seemed to understand.

Zach wondered about her motives, but not her concern. It was obviously genuine. He'd gotten several phone calls from people who wanted to purchase Rosebud, but nobody had yet had the brass to show up on his doorstep. Had this lady staged the car trouble to gain access to the ranch proper and make an offer for Rosebud in person?

At any other time, the possibility might have upset Zach. He detested subterfuge and liars. But he was too worried about his horse right then to focus on it. What mattered to him was that she'd pitched in without hesitation, and it was obvious that Rosebud had accepted her. Horses had good instincts about people.

Cookie helped himself to a mug of coffee, splashed in a generous amount of whiskey, and took a seat at the table. Judging by the worried expression on the foreman's craggy face, he'd become as fond of Rosebud as Zach was.

At last, Tucker carried the bucket out to the porch

and poured off most of the water. When he reentered the kitchen, he tipped the container toward the light. "Sand. Not much, only about a half teaspoon. Normally I'm not alarmed unless I see a tablespoon. But she's tiny, so I'm guessing this is a lot for her."

Zach crouched beside his horse. Rosebud pressed her forehead against his arm. Zach swallowed hard. "Now what?"

"I'll start by administering psyllium via a nasogastric tube. You got any psyllium?"

"Out in the stables." Zach patted Rosebud's shoulder. "I'll go get it."

Minutes later, Tucker gave Rosebud psyllium mixed with water. He chose a nasal tube normally used with newborn foals. Rosebud accepted the treatment like a grand little lady, not resisting when Tucker fed the tube into her nose. Her resigned behavior brought a sting of tears to Zach's eyes. It broke his heart to think she might die.

"She's little, man. Don't give her too much."

Tucker nodded. "I've reduced the amount according to her size."

"What'll it do?" Zach asked. "The psyllium, I mean?"

"The idea is to get a lot of digestible fiber into her gut to aid in motility and water retention. Psyllium forms soft stools that move along the intestinal walls. Our aim is to get rid of the loose stools, form solid ones, and get lots of water into her. You ever built castles on the beach? Wet sand breaks apart. To shape a castle you need damp sand, because it packs and forms shapes. Right now, she has perfect castle-building sand in her gut. It packs down like concrete. We want to get it really wet and keep adequate amounts of psyllium moving through so she can pass it. Lots of water, lots of psyllium."

Zach released a shaky breath. "She's not big on water. I give her fresh water several times a day, but she doesn't drink that often."

"Try room-temperature water," Tucker advised. "Some horses don't like it real cold." He arched an eyebrow at Zach. "You got any Gatorade in the house?"

"Yeah, I've got some."

"You got any strawberry flavor?"

While Zach stepped to a cupboard to check, Miranda picked up Rosebud's drinking bucket and, without being asked, filled it with warmer water. "Yeah, I've got several bottles," Zach said over his shoulder.

Tucker inclined his head at the bucket the woman set on the floor. "Thanks, uh . . ."

"Miranda."

"Miranda. Right. Zach, lace that with a whole bottle of strawberry. What do you want to bet she goes for it like I do Jack Daniel's?"

Zach produced a laugh, but it took effort. He'd never forget this night. His hands shook as he mixed Rosebud's spiked water. He doubted she'd drink the stuff, not with a bellyache. But when the psyllium had been administered and Zach nudged the bucket in front of the mini, she started sucking water as if she'd just crossed the Mojave.

"I'll be damned."

"She *loves* it," Miranda chimed in.

"I ain't never seen the like," Cookie said.

Tucker chuckled. "Stock up on strawberry Gatorade." He patted Rosebud's back. "She sure is cute, Zach. Don't let Sam meet her. I'll end up with a horse in the house."

Zach wanted to turn loose of his fear and pretend everything would be okay, but over the years, he'd lost two horses to colic, and he had never forgotten the agony of it, not only for his horses, but for himself as well. "You think she'll live to meet Sam?"

Tucker began repacking his medical bags. "Truth?"

Zach swallowed hard. "Of course, truth. You've always told it to me straight."

"This little lady is special to you. Maybe the truth is a bit harsh right now."

"Give it to me." Zach's voice twanged in his ears like a taut fiddle string.

"Colic is a bastard. Her symptoms seem fairly mild to me, but if that sand forms an impaction, she could turn in a New York minute." Tucker snapped the bag closed. "Watch her like a hawk. Continue to dose her with Banamine to keep her comfortable."

Zach's brain froze. "How much do I give her?"

"Get a grip. You've dosed dozens of big horses. Figure out her weight and do the math." Tucker studied Zach's face. "Okay, okay, I'll write down the amount. Keep offering her water laced with Gatorade." He glanced at his watch. "Every four to five hours, give her more psyllium." Tucker jotted down the instructions and handed Zach the paper. "If she turns south, call me. We'll take her in, and I'll open her up."

Zach's stomach lurched. He stared at Rosebud's fluffy forelock. The first time he'd clapped eyes on her, that mass of flyaway hair had struck him as being the silliest thing he'd ever seen on a horse. Now he thought it was beautiful, and the thought of shoveling dirt on top of it as it disappeared forever made him feel as if he might puke.

"Cookie, can you spell Zach during the night?" Tucker asked.

"Darn right," the foreman said. "If he calls, I'll be back over here in two shakes."

Zach sighed. "Cookie will have his hands full overseeing the hired hands tomorrow. I'll just pull an all-nighter. If Rosebud isn't better by morning, I'll have someone come over from the stable to watch her while I grab some sleep."

"If Rosebud isn't better by morning, she'll be at my clinic," Tucker stated.

Zach nodded. He thrust out his hand. "Thanks for coming so fast, Tucker."

"That's my job," Tucker replied as they clasped and shook, "and the only thanks necessary is the check you'll soon be signing to cover my fees."

Zach managed a shaky laugh. "Don't gouge me, you mercenary son of a bitch."

"Ah, well," Tucker said as he ambled toward the door, "I reckon since you're my wife's brother, I can give you a ten-percent discount. I'm less than three minutes away. I'll sleep with my pants on. If she gets worse, call me."

"You don't need to worry about that. I'll be on the horn in two seconds flat."

With a gruff good-night, Cookie followed Tucker out. When the door closed, Zach dropped onto a chair, feeling like a bag of cement mix that had just been tossed from the back of a truck. He gazed at Rosebud, now standing comfortably with one hip dropped. She sure seemed to feel a lot better than he did. She'd stopped pawing and kicking at her belly. She stood guard over her water bucket as if fearful someone might drain it while she rested. Strawberry Gatorade. *Who would have thunk it?*

Belatedly Zach realized that Miranda was still in his kitchen. She stood well away from the table, arms crossed at her waist, the rounded front panels of the bolero draping over her wrists. "I'm so sorry she's sick," she offered in a tremulous voice. "I'll keep her in my prayers tonight."

Zach fixed a blurry gaze on her delicately sculpted face. "You jerked that battery cable loose on purpose." He didn't pose it as a question, but he was too weary to lace the words with accusation. "You're hoping to buy Rosebud, aren't you?"

Zach half expected her to lie. In his experience, most people wouldn't hesitate. Instead her pointy chin came up. Her gaze never left his as she replied, "Lousy timing. I saw on TV that she had loose bowels, but I had no idea she was this sick."

Zach gestured limply for her to continue. She shook her head slightly. "It'll wait. I just—" She caught her lower lip between her teeth, drawing his attention to her mouth, which had "kiss me" written all over it. "You see, Mr. Harrigan, my brother was blinded at six years of age. Now he's nineteen and should be starting college, but he isn't a take-charge individual, and he worries about finding his way around the campus. There's just the two of us. Our mom took off when I was thirteen, and our dad—well, he's otherwise occupied at present. Rosebud would change Luke's life. During the newscast, you said that other people have been trying to buy her, and I—"

"Hoped to get first crack?" Zach finished for her.

She nodded and shrugged. "Like I said, lousy timing." Her lips curved in a self-deprecating smile. "I don't have much money. I thought maybe you'd agree to let me make payments." She drew one arm from around her waist to push at her glorious mane of hair. "Now that I'm here, it seems stupid—and inexcusably presumptuous." She bent to stroke Rosebud's mane. As she straightened, she added, "Forgive the intrusion. Next time, I'll behave like a normal person and telephone. I had a confrontation with Luke today about guide dogs, and when I saw you and Rosebud on TV it seemed like the answer to a prayer. You see, he was attacked by a Doberman when he was very young, and he's terrified of dogs as a result."

Brain fuzzy with exhaustion, Zach settled a worried gaze on his horse. "Right now, I'm not even sure Rosebud will live, and if she does, she'll still be a long way from being a trained guide horse. But *if* she lives and *if* I can get her up to speed, how much money I make won't matter a whit to me. I just want a good home for her."

"She's such a sweet little thing," Miranda said softly. "If she were mine, I'd feel exactly the same way."

She'd lied to gain access to the property, but for reasons beyond Zach, that strengthened her case in his eyes, telling him she desperately wanted Rosebud for her brother. Someone who would go to those lengths to acquire a horse would probably go the extra mile to give it a wonderful home. Despite her poorly executed attempt at subterfuge, he decided to say what was on his mind.

"If the wrong person offers a fortune for Rosebud, I'll turn him down. If the right person comes along, I'll let her go for free. Is your brother the right person?"

Miranda's eyes went round. "Are you serious? You'd give her away?"

Zach nodded. "It's not about the money. I make plenty on my big horses." After letting that hang there for a moment, he added, "You obviously found me in the phone book. Call tomorrow to see if she makes it through the night. If she does, we'll talk. Don't take that to mean it'll be anywhere close to a done deal. Rosebud hasn't finished her training yet, and I'll have to meet your brother to judge his suitability. Before I'll allow that horse to end up in a bad situation, I'll keep her, simple fact."

She splayed a slender hand over the center of her chest, her eyes filled with such incredulity that Zach felt oddly uncomfortable. "Thank you so *much*, Mr. Harrigan. I will call. You can count on it."

"If I turn on the yard lights, can you make it safely back to your car? I can't leave Rosebud. She might start to roll. About all I can do is lend you a flashlight."

"I'll be fine. Stay with her. It's not that far to the gate."

Despite her objection, Zach rummaged in the junk drawer for a flashlight. She accepted the torch and smiled at him. "Thank you. This will be a big help."

Zach was too tired to muster up a reciprocal smile. He escorted her to the door, flipped on the yard lights, and then stared blearily at her through the screen. "At the gate, you'll see a post on the driver's side. Push the button, and the gate will open."

"Good night, Mr. Harrigan."

As she switched on the light and went down the steps, he almost told her to call him Zach, but he didn't have the energy. "G'night," was all he managed to push out.

He watched the bob of the flashlight long after she was absorbed by darkness. *Pretty*, he thought again, and unless she was a consummate actress, that innocence in her eyes was real. *Hello?* She looked to be in her late twenties. How could a beautiful woman that age still be sexually inexperienced? Maybe his judgment was slipping.

It was a question for another day. Zach returned to the table and poured himself some whiskey. Rosebud had her pain reliever; he had his. As the liquor burned a path down his throat, Zach thought of Miranda again. She'd looked so over the moon about her brother possibly getting Rosebud for free. Zach could only pray he wouldn't have to give her bad news when she telephoned tomorrow.

After paying the sitter, cleaning up the kitchen, and working on the computer for two hours, Mandy was exhausted but also so excited she couldn't sleep. She'd gotten on her knees earlier, crossed herself, and offered up prayers for Rosebud's deliverance. It had felt strange to pray after so many years of not going to Mass. But it had also felt good, driving home to her how much she missed practicing her faith. She'd quit going to church because her father was a cradle Catholic, and she'd been determined to be nothing like him. Dumb, she realized now. Why abandon her faith because her father was such a maniacal jerk?

Now Mandy lay snuggled under her comforter, grinning like an imbecile at the crack of moonlight that leaked into the bedroom under the pull-down shade. Zach Harrigan had seen straight through her ploy to gain access to his ranch, but he hadn't been angry. Even better, he'd implied that he might be willing to give Luke the horse for free. She couldn't believe it. Nobody gave stuff away anymore. But if Harrigan made the offer again, she'd jump at it. Just sending Luke to college and paying for his special expenses would drain her savings and mortgage her future earnings.

Mandy shivered. *Oh, God.* Would she ever forget the sight of Zach Harrigan in nothing but jeans? He had skin the color of polished teak. *All that muscle.* In a shirt, he looked trim and nicely toned. Without a shirt, he could make any woman's heart skitter and miss beats. Normally Mandy didn't feel attracted to men, but there was no denying the impact that Zach had had on her senses. She wasn't comfortable with that and decided what she'd probably found most appealing about him was his complete and absolute devotion to Rosebud. His looks were just frosting on the cake.

It would be hard for anyone to resist a strong, work-hardened man whose heart shone in his eyes when he looked at a sick little horse. He *loved* Rosebud. To him, it truly wasn't about making money. He'd clearly meant what he said during the news interview: that he'd set out to train a guide horse because he wanted to make a difference in someone else's life. And what if that fortunate *someone* was Luke? It boggled Mandy's mind.

She dragged in a calming breath, determined to keep a level head on her shoulders. Her attraction to him was nuts. Men were treacherous. If anyone knew that from bitter experience, she did. It made no sense for her to feel so captivated by Zach Harrigan, and she was nothing if not sensible. Even so, untangling her emotions was like trying to straighten a skein of knitting yarn after a kitten had batted it into a hundred knots. *Too handsome for words, caring, and gentle.* And more important, he hadn't touched the whiskey on the table. Mandy detested spirits of any kind and trusted no man who drank the stuff. Zach Harrigan hadn't, and even she would have given him a pass tonight. A tiny horse he loved deeply was possibly at death's door. Mandy had wished for a tranquilizer. Only for her, warm milk was the nerve-numbing agent of choice.

Okay, okay, time to stop thinking about it and get to sleep. Luke would be yelling loud enough to wake snakes in five counties at six sharp in the morning. Time for rest now, no matter how exciting the evening had been.

She forced herself to go still. Why had counting sheep never worked for her? Instead she conjured up little palominos and sexy cowboys as she drifted off to dreamland, smiling happily, halfway convinced that Santa Claus truly did exist, after all.

Sometime later, she jerked awake. *A noise?* Mandy had been on her own for so long that she seldom got night terrors, but her sleep-fogged brain was being assailed by them now. She jerked upright in bed, heart slamming as she strained to listen. *Oh, God.* She heard a muffled thump come from the kitchen. Luke never got up without yelling for her to come help him, not even to go to the bathroom.

An intruder was in the house.

Chapter Four

Mandy inched out of bed. *Please, God, don't let the box spring squeak, and don't let Luke wake up.* Bypassing slippers, she forced her sleep-dazed brain to focus. She needed a weapon. She'd read about women confronting assailants with hair spray, but that was beyond dumb. Besides, there was only one bathroom, and in order to reach it, she'd have to pass through the kitchen, which was where the intruder seemed to be.

Icy sweat made her shiver. Clubbing someone with a nightstand drawer sounded less than optimal. She'd been at the receiving end of a man's strength too many times to overestimate her own. She needed something smaller, but heavy, with a good handhold. Something that, combined with the element of surprise, would quickly disable a burglar before he had a chance to turn on her. She grabbed her bedside lamp, jerked the plug from the socket, and wrapped the cord around her wrist. If worse came to worst, the intruder wouldn't be able to wrest the weapon easily away from her.

Making sure to avoid the squeaky spot on the scarred wooden floor, Mandy crept to her door, which opened onto the kitchen. She'd need to take him unawares. She grasped the brass knob, held her breath to give it a turn, and eased the door open.

A man. He was silhouetted in front of her window, tall, broad-shouldered. *Memories.* Oh, how she wanted to ease the door closed and lock it. Nothing she owned was worth much. Why risk her life? Maybe she could call the police. They'd arrive in five minutes. In the meantime, she could hide in the closet. She was an expert at hiding. She had perfected the art when her father was on his drunken rampages.

Only—*oh, God*—Luke's bedroom was even closer to the kitchen sink than hers. What if he heard the noise and got up? He might startle the burglar. He'd be totally helpless. Mandy had been protecting him all his life. She wasn't about to leave him at the mercy of a possible killer just because her legs felt as if they'd turned to water.

She drew the door farther open and raised the lamp above her head. When she was two feet from the intruder, he made a choking sound and whirled around. Only moonlight illuminated the room, but, as terrified as Mandy was, there was no mistaking that profile.

"Luke?"

The choking sound came again. Her brother hunched over the sink. Mandy ran for the light switch. Luke had one hand clamped at his waist while the other gripped the counter. His face was crimson with faint splashes of chartreuse around his lips. He sucked for air, and again she heard the clogged sound.

Choking. Mandy tried to drop the lamp and couldn't. So she raced to the sink with the cord still encircling her wrist, the lamp clunking on the linoleum behind her.

"Luke? For heaven's sake, what on *earth*?"

She whacked her brother on the back. He coughed and gagged. Mandy stared in incredulous shock as he puked up a half-chewed mass she identified as chocolate-chip cookie. The raspy sounds as he fought for air scared her.

Suddenly her brother caught his breath. "Sorry," he managed. He gulped and gagged again. "You . . . startled me . . . choked . . ."

Mandy gave his back another whack, resisting an ill-advised urge to bring the base of the lamp down on his head. Murderous thoughts slipped into her mind. Luke couldn't go anywhere in the house by himself, but he'd managed to find the cookies? She gulped back expletives, untangled her wrist from the cord, and settled her hands on her hips. "What *is* this? You're up in the middle of the night, stuffing your face with *cookies*?"

Luke gagged again. Mandy cranked on the cold water to wash away the evidence of his treachery. When he could speak, he said, "They smelled so good, and you didn't give me any, so I came out to find them. Sorry, Mands. I didn't mean to wake you up."

I'll kill him. The thought sprang unbidden into her mind. Mandy booted it out, aware that her legs trembled. No intruder to take on, only her blind brother, who'd suddenly developed an amazing sense of smell, not to mention an incredible ability to find his way around the kitchen. She sank onto a chair and stared at him in disbelief. He wasn't anywhere close to being as helpless as he pretended to be. On some level, she'd suspected this, but she'd always shoved the thoughts away because she didn't want to believe her brother was using his disability to make her kowtow to him. Now she could no longer kid herself. He used his blindness as a weapon. Against her. He'd been doing it for years. The realization bewildered her as much as it angered her.

She checked her watch. Three o'clock. Luke insisted on rising at six. Fresh surges of rage welled within her, but now wasn't the time to address this problem. She should wait until she was wide-awake and her heart wasn't stampeding. Willing the tension from her muscles, she glared at her brother's back. He still hung his head over the sink. She no longer feared that he might choke to death.

She dredged up as neutral a tone as she could. "Well, have you had enough cookies now to satisfy your craving?"

His hanging head bobbed up and down. In a hoarse voice, he said, "Plenty."

Mandy pushed up from the chair. She hadn't known until now that outrage could make a person icy calm. "Well, then, I think we should both go back to bed."

She grabbed the lamp and turned to leave the kitchen. Hearing her retreating footsteps, Luke swung erect. "Well, come on. Aren't you going to take me to my room?"

"Don't even go there with me," she snapped. "You managed to find the cookies. I'm sure you can find your bed."

Mandy stepped into her bedroom and slammed the door shut with more force than she intended. Silence from the kitchen.

She sank onto the edge of her mattress as realization overwhelmed her. Luke was navigating the house without her assistance. Even worse, she had put the cookies in a plastic container, and he'd still located them. Given the fact that she kept a lot of stuff in airtight plastic, Luke had to be familiar with the contents of the cupboards to identify a new addition to the clutter. How many times had he made kitchen raids? Thinking back, Mandy could recall a few times when she'd thought food might be missing, but she'd never paid close enough attention to be certain.

Helpless? It was all an act, Luke's way of trying to control her. A young man who could locate a bin of cookies should have no difficulty finding the wastebasket at the end of the sofa. He tossed the wrappers on the floor *deliberately*. If he could find cookies, he could find the bathroom. This helpless business was a fraud.

Thirteen years after the accident, Luke was still making her pay.

She lay on her bed. She heard Luke making a racket in the kitchen. Well, she would *not* race out there. He'd just been found out and was trying to bring her back to heel. Let him stew.

"Mandy, I fell. I'm on the floor and don't know where I am."

Oh, right. "You know exactly where you are. Now get up and go back to bed."

"I *need* you. You aren't going to leave me out here, are you?"

Mandy wasn't going to fall for it, not this time. "Maybe if I put a cookie on your pillow, you could smell your way back to bed."

"Mands, you're just being mean. I'm cold. Don't feel good. Please come get me."

And so it went until four in the morning, when Mandy's eyelids grated against her eyeballs like sandpaper. The voices of Luke's counselors bounced around in her brain. *Don't enable him.* But, damn them, they weren't here. For nearly an hour, her brother had been lying out there, on the linoleum, on a chill February night. What was she supposed to do, cram wax plugs into her ears and drift blissfully off to sleep?

"Mands?"

Hearing the tremor in his voice, Mandy sat up. *Okay, I'm an enabler. So hang me.* Her teeth clamped down on her lower lip. She'd tried so hard to encourage Luke to be self-sufficient, and he'd always played the guilt card. Despite that, she couldn't leave him lying on the cold floor. Maybe when she met her Maker, she'd be condemned for going out there to help him. But what if he really had become disoriented, and she ignored his plight? Only a heartless person could do that.

She returned to the kitchen. Luke lay on the linoleum, shivering convulsively. She knelt beside him, curled her arms around his shoulders. He was crying, and even though visions of him gobbling cookies still filled her head, she felt sorry for him.

"Luke, I'm here. I'll help you back to bed."

"Why'd you leave me so long? I'm so cold I'm shuddering."

Even though Mandy believed that Luke could find his way back to bed alone and that his tears were of the crocodile variety, he truly was shivering. Guilt settled over her like thick fog. She strained to help him gain his feet. And then, together, they went to his room. As Mandy helped him into bed, she accepted on some level that they would probably live like this for the rest of their lives, Luke deliberately helpless, she his faithful caregiver, bound to him by chains that were no less real for being invisible.

At seven a.m., Zach was still slumped on a kitchen chair, staring with reddened, aching eyes at his horse. She'd stirred during the night, mostly to move her legs a bit before going back to sleep. Now she tapped her hooves, not energetically, but with listless sidesteps. She looked expectantly at him. This morning, he said to hell with the stairs and picked her up to carry her outside. She dumped a huge load, the size of which amazed even Zach, who was accustomed to big horse droppings.

He scooped a measure of the dung into a bag. Tucker would want to know how much sand settled in the bucket. Zach didn't relish the thought of stirring manure water, but a guy had to do what a guy had to do.

Cookie called at seven thirty on Zach's cell. "Well, son, how's our little girl doin'?"

"I think she's a bit better," Zach replied. "Not kicking at her belly or staring at her flanks. But she still isn't back to normal. I'm taking the day off to keep an eye on her."

Cookie huffed into the phone. "Well, friggin' hell! If you think she might still go down, maybe you should call Tucker and take her to the clinic. We don't want to lose that pretty little lady. She's a sweetheart."

Zach passed a hand over his eyes. "I'll ask Tucker what he thinks."

"Keep me posted," Cookie said gruffly. "If you need help, just holler."

"Thanks, Cookie. I appreciate the offer."

Zach disconnected and settled a bewildered gaze on Rosebud as she proceeded to drain what remained in her water bucket. More strawberry Gatorade, coming up. After refilling her pail, he gave her a dose of Banamine and fed a tube into her nostril to administer more psyllium mixed with water. As he worked, he envisioned sand flooded with enough water to break it apart and prayed Tucker's remedies would work.

By noon, Rosebud's appetite was picking up. When Tucker called to check in, Zach couldn't keep a note of exhilaration out of his voice. "I think she's better, drinking tons of water and passing sand. The psyllium seems to be moving it out of there."

"Good, good. What's her temp?"

"Normal," Zach replied. "Her heart rate is still a little fast, but nothing alarming now, and her gums look better."

"Belly?"

"It feels softer to me. She's not tensed up from the pain like she was."

Tucker laughed. "Congratulations. You're going to pull her out of it."

"I hope so." Zach's sincerity alarmed him. He'd come to love the horse far more than was wise. When training ended, she would become someone's service animal, and Zach would never see her again. "I'll keep a close eye on her."

"Good man." The sound of a honking horn came over the airwaves, and Tucker mumbled expletives under his breath. "People are driving like maniacs."

"Full moon. You out making farm calls?"

"I am. You can reach me on my cell if anything goes wrong."

After the call, Zach carried Rosebud outdoors. Winter sunlight pooled like melted butter on the frosted grass, and the breeze carried scents of pine and hay to Zach's nostrils. Walking beside the mini, he drew in deep breaths, savoring each smell, which had become part of the fabric of his life. He couldn't imagine living where exhaust fumes overrode nature's fragrances. Even the odor of horse dung appealed to him.

Rosebud's movement was firm, but Zach still collected it for analysis, hoping he'd find more sand. An hour later, he'd just drained off the water and was grinning over the substantial amount of grit he'd found in the bottom of the bucket when his landline phone rang. He grabbed the portable, hit the talk button, and said, "The Crooked H, Zach Harrigan speaking." His main line was essentially for business, the number listed in the phone book for the public. Only family, friends, and business associates with whom he was already interacting had his cell phone number. "How can I help you?"

"Hi, Mr. Harrigan," a woman said. "This is Miranda Pajeck, the lady with the fake car trouble last night."

Zach had already recognized her soft, lilting voice. *Pajeck?* Somehow that rang a bell, connected with something vaguely unpleasant, but he couldn't think why. When he'd heard her surname last night, it had gone in one ear and out the other.

"I waited to call as long as I could stand it. How's Rosebud doing today?"

The concern in her voice tipped Zach's lips into a grin. Maybe he was nuts, but something about this lady spoke to him, and it sure as hell wasn't only her looks. He'd bedded some gorgeous women. None of them had ever made him feel this way. Just the sound of her voice over the phone got to him. Almost as much as the gentleness in her tone last night when she soothed Rosebud.

He glanced down at the mini. "She's eating and accepting her treats. Not eagerly, mind you, but she seems to be on the mend, and Tucker thinks she's out of the woods."

Zach heard her breath catch. Then she whispered, "Oh, thank you, *God*." Then she laughed shakily. "I was so afraid you'd tell me she was dead. I know zip about horses and even less about colic, but it sounded extremely dangerous."

"It definitely can be." Zach settled his hand on Rosebud's head, threading his fingertips through her forelock. "But Tucker thinks we caught it in time. She's probably going to make it. Keep your fingers crossed."

"I think I'll just continue to say Hail Marys," she replied. "I've found that to be more effective than finger crossing."

She was a Catholic? He couldn't remember seeing her at St. Catherine's, the only Catholic church in Crystal Falls. "Well, I'm glad you've been saying Hail Marys. I'm so sleep deprived I caught myself saying the meal blessing instead."

She laughed lightly, the sound almost musical. "Uh-oh, you must be on autopilot. That's okay. I'm sure God understands how exhausted you are."

Zach grinned, then turned his mind to their conversation last night. "If she makes it, and it appears that she will, maybe your brother will end up with her as his guide horse."

"Oh, I hope so." A long silence ensued. Then he heard her sigh. "I just hope Luke behaves himself when you first meet him."

Zach frowned slightly. "Do you have a reason to think he might not?"

"When it comes to getting an assistance animal, Luke is . . . well, *resistant*, I guess is the word. To be fair, we were talking about a dog when he got his back up, and he has good reason for fearing dogs. I can only pray that he'll feel different about a horse."

"He'll have no reason to be afraid of Rosebud," Zach replied, "so you're probably worrying about nothing."

"Would you object to a meeting? A casual, no-

pressure kind of thing? I'd love for Luke to meet Rosebud to see how he reacts to her and how she reacts to
him. I think Rosebud is the perfect answer for him, but
he has to be on board. You know?"

Did he ever. There was no way his mini was going to
end up with anyone who wasn't enthusiastic about getting her. "I see no harm in letting the two of them meet."

"I'd be happy to drive out to your ranch. Name the
day and a time that's good for you, and Luke and I will
be there."

Zach was thinking about a few months down the
road. Rosebud still had so much to learn. Conditioning
the mini to large cities would take time, and that wasn't
to mention all the different modes of transportation that
the horse hadn't yet experienced.

"How does next Wednesday sound to you?" she
asked.

Zach's first thought was that next Wednesday was
too soon, but then he envisioned Miranda's lovely face,
that glorious hair, and those huge hazel eyes. Wednesday wasn't soon enough. Okay, maybe he was thinking with his hormones, but he heard himself say, "Sure,
next Wednesday works. Just please bear in mind that
Rosebud is still in the early stages of training. It will
be months, possibly as much as a year, before she'll be
ready for placement."

"I understand. Luke is only nineteen. If he has to wait
a year for college, it won't put him that far behind. And
in a way, the time lag may be a good thing. It'll give him
and Rosebud a chance to become friends long before
anything is finalized."

Zach liked the thought of Rosebud going to someone
she already knew and loved. He didn't want the move
to be traumatic for her. "I'm tied up with my quarter
horses until midafternoon. How does three o'clock next
Wednesday sound?"

"Three sounds fabulous!" Her voice rang with pleasure and excitement. "We'll be there with bells on our toes. Unless, of course, Rosebud isn't completely well by then. You've got my number on your phone now. If she's still a bit peaked, just give me a call, and we can plan it for another time."

Just then, Rosebud nuzzled the treat pouch on Zach's belt with an eagerness that lifted his spirits. "I think she'll be feeling great by next Wednesday. See you then?"

"Absolutely. I'm so excited for Luke to meet her!"

After ending the call, Zach put down the phone and offered Rosebud a treat pellet. She gobbled it down and nudged him for more. He chuckled. She was definitely on the mend. He started to enter his appointment with Miranda and her brother into his BlackBerry, but before he could punch a button, Cookie's signature ring pealed.

When Zach answered, Cookie gave him no opportunity to speak. "Get your ass over here," he yelled, almost blasting out Zach's eardrums. "Tornado's throwin' another fit! He broke through his stall gate and has Mike penned in the tack room!"

Tornado was a stallion Zach had purchased recently for breeding purposes, a decision both he and his employees had regretted ever since. "I'm on my way."

Zach raced for the stable. Rosebud would be okay for a little while, and she'd be safer at the house. When that big sorrel stud went ballistic, it was best to stay clear unless you had to intervene, and that was Zach's responsibility. If anyone was going to get hurt, it was going to be him.

Over the next few days, Zach issued frequent stern reminders to himself: Rosebud was not a permanent resident. He was training her to be a service animal. She would leave the ranch when her training was finished. But the lectures did no good. As soon as she'd recovered from the colic, she was ready to work again, so eager to please him that Zach found her almost irresistible.

Each morning when he led her to her stall and exercise paddock in the stable, she walked at his side like a well-trained dog. It was only when he started to leave her to work with his other horses that she exhibited anything close to bad behavior, whinnying, nickering, and neighing as he walked away. She didn't want Zach to leave her. The feeling was mutual.

Zach fell into the habit of carrying Rosebud's treat pouch, target wand, and clicker with him in order to sneak moments with the palomino throughout the day. His heart always lifted when Rosebud ran to the gate to greet him, shoving her nose through the slats and nickering with delight. No matter what he asked of her, she responded. Sometimes it was nothing more than asking her to touch her target. Other times he'd think of something else—dropping an object on the floor of her stall and asking her to pick it up, or stepping inside the enclosure and encroaching on her space so he could ask her to give him room. She responded beautifully every time, picking up on new tasks so fast that he was amazed. Either he was a fantastic guide horse trainer or Rosebud was an equine genius.

At half past two on Wednesday afternoon, Zach was working with Rosebud on the overhead obstacle course when his father, Frank, suddenly spoke from behind him. Zach nearly whacked his head on an overhang as he spun around, startled.

"So this is the infamous mini horse."

"Dad! Hey, nice surprise. I didn't expect to see you today."

Except for silver at his temples and lines on his sunburnished face, the family patriarch was a dead ringer for his sons, sporting a lean but muscular build, jet-black hair, and dark eyes. Tugging on the brim of his brown Stetson to shade his face from the sun, Frank grinned, flashing a dimple in his cheek that had long since become a deep crease, compliments of too many hours of exposure to the elements.

"I just moseyed over to meet the half-pint celebrity." His eyes warmed with amusement as he perused Rosebud's stocky body. "I hear she's sharp as a tack."

Zach settled a hand on Rosebud's head. "Sharper," he said proudly. "I've never seen a horse learn as fast as she does."

Frank folded his arms, took a step back, and cocked a hip. "Show me her stuff."

Zach tugged on his ear, a habit of his when he grew tense. "Right now, we're not doing anything too exciting, just some overhead obstacle work."

Frank gestured with a hand for Zach to proceed. Zach had a course mapped out that led around outbuildings with eaves that sloped low enough to strike a person on the head. He urged Rosebud forward. As she led him around the first corner of a shed, she pressed her body against Zach's leg to make him swing wide of a support beam.

"Well, butter my ass and call me a biscuit." Frank whistled softly. "She steered you around that slicker than greased owl shit."

"She's doing great, isn't she?" At just that moment, Rosebud came upon a crisscross of pipes left on the grass earlier in the day. Performing as she'd been trained, she pawed the steel and then angled her stout body in front of Zack's knees, refusing to let him step forward. *Click.* Zach gave the mini a treat.

"Good *girl.*" Using the leash attached to the halter under the mini's chin, Zach purposely signaled her to circle left. Even he was surprised when Rosebud did the unprecedented, cutting in front of him to walk at his right to keep her body between him and the pile of pipes. *Click.* Zach couldn't keep the edge of excitement out of his voice. "Do you see this, Dad? She's supposed to stay to my left. She's making an executive decision to break that rule to keep me from tripping over the debris."

Frank chuckled. "Boy, howdy, she really is quite somethin', ain't she? Looks to me like she's damned near trained."

"Not even close," Zach replied. "She still has countless tasks to master before she'll be bulletproof in any environment. I'll have to take her where she can learn how to guide on crowded sidewalks and in heavy traffic, how to board transit buses and airplanes, even from the tarmac. I doubt she's ever seen a train or been in a taxi. Hell, I even need to slick up and start taking her to fancy restaurants."

"Sounds like you'll be doing some traveling before this is over."

"Quite a lot," Zach agreed as he worked with the horse. "Mostly just weekend trips. When she's ready, we'll have to spend at least a week down in Los Angeles, and I'll probably take her to Portland several times. Even if she's placed with someone who lives in a smaller town, she may have to work in large cities if her new owner travels."

"What's that noise you make?" Frank asked. "Sounds like a frustrated bullfrog."

Zach explained about clicker training. "I guess you missed the newscast?"

Frank nodded. "That evenin' I was kicked back in my new recliner, checkin' my eyelids for pinholes. I learned about the disgrace to our family secondhand."

Zach signaled Rosebud to stop, braced for the worst, and turned to face his father. "And it's taken you this long to come over to read me the riot act?"

The breeze kicked up, tugging Frank's blue chambray shirt against his chest. For a man of sixty-three, soon to be sixty-four, he had well-padded pecs and shoulders, a result of hard physical labor, which continued even now that he had retired. A horseman never stopped being a horseman. Frank ran a calloused hand over his jaw.

"Well, now, put like that, I reckon I'm about to disappoint you. I'm not here to scold. I think what you're tryin' to do is a fine thing. So does Dee Dee."

Dee Dee had been the Harrigan family housekeeper for aeons, a position she'd finally relinquished to become Frank's wife. "Seriously? You both approve?" Zach asked.

"Hell, yes. You're takin' your God-given gift with horses and tryin' to do somethin' spectacular with it." Frank met his son's gaze. "Maybe you think I haven't noticed that you've backed off on the drinkin' and carousin'?"

"The thought did cross my mind. Nobody else in the family seemed to notice."

"I'm not everybody else. I'm your old man. I pay closer attention." Frank bent his head and dug a trench in the dirt with the heel of his boot, something he did only when he groped for words. When he looked back up, there was a suspicious shine in his eyes. "For a time, you played fast and loose, but I knew you'd come around. I've always been proud to say you're my son, but I've never been prouder than now."

A sting came to Zach's eyes, too, and he bent his head to scuff at the dirt himself. It was true, he guessed; he and his brothers were all carbon copies of their father. If Frank had a habit, they had it, too. "Thanks, Dad. Means a lot, hearing you say that."

"You deserve to hear me say it." Frank inclined his head at Rosebud. "Not every man sets time aside to help someone else. What other tricks does she have up her sleeve?"

Zach was about to demonstrate a few more of Rosebud's talents when he heard the crunch of tires on gravel. He turned to see a dented gray Honda Element passing through the front log arches. As the car bumped along the rutted road, he glimpsed the silhouettes of two people behind the sun-washed windshield.

More to himself than to his father, he said, "I wonder who the hell let them in? I don't know anyone with a car like that."

"That's a car?" Frank chuckled. "Looks more like a thimble on wheels to me."

The Element drew to a stop in the parking lot between Zach's cedar home and the arena. The driver door opened, and a woman emerged. The instant Zach glimpsed the shine of her sorrel-colored hair, caught with a clip at the crown of her head, he realized it was Miranda and recalled that he'd agreed to meet with her and her brother today.

Though not tall, she had legs that seemed to go on forever as she walked toward them. Snug jeans, a tailored blue-plaid blouse tucked at the waist, and a blue parka showcased her slender, tidy figure. Worn running shoes lent a bounce to her step. Glancing at the footwear, Zach noted that the shoes were more practical than the pumps she'd worn the other night, but he was still thankful it hadn't snowed in a while. Otherwise, she might have slipped and landed on her ass.

Frank whistled low under his breath. "Wow."

Zach couldn't quarrel with that assessment. *Wow* was right. He walked out to meet her. She stopped about ten feet away, prompting him to halt as well. With the efficiency of long practice, Zach took quick inventory of her pretty, wholesome face, her almond-shaped hazel eyes, and the sweet, perfectly shaped bow of her full mouth. Even in the bright glare of sunlight, he could detect no trace of makeup on her face, but despite the lack of embellishment, she packed a wallop.

"Hi," he said.

Her face transformed with a glow of radiance as she smiled. Stepping closer, she extended a hand. "It's good to see you again. I hope you don't mind that we're a bit early. I wasn't sure how long the drive would take, and I didn't want to be late."

As Zach enclosed her fragile fingers in his own, he thought, *Early, late, I wouldn't have noticed, because I totally forgot our appointment.* Aloud, he said, "No problem. I keep a pretty relaxed schedule out here."

She slipped her hand from his and glanced at Frank, who stood slightly behind Zach. Her eyes filled with a question. "If this is a bad time, we can reschedule."

"No, it's not a bad time. I'm not tied up or anything." Normally Zach liked his women a little on the trashy side, but Miranda Pajeck was enough to make a man reconsider his preferences. "I hope you had no trouble getting in the gate."

The breeze picked up, trailing strands of auburn hair across her cheek. "Cookie spoke with me over the intercom and was kind enough to let me in."

Zach turned slightly toward his dad. "Dad, I'd like you to meet Miranda Pajeck. Miranda, my father, Frank Harrigan."

Frank jerked off his hat and strode forward to shake hands. "Good to meet you."

"Likewise." Miranda searched Frank's gaze. "You're nothing like I pictured."

"Oh?" Frank looked bemused. "What were you expectin'?"

"Someone in a fancy Western suit." Her cheeks went pink. "I mean—well, you're something of a celebrity in Crystal Falls."

Frank chuckled. "I only wear a suit to weddings and funerals." He swatted his pant leg with the Stetson. "Jeans and boots are the standard dress. We Harrigans don't do fancy. Got no time and even less inclination."

Zach ran a hand over his mini's back and grinned at his guest. "Judging by the way Rosebud's acting, she remembers you and can't wait for more petting."

Miranda laughed. "I'll be happy to oblige. It may

sound silly, but I lost my heart to her the night she was sick."

Instead of immediately reaching out to pet the horse, as most greenhorns would have, Miranda dropped to one knee, the movement fluid and graceful. For a long moment, she only smiled slightly, searching the mini's gaze. Then she extended her hand, palm up, just under the horse's nose.

Zach liked her approach. She was giving Rosebud an opportunity to initiate contact. He'd brought only a handful of women out to his place to meet his horses, and despite their "cowgirl" apparel, they'd behaved like imbeciles, hugging his horses' necks and kissing their noses, startling the animals half to death. Miranda didn't do that.

"Hi, Rosebud," she said softly. "Do you remember me?"

Rosebud obviously did remember. Zach half expected the mini to sniff the lady's palm for treats. Instead the little horse astounded him by gently placing her right front hoof in Miranda's hand.

"Oh, how *sweet*. You've taught her to shake hands!"

Zach hadn't taught the mini that trick. He guessed it was a hangover from her stint as a circus performer. But when a single man found himself in the presence of a beautiful lady, pride took a backseat and he accepted all the kudos he could get. "She's pretty smart and learns fast." Hell, it wasn't actually a lie.

As Miranda shook the horse's hoof, she beamed a delighted smile. "Of *course* she is. Such a smart, special, precious girl."

And then the petting and hugging began. Rosebud ate it up. The mini seemed to trust this lady who smelled like—Zach called up his mental perfume identifier—roses. Oh, *yeah*, a tasteful, faint scent of roses. He found that refreshing.

When the *ooh*s and *aah*s had run their course, Miranda pushed erect again. Rubbing the sleeves of her jacket, she quirked her delicate brows into a slight frown and met Zach's gaze, giving him a jolt. What had he ever seen in blondes?

All trace of humor gone from her voice, she said, "I'll apologize for my brother in advance." She gestured at the car. "He's not enthusiastic about a guide horse yet. Like many disabled, he resists change, and he doesn't want to get out of the car." She lifted her shoulders in a shrug. "I'll convince him, but please don't get the wrong idea. He'll *love* Rosebud once he gets to know her. He can just be ..." Her voice trailed away. Then her face went bright with another smile. "He'll come around. You'll see."

Zach's first thought, before he even met Luke, was that the kid sounded a little spoiled. Seconds later, Luke did nothing to change that impression. When Miranda opened the passenger door, her brother refused to get out and took a swing at Miranda when she insisted. Zach's body snapped taut. Where he came from, no man tried to slap or punch a woman.

"Hold your temper, son," Zach's father said from behind him. "Even if he lands a blow, it ain't your stall to muck out. You hearin' me?"

Zach heard, all right, but as he watched Luke fling his hands blindly at the air, narrowly missing Miranda's delicate face, he wanted to jerk that kid out of the car and give him a quick, hard lesson in how to treat a lady. Blindness was no excuse for bad behavior.

Miranda finally coaxed her brother out of the vehicle. Tall, with shoulders twice the span of hers, he bore a marked resemblance to his sister, with the same reddish brown hair, fine features, and nicely shaped mouth. All resemblance ended there. In contrast to her glowing warmth, Luke's expression was mulish. His bright yellow parka, open at the front to reveal a green plaid shirt, did nothing to make the picture more cheerful.

Luke clung to Miranda's arm and leaned against her as if she were a pillar, yet another count against him in Zach's book. She wasn't large enough to bear the weight of a grown man, and Luke was definitely full-grown, a couple of inches taller than Zach. Soft, with little muscle tone, though, Zach noted.

As Miranda led Luke forward, the kid felt the ground ahead of him with pats of his feet. When he felt a dip, he tightened his grip on Miranda's arm, digging his fingers in so deep it nearly made Zach wince. Why didn't he use a cane and give his sister a break? As Zach recalled from his first conversation with Miranda, Luke had been blinded at six and was now nineteen. He'd had thirteen years to adjust to his disability. Zach didn't know many blind people. Only one, in fact. His sister Samantha's husband, Tucker, had a blind sister-in-law, Carly. Born blind, Carly had received sight restorative surgery a few years ago, but she'd still endured periodic bouts of blindness between corneal transplants. During those times, she navigated with a cane, taught the sight impaired, kept house, cooked, and cared for her family. Luke acted as if he could do nothing for himself.

Zach considered himself a compassionate person, but something was totally out of whack here. And his sympathies were all with Miranda.

After leading her brother up to Zach, Miranda flashed one of her amazing smiles. "This is Luke, Mr. Harrigan. He's a little hesitant right now about Rosebud, but I'm sure that once he meets her, all his misgivings will melt away."

"Fuck that!" Luke said. "Nothing about my situation is going to melt away. You want me to walk around a campus, making a spectacle of myself with a dwarf horse? Yeah, right. Anything to get me out of your hair!"

In Zach's family, the F-word was never uttered around women, and for a moment he saw red. He also had to bite his tongue to keep from informing the spoiled little bastard that Rosebud was *not* a dwarf. But in the end, his father's warning helped him to remain silent.

The initial visit was shaping up to be a disaster. Zach felt certain there wouldn't be a second. Give Rosebud to this spoiled, petulant brat? No way. With a sharp pang of regret, he glanced at Miranda's hazel eyes, lovely face, kissable mouth, and glowing smile. Eventually, Rosebud would be placed with a blind person, but it would never be with someone like Luke. No matter how badly it disappointed Miranda, Zach would make damned sure of that.

Chapter Five

Telling Miranda up front that there was no way her brother was a good match for Rosebud would make Zach look like a jerk, so instead he focused on getting through the meeting without losing his temper. Though Luke's hazel eyes had an opacity that made it tough to get a read on him, the kid seemed intelligent enough to realize he was behaving like an ass. But apparently Luke didn't give a rip about the impression he made on others. Head hanging, shoulders hunched, he crossed his arms, leaned heavily against his sister, and refused to pet Rosebud. Zach got a strong urge to apply his hand with vigor to an appropriate part of the little pill's anatomy.

"Please, Luke," Miranda coaxed. "Just let her smell your fingers."

"No," Luke cried. "She probably has germs. I don't want a guide animal. This is a total waste of time. What about that do you fail to understand?"

"I'd just like you to give it a chance. Luke. What harm can it do to touch her?"

Catching movement from the corner of his eye, Zach turned to see his father lifting a hand in farewell. Frank's brown eyes danced with laughter. *Thanks, Dad.* At least someone thought this whole mess was funny. Zach certainly didn't, and judging by Miranda's strained smile, she felt just as uncomfortable.

When Luke persisted in his refusal to touch Rosebud,

Miranda led him back to the car. In Zach's estimation, it was just in time. Blunt words to inform the kid exactly what he thought of both his manners and his treatment of his sister were crowding Zach's throat. If Frank Harrigan had ever caught his boys behaving like that to a woman, they wouldn't have been able to sit down for a week. There were lines a man never crossed, and Frank had always made sure his sons knew precisely where those lines were drawn.

After getting her brother deposited on the passenger seat and belted in, Miranda retraced her steps to where Zach stood with the horse. Cupping her elbows, she said, "I'm so embarrassed. Luke can be . . . well, difficult sometimes."

Difficult? How about rude, disrespectful, and a whole string of similar qualifiers?

"No worries. Guide horses work well for some and not for others."

Her eyes went bright, and Zach feared she might burst into tears. He hated it when women cried, always had. Instead she pulled a tremulous smile out of the hat. "Please don't let Luke's behavior put you off. He has some issues. I can't deny that. But he's a good kid. In time, he'll warm to the idea of a guide horse. I just know he will."

On the verge of announcing that he didn't give a tinker's damn any longer if Luke warmed to the idea, Zach leaned over to make an unnecessary adjustment to Rosebud's halter. It gave him a second to calm down and collect his thoughts. Even a small horse like Rosebud required care and attention. Luke struck Zach as being far too self-centered and spoiled to give a hoot about anything but himself.

As cowardly as it was, instead of dashing her hopes, Zach dredged up a smile. "We'll see how it goes. Rosebud still isn't trained, so there's plenty of time."

She extended her hand. "Thanks so much, Mr. Harrigan. I'll be in touch. Okay?"

That was what she thought. When and if the lady called, Zach wouldn't answer. He felt a stab of regret as he enfolded her slender fingers in his. Maybe he'd been looking in all the wrong places, but even at church, ladies like her were hard to find. She was pretty and sweet, a heady combination for a man who'd dated busty blondes who were as casual about sex as they were about getting their nails done. Was he out of his mind to be telling her good-bye, with no intention of seeing her again?

No. Rosebud depended on Zach to find her the perfect home with a loving and appreciative person. Luke Pajeck didn't fit the bill. Zach wouldn't sacrifice Rosebud because Miranda Pajeck was the most delectable package he'd come across in years.

As Miranda walked away, Zach gazed after her, feeling oddly depressed. Meeting her had been like glimpsing a splash of sunlight on a dreary day, and he couldn't shake the feeling that he might regret passing on this opportunity to get to know her better. For an instant, he strongly considered asking her out on a date; then he kicked the thought from his mind. When she learned that he had no intention of letting her brother have Rosebud, she'd be pissed, and Zach couldn't change his mind about that.

Rosebud wasn't going to be placed with that smart-mouthed kid.

The instant the Element was out of sight of Zach Harrigan's ranch, Mandy jerked the wheel to the right and white-knuckled the car onto the narrow shoulder of the road. She slammed her foot down on the brake so hard that Luke, unprepared, pitched forward and nearly smacked his head. With a jerky shove, she shifted into park.

"Shit, Mands!" he yelled. His head slewed around, his eyes huge. "Are we having a wreck?"

Mandy slammed her hands down on the steering

wheel, inadvertently blasting the horn. Luke jumped and hit his elbow on the door. She didn't care. Normally when she was this angry she held her tongue until she calmed down. *Not this time.*

"Your behavior was absolutely *inexcusable*. I can't believe you acted that way!"

"Like I give a shit?"

Remembering Zach Harrigan's expression of astonished distaste, Mandy fought down an unfamiliar urge to slap her brother. She couldn't remember the last time she'd been so embarrassed. "Watch your mouth! If you *ever* use the F-word in my presence again, you'll go without dinner or get your own for a week. Is that crystal clear?"

"It's called an F-bomb, and yeah, it's clear, and I've heard that crap before, but you always end up feeding me." Luke bunched his fists on his spread knees, his sightless gaze fixed on the dash. "Lots of other things are clear, too. Think I don't know why you're all of a sudden pushing so frigging hard to get me to be self-sufficient? It's not because you care about me! You just want me off your hands!"

Well, this was a new line of attack. Luke knew better, and she knew not to believe what he said when he was angry and upset. But it still hurt. "You know that's not true!"

"Not true? Of course it's true! All you talk about is college. For my own good, you say, but my own good doesn't have much to do with it. After I'm in some dorm, you'll be *free*. No more helping me, no more leading me, no more fixing my meals, no more being tied down. Once you're rid of me, do you really think it will ever be the same?"

"Stop it!" Mandy heard her voice shoot up, and she snatched at her self-control. "I do *not* want to get rid of you, and I have never *once* so much as *hinted* that I do."

"The hell you don't!" Now Luke was yelling, too,

his fists beating impotently against his knees. "No, you never hinted at it, but Mom never gave us any hint she wanted to get rid of us, either, and look what happened. She was all hugs and kisses one day, then gone the next. She didn't want us. And she . . . she never came back."

The pain in Luke's voice caught Mandy off guard. A hot lump that felt the size of a grapefruit jammed in her throat as ideas she'd never even considered began falling into place. She stared at her brother for a long moment. "Oh, Luke," she said shakily.

"It's true and you know it!" he cried. "*She* never let on that she didn't want me, either, but that didn't stop her from taking off and leaving me behind, did it? Maybe you're the same way. You're her *daughter*, after all. Every morning I wake up scared to death until I know you're still in the house! And now you keep saying you want to send me away! Do you think I don't know you won't be around when I'm done with school?" He made a choking sound and put his hands over his face.

So that was it. He really believed she would abandon him like their mother had. Scalding tears welled in Mandy's eyes. His mother hadn't wanted him, so why should his sister, especially disabled as he was? Every time she encouraged him toward independence, he interpreted it as being rejected. He truly believed she was eager to be rid of him.

With a concentrated effort, she loosened her grip on the steering wheel. The anger that had surged through her earlier evaporated, replaced by a flood of tenderness. She knew now what he'd been thinking all these years. If anyone could understand how painful it was to feel insecure, it was Mandy. Luke hadn't been alone that long-ago morning when he'd awakened to find his mother gone. There had been a frightened, teenage Mandy there, too. She'd just been older and better able to deal with her emotions.

Mandy opened her mouth, but the words couldn't

get past the logjam in her throat. She gulped and tried again. "So that's what this has always been about," she said. Her voice quavered, and Luke turned his head toward her, his expression suddenly alert. "That's why you won't try a service animal or anything else that will make you self-sufficient. If you don't need me, you're afraid I'll take off, just like Mom did. Oh, Luke, I *love* you! I want you to be independent for *you*, not for me! Don't you know I'd never abandon you? You're all I have!" The last words came out on a strangled sob.

"Mands? Are you crying? I didn't mean to . . ." Luke reached out for her. Mandy scooted over, flung her arms around him, and held him as tightly as she could. She wasn't sure whose tears were on her face. Her brother's body trembled, and she felt a searing pain in her midsection, as if something tight within her was breaking apart.

She had no idea how long it was before they drew apart and began mopping their eyes. She put a wad of tissues in Luke's hand and gave it a squeeze. He returned the pressure in an answer that touched her more deeply than words. They'd crossed over some invisible barrier, and now they had a better understanding of each other.

"Do you believe me now?" she asked.

Luke kept hold of her fingers. "Yeah. I guess. I'm sorry, Mands. Don't start trying to analyze me, though, okay? I get enough of that with the shrinks."

Mandy saw nothing to be gained by reminding Luke that he hadn't seen a counselor in nearly a year. "I have no intention of making you go away to college. You can go to the university right here in Crystal Falls and continue to live at home."

"Well . . . yeah, I guess I could. Maybe. But Mands . . . I mean, okay, I understand now about you wanting me and stuff. But without me as a ball and chain around your neck, you could get married and have a family of your own. That'll be a *huge* temptation."

"Never."

Luke went silent, his expression bewildered. "Why not? You're still young enough."

"After all Mom went through, how can you think I'd ever be dumb enough to marry?"

He was silent for a few moments. Then he said, "Not all men are like Dad."

"Not all, possibly, but some are. How does a woman know the truth about a man until it's too late? Dad never showed his true colors before Mom married him. I will *never* put myself in a situation like that. The day I turned eighteen, I grabbed hold of my independence and never looked back. I like being my own person. I like making my own decisions. I'll never give up my freedom and let some lunatic run my life."

"You're serious." Luke sank back in the seat. "I never knew you felt like this." He cleared his throat. "I guess I'm learning today there's a lot of stuff I never knew."

Mandy rested her throbbing forehead on the steering wheel. She felt so exhausted, as if her bones had dissolved. "Me, too. That's what this has been about, all these years. You've always been scared that I'd leave you."

"No big surprise. I've told you before."

"Yes, but . . ." Mandy started to choose her words carefully, but she was as tired of doing that as she was of everything else. "You say lots of stuff to get back at me. I didn't know you believed it. A husband? I don't even go out on dates."

"Only because you have me to take care of, and you can't afford a sitter very often." Luke's larynx bobbed. "If I were gone, you could do whatever you want."

"Oh, Luke," she said shakily. "Listen to me. No matter how independent you become, I'll always want you with me. I'd be lost without you. If you go to college and land a great job, my biggest fear will be that you'll decide you no longer need *me*."

Luke's auburn brows drew together in an incredulous frown. "That's stupid. Where would I go? Living alone would be . . . lonesome."

Mandy knew it wasn't funny, but a giggle pushed up the back of her throat.

"What's so funny?" Luke demanded.

"This," she said with a limp wave of her hand. "*Us*. We talk to each other all the time but never hear each other. Without you in the house, I'd go out of my mind."

"Not if you had a husband and kids."

"I don't *want* a husband. Kids, maybe, but I'm not in a position to support any on my income. Take the cotton out of your ears! I love you. Always have and always will. I prefer to remain in control of my future, and you are always going to be a part of it. You know how I picture that future, Luke?"

"No, how?"

Mandy gazed out the windshield across a winter-yellow field splashed with patches of snow. Lining the drainage ditch, metal fence posts leaned willy-nilly, strands of barbed wire sagging like rusty necklaces between them.

"I see you getting a fabulous education and becoming a respected professional."

Luke muttered a comment under his breath that she didn't ask him to repeat.

"You'll come home at night—maybe with a guide horse—and I'll have dinner on. We'll eat and talk about our day. With you contributing financially, maybe I'll be able to go back to school and get into another line of work."

"You don't like your work, do you?"

Mandy bit the inside of her cheek. How could he think she actually enjoyed her job? "Luke, I'm a medical transcriptionist. Maybe some people love it, but for me, it's drudgery. I'm good at it, but that's as far as it goes. I'd love to do something different."

"Like what?"

"You'll think I'm nuts." She moistened her lips. "I, um . . . Well, remember how Dad made me take over the gardening and all the yard work after Mom ran off?"

"Yes. You hated it. Whenever he wasn't around you were always complaining."

Mandy smiled. "I did, but only because I was so loaded down with everything else. Somewhere along the way, I developed a love for plants—not vegetables, but flowers and other ornamentals. I'm never happier than when I'm working out in our yard."

"You want to be a *gardener*?" Luke's tone suggested he equated this career choice with snake charming or fortune-telling.

"No, I want to run a nursery. I'd have to get a degree in horticulture, I suppose, but I think I'd enjoy the coursework. That's my dream, to raise and sell beautiful plants. Maybe if I got good enough, I could even do some landscape design."

Luke hung his head for a long moment. "You'd be good at it without a degree. You're really smart, Mands. You could be anything you want, even a horticulturist."

She ached to try. She nursed seedlings to life and turned her yard into a showplace every summer. She dreamed of owning a nursery almost every night. But as things stood, it was out of the question. Her present job paid the bills, bought food, and added a monthly trickle of cash to Luke's college fund. There wasn't much left over.

Luke sighed. "Swear it," he whispered gruffly. "Swear to me that you'll never make me move out if I go to college and get a job."

Mandy studied her brother's haunted expression. He'd never even admitted to the possibility before, and now he was trying to put his fear aside and actually consider it. Oh, *God*, what a number their mother had done on him—and on her as well. Mandy wondered if Sharyn Pajeck was happy in her new life. Then she realized she didn't care. Any woman who would abandon her kids, leaving them with a violent alcoholic father, didn't deserve happiness or any semblance of peace. "I swear it, Luke."

"No, I need you to say it and then swear it."

"If you go to college and get a job, I'll never, *ever* make you move out of the house. I swear it."

He nodded slightly. "All right. Next time, I'll pet the horse. That's all I promise, though. If I don't like her, I don't want to hear any more about it. Deal?"

Mandy could barely speak. "Deal," she whispered.

Zach wasn't enjoying his evening. He had a new DVD, and he'd had a good dinner chased by a cold beer, but it didn't matter. Miranda Pajeck kept elbowing her way into his mind, and every time he booted her out, she sneaked back in. He kept remembering things—her graceful movements, the lilt of her voice, the way her face glowed when she smiled. As he unwrapped the DVD and tossed the cellophane in the trash can, he tried to pinpoint what he found so attractive. She wasn't the most beautiful woman he'd ever seen, so why had two occasions in her company made such an impression? Hormones, he decided. It had been way too long since he'd dipped the old oil stick. He'd react the same way to any pretty female.

He let out an exasperated sigh. That explanation didn't work. His thoughts of Miranda weren't of a sexual nature. He felt physically attracted, of course. Any man probably would. But overall, it was more a sense way deep within him that she was someone special and that he'd been stupid to let her slip through his fingers.

That feeling followed him into his dreams and was still with him the next morning when he got up an hour before daybreak. He tried to wash it away with two cups of strong coffee. When that failed, he went to the stable, convinced that a long day of hard labor might cure what ailed him. If not, he'd go to a honky-tonk tonight and find a cowgirl looking for a ten-minute rodeo.

Cookie often checked on the animals while his morning coffee perked, so Zach wasn't surprised to find the lights on in the arena. A glow of yellow spilled from the rafter fixtures, creating an impression of daylight even though it was dark outside. Several horses stood at the stall gates, heads high, ears cocked. They greeted Zach with whickers of welcome. Only Tornado, Zach's nemesis, didn't appear at his gate.

Zach spoke to the horses that came forth to greet him as he led Rosebud to her daytime stall. After getting her settled, he took time to stroke necks as he retraced his path to the front of the building. Ah, how he loved the smells in here—the scent of hay, the hint of molasses-coated grain, the pungent odor of vitamin powder, and the faint traces of saddle leather, all mixed with the ever-present musk of manure. As he walked, sending up puffs of dirt, he breathed it in. He felt at home here as he did nowhere else.

The door of Cookie's loft apartment stood open, a signal that breakfast was on and Zach was invited. As he started up the stairs, he caught the scent of bacon frying.

"Hope you're hungry. I cooked for two," Cookie said when Zach stepped through the doorway. "Had a hankerin' for Southern-style this mornin'."

Built like a tree stump, with a butternut brown complexion and faded blue eyes, Cookie looked more like a gnarly old gnome than a cowboy, but his talent with horses knew no equal.

"You sure you've got enough?" Zach asked.

"Don't I always? Hang your hat and elbow up."

Cookie's apartment, tidy as always, exuded inviting warmth. The leather sofa and matching recliners were a dark cream color that struck just the right contrast to the dirt-brown carpet. The kitchen, open to the rest of the flat, was divided off by a curved bar fronted by four stools, upholstered in the same leather as the furniture.

Zach hung his hat on a horseshoe hook just inside the door, swung onto a stool, and accepted the mug of coffee his foreman slid toward him over the hickory counter.

"Why are you so glum?" Cookie asked. "You're frownin' like a mule with a burr up his ass."

Zach took a sip from the mug, ignoring Cookie's unflattering metaphor. "You ever meet a woman and get the weird feeling that you shouldn't let her slip away?"

Cookie ran a hand over his flyaway hair, then grabbed a spatula to flip the eggs, which he fried in the bacon drippings. "If they're purty, I never want 'em to slip away. But I've learned over the years that life is better if I pretend it's a smorgasbord, enjoyin' a taste of this and then a taste of that."

Zach laughed and shook his head. "Not like that, Cookie. I mean a special feeling, like you'd been waiting all your life to meet her." Turning the mug in his hands, Zach added, "You know it's crazy, but you just can't shake it off."

Cookie filled two plates and circled the bar with them to sit beside Zach. Sliding one plate over and claiming the other for himself, he said, "I felt that way once."

Zach prayed over his food. "When you felt that way, what'd you do?"

"Married her. Worst thirty seconds of my life."

Zach grinned. "You were married for only thirty seconds?"

" 'Bout six months, but I was callin' myself a dozen kinds of fool in thirty seconds. The woman didn't like nothin' about me—the way I walked, dressed, talked. You name it, she hated it. I reckon she thought she'd change me. When she couldn't, she filed for divorce. When I got them papers, I went on a three-day drunk to celebrate."

Zach shifted his plate, a chipped beige stoneware thing with a ring of darker brown at the edge. He crunched down on a delicious piece of bacon. Cookie's talents weren't limited to working with horses. "It doesn't always end up that way."

"Not for everybody." Cookie bent over his plate, pushing a folded piece of bread around in runny egg yolk. "I just ain't cut out to ride double, I reckon."

Could the same be true of Zach? So far, he'd never found that one special person.

"Enjoy the ladies as much as the next fellow," Cookie went on, "but after a quick dilly and dally, I always make tracks before the sun comes up." Cheek bulging, he gave Zach a measuring look. "I'm different than you, though. Ran away from home at eleven. Worked on ranches in Montana until my green wore off. Never had a pa like yours to teach me manners, polish my edges, and send me off to college to get book learnin'. Horses love me, but the ladies ain't never interested in more than one ride."

"Maybe you just never gave the right lady a chance."

"Could be." Cookie shoved another piece of bread in his mouth. "But I ain't mournin' the loss. Like my life just the way it is. I got nobody but you to fuss at me."

Zach resumed eating. Having a conversation with Cookie was like spinning a spur; you never knew where the rowels would land. Even so, the old codger had a way of cutting right to the heart of a matter. Zach's strange feelings about Miranda were just that, strange feelings. They weren't something he should act upon or take seriously.

After helping clean up the breakfast mess, Zach began his day with Tornado, whose name should have been "Impossible" and probably would have been if not for Zach's practice of naming his horses after weather patterns. His sister, Sam, had a theory that every stable needed a theme for the quarter horse registry, and all the Harrigans except Frank had followed her lead. All Sam's animals were named after kitchen spices, sauces, or flavorings; Clint had gone with a biblical slant; Parker named his horses after cities and states; and Quincy, the health nut, had a stable filled with fruits and vegetables. How could anyone name a gorgeous stallion Rutabaga and expect the poor critter to hold its head up high? Asparagus was even worse.

Tornado had gotten his name by the luck of the draw, before Zach realized how apt it would end up being. He'd already used Hurricane, Whirlwind, Typhoon, Cyclone, and Tempest. Tornado had been the next unused name. Sadly, the five-year-old horse had soon proven to be deserving of the handle, exhibiting violent and unpredictable behavior that Zach had spent nearly two months trying to resolve without a lick of success.

"Easy, boy," Zach said as he entered the stall, knowing even as he spoke that he was wasting his breath. Nothing with Tornado went easy. Unlike the stable-born Crooked H horses, Tornado had evidently not been imprinted at birth or as a young foal, and he'd apparently received no effective training as an adolescent. Despite all Zach's efforts, the stallion remained a twelve-hundred-pound bundle of trouble, the equine version of Jekyll and Hyde. Zach allowed no one else to enter Tornado's stall. When the stallion needed farrier or veterinarian care, three people hazed him into a hydraulic box stall, Tucker sedated him, and only then did the animal receive the attention he needed.

Every time Zach thought about it, he did a slow burn. *Live and learn.* Tornado's previous owner had been ill when Zach first went to examine the stallion, named Morpheus at the time, and the ranch foreman, given power of attorney to transact sales, hadn't seen fit to tell Zach that he was about to purchase a nightmare. During that first viewing, Tornado had exhibited no bad behavior. Zach suspected the stallion had been sedated, but when Tucker had gotten back from a cruise with his wife two weeks later and done a drug test, he'd found no trace of a sedative in Tornado's system. That had been disappointing, because some drugs remained detectable for as long as ninety days. If Zach could have proved that he'd been ripped off, he might have been able to return the horse and get his money back. But as things stood, Zach was stuck with a crazy horse.

The sad part for Zach wasn't the financial loss, though. Hell, no. It was the stallion's probable fate that broke his heart. If Zach couldn't help Tornado, probably no one could, and on his present course, Tornado would eventually hurt somebody. When a horse was that dangerous, the eleventh hour eventually led to midnight. Ending the stallion's life would be one of the most difficult things Zach had ever done. He hated to even *consider* it, which was why he worked with the horse daily, hoping for a breakthrough.

This morning, all Zach had in mind to do was some routine grooming. With Tornado, that was dicey. So dicey, in fact, that the animal's coat and mane were a mess. One time, the stallion would docilely accept being touched in certain places. The next time, he blew up for no apparent reason. There was just no figuring him out.

The moment Zach closed the stall gate behind him, the sorrel snorted and spun on his hind legs, slashing the ground with his front hooves. Zach had no idea why the horse was in a snit. Knowing Tornado, it could be anything from the way Zach wore his hat to a movement he made that the animal didn't like.

"Easy, boy. It's okay." Zach had learned as a youngster to develop eyes in the back of his head when he was around horses, so he kept the stallion in sight as he moved slowly toward the currycomb that hung high on the right wall. "No worries," he soothed. "I'm just going to brush you down."

As Zach closed his fingers over the handle of the

sawtoothed grooming tool, Tornado reared on his hind legs, screamed, and came at Zach with a lightning-quick slashing of his front hooves. Zach ducked sideways, but not quickly enough to avoid a blow to his shoulder that sent him reeling. He dove to the right, rammed his arm against the wall, and took another strike to the back before he could roll clear. For an instant, all he could see was a funnel storm of straw and dust. Then he glimpsed the stallion's front hooves suspended directly above his face. He rolled again, sprang to his feet, and ran for the gate, barely managing to vault over the barrier before Tornado reached him.

Landing in a sprawl outside the enclosure, Zach spit dirt and hay, trying to get his lungs to work again before he moved. *Pain.* Fortunately, the stallion's hooves had glanced off, sparing Zach the full impact of the strikes, but it still hurt like hell. When he'd recovered enough to move, he gained his feet and began berating the stallion.

"You ungrateful, rotten, misbegotten *bastard!*" Furious, Zach drew back his foot and sent a feed pail flying. The bucket arced high and landed at the center of the arena with a metallic *thunk.* "One of these days, I'm going to put a bullet between your eyes!" Zach kicked the dirt, settled fists at his hips, and grabbed for breath. "Son of a *bitch!*"

Cookie sauntered from a mare's stall well away from the stallion section. As he fastened the gate, he shook his head. "You kickin' buckets again? If you want your toe broke, come out with me to the choppin' block, and I'll just whack it with the sledge."

Zach leveled a burning gaze on the older man. Atop Cookie's head sat a battered tan Stetson that Zach knew for a fact had served him winter and summer for more than thirty years. Thinking of hats, Zach shot a look into Tornado's stall. His brown Stetson, knocked from his head during the brouhaha, was now flatter than a pancake, and Tornado was still pawing it to do further damage. Zach made a mental note to grab another Stetson from the stable office, where he always kept spares.

"It's called venting, Cookie. That damned horse just tried to kill me."

Cookie arched a grizzled brow and spewed tobacco juice from between his front teeth. With his usual good aim, he nailed the bucket Zach had just sent flying. "You got two choices, way I see it. Work the meanness out of him or have Tucker put him down."

Zach hooked his thumbs over his hand-carved leather belt, which he'd won during a challenging bout of cutting competition a few years ago. The reminder only made him feel more frustrated. He was renowned for his ability to train any horse he came across. It was pretty damned humiliating to fail day after day with Tornado.

"I've tried everything. He's impossible, and nothing I do is going to change him."

Dawn was breaking, faint streaks of pearly pink light spilling into the arena through skylights and open paddock doors. The other employees hadn't arrived yet. Zach and Cookie opened shop each morning, and the hands started trickling in around seven.

"Ain't many horses truly ruined beyond repair." Cookie spit more tobacco juice. "Even well-trained stallions can be temperamental. Give 'em a sniff of a mare in estrus, and they're popcorn farts. You Harrigans have a way of breedin' docile ones. Maybe it's the handlin' they receive from birth. But as a general rule, stallions are difficult."

Zach passed a hand over his eyes. "Tornado's beyond difficult."

"Since nothin' else has worked, why don't you try some of that newfangled clicker stuff on him? Works with Rosebud, don't it?"

As the old foreman turned and walked away, Zach glared at his back. *Clicker training?* It was the craziest suggestion Zach had ever heard. Or was it?

A few minutes later, when Zach had cooled off, he approached Tornado's stall with Rosebud's tennis-ball target. The stallion snorted and threw his head, sidestepping inside the enclosure. Softly whistling, Zach opened the gates and strung a heavy chain across the opening, which was about as effective as stringing dental floss in the path of a rhino. But Zach trusted the other horses, and he needed to pretend that he trusted Tornado. Mind-set was sometimes everything.

Zach scooped some pellets from the pouch at his belt and extended an open palm to the horse. Tornado snorted and backed up several steps. But then his nostrils quivered, and he elongated his neck, trying to get a whiff of what Zach had in his hand. *Stubborn, mean-hearted beast.* But Zach had decided to give this a try, and he was as stubborn as any horse. He waited until Tornado gave in to curiosity and came over to eat the pellets. Then Zach slowly drew Rosebud's training wand forward, allowing the stallion to see and grow accustomed to it while he ate a second handful of goodies.

Before the session ended, Tornado was touching the tennis ball to get rewards, and Zach was congratulating himself on a job well-done. The quarter horse had locked onto the target just as quickly as Rosebud had during her first clicker session. Was it possible this might work? Zach cautioned himself not to get his hopes up. Tornado had a temperament as volatile as nitroglycerin. Unless the equine equivalent of Dr. Phil dropped by, Tornado might never get better. Even so, Zach felt a surge of excitement as he went to work with Hurricane, a dream stallion Zach had started training at birth. What if? The question circled endlessly in Zach's mind.

Once Zach finished with Hurricane, it was time for his hands to start arriving. Ethel De Mario appeared first, running ten minutes early. A slender brunette who wore her long hair in a braid down her back, she waved and called, "Good morning!"

Zach latched Hurricane's stall gate. "Morning! How'd the dinner go last night?"

Ethel's Italian parents-in-law had dined at her home the previous evening, and they tended to be critical of her culinary skills. "Let's just say Michael's mom left for home before I strangled her." She tugged a pair of worn leather gloves from the waistband of her jeans. "Didn't like my lasagna. Said my pasta was rubbery. Detested the bread because I didn't bake it. Didn't care for the dipping oil. You name it, she hated it."

Zach laughed. "Don't let her upset you. Your lasagna is perfect!" Ethel often brought in dishes to share with everyone at lunch, and Zach loved her cooking. "She probably just has her nose out of joint. Her non-Italian daughter-in-law can make lasagna that rivals her own. That's bound to stick in her craw."

"I wish something would. Some rubbery pasta, maybe? Trust me when I say I would *not* be the first person to jump up and administer the Heimlich maneuver."

Zach ambled across the arena, grinning at the spark of anger in Ethel's blue eyes as she tugged on a glove. She flexed her shoulders and stretched her neck, an obvious attempt to readjust her mood before she went near the horses. She never allowed her personal problems to interfere with her work. "She raised a wonderful son. I'll give her that." She flashed a smile. "What's on the agenda today?"

Zach crooked a finger at her and led the way to Tornado's stall. After briefing Ethel on the blowup that had occurred earlier and Cookie's suggestion that Zach try clicker training, he gave her an inquiring look. "You're great with horses. I respect your opinion. Do you think there's a chance in hell it might work on him?"

Ethel settled a gaze on the sorrel. "Anything's worth a try." She watched the horse circle inside the enclosure. "I hear the talk around here, Zach. Everyone's afraid of that animal, including me, as ashamed as I am to admit it. One of these days, he's going to hurt somebody. I mean *really* hurt somebody. The worst part is, you'll never see it coming. He's fine one minute and maniacal the next."

Zach's throat went tight. As infuriating as Tornado could be, Zach didn't want to see the stallion come to a bad end. "I hate the thought of putting him down."

A singularly plain woman who never wore cosmetics, Ethel always seemed beautiful when she smiled. She rested a gloved hand on Zach's arm. "If anybody can turn him around, it's you. Don't give up on him quite yet. We can all be careful and stay clear of his stall. Maybe the clicker training will be a turning point for him."

"I hope so. I've tried everything else for almost two months, no headway."

"No headway with what?"

Zach turned to see his hired hand Tony Spellman sauntering toward them. Tony was a big man, as square and solid as a brick outhouse, but despite his size, he was agile and a damned fine horseman.

"Tornado almost took me out this morning," Zach replied. "Ethel and I are discussing plans of action."

"A tranquiilizer gun followed by lethal injection?"

"Shut up, Spellman." Ethel shot her fellow employee a warning glare. "He hasn't seriously hurt anyone yet."

"*Yet* being the key word. Nobody wants to work with him. Even with the hydraulic box stall and sedation, the farrier shook in his boots while he trimmed that monster's hooves. Hell, even Tucker walked a wide circle around the son of a bitch that morning, and he's one of the finest vets I've ever known." Tony lookcd Zach dead in the eye. "He's loco. You know it, and I know it. There's only one thing to be done with a horse like that. I just hope you get your mind wrapped around it and act before it's too late." He gave Zach a level look. "He will hurt someone. It's just a matter of time."

Tornado chose that moment to blow up again. The

thunderous reports of his rear hooves on the walls of the stall rolled across the arena. Startled, Tony fell back a step. "He's a killer, I'm telling you."

Zach clenched his teeth as he watched Spellman walk away.

"Don't listen to him," Ethel said softly. "You can turn Tornado around. You just haven't hit on the right method yet."

Zach turned to watch the stallion rear up and strike the air again. He could only pray Ethel was right. It wasn't fair to his employees for him to keep a dangerous animal on the premises and put all of them at risk.

Chapter Six

While waiting for his employees to leave for the day, Zach finished some desk work in the arena office before approaching Tornado's stall for another session of clicker training. In both hands, he carried plastic bags filled with different treats—baby carrots, apple slices, grain pellets, and a mixture of oatmeal and chopped apples laced with molasses, which was to equines the equivalent of fine wine and dark chocolate.

At this time of evening, the cavernous arena was serenely quiet. The smell of alfalfa drifted on the air. The horses had already received their nightly ration of grain, and each of them was now munching happily on two flakes of hay. The sound of their molars grinding the fodder always comforted Zach, but he found it particularly soothing in the evenings for some reason, possibly because he associated it with the end of the day, when all the work was done and his horses were safely tucked in for the night.

His belly rumbled as he strode toward the front of the building. He ignored the pangs of hunger. It wouldn't be the first time he'd gotten a late supper, and it wouldn't be the last. When you had a stable filled with horses, your own needs took second seat. Tornado needed help, and Zach was bound and determined to give it to him.

Once outside Tornado's stall, Zach put the treats on the ground and then considered leaving the gate latched. Given Zach's agenda for this session, Tornado would probably blow up not once, but several times, and the barrier would at least give Zach some protection. But no. Zach refused to go there. He had to give this horse every possible chance.

Like his stable mates, the sorrel was munching hay. When Zach opened the gate, the stallion wheeled his rump around. Zach strung the chain across the entrance. Tornado abandoned his meal to watch Zach's every movement. Zach bent to pick up a bag of pellets. He scooped some onto his palm and extended his hand. Tornado elongated his neck, sniffed, and backed into a corner, shaking his head and snorting.

"Come on, Tornado, we did this once already today. It's fun. Remember?"

Watching the horse, Zach wondered, not for the first time, what went on inside the animal's head. In the overhead light, the sorrel's body rippled with power every time he moved. He would throw gorgeous foals, but what if they were as crazy as their sire? No matter how beautiful the stud, no ethical breeder played this kind of genetic roulette.

The stallion smelled the pellets and obviously wanted them. His nostrils flared to catch their scent. He pawed the dirt and whinnied. But still he held back.

Eventually the horse could resist the temptation no longer and stepped toward Zach's outstretched hand. Zach allowed Tornado to enjoy the first handful of pellets, then offered him another. As the horse began to eat, Zach drew the training wand from his belt. The stallion wheeled away, grunting and kicking with his rear hooves. Zach jumped clear, waited for the animal to relax, and then approached the chain again.

"Come on, boy. You touched the ball this morning and know it won't hurt you."

Tornado stretched his neck, trying to steal the pellets without getting too close to the yellow orb. When that tactic failed, the horse eventually moved closer, tense and jumpy, but determined to get the treats.

It took Zach nearly an hour to get Tornado to bump his nose against the tennis ball accidentally. *Click.* "Good boy, Tornado, good *boy*," Zach said, picking up a package of sliced apples. He gave the stallion three tastes and then zipped the bag closed. The idea was to keep the stallion wanting more so he would remain eager to work.

Zach's goal tonight was to get Tornado to touch his nose to the halter hanging on a hook inside the stall. From day one, Tornado had exhibited an abhorrence of halters. Hoping to desensitize the stallion to the sight of one, Zach had hung the headgear there when Tornado first arrived. Sadly, it hadn't worked. Tornado simply avoided that side of the enclosure. Zach didn't know why the animal despised the leather straps. The only way Zach could put gear of any kind on the horse was to confine him in a box chute, call in help to run a rope under the animal's chin to force his head up, and then ear him until the halter was on. Earing a horse, twisting the ear until it caused pain, was a practice Zach detested, but with Tornado there was no choice.

To Zach's relief, the stallion began cooperating quickly. *So far, so good.* He had been working with the stud for almost another hour when Cookie spoke from somewhere behind him.

"Don't you pussy out on him," the older man said softly.

Zach twisted to look over his shoulder. Cookie stood about fifteen feet from the stall entrance. "Pussy out? You should try this. My arm feels like it's about to fall off."

"If you give up, that stallion's days are numbered."

A chill washed over Zach's scalp. "You think he's loco, Cookie?"

The older man sighed. Judging by the sounds, he was

scuffing his boot heel in the dirt. "Sometimes a horse is born with a screw loose," Cookie finally replied. "Ain't no denyin' that. I had me a horse like that once. Raised him from birth. Never mistreated him or gave him any cause to be crazy." Cookie made a choked sound. "Lord, he was a beauty. But he was plumb loco, and there wasn't no fixin' him."

"You have to put him down?" Zach asked tautly, dreading to hear the answer.

"Nope. He died in an accident, broke his neck. Maybe it was a blessin' in disguise, as they say."

Zach hadn't raised Tornado from birth, but he still felt an overwhelming sorrow when he thought about having to end the stallion's life. Tornado was only five, and he was physically amazing. If only Zach could turn him around, the horse could live to be thirty. Trying to ignore the cramp in his shoulder, he said softly, "If some people are born with a screw loose, I guess the same thing can happen with horses."

"True," Cookie agreed. "But I have to say, in all my years of trainin' 'em, I've only seen it that one time. That ain't to say Tornado ain't loco. Way he acts, he's crazier than a loon. But when you bring an animal into the fold from another ranch, you're never really sure what happened in its past to make it quirky."

"His previous owner, Pat Jones, checked out," Zach replied, rubbing his upper arm. "He's got a reputation that would make Mother Teresa look like a mugger. Otherwise I'd never have bought a horse from him."

"Sometimes the way things seem ain't the way they really are."

Zach knew that was true. Despite Cookie's warnings, he lowered his arm. "I'm due for a break."

Cookie inclined his head at the wand. "Just so you know you're not finished yet. Before you call it a night, you need to make him touch that halter."

"I will," Zach assured the older man.

Cookie knuckled the brim of his hat. "Have fun. I'm headin' upstairs for a shower, some supper, and a little kickback time in my recliner."

Zach drew Tornado's stall gate closed. "I'll see you in the morning, then."

As Cookie started up the stairs, Zach headed for the stable office to get a cold soft drink from the fridge. After gaining the landing, Cookie hollered, "Don't take too long a break. Continuity is important."

Zach chuckled and repositioned his hat, which he'd confiscated from the office—a new black one he usually wore for church or nights out. "I won't, old man."

As Mandy drew her Honda to a stop by the intercom box just outside Zach Harrigan's front gate, she once again felt a little spooked by the utter blackness that blanketed the landscape. In town, there were street lamps to illuminate the sidewalks and curbs, and light from the windows of houses spilled over the yards. Out here, she could see nothing beyond the yellow swath of her car's headlights.

She pushed the red call button. The gruff voice of the ranch foreman came from the speaker. Mandy leaned out the window to identify herself and ask to be buzzed in.

"I know it's a little late, but I really need to talk to Mr. Harrigan," she explained. "He is at home, I hope. It's very important."

"He know you're comin'?" the foreman asked. "I just got out of the shower, and I'm buck naked. Can't go downstairs to ask if it's okay to let you in, and he's got his cell phone turned off, so I can't call him."

Buck naked? Mandy gulped back a startled giggle. "No, he doesn't know I'm coming. I tried to call his house. All I got was the answering machine." Stomach fluttering with nerves, she tried to think of something she might say to convince the foreman that it was okay to let her pass. "It truly is very important that I speak with him."

The foreman grunted and then sighed, the sound a static-laced *whoosh*. "He's workin' with a restive horse. It's not a good time for visitors."

Mandy wilted with disappointment, convinced the foreman would turn her away. Surprise sent a pleasant tingle up her spine when he said, "Ah, hell. It ain't like he don't know you. I'll buzz you in, I reckon. Go in the front entrance of the arena and stay by the personnel door if he's still workin' with the horse. The stud spooks easy, so don't holler out. The boss will notice you're there sooner or later."

"All right," Mandy agreed. "I'll be quiet as a mouse until he sees me. Thank you!"

"You're welcome."

The gate began to swing open. Mandy waited until the way was clear and stepped on the gas pedal. As the Element bounced over the rutted gravel road, the headlights danced over the buildings ahead, illuminating the ranch house and an open-sided pole barn filled with hay. She parked by the arena, a massive building ringed on three sides with wooden fences. Toward the roofline, windows emitted a butter yellow glow.

Leaving her purse, she exited the car and headed for the building. It was so dark she couldn't see her hand in front of her face, let alone the ground. As she rounded the corner, an outdoor light brightened her way, casting a swath of illumination over the white personnel door. She grasped the doorknob, then paused to take a deep breath. She couldn't argue a case on Luke's behalf if she was quaking and stammering.

As she pushed open the door, it took a moment for her eyes to adjust to the brightness. She stepped inside, drawing the portal closed behind her as she panned the massive interior. A few horses nosed their heads out over their stall gates to study her, but their owner was nowhere to be seen. As per the foreman's instructions, Mandy remained by the entrance. The last thing she wanted was to get on Zach Harrigan's bad side before she even had a chance to talk to him.

To her left, a reddish brown horse whinnied, the sound laced with excitement. Startled, Mandy jumped so violently she nearly parted company with her shoes. She'd never been around big horses. Their size intimidated her. This one seemed friendly, though, almost as if it were calling to her. She determined that it was a stallion. Muscle rippled under his shiny coat. He was absolutely gorgeous. A bewildered smile curved her lips when the horse called to her again, this time with a pleading, frantic shrillness.

"Hey, big guy," she called back softly.

The stallion tossed his head, lifted his tail, and pranced in a circle within his stall. Then he returned to the gate and whinnied at her again, an invitation to come closer, she felt sure. Glancing around, she noted that the other horses had already disappeared into their shelters. Not the stallion. He whickered and chuffed, pressing his chest against the gate and extending his neck as if reaching out to her.

Mandy hesitated to leave the personnel door, but the stallion's whickering was difficult to resist. She saw no harm in petting him. As she moved toward the animal, he quivered with delight and made happy little grunting noises. Mandy couldn't help but smile. How sweet! She noticed a pile of sandwich bags just outside the gate, but she barely looked at them. The horse had her full attention.

"Hello," she murmured as she closed the distance. Nodding his massive head, the stallion blew out through his nostrils. She grinned and stepped closer. Through the rungs of the gate, she saw a battered brown hat lying on the stall floor. "Aren't you too beautiful for words?"

she whispered as she reached up to rub the flat area between the animal's soft brown eyes.

The horse shuddered and shoved his nose under Mandy's right arm, nearly knocking her off balance. She laughed nervously. "Hey, big guy, no armpit sniffs on the first date. Okay?"

The stallion shuddered again, and Mandy's smile faded. She couldn't explain the feeling that washed through her, but she was suddenly certain that this animal was frightened, horribly frightened. Of what, she couldn't fathom. But she'd been terrified too many times herself not to recognize fear in another creature. An ache filled her chest and formed a lump in her throat.

"Oh, sweetie," she murmured. "What's *wrong*? Has someone been mean to you?"

The horse huffed and pressed his nose deeper into the fluff of her parka. It was as if he were trying to melt into her and hide. And just that quickly, Mandy fell in love. She stepped up onto a gate rung so she could more easily pet him. *Poor baby*. He had little scars all over his head, barely visible under his hair, but she could feel them with her fingertips. His mane was a tangled mess. Anger burned through her. Was Zach Harrigan abusing this poor horse?

Thirst quenched, Zach made his way along the hallway that divided the stable office from the tack and feed rooms. As he stepped out into the arena, he glimpsed movement, a flash of light blue. For an instant, he thought Cookie had come back downstairs, but then he focused and stopped dead in his tracks. *Shit*. His heart shot into his throat. Miranda Pajeck stood on a rung of Tornado's stall gate, her right arm hooked over the stallion's neck. If she made one wrong move, the horse might blow up. Didn't she realize how powerful a twelve-hundred-pound stallion was? If Tornado threw his head, he could flip her up and over the damned gate.

Once inside the stall, she'd have no protection against those lethal hooves.

Afraid to move, Zach said in a low but firm voice, "Miranda, take your arm off the horse. Slow and easy, no sudden movement. Okay?"

Arm still encircling the horse's neck, she sent Zach a burning look. "Afraid your secret will get out, Mr. Harrigan? Well, too late. No wonder you're renowned as a trainer. If you're cruel to an animal, you can make it do almost anything, can't you?"

Zach nudged up the brim of his spare black Stetson to gape at her. Unless he'd misheard her, she had just accused him of abusing his horse. The charge was ludicrous, but Zach would address that later. Right now, his only concern was getting her safely away from the stallion. "Miranda, that horse is dangerous. Very slowly, take your arm from around his neck and get off the gate."

As if Zach hadn't spoken, she went back to petting the horse. "Oh, yes, he's a dangerous one, all right. I'm trembling in my shoes!"

Zach's throat felt as if it had been swabbed with glue. "Get away from that horse," he said. *"Now."*

She shot him another heated look but finally did as he said. When her feet touched the ground, she turned to face Zach, her hazel eyes sparking fire. Zach's gaze shot past her to Tornado, who was now nuzzling his visitor's hair. The stallion had bitten Zach more than once and was fully capable of ripping off the top of Miranda's head. Sweat trickled down Zach's spine, dampening his shirt.

"Step away so he can't reach you," he told her.

She placed her hands on her hips, her arms hiking up the sides of her parka. "I'm not afraid of this horse. He's the one that's terrified. What have you done to him?" She'd no sooner asked the question than she threw up a hand. "Scratch that. You've beaten him. He has scars all over him. I felt them when I was petting him."

"Get away from that damned horse," Zach said more loudly. "Right *now*, before he hurts you."

She finally stepped away from the gate. The instant Zach felt certain she was out of danger, he pried his feet loose from the dirt. His boot heels kicking up dust with every step, he took long, measured strides toward her, so furious he could have pulverized lug nuts with his front teeth.

Jabbing a rigid finger at the air, he said, "Don't you *ever* go near one of my horses again without my permission. It's a good way to get killed. That stallion tried his damnedest to trample me this morning!"

She jutted her chin. "Good for him. Maybe he'll teach you a much-needed lesson! If you mistreat anything, animal or human, eventually it fights back."

Zach drew up three feet from her. Two things registered in his mind: Tornado was whickering and hammering the gate with his chest, and the sweet-natured Miss Pajeck had morphed into a hundred-plus pounds of pissed-off female.

"I don't have any idea what the hell you're talking about," he found the presence of mind to say. "I have *never* mistreated that horse."

"Well, someone has! And since he belongs to you, you're the number one suspect." She doubled her hands into tight fists at her sides. "To think I came here to appeal to your good nature. Ha! I'm out of here." Whirling to leave, she threw back, "Expect visitors in the morning, Mr. Harrigan. I'm reporting you to the Humane Society."

Zach had an insane urge to burst out laughing. But this was no joking matter. The lady was serious. "You're going to *what*?"

She whipped back around. "You heard me!"

Tornado neighed loudly and rammed the gate again. Zach was too focused on the woman to glance at the stallion, but he was still acutely aware of the horse's grunting and whickering. He'd heard other horses make similar sounds over the years. Incredulous, Zach shifted his gaze from Miranda to the animal. There was no mistake. The stallion was staring at Zach's unexpected visitor as if she'd just hung the moon.

"I'll be damned," Zach whispered.

"Oh, yes," she agreed. "You'll be damned straight to hell. How could you do that to a helpless animal?"

Helpless animal? Zach was still staring at Tornado. The stallion had eyes only for Miranda, and the noises he made were, without question, love talk.

"I'll be damned," he whispered again. "He's taken a shine to you."

"No big surprise. He knows I won't hurt him!"

She turned to leave again. Zach stepped after her. "Miranda, hold up a second."

She kept walking. "Why? So you can lie through your teeth and convince me it wasn't you who abused him?"

"Yes, damn it, that's exactly why!" Zach winced. That sure came out wrong. "I mean, no, it's not why. I mean, yes, but I don't lie through— Damn it, lady, will you *listen* for a minute? Ask anyone who's ever known me. I've never abused a horse in my life."

She pivoted on a well-worn sneaker, the sole of which was now smudged with dust. Arching her brows, she said, "Really? Then explain those scars!"

Zach had felt the scars on the horse's head and neck, but only in passing. Tornado had never allowed Zach to handle him very much. "It's not unusual for a horse to have scars. They kick and bite each other. Sometimes they injure themselves. I know Tornado has a few nicks here and there, but—"

"A *few*? It feels like someone stabbed him repeatedly with an ice pick!"

Zach glanced at the horse again. Never in all his life had he seen anything so amazing. Tornado was about to crawl over the gate to reach his lady fair.

"I've had Tornado for only two months," he told her,

"and I've never been able to really pet him. He's loco. I've tried everything I know to turn him around, but nothing has worked. I'm trying clicker training on him now as a last resort. If I can't get him straightened out, I'll have to ask Tucker to put him down."

Her eyes widened. In the overhead light, they shimmered like fine scotch shot through with firelight. Her hair, mussed by the horse, glistened, some of the strands the same color as Tornado's coat. In that moment, Zach could totally understand the stallion's sentiments. Even pissed off and spitting fire, Miranda Pajeck was one beautiful woman.

"Put him *down*?" she cried. And a heartbeat later, Zach was on the receiving end of a jabbing finger. "If you *dare*, I'll notify every news channel in this country! That horse is a big old love, as sweet and dear as he can be."

Tornado, a big old love? Zach couldn't credit his ears. He'd said that about many of his stable-bred horses, but Tornado did *not* fall into that category.

"I *know* he's been abused," she threw at him. "You ever heard that old saying that it takes one to know one? Well, he and I are soul mates. He's frightened. I sensed it the instant I touched him."

It takes one to know one? Zach zeroed in on her lovely face. What the hell was she saying, that she felt frightened? "Miranda, if the horse is afraid, I swear to you I'm not the person who made him that way." Zach inclined his head at Tornado's stall. "You see that halter hanging in there? From day one, he's blown up every time anyone tried to put it on him. I've been working with him tonight with the target and clicker, trying to get him to touch it. Trust me, I've done everything I know to help that horse."

"Really?" Her beautiful eyes still smoldered as she thrust out a slender hand. "Give me a halter."

"What?"

"You heard me. Give me a halter. If I can put it on

him, then I call baloney on your story and contact the Humane Society. If I can't, which I seriously doubt, then maybe—just *maybe*—I'll believe you."

Zach knew damned well she couldn't put a halter on that horse. And now he was starting to get pissed off. Nobody had ever accused him of mistreating an animal, and he wasn't about to take it from her. He spun on his heel, heading for the tack room. "You asked for it. You got it!"

Seconds later, when Zach returned to the arena, Miranda Pajeck was still standing there. As he drew near her, she thrust out her hand for the halter. He slapped it onto her palm.

"Go for it." Zach wasn't worried that she might get hurt. She wouldn't get close enough. Tornado would take one look at that halter and fly into a frenzy. "If you can put a halter on him, I'll kiss your bare ass on the courthouse steps in broad daylight."

She shot him a startled look. Zach was too mad to apologize for the crudity.

"Go on," he told her. "Try to approach him now."

She held up the crisscross of leather straps to study it. "Which part goes on first?"

Impatient and angry, Zach grabbed the headgear. "His nose goes through here, and this part goes up behind his ears." He shoved the thing back at her. It rankled that the only person who'd ever managed to get cozy with that damned stallion didn't know one end of a halter from the other. He'd worked with that miserable beast every day for nearly two months, and never once had he been able to hook an arm around his neck like Miranda just had. She was still turning the leather straps in her hands, studying the layout with a frown. "Go on," he challenged. "You won't get within five feet of him anyway, so you'll never get a chance to put it on him."

She flashed him a challenging look. "Wanna bet?"

She turned and marched back toward Tornado. Zach

smothered a grin, folded his arms across his chest, and
cocked a hip for good measure, assuming a tougher-
than-shit cowboy stance so he could smirk at her when
she failed. Tornado remained at the gate, head forward,
whickering as she walked toward him. *Countdown.* Zach
visually measured off the distance between her and the
stallion. Ten feet, nine feet, eight feet. When he got to
five and Tornado was still standing at the gate, calling
to Miranda, Zach straightened, dropped his arms, and
gaped in startled disbelief.

She walked right up to the horse with the halter in
plain sight. Tornado emitted soft huffing sounds and began nudging her with his nose. Zach couldn't believe it.
Miranda held up the halter and tried to fit it backward
over the stallion's nose. Tornado just stood there, apparently as happy as a worm in a compost heap.

"I'll be pickled and bottled."

Zach glanced up to see Cookie on the landing. The
old fart wore a ratty plaid robe over white pajamas with
hearts all over them. At any other time, Zach would
have made a wisecrack, but the sight of Tornado lowering his head for the halter was so astounding Zach
couldn't get past it.

"I ain't never in all my born days." Cookie watched
Miranda trying to shove the halter onto the stallion's
nose and shook his head. "Tell her how it's done, son,
and then, if you got anything resemblin' brains betwixt
your ears, hire her on the spot."

"Hire her? To do what?"

Cookie inclined his head at the woman and horse.
"To work with that stallion, of course. She'd have him
gentle as a lamb within a week."

Zach shook his head. "She doesn't know one end of a
horse from the other."

"Don't matter. Look at them."

Zach's stomach churned again, maybe from hunger,

but he suspected it was more from shock. Had Tornado been abused?

Zach couldn't go too close to the stall gate. So he angled off to the left a few paces so he could see Miranda's hands. "Turn it slightly," he told her. "See the smaller cross straps? They go over the nose. Then you pull it up over his ears and fasten the chin strap."

To Zach's utter disbelief, Miranda did exactly that, and Tornado kept his head down so she could accomplish the feat. When she had the headgear on the horse and was fastening the buckle, Zach let loose with a sigh. He'd spent his entire life around horses, and he'd never witnessed anything like this. Tornado was putty in her hands. Granted, some horses responded better to women than men, and vice versa, but Tornado didn't behave any better with Ethel than he did with Zach. No, it was something about this particular human that somehow—*how?*—reassured the horse.

Miranda swung down from the gate and fixed a gaze bright with anger on Zach. "Well, now what's your story, Mr. Harrigan? Is it possible that this horse objects only when it's *you* coming toward him with a halter?"

Zach took a moment before answering. "No. He pitches a fit no matter who it is."

"I call malarkey on that." She swung a hand toward the horse, a gesture that normally would have sent the stallion into a frenzy of kicking. "Look at him. He's perfectly calm."

"Are you calling me a liar?"

"If the shoe fits—and I'll toss in 'bastard' for good measure."

Zach had been called worse, but usually with better reason. Oddly, he wasn't offended. He was so stunned by what he'd just witnessed, in fact, that he wasn't sure how he felt. Bewildered, mostly.

"You want a job?" he asked jokingly.

"Doing what, teaching you how to treat animals properly?"

Zach heard Cookie snort. The ornery old codger probably found this more entertaining than FOX News. Zach wouldn't hear the end of it for weeks.

She hugged her waist, pulling the open front panels of the parka snug over her breasts. "You don't put down a horse because it's afraid, especially if it's your fault."

"Miranda, if that horse has been abused, I wasn't the guilty party."

Zach launched into the story of how he had acquired Tornado, and how the horse had turned into a nightmare overnight. "I think they drugged him when I went to look at him," he allowed. "And maybe again before I loaded him into my trailer. To be honest, I trusted the former owner so much I didn't look for signs of sedation."

"It's true," Cookie said from the landing. "Zach, here—well, he ain't perfect, mind you."

Zach threw a warning look at the older man. Cookie ignored him to add, "Got a temper, no question about it. But he's no horse abuser. If he mistreated an animal, his daddy would kick his ass. Course, he'd have to wait his turn if I got there first."

Great, Zach thought. He was well over thirty years old, and everyone still talked about him as if he were a wild teenager with scrambled eggs for brains.

Miranda was up on a gate rung again, hugging Tornado's neck, only now Zach no longer feared for her. The stallion was talking to Miranda, emitting little grunts and moans, as if he were telling her all his woes. Even more bewildering, she seemed to understand horse-speak. She whispered into the stallion's ear and loved on him as if she could undo all the wrongs he'd endured with the mere touch of her hands. Fascinated as he was with the whole uncanny performance, Zach realized with no small amount of disgruntlement that he was picturing those same hands touching *him*.

"All right," she finally said to Zach over her shoulder. "With Cookie vouching for you, I have no choice but to believe you." Noting sourly that Cookie's words carried more weight than his own, Zach watched as she climbed down from the gate and turned to face him. "If you didn't hurt him, though, someone else did."

Zach looked deeply into her eyes, and he saw pain there. Only a glimpse, but he saw it, and then she lowered her lashes.

Her mouth trembled. She licked her bottom lip. "If I jumped the gun, I apologize." She pushed the words out, a telltale sign that he wasn't off the hook yet and her apology wasn't completely heartfelt. "I definitely shouldn't have called you names."

Zach suppressed a smile. Being called a liar hadn't sat well with him, but *bastard* was a stable byword, uttered so often that Zach barely noticed. In fact, compared to some things he'd been called, *bastard* could sound downright friendly at times. Damn, but she was pretty, all softness and tempting curves, with a face that a man's dreams were made of. Under the parka, she wore a pink knit top that skimmed her breasts and nipped in at the waistband of her jeans, which showcased her rounded hips and shapely legs. Little wonder Tornado, still whickering at the gate, found her irresistible.

"Name-calling doesn't bother me much," Zach replied. "I'm a little too country to take offense. As for your jumping the gun, I'm kind of glad you did." He looked at Tornado. "I didn't think of abuse as being a possible cause for his crazy behavior. I bought him from a reputable breeder, and I checked the guy out nine ways to hell. If abuse occurs in a stable, sooner or later someone reports it—an employee, a buyer, or some neighbor who happens to witness it. The man's record is so clean, it squeaks."

"Well, you overlooked something. Someone has been horribly cruel to that horse."

"It wasn't me," Zach assured her, "and trust me, I've had plenty of reason. He's pushed me to the point of almost losing it a few times, *almost* being the key word. I don't beat my horses. Never have and never will."

From the landing, Cookie laughed and said, "I've had to bail him and his daddy out of jail a fair number of times for goin' to fisticuffs in defense of a horse. He's tellin' it true. When Tornado pushes the boss too far, he yells a lot, but the only violence he commits is when he goes to kickin' buckets."

Zach turned to glare at his foreman. "Does it ever occur to you, Cookie, that there may be some things I'd prefer the whole world doesn't know?"

Cookie tightened the sash of his robe and straightened from the railing. Hanks of his hair, starting to dry, stood out from his head like gray wisps of cotton candy. "Well, you do kick them buckets when you get mad, and I was only tryin' to help. As for the jail stuff, you did pound the shit outa Mose Breckenridge when you caught him beatin' on his cuttin' horse at the Salem show two years ago, and it took three men to pull you off. Ain't like I told her you pick your schnozzle in public and eat the proceeds."

Zach winced. He jerked his gaze to Miranda. "Strike that. I do *not* pick my nose."

Faint splashes of pink colored her cheeks, and a sparkle of laughter now brightened her eyes. "Now I *know* you're a bald-faced liar. *Everyone* picks his nose sometimes."

Zach chuckled. He couldn't believe the turn of this conversation. The foreman started to speak again. Zach threw up a hand. "Enough. One more helpful word out of you, Cookie, and I'll can your ass."

"Promises, promises." Cookie turned toward his apartment. "I'll never get to retire. You can't pour piss out of a boot without instructions on the heel." He stepped inside, poked his head out around the door-frame, and said, "Don't convict him without a fair trial, honey. He's gnarly, with a few rough edges, but he's got a good heart." Cookie started to close the door, then poked his head back out to add, "Before you go, missy, it'd save Tornado a lot of heartache if you'd remove that halter. He hates 'em so bad that he goes crazy tryin' to get one off, and we worry he'll hurt himself."

Zach sighed and shook his head. When Cookie had finished making his exit, he smiled at Miranda. "My turn to apologize. Cookie thinks polish is the shine on his go-to-meeting boots."

A dimple flashed in her cheek. Just a flash, and then it vanished. Zach found himself staring at the spot, wanting to see it again.

"You haven't seriously considered putting Tornado down, have you?" she asked, her eyes dark with apprehension.

"With horses, there's not always a choice. No matter what caused it, he's dangerous, and nothing I've tried has changed that. He's about out of chances at this point. I have to think about the safety of my employees." He hooked a thumb toward the landing. "If he took after Cookie the way he did me this morning, Cookie couldn't move fast enough to save himself. As sad as it makes me to think about euthanizing Tornado, I may end up there. I couldn't live with myself if he killed somebody."

She shook her head, sending her hair into a glistening tumble around her shoulders. "You need to readjust your thinking, Mr. Harrigan. Maybe Tornado *is* dangerous, but it's due to fear, not viciousness."

"The reason's not going to change the outcome if he seriously injures anyone."

She shot him an unfriendly look and retraced her steps to Tornado's stall gate, crawled up onto a lower rung, and began removing the halter. The stallion whickered and fluttered his lips over her hair as she struggled with the clasp. When the headgear was finally removed, she hugged the horse's neck and kissed him on the cheek, whispering words of farewell that Zach couldn't quite catch.

Moments later, when she handed Zach the halter, she brought her dainty chin up, met his gaze, and said, "I'll accept that job. Working with him, I mean. I know nothing about horses, but if you think I can help, I can't turn my back on him. And, Mr. Harrigan . . ."

"Make it Zach. Yeah?"

"About what you said earlier. I mean, about what you'd do on the steps of the courthouse. I won't hold you to it."

Zach felt a surge of heat come up his neck. "Sorry about that. I was mad when I said it. I don't usually talk to women that way. And I was only joking about the job. It'll take someone with a lot of experience to turn him around." He fiddled with the halter, straightening the straps, then tucked them over his belt. "If I do some checking and discover he truly has been abused, it'll give me a leg up. I'll go at everything differently."

"Can a badly abused horse be turned around?" she asked, her gaze clinging to his in hopeful appeal.

Zach nodded. "Sometimes, sometimes not." The concern that flashed across her face had Zach readdressing the question. "I think I can do it, though. It won't be easy, but yeah, I can probably turn him around. I just never thought—" He broke off because his throat had gone tight. If Tornado had been abused, Zach had done absolutely everything wrong. That bothered him. Other people paid big bucks to have him work with their animals. How could he have had Tornado for nearly two months and failed him so miserably? Swallowing hard, Zach decided to change the subject before his emotions got the better of him. "With all the hullabaloo, I never thought to ask what brought you out here. I'm assuming you had a reason for coming."

*   *   *

Until that instant, Mandy had all but forgotten why she'd come to see Zach Harrigan. Now her brain went blank. She stared at him, trying to collect her thoughts. That was nearly impossible. She'd never been a great admirer of cowboys, but Zach Harrigan was, hands down, one of the handsomest men she'd ever seen.

Thumbs hooked over his belt, he stood with one hip cocked, his opposite leg bent. A wash-worn blue shirt, partially unbuttoned to reveal a sun-bronzed chest furred with black hair, clung to his muscular shoulders. The cuffs, folded back to the elbow, showcased the hard thickness of his wrists, the square breadth of his hands, and the grace of his strong fingers. His jeans, dusty from a day of hard work, were covered by chaps to below the knee, the front cutout in the soft, worn leather showcasing the fly of his Wranglers—and the bulge beneath it. Mandy tried not to look there, but controlling the direction of her gaze was difficult.

He tipped back the brim of a new-looking black Stetson, which was flecked with bits of hay, to give her a questioning look, his dark eyes searching hers. Miranda struggled to regain her composure. What on *earth* was the matter with her? He was incredibly attractive. But so what? When she spotted a beautiful dress, she didn't drool over it unless she happened to be shopping for one. Well, hello, she absolutely, positively wasn't shopping for a man. So why did his appearance unnerve her so?

She took in his face, all masculine planes and sharp angles, and decided it was the raw power that seemed to emanate from him. Then she realized he was staring at her, one eyebrow elevated slightly, waiting for her to speak. Oh, nuts, what if he'd guessed why she was gaping at him like a tongue-tied schoolgirl? She rushed into unplanned speech. "I, um—" She broke off, pushed at her hair, and swallowed to steady her voice. *Don't look at his fly.* "I came to talk to you about Luke."

His cheek muscle bunched, a telltale sign that her

brother wasn't on his list of favorite people. His tone wasn't encouraging, either. "What about him?"

Mandy clasped her hands, decided that would make her look nervous, disentangled her fingers, and crossed her arms instead. *Perfect.* A defensive posture. That wasn't the message she wanted to convey. She jerked her hands free and stuck them in her pockets. "After the way I acted, you probably don't even want to hear it."

"I just asked, didn't I?"

She pulled her hands from her pockets and forced her arms to her sides. They hung from her shoulders like stiff boards. "It's just . . . well, I know Luke made a very bad impression yesterday. I also sensed before we left that you'd decided he isn't suitable to have Rosebud."

"That was intuitive of you."

Mandy's heart sank because he didn't deny the charge. She could also tell by the set of his mouth that he had no intention of changing his mind. "Mr. Harrigan, I don't blame you for deciding Luke shouldn't have Rosebud. His behavior was deplorable, and afterward, I jumped all over him. During that exchange, I found out—" His eyes narrowed as she broke off, gulped, and took a different tack. "He said things to make me realize—" Mandy threw up her hands. "I'm making a mess of this, aren't I?"

His lips curved into a crooked smile. "The truth? Yes. But I have a talent for making a mess of things, too, so I'll cut you some slack."

Mandy took a bracing breath, wishing the shadow of his hat brim weren't hiding the expression in his eyes. Her brother's entire future hung in the balance. She had to convince Zach Harrigan to give him another chance. She simply had to.

"Then please," she said just above a whisper, "give me five minutes and listen to me. Just listen to me. Nothing's the way I thought it was, and I have to make you believe it."

Chapter Seven

Gazing down at Miranda's lovely face, Zach felt as if he were walking on a frozen pond about to crack beneath his weight. He wasn't sure if he wanted to speed for the edge and safety, or stay where he was. He had an idea what she wanted to ask him, and with those big hazel eyes pinned on him, he wasn't sure he'd be able to say no.

She stopped, started, and then caught her lush lower lip between small, perfectly shaped white teeth. Then she pushed at her tousled hair, which he thought looked fine just as it was. *Too fine.* He could barely think straight around her.

During her visit tonight, he'd experienced a gamut of emotions—paralyzing fear, disbelief, amazement, outrage, and an inexplicable attraction. Now she was going to try to pitch her snotty brother to him.

"You know," she finally said, "not all of us are fortunate enough to have a father like you do. I mean, well, I don't really know him, but I could tell you and he are very close."

Zach couldn't see how his relationship with his dad had anything to do with anything, but he nodded to indicate he was listening.

"Luke got a raw deal when it came to parents. His father is abusive, and his mother took off when he was four. I was thirteen at the time and the only person he had left to count on. I was fifteen when he was blinded. Mature for my age. I had to be. But I was still a kid and knew nothing about raising a sight-impaired child. I tried so hard to be his eyes, to help him every way I could ... but I didn't understand he needed discipline, too. And I didn't have a clue about the emotional scars he'd suffered when our mother abandoned him." Her eyes went bright with what Zach suspected were tears. "She was his whole world, and one morning when he woke up, she was just ... just *gone*."

Zach wanted to interrupt for clarification. *What about you? Weren't you abandoned, too?* But he managed to keep his mouth shut. Better to let her tell the story her way.

"Anyway, Luke has issues. But until yesterday when we quarreled, I didn't understand that most of them are my fault. I should have realized long ago how insecure he is and known that was why he refused to become independent." Her small larynx, about the size of a shooting marble, bobbed in her throat as she swallowed. Her gaze chased off to the far end of the arena. "If he learns to use a cane and do everything for himself, he won't need me. If he agrees to get a guide horse and attend college, he *truly* won't need me. In that event, what will stop me from abandoning him just like our mother did? And that's what he thought I was planning to do."

Zach tilted his head to study her delicate countenance— the bridge of her small nose, the angle of her fragile cheekbones, and the arch of her fine eyebrows. *Yep*. He was on thin ice, and if he listened to much more, he'd be astraddle a widening crack.

"I'm sorry to hear all that. But where are you going with this, Miranda?"

She scooped her hair back from her forehead. "I hired a sitter for Luke tonight so I could come here and see you, face-to-face, and ask you—no, *beg* you, Mr. Harrigan—to give my brother one more chance. If he blows it again, and you walk away, then I won't blame you. But *please*, won't you let him meet Rosebud one more time?"

It was Zach's turn to gaze off, his attention fixed on Tornado, who had stopped whinnying and pressing against the gate now, but still watched Miranda with unmistakable yearning. A rush of fellow feeling for the stallion swept over him.

"What can it hurt?" she pleaded. "Just one more meeting. If Luke misbehaves, that'll be it. Sometimes all of us need a second chance. Right? All I'm asking is that you give Luke one."

Zach released a taut breath. He'd given that horse countless chances, and if he learned Tornado had been abused, he'd surely give the stallion many more. If he was willing to do that for an animal, how could he refuse to do it for a human being?

"All right," he heard himself say.

"I mean—if you think about it—we'll both be there. It's not as if Luke will have a chance to hurt Rosebud or anything. Not that he ever would. Whatever you might think, Luke likes animals, and he's always been gentle with them."

Zach brought his gaze back to hers. "I said all right. I'll give Luke another chance."

"And if you'll only—" She broke off. Lips parted, she looked blankly up at him for a long moment. "What?"

Zach couldn't help himself. He chuckled and barely stopped himself from ruffling her hair. "When would you like to bring Luke back out?"

"Oh, Mr. Harrigan, thank you!" She beamed one of those smiles that somehow made Zach feel warmed through and through. "You won't regret it, I promise."

"The name's Zach. I'm not much for social graces." He drew out his cell phone, which he'd turned off so it wouldn't startle Tornado. With a push of a button, the screen lit up. Zach checked his schedule, turned th phone back off, and returned it to its case. "Except for working here, I'm free every late afternoon and evening until next Thursday. Pick your day, and I'll set aside some time."

She clasped her hands at her waist, cluing Zach before she spoke that she had another favor to ask. *In for a penny, in for a pound.*

"Actually," she said, "I was hoping you might bring Rosebud to my house. Luke is more at ease there. I think he might be more receptive if he's in a familiar setting."

Zach had no problem taking Rosebud to the lady's house. The mini needed to experience different environments. "That works. What day and what time?"

"Tomorrow? Seven would be perfect. I usually have supper done by then."

"Sounds good," Zach agreed.

She flashed another brilliant smile and then startled him by suddenly going up on her tiptoes to hug his neck. Her lips pressed briefly against his jaw. "Thank you, Mr. Harrigan! *Thank* you. This is so good of you."

She drew away and began backing toward the door. "Tomorrow night, seven," she said. "We'll be expecting you."

Zach hoped he wasn't turning lobster red, and barely caught himself from pressing a hand to the place her lips had touched. To his dismay, he also realized that the brief physical contact had given him a hard-on. Not a good thing when a guy was wearing chaps. He swept off his hat and held it in front of his groin, making a show of finger-combing his hair. "Don't take off just yet. Aren't you forgetting something?" When she looked bewildered, his smile widened. "Your address."

"Oh! Of *course.* You need to know where we live." She patted her pockets, then held up a forefinger. "One second. I need a pen and paper. My purse is in the car."

"I don't need it written down." When she looked dubious, Zach gestured at all the horse stalls. "When you work with this many animals, there's a lot to remember, and it takes too much time to check charts constantly. I've got a mind like a steel trap."

She gave him the address. Zach recognized the street as being in an older section of town, which reminded him of a concern that he couldn't recall having mentioned to her yet. "I may be getting the cart before the horse, pun intended, but just in case I change my mind about Luke, horses aren't allowed to be kept inside the city limits."

"I already called the city. I can get a special permit for a service animal."

Zach was surprised she was already thinking that far ahead. "She'll also need a fenced outdoor exercise area and a shed for shelter," he told her.

"I figured as much. Luckily, where I live, the lots are really large, and I have a huge fenced-in backyard. Rosebud will have *lots* of room to exercise, and I'll get a shelter constructed for her. A really nice one, guaranteed."

Zach finally felt it was safe to return the hat to his head. "No worries, then."

"Nope." She retreated another step. Then she turned to head for the door. As she slipped out into the night, she waved good-bye and called, "Thanks again, Mr. Harrigan."

"Zach," he reminded her, but she was gone before he got the word out.

Tornado let loose with a pathetic whinny. Then the stallion shrieked and began kicking the walls of his stall, making such a racket Zach could barely hear himself think. No matter. There wasn't a thought in his head that made much sense, anyway.

Miranda's departure made him feel as forlorn as the horse did.

Cookie reappeared on the landing. Hooking his elbows over the railing, he smiled down at Zach. "I can see why you didn't want to let her slip through your fingers."

Zach glared at the old foreman. "Oh, stuff it, Cookie. You were a great help. Telling her I kick buckets and get into fistfights. Thanks a bunch."

"Ah, now, I got her to laughin', didn't I? Way you were handlin' her, she was about to bring the law down on your head."

Zach grinned at the memory. "She *was* riled up, wasn't she?"

Cookie studied the stallion. "You gonna work with him some more tonight?"

Zach shook his head. "I've got some research to do on Pat Jones, the breeder. If that horse has been abused, clicker training may help, but it'll take a whole lot more than that to turn him around. I'll have to change my tactics."

"First thing is to gain his trust," Cookie mused. "That'll take some doin'. You gonna rescue your other bonnet, or leave it in there for him to stomp on some more?"

"Nah." Zach glanced at the stall as he began taking off his chaps. "I have a feeling it's a goner, and maybe it'll get him used to my smell. It's lucky I've got more than one hat. Need to buy another brown one, though. Okay, lights out. I'm going to collect Rosebud and head for the house."

Cookie lifted a hand in farewell and disappeared back into his apartment.

Thirty minutes later, Zach dumped the remains of a TV dinner in the trash and glanced toward his office. He planned to spend the rest of the evening deep in the bowels of the Internet to find any dirt he could on Tornado's former owner. Before leaving the kitchen, he poured himself a cup of coffee so he wouldn't get drowsy, then headed up the hall.

Rosebud followed him, the taps of her hooves on slate becoming muffled as they stepped onto the thick office carpeting. After Zach turned on the lamp, golden light spilled across the ash surface of his cluttered desk, piles of papers casting square-edged shadows onto the leather blotter. He sank onto the leather chair, set his mug off to one side, and reached for his landline phone to check his business messages.

The first two were from people with horse problems; another few were from people in the quarter horse industry shopping for a quality stallion or brood mare. Zach listened with bored distraction, taking notes so he could get back to each person later. Then a voice came over the line that swept the cobwebs of routine from his mind.

"Hello, Mr. Harrigan, this is Jarrod Black calling from the Malheur County district attorney's office. It's imperative that I speak with you about a horse you purchased a couple of months ago from Patrick Jones in Ontario, Oregon. Please get in touch with me as quickly as you can, regardless of the hour."

The attorney left his cell number and bade Zach a hasty, taut-with-tension farewell.

The next messages alarmed Zach even more. The Malheur County sheriff wanted to talk to him. The final recording was from Zach's attorney, Carlo Bergetti. "Damn it, Zach, where the hell are you? Tried to reach you on your cell around six. You must have it turned off. All hell broke loose in Ontario. The county sheriff and the district attorney need to talk to you about Morpheus, that stallion you bought a while back. Call me. Doesn't matter how late. The shit has hit the fan."

Zach sat there a moment, dreading what Carlo might tell him. He had a bad feeling, a very bad feeling. The only sounds in the room were the soft huffs of Rosebud's breathing, the tick of the grandfather clock, and an occasional squeak of the chair when Zach shifted his weight.

His hands felt oddly numb as he punched in the attorney's phone number. The man answered on the second ring, barking, "Hello."

Carlo had been Zach's lawyer for years, and they'd fallen into a relaxed relationship with no pretense. "Carlo, Zach here. What the hell's going on? Had my phone off while I worked with a horse and didn't know you were trying to get in touch with me."

Zach heard Carlo chew and swallow. "*Finally* you call. Took the wife to Diamond Lake for a two-day getaway, and we no sooner got home this evening than both my phones started ringing off the hook. The sheriff and D.A. are frantic to get in touch with you."

Zach pinched the bridge of his nose. "How did they get *your* number?"

"One of Jones's employees must have gotten it off the stable phone, I guess, from that time when I called there to rattle cages about the horse being crazy." Carlo expelled a tight breath. "Brace yourself, buddy. I've got bad news. Pat Jones is dead, and that's only the tip of the iceberg."

Zach was stunned. "I knew the guy was ill, but I had no idea he was that ill."

"Lung cancer. Heavy smoker, I guess. Kicked the bucket two days ago. Did you ever even meet the man?"

"Actually, no. He was so sick when I bought Tornado that his stable foreman had been assigned temporary power of attorney for all the ranch business, and I dealt with him, a fellow named Steve Ristol."

Zach heard the sharp rap of Carlo's footsteps and envisioned the lawyer walking across the large expanse of living-area terra-cotta tile to his elegant home office. "They told me the horse is called Morpheus."

"I got the name changed," Zach explained. "Can you get to the point, Carlo?"

"Ristol was arrested this afternoon. Apparently Jones was out of commission for months, trusted Ristol implicitly, gave him total control of the ranch operations, and the man turned into a cowboy version of Hitler, mistreating the horses and terminating any employee who bucked him. All his subordinates were afraid of losing their jobs, so they didn't report him, but after Jones died, they must have figured their jobs were history anyway and started talking."

A cold chill washed over Zach. He remembered the fiery anger in Miranda's eyes as she bellied up to him. *Someone has abused this horse.* Zach couldn't believe this. He just couldn't believe it. A choking sensation filled his throat. He leaned back in the chair and closed his eyes. "So Tornado *has* been abused."

"The term 'abused' fails to describe it," Carlo retorted, and then began giving Zach details that made him feel sick to his stomach.

A female stable hand had been the first employee to call the authorities that afternoon to blow the whistle on Ristol. She'd even volunteered to testify in court. According to her, Morpheus, aka Tornado, had been haltered and snubbed to a post, then hobbled to receive his punishment. Ristol had allegedly used an electric prod on the stallion, sometimes holding the ignited tip against the horse's underbelly so long that it burned the animal. He'd whipped the stallion with a pronged dog collar until he brought up blood. *It feels as if he's been repeatedly stabbed with an ice pick*, Miranda had cried angrily. Ristol had even denied Morpheus meals, not often enough to make the horse gaunt, but occasionally as a punitive measure. He'd also put him in small enclosures and tossed lighted firecrackers at his feet. The list went on, and Morpheus hadn't been the only horse to endure such horrible treatment.

Battling waves of nausea, Zach leaned forward on the chair to brace an elbow on his desk. "Oh, dear God," he whispered. "No wonder the horse acts so crazy."

Carlo fell quiet for a moment. "I'm sorry, Zach. I hate to hit you with this all at once, but you need to get Tucker over there right away to examine that horse from head to toe for signs of abusive treatment. Apparently when Ristol realized a few months back that Jones might die, he started selling off the horses that bore physical signs of his abuse. The authorities are trying to track down the other buyers, but it'll take time. The ranch employees remembered you because you're something of a celebrity, but they're hazy on the names of the other folks who bought mistreated horses."

Carlo sighed before he continued. "The cops are scrambling to get a search warrant to look at the ranch files. Jones's wife refuses to cooperate. She's probably afraid charges will be filed against her and is conferring with a lawyer who has advised her to protect the records. Or, hell, who knows? Maybe she and Ristol had something going while her husband was sick, and she's trying to buy him some time. Anyhow, in the meantime, the county sheriff is holding Ristol without any hard evidence, and in Malheur County, arraignment hearings take place every afternoon at one, Monday through Friday. The Malheur County D.A. wants Ristol's head on a platter. When I spoke to him this evening, he told me he thinks Ristol will run if he's released from jail. They need some irrefutable physical evidence before that hearing tomorrow."

"The testimony of all the employees isn't enough to hold the bastard?"

"The testimony of that many people constitutes probable cause for arrest, but for the hearing, they need hard proof to back up the allegations. Without it, Ristol's attorney can argue that the employees dislike Ristol and the allegations are all a pack of lies. If you can't get some evidence to them before one tomorrow, Ristol will be released and will probably skip out."

"Why can't they just postpone the hearing until Monday?" Zach asked.

"No way. When a person is arrested, they're entitled

to go before a judge at the next scheduled arraignment hearing. It's the law. If the arrest had been postponed until tomorrow, Ristol could have been held until Monday, but the sheriff may have been afraid the guy would skip out."

"I'll get Tucker on the horn, ASAP," Zach said wearily. Remembering Miranda's avowal that Tornado's head was covered with scars, he added, "I'm confident we'll find plenty of evidence to keep the bastard in jail. Will digital photos sent as e-mail attachments and a faxed statement signed by the vet be sufficient for now?"

"Can you get your hands on a camera that shows the date and time at the edge of the photo?"

"No worries," Zach assured him. "Tucker is often asked to document equine abuse for the local Humane Society. I'm sure he has his camera set for that."

"You'll also need to sign a statement verifying that the photos are of the stallion you bought from Pat Jones."

"Done," Zach said. "I have a message from the D.A. of Malheur County. He wants me to call him."

"I'll take care of it," Carlo assured him. "You concentrate on getting the evidence they need for that hearing tomorrow."

After ending the call, Zach phoned Tucker and Cookie. Ten minutes later, they met in the arena. Samantha had come with her husband. When she met Zach's gaze, the expression in her dark eyes told him she understood, possibly better than anyone, how bad he felt. In Zach's mind, it wasn't only about the abuse Tornado had endured, but also that he'd failed to recognize that the stallion's behavioral issues stemmed from it.

In order to get close enough to sedate the horse, they had to haze him into the hydraulic box chute. As expected, Tornado went nuts. After the third unsuccessful and undeniably dangerous attempt to get the stallion into the enclosure, Cookie said, "You should call that girl, Zach. I'd bet next month's paycheck that she could keep him calm while Tucker gives him the shot. Easier on the horse, and a hell of a lot safer for us."

Zach considered the suggestion and ran back to the house to get Miranda's number off the main line. After checking on Rosebud, he hurried back to the arena, calling Miranda on his cell as he went.

Mandy had just flipped on the computer for another session of medical transcription when the phone rang. She grabbed the receiver out of its base.

"Hello."

"Hey, Miranda, it's Zach Harrigan."

Mandy's heart sank. She feared that he'd changed his mind about giving Luke a second chance. "Hi, Mr. Harrigan. What a nice surprise."

"Not really. I've got a problem over here, and I'd really appreciate it if you could help me out."

Relieved that he wasn't calling to cancel their meeting tomorrow night, Mandy said, "Certainly. What do you need?"

She listened as Zach briefed her on the developments that had unfolded earlier. Her stomach lurched when she heard about the terrible things Tornado had endured.

"Anyway, the Malheur County sheriff has the jerk in jail, but without some solid evidence for that hearing tomorrow, they won't be able to hold him. I've been asked to take photographs of Tornado to document that he's been abused. In order to do that, we need to sedate him, and Tucker can't get close enough to give him the shot unless we put him in a box chute. *That* is damned near impossible, and Cookie came up with the idea of calling you. Tornado trusts you. Why, I don't know, but he does. If you were here, maybe he'd remain calm enough to let Tucker stick him."

Mandy was already on her feet. "I'll need to get a sitter to stay with Luke. If I can't, I'll have to bring him along. I suppose he could sit in the car if he wears a heavy coat."

"That, or he could stay in the stable office. It's warm in there."

Mandy glanced at her watch. "I'll be there as fast as I can."

"I owe you one," he said, his voice growing husky. "Drive safe. It's important that we get this done ASAP, but it's not so urgent you need to break the speed limit."

After disconnecting, Mandy called her usual sitter but the woman didn't answer. She was either out for the evening or had already gone to bed. As a second resort, Mandy phoned another lady who occasionally stayed with Luke. She was less pleasant and Luke didn't like her, but given that he had already gone to bed, he wouldn't have to interact with her. Luckily the woman answered and agreed to come over.

"My nighttime rate is more," she said.

"I don't care," Mandy informed her. "Just get here as fast as you can."

After ending the call, Mandy dashed to her bedroom to jerk off her pajamas and throw on jeans and a sweater. She was dressed and ready to leave when the sitter showed up.

When Mandy pulled up in front of the ranch gate, Zach was waiting on the opposite side to let her in. Once she was on the property, she stopped the Honda and rolled down her window. "You want to ride back with me?"

"Sure." He loped around the vehicle, opened the passenger door, jerked off his hat, and swung in beside her. "I really appreciate this, Miranda. Tornado is beside himself. Each time we tried to get him into the box chute, he got more and more upset."

The scent of Zach filled Mandy's nostrils—a pleasant blend of leather, hay, grain, aftershave, and male musk.

As she eased the Honda forward, her hands tightened on the wheel. She was unaccustomed to being in such close quarters with any man other than Luke.

"I'm so sorry about Tornado," she told him.

His voice ached with regret as he replied, "I feel awful for not recognizing the signs. You nailed it right on the head. Tornado isn't crazy, only terrified. I've been working with him all wrong. The first things an abused horse needs are unconditional love and unfailing patience. All this time, I should have been trying to gain his trust, and I—"

Mandy heard his voice catch as she parked outside the arena. She cut the engine and turned to peer at him through the darkness that suddenly enveloped them. Though his face was lost in the gloom, she suspected he was battling tears. "It isn't your fault, Mr. Harrigan. You had no way of knowing. Tornado couldn't tell you what had happened to him."

"He talked to you," Zach retorted. "How, I don't know, but I was watching, and there's no doubt in my mind that he was somehow communicating with you."

"Yes," she confessed. "In a way I can't explain, he did. But that's only because—" Mandy caught herself. Zach Harrigan had no need to know about her past or the incidents that had molded her into a person who could sense fear in others. She settled for saying, "Shall we?" The conversation ended when she opened her door.

Zach walked beside her to the personnel door and held it ajar so she could precede him into the building. The instant Mandy stepped inside, she heard Tornado shriek. Tucker Coulter, a petite, dark-haired woman, and Cookie stood well back from the stallion's stall gate. Conscious of Zach right behind her, Mandy hurried over to them.

When Tornado saw Mandy, he stopped rearing. A tremor shook his huge body, and he emitted a beseeching little grunt. Mandy went to the gate, stepped up onto a rung, and stretched out her arm. "Hey, big guy," she said softly. "What are you throwing such a big fuss about?"

The stallion grunted again and elongated his neck but remained where he was. Mandy glanced over her shoulder. "Would you mind stepping back a bit more? I think your nearness to the gate is making him nervous."

Everyone obliged, and Tornado's reaction was almost immediate. He hurried over to the gate, whickered and chuffed, and thrust his nose under Mandy's arm. Tears stung her eyes as she rested her cheek against the animal's temple.

"Ah, Tornado," she whispered, "you have to trust me, okay? That awful man who hurt you is in jail, but they'll have to turn him loose if we can't get some pictures of your scars. Cameras are kind of scary." She ran a hand along the ridge of the stallion's neck. "They flash and make little clicking sounds. But I promise nothing bad will happen. Okay?"

Mandy waited until she felt all the tension leave the horse's body. Then she glanced back at Zach. "How do you want to do this?"

"You think you can get a halter on him again?" Zach asked. "If you can, maybe you can move far to the left and get him to stand sideways to the gate. Tucker can give him the shot through the rungs."

"Will that hurt him?" Mandy had just promised Tornado that he wouldn't be hurt, and it was a promise she meant to keep.

"No. A tiny prick on the rump," Tucker assured her. "He'll barely feel it. Once the sedative takes effect, which will take a while because I can't give him anything intravenously, he'll go down and be so sleepy for a while that he won't really care what we do with him."

Zach brought Mandy a halter. As had happened earlier in the evening, Tornado didn't object when she slipped the leather straps over his nose and fastened the buckle. When Mandy moved to the far left end of the gate, the stallion followed her without question. She grabbed his cheek strap and began scratching his shoulder and side to get him to stand parallel to the gate. When the horse was in position, Tucker circled around to the right and slipped up behind the stallion with the hypodermic needle. The stallion chuffed when he felt the prick, but he seemed to be so intent on the petting from Mandy that he didn't act up as the large amount of medication was administered.

Tucker backed away, shaking his head in amazement. "I've never seen anything like this. He's putty in your hands. What did you do, cast a spell over him?"

Mandy smiled sadly. "No black magic involved. He just senses that I won't hurt him, is all. How long will it take for the sedative to work?"

"It won't be as fast as something straight into a vein. Thirty minutes, I'm guessing. And it's short duration, so he won't be groggy for very long."

Tucker slipped an arm around the dark-haired woman's slender shoulders. The gesture conveyed affection. The expression that softened his handsome features spoke of deep love. The woman—Mandy suspected she was Zach's sister, Samantha—smiled up at him, his feelings for her mirrored in her expressive brown eyes. Mandy fleetingly wondered how it might feel to share a love like that, to know, way deep in your heart, that a man's devotion to you would never falter. Being in love with a man was an experience Mandy had never hoped to have, but for an instant, watching Tucker and Samantha together, she felt empty inside and envied them a little.

When the sedative finally began to take effect, Tornado hung his head and weaved slightly on his feet. Mandy was forced to stand back and watch, fascinated, while the other four people went to work. Zach led the drugged horse to the center of the enclosure. Samantha spread a towel on the stall floor to the left of the horse. Tucker stood at the stallion's left shoulder.

The vet checked to make sure Samantha was out of the way and then pressed the palms of both hands against Tornado's left side. Even sedated and groggy, the stallion braced against the pressure, and when Tucker suddenly removed his hands, Tornado went down as if a hard wind from the right had knocked him over. When he landed, Mandy saw that the towel had been carefully positioned so his head would lie on it.

It was the slickest trick Mandy had ever seen. Tornado whinnied and struggled to get up, but he was too out of it to gain his feet. Samantha beckoned to Mandy.

"I know you want to be with him. Come on in. He'll feel calmer if you're here."

Mandy hurried inside and knelt at Tornado's head. He trembled and chuffed when she began petting him. That told Mandy that the stallion still recognized her. More important, he still trusted her. She'd been afraid he might resent that she'd tricked him.

Samantha crouched beside Mandy. "I'm Zach's sister, Sam." She held out a small but strong-looking hand. "Somehow, we bypassed introductions."

"I'm Miranda Pajeck." Mandy shook hands with her. "I'm pleased to meet you."

Sam fingered the horse's tangled mane. "Poor fellow. He's so scared of everyone, he can't be groomed much."

Tucker approached with an electric clipper. Hunkering beside his wife, he turned his gaze to Mandy. "Zach says you felt scars under his coat. You remember where?"

"All over his head." Mandy pointed to a spot she knew was peppered with marks.

Tucker shaved a small place on Tornado's forehead to reveal at least a dozen scars, each about the diameter of an ice pick. "Pay dirt."

Zach moved in to take pictures. Next Mandy directed

Tucker to the stallion's neck. Tucker chose to shave away the hair beneath the fall of Tornado's mane. "This way, the mane will hide the bald spots."

Once again, the clipping revealed a mass of scars. Zach swore under his breath as he took pictures. "Ristol whipped him with a pronged dog collar," he said angrily. "Sweet Jesus, is this poor horse scarred from head to toe?"

The next revelation was the scars on the horse's underbelly. Hair wouldn't grow where Tornado had been burned by the electrical prod. The marks weren't visible when the horse was standing, but they were very apparent with the stallion lying on his side. The instant Tucker hoisted one of Tornado's hind legs, Mandy gasped. The scars were near, even on, the animal's privates. Tears burned her eyes as she stared at the evidence of Ristol's merciless treachery. How could anyone be so cruel to an animal?

When Zach had taken all the pictures necessary, he left for the house to tag the photos with identifying captions on his computer. After Tornado was back on his feet, Tucker would join him there to compose their individual statements and send the information to the authorities in Malheur County. Cookie and Samantha stayed to help with Tornado until the sedative wore off. Mandy's presence was no longer needed.

Even so, she lingered for a while, her heart aching as she stroked Tornado, her fingertips lightly grazing the scars Tucker's clippers had revealed. Her heart caught each time Tucker used a stethoscope to check the stallion's heartbeat.

"Is he okay?" she asked faintly.

"Right as rain," Tucker assured her. "This is only routine."

When Mandy finally left for home, the tears she'd held at bay slid silently down her cheeks. The world could be such a cruel place. She'd learned that long ago.

But that didn't make it any easier to accept what had happened to Tornado. She hoped Steve Ristol received a very long prison sentence.

By the time everything had been sent to the Malheur County authorities and Tucker and Samantha had left, Zach was completely exhausted. He flopped down onto his office chair and stared stupidly at nothing. His chest felt as if someone had injected his rib-cage cavity with molten lead that had cooled and hardened into a massive lump. If he lived to be a hundred, he'd never forget Tornado trying to hide his head under Miranda's arm. The stallion sensed that he'd get nothing but love from her without any expectations riding double. With her, the horse could just be himself, a huge, angry, frightened mass of muscle that wanted to be comforted.

Miranda had delivered. Zach sure as hell hadn't.

He shut down the computer. Staring past the desk light into the shadowy end of the room, he had to face and accept that he was a horse trainer and an authoritative figure, which made him a fearsome person to Tornado. The horse didn't know what mean trick Zach might pull on him next. Had Tornado been beaten with a currycomb at some point? Zach's muscles knotted as waves of sheer rage crashed over him. Men like Ristol grew violent with their fists and with anything they held in their hands. A currycomb could have been used as a punitive instrument at some point.

Now armed with the knowledge of Tornado's background, Zach realized something else that made him feel small. Tornado had already come a long way by allowing Zach to touch him sometimes. For the stallion, that must have taken tremendous courage, because the horse had learned firsthand how evil and unpredictable men could be.

Zach picked up the phone, hit "menu," and then scanned the list of callers until he found Miranda's number. He punched "send" and rocked back on the chair while the phone rang. Finally, her sweet voice came over the wire. "Hello?"

"Hi." Zach's voice rasped like a rusty tin can being dragged across bumpy concrete. "It's Zach. I hope you weren't asleep. Any normal person would be."

"I'm not normal, I guess. I had some work to finish up." She hesitated and her voice tightened. "Did something go wrong with Tornado after I left?"

Zach smiled. "No. He came out of it just fine. I just called to thank you. We could have hazed him into the chute, but it would have been traumatic for him. You saved him from that. He was calm, unafraid. I can't tell you how much I appreciate that."

"There's no need to thank me. I was glad to do it. This may sound silly, but he's special to me."

"Even so, it was late when I called. You could have said no." Zach raked a hand through his hair. "I, um, was thinking. You had to pay for a sitter." Zach didn't get *why* a nineteen-year-old boy needed one, but he accepted that Miranda never left the kid alone. "I'd like to cover the cost of that." He suspected she didn't have much money. "And, please, don't refuse. My horse, my expense."

"Don't be silly. Having the sitter here didn't cost *that* much."

Zach pinched the bridge of his nose. "Well, thanks for coming. You made the whole mess a lot easier for my horse."

"My pleasure. I'm just glad to know he's awake now and doing well."

Silence came over the line. Zach tried to think of something else to say and couldn't. For some indefinable reason, he didn't want to hang up. The sound of her voice eased the ache in his chest. *Crazy*. They were veritable strangers. Hell, he didn't even know her well enough to chitchat.

He settled for saying, "I'll be there tomorrow night as agreed."

"We'll be waiting," she replied softly.

Another silence. Zach listened to her breathing, realized he was clinging to the sound as if it were a lifeline, and tightened his grip on the phone. He felt so awful about not realizing what was wrong with Tornado, and somehow she was like balm on the wound, soothing away the hurt. "Good night, then," he forced himself to say.

"Good night," she told him, her voice sweet and as soft as a caress.

Zach disconnected but kept the phone pressed to his ear for a second, not wanting the contact with her to end. Finally he shoved the cell back in its case and pushed wearily to his feet. Ruffling Rosebud's flyaway forelock, he said, "Come on, sweetheart. We're bunking in the arena tonight."

Rosebud followed him into the kitchen. Zach left her there to collect a sleeping bag from the storage room. Ten minutes later, he and the mini were walking to the arena. Once inside, Zach fetched Rosebud's bucket and hay feeder from her daytime holding area. Then he set up a makeshift camp for himself and the tiny horse outside Tornado's stall. The stallion chuffed and wheeled away as Zach unrolled the sleeping bag and unzipped it. Zach ignored his protests. The stallion would eventually get used to this ritual. For an indefinite time, Zach would be sleeping here every night.

After dousing the lights, he decided to keep his boots on. Sleeping around horses barefoot felt all wrong to him. After he climbed into the sleeping bag and pillowed his head on his crossed arms, Rosebud came over to sniff him. In the wash of moonlight coming through the skylights, her expression looked bewildered.

Zach chuckled. "I know it seems strange to you sleeping out here, but the big guy in there needs a couple of friends. You and I are elected."

Rosebud, left to wander at will inside the huge building, chose instead to thrust her head through the rungs of Tornado's stall gate. Zach tensed. The mini and stallion had never met, and Zach feared Tornado might kick or bite her. Instead the big lug touched his nose to Rosebud's, whickered, and nibbled at her lips. The mini nickered and nibbled back. Zach watched the exchange in wonder. *He's so sweet*, Miranda had said. Until tonight, Zach had never seen the gentle side of Tornado, but watching him now, he couldn't deny that the stallion was being very careful with the mini.

Strange. Apparently Tornado felt that he could let down his guard with Rosebud because she posed no threat to him. The two animals exchanged breath, bumped each other, made odd little sounds, and, just that quickly, seemed to forge a fast friendship.

Zach drifted off to sleep, images of Miranda moving sweetly through his mind.

Chapter Eight

The next evening, Mandy's doorbell rang at precisely seven. She wondered whether Zach had parked at the end of the block and waited in order to be right on time. Sniffing the air in hopes that the cookies she'd just removed from the oven would camouflage any lingering fishy odor from dinner, she raced through the dining room, detoured in the living room to pick up candy wrappers, and then hurried to answer the door.

The sound of her rapid footsteps caught Luke's attention. "What are you so nervous about? It's not like he's the president of the United States or anything."

Mandy wiped her sweaty palm on her slacks and then grasped the doorknob. In a low voice, she said, "Stuff a sock in it. You promised to be on your best behavior."

As she drew open the door, Mandy pasted on a smile, praying it didn't look as stiff as it felt. And then she forgot everything but the cowboy on her steps. Haloed by the porch light, he looked so incredible that *handsome* didn't begin to describe him. The Wranglers, riding boots, and Stetson seemed natural on him, and his loose-hipped stance displayed his trim, muscular build to perfection. His eyes, gleaming in the light, were what really made her heart race, though. Coffee dark, they had a way of looking *into* her instead of *at* her, making her feel transparent and a little breathless. Rosebud stood beside him. One of his big hands gripped the handle of her harness.

"Hi," she pushed out, and then wished she'd said something else. What, she didn't know. She drew the door wide and gestured to welcome him in. "You're right on time."

"It's a failing of mine," he said. His voice, laced with amusement, made her wonder whether he knew how nervous she felt.

Mandy realized she hadn't stepped back to allow him in and kicked her feet into reverse so fast that she snagged the two-inch heel of her left slip-on sandal on the carpet. Low-heeled shoes were a weakness of hers. Because she didn't often go to an office, dressing up a bit made her feel more professional and productive. For a horrible second, she pictured herself falling backward in a sprawl, but Zach snaked out a hand to catch her arm and steadied her just in time. At his touch, a tingle of warmth shot from her elbow to her shoulder. She was glad when he quickly released his hold on her.

"Careful, there." He glanced down at her shoes and quirked an eyebrow. "Ankle breakers again? What you need are some nice, sensible boots."

Mandy figured she was more in need of lessons in graceful comportment. "Come in, come in. Luke and I are so excited to have you here." She smiled at Rosebud. "Both of you." Turning toward her brother, she cued him with, "Aren't we, Luke?"

Luke didn't strike Zach as being very enthusiastic. He slumped at the end of a tweed sofa, not even bothering to turn his head in their direction. Zach wondered if the kid spent most of his life there, letting his sister wait on him. But then he gave himself a hard mental shake. He'd come here determined to give Luke a fair chance, and he would do exactly that.

"Hi, Mr. Harrigan," Luke said, his tone not exactly warm, but not cold and resentful, either. "I'm glad you agreed to come."

"I'm glad to be here," Zach replied. "Good to see you again, Luke."

Luke's mouth curved in a tight smile. "Sorry about my behavior the other day."

Mandy released a little laugh and pressed her palms together. Then she circled Zach and Rosebud to close the front door. With a wave of her hand, she said, "Excuse the house. I cleaned today, but it's small, and we clutter it up pretty fast."

On the way to her door, Zach had admired the fresh paint on the exterior siding and the tidiness of the yard. He could tell she spent a lot of time on maintenance. The interior, filled with what looked like garage-sale purchases, had a warm, cozy ambience that Zach's expensively furnished house lacked. He had no idea what Miranda did for a living, but if she worked all week, how did she keep everything so nice? From what he'd seen so far, Luke himself was a full-time job and then some.

She smiled at him, apparently uncertain what to do or say next. That made two of them, an unfamiliar experience for Zach. As he looked at her, he got the same feeling he'd gotten the first time he saw her. With her auburn hair loose around her shoulders and her face flushed with excitement, she was even lovelier than he remembered, not in the flashy way he'd always preferred, but in an understated, classy way. Searching her gaze, he once again noticed that innocent look, which baffled him. He guessed her to be in her late twenties. Such a pretty woman had to have had her share of boyfriends. But something about her told Zach that wasn't the case. Wearing an off-white cotton-knit sweater and tidily creased gray slacks, she emanated a schoolgirl sweetness that was totally at odds with Zach's knowledge of women her age.

The house smelled faintly of fish, but the scents that made Zach's empty belly rumble were those of warm-from-the-oven chocolate-chip cookies—he could recognize that smell from a mile away—and freshly brewed coffee. Unlike the Pajecks, he hadn't had dinner. He'd worked with Rosebud from two until four thirty, then had spent two frustrating hours with Tornado. He'd lost track of time, and when he checked his watch, it had been half past six. After a mad dash to the stable restroom to wash up, he'd finger-combed his wet hair, plopped his hat back on, and driven here. It was just as well. Otherwise he might have considered a shower, a change of clothes, and a shave to impress Miranda, and he wasn't entirely sure that would have been a good idea.

Cookie's story about the worst thirty seconds of his life had Zach determined not to make the same mistake. Yes, Miranda Pajeck stirred something within him, and yes, he found her attractive, but that was as far as he wanted it to go. It had taken him a while to learn that his dick wasn't equipped with brains, but now that the lesson was driven home, he no longer allowed that part of his anatomy to do his thinking for him.

"Are you hungry?" Miranda asked, her guileless hazel eyes fixed on his in question.

Damn. Zach wondered if she'd heard his stomach growl. *Nailed.* "Yeah, I am a little. I keep rancher's hours, which means I eat supper whenever the day is done, and sometimes that's midnight or after."

"Well, I can fix you right up. I put the food away after dinner, but I'm sure it's still fairly warm, and we have coffee and cookies for dessert."

Zach detested fish and would have preferred going straight for the cookies. "That sounds great."

He bent to remove the guiding gear from Rosebud's stout little body. The moment the palomino sensed freedom, she made a beeline for Miranda, who welcomed her with the hugs and scratches that Rosebud loved to receive. Then, to Zach's surprise, the mini went directly to Luke, exhibiting no hesitation at all before she nudged his bony knee. Luke started as if he'd been stuck with a pin. But Rosebud wasn't going to be put off by shyness. She stretched her neck to nuzzle Luke's hand and whickered.

Zach didn't understand Rosebud's apparent eagerness to make friends with Luke. The kid was a jerk. But the mini seemed to think otherwise. The worry within Zach eased somewhat. Maybe Rosebud sensed something in Luke that Zach couldn't. She didn't get sidetracked when the youth jerked his hand back. She just nudged his other hand and patiently waited for him to reciprocate with a friendly hello.

Luke clamped both hands to his chest, his expression appalled. "What's it *doing*? That's the horse, right? Why's she bumping me? Does she bite?"

When Miranda didn't speak, Zach did. "No, she doesn't bite, Luke. She never has. I think she's taken a liking to you. She's just trying to make friends."

The tension eased from Luke's body. "I don't know if I want to get friendly so soon."

Fortunately, Rosebud's vocabulary was limited to commands and words of praise, so she took no offense at the comment. Watching his horse, Zach almost chuckled. Rosebud seemed to know somehow that Luke was different from every other human she'd ever met. It was almost as if the mini realized that Luke, or someone like him, was her destiny in life, and she was determined to get off to a good start with him.

The palomino lifted her right front hoof and plopped it on Luke's thigh. The kid jumped. "What's *that*?" he cried. He tried to move away but he was already at the end of the sofa and succeeded only in bunching himself into the corner.

Miranda laughed. "She wants to shake hands, Luke. You're being very rude. You don't want to hurt her feelings, do you?"

Luke looked none too concerned about hurting Rosebud's feelings, but to his credit, he extended his hand, which hung in the air above Rosebud's hoof. Rosebud rectified that by placing her foot in the loose curve of Luke's palm. Luke gave a nervous laugh.

"She really *does* want to shake hands." The kid carefully pumped the mini's foot up and down. "Wow. Hi, Rosebud. My name's Luke."

Rosebud nickered, withdrew her hoof from the kid's grasp, and went for more satisfying physical contact, burying her muzzle in the vee of Luke's thighs, perilously close to his crotch. Luke almost came up from the sofa, but then he laughed and relaxed, hesitantly feathering his fingertips over Rosebud's fluffy forelock and tracing the bony lines of her head and face. Rosebud ate it up.

"She's little," Luke said, clearly fascinated. "And she likes being scratched."

The youth found the hollows behind Rosebud's ears and rubbed vigorously. Rosebud grunted and pressed closer.

"I think she likes you, Luke," Miranda inserted.

Luke smiled. Rosebud almost crawled up in his lap. At that juncture, Miranda turned to Zach, gestured toward the kitchen, and said, "Shall we? It'll give them some time by themselves to get acquainted."

Zach still wasn't sure he wanted to leave Rosebud alone with a kid who had taken swings at his sister, but he figured he'd be close enough to come to his mini's rescue if Luke got out of line. He fell into step behind his hostess. His gaze dropped to the tantalizing swing of her hips. *Hot damn.* She was put together nicely.

"Have a seat." She gestured at a small round table encircled by four chairs. "Heating everything up won't take but a minute."

Zach deposited his hat on an adjacent chair and sat down, smoothing his hair as she opened the old refrigerator to remove plastic storage containers. While she bustled about, he gave her kitchen a once-over. Because his sister-in-law Loni was an interior decorator, Zach now knew more about tasteful color schemes than he'd ever dreamed he might. Miranda had a talent for it. The

sink wall was painted a dark green that set off the window frame, which had been stripped down to bare wood,
stained light maple, and was lined with tiny pots produc-
ing tender green shoots. The scalloped valance, bright
with a flowery pattern of rusts, oranges, reds, greens, and
creamy white, reflected the more muted green of the
other walls. She'd carried out those colors with accents
around the room—crimson pot holders, a rust tablecloth, off-white towels, and strategically placed knickknacks. A person barely noticed the chipped surface of
the white range, the yellowed enamel of the fridge, or
the cracked linoleum.

As she worked, she moved with brisk but graceful
efficiency. While stuff heated in the microwave, she ar-
ranged a china place setting in front of him, complete
with a linen napkin. Given that there were paper ones in
a wicker holder at the center of the table, Zach said, "No
need to get fancy. At home, I just grab a paper towel."

"We use paper napkins during the day, but for dinner,
we always use cloth."

The dimple flashed in her cheek as she leaned around
him to arrange the flatware. Her breast grazed his shoulder as she straightened. Her scent—that faint hint of
roses—had an intoxicating effect and filled his mind
with X-rated thoughts he prayed didn't show on his face.
He was grateful to be sitting down with the tablecloth
draping his lap. She snatched up a gardening magazine
that had lain open to his right and put it on the lower
shelf of a telephone stand between the kitchen and dining area.

When she'd finished arranging his place setting, all
that was lacking, in Zach's estimation, was a wineglass.
Every other detail was perfect. As she began dishing up
the food, the smell of her perfume was eclipsed by the
tantalizing aroma of the fish she spooned onto his plate.
It was like no fish Zach had ever seen, chunks of white
in a creamy sauce, served with steamed asparagus stalks

drizzled with hollandaise, mashed potatoes topped with grated cheese, a green salad in a separate bowl, and slices of sourdough on a bread plate with pats of real butter.

As she set a selection of salad dressings on the table, she said, "Sorry. Normally I put the dressings in small ramekins."

Zach flashed a grin and reached for the creamy ranch. He was unaccustomed to so much folderol. At formal family dinners the Harrigan women went all out, but for everyday meals, eating was a casual affair. "Salad dressing in a bottle is fine by me."

She sat across from him. The habits of a lifetime had Zach making a quick sign of the cross to say a silent meal blessing before he dug in. *Get the worst over first.* He went for the fish. After chewing and swallowing, he gave her a wondering look. "What *is* this stuff? It's fabulous!"

"It's just fillet of sole in a cream sauce. Nothing fancy, but I'm glad you like it."

Zach *loved* it. "I dread Lent every year because I *hate* fish. On Fridays during the season, I avoid fish by filling up on eggs and peanut butter."

"Would you care for something else?"

Zach chuckled. "Try to touch this plate and I'll bite your arm off. This stuff is delicious. What'd you do, attend a gourmet cooking school?"

A shadow crossed over her face but vanished so quickly Zach wondered if he had imagined it. She sat back down. "My father entertained. After my mom left, the cooking fell to me. She'd already taught me a lot. The rest I learned by trial and error."

"Not much error, if this is any example."

She laughed. "Oh, yes, lots of error. No one's born knowing how to cook." Her small white teeth closed for an instant on her full lower lip, and she looked away. Then the hostess took over again, and she smiled at him.

"I learned quicker than most, I suppose. My father was a stickler for perfection, especially when we had guests."

As Zach enjoyed a bite of the asparagus, he did some quick mental calculations. If he remembered correctly, Miranda had been only thirteen when her mother left. Had she been put in charge of the kitchen at that age? Surely not, but Zach didn't know her well enough to ask. So instead he simply enjoyed the meal, which ended with a dessert of delicious chocolate-chip cookies and a mug of perfectly brewed coffee.

"Chewy, just the way I like them," Zach told her as the chocolate chips melted over his tongue. "I hate when people bake them to a crisp."

Luke, who'd been served cookies in the living room, called out, "Rosebud wants a cookie, Mr. Harrigan. Is it okay to give her one?"

Zach's big horses could eat chocolate with no ill effects, but given Rosebud's diminutive stature and her recent bout with colic, he didn't want to take any chances. "No," he called. "Be right there." Pushing up from his chair, he went to the living room to give Luke a handful of the mini's training treats from the pouch on his belt.

"She won't like these as well," Zach explained as he dumped them into Luke's cupped palm, "but I don't want her getting sick again."

Luke nodded. "How many does she get at once?"

"A couple. When she nudges you, give her more."

"She's nice," Luke said. "Doesn't stink, either. I thought she might."

Zach patted the mini's head. "She gets fairly frequent baths. At my place, I have facilities for that. If you end up having her with you someday, you'll have to take her into the shower stall and wash her down in there."

A look of horrified fascination crossed Luke's face. "Together, me and her? In the shower? Are you serious? What if she steps on my feet?"

Zach bit back a grin. "She won't, Luke. She's trained

for that. If the time ever comes, you'll be ready for it. Horses need baths, just like we do."

When Zach returned to the kitchen, Miranda arched an eyebrow at him, her cheek dimpled in a smile. "He's warming to the idea, isn't he?"

"Seems to be." Zach wasn't yet ready to change his mind about Luke, but he did have to concede that the young man was making an effort. "We'll give it some time." He stared at the spot where the dimple had flashed and scrabbled for some brilliant remark that would make it appear again.

"His initial reluctance really was mostly my fault," she said softly.

Zach wanted to learn more about why Miranda believed that, but he wasn't sure he wanted to have the conversation where Luke might overhear. "How about showing me the backyard?" he suggested.

"Oh, certainly!" She bounced up from her chair. "It's out this way."

Grabbing a thick cardigan from a wall hook, she led him to an old door that, like the window frame, had been stripped down and stained. As she opened it and moved out onto a concrete porch, she gestured at the steep, narrow steps. "If we bring Rosebud here, I hope to build her a ramp with a nonslip surface. And I was thinking that an oversize doggy door might work really well for her, too. That way, she could come and go as she pleased."

Zach had no reservations whatsoever about Miranda's suitability to be Rosebud's next owner. It was her brother who posed the worry.

She leaned back in to flip on the yard lights. As Zach closed the door behind them and followed her onto the lawn, still patchy with snow from the last storm, he worried about her falling. Her footwear wasn't suited for walking over uneven ground.

"This is it," she said, gesturing expansively at the yard. "I told you it was large."

Zach surveyed the area, enclosed by a tall wooden fence. She hadn't exaggerated. It was big and blessedly uncluttered. One large tree, nude branches stark against the night sky, offered the promise of shade in summer. Fog had moved in, hanging low to create orbs of yellow around the street lamps on the next block. The smell of wood smoke drifted on the air, conjuring images in Zach's mind of families gathered around fireplaces, their faces washed with gold from the flickering flames.

"Very nice," he told her, and meant it.

There would be plenty of room for Rosebud to run and play, *if* she ever lived here. "Where would you locate her shelter?" he asked.

"There." She pointed to a far corner of the yard. "I have a little snowblower. I can create paths so it'll be easy to walk out there."

"It'll be up to Luke to care for her, you know. That *must* be his responsibility. It's necessary for the horse to form a bond with him."

She gave Zach a sidelong glance. "And you aren't certain Luke is capable of that."

"No, I'm not." Zach saw nothing to be gained by lying. "Are you?"

"He isn't at the moment," she conceded. "But with work, he'll get there."

"In my experience, no one works for something he doesn't really want."

Miranda smiled sadly. "I know Luke made a horrible first impression, Mr. Harrigan, but as I said, his initial reluctance to befriend Rosebud was mostly my fault."

"The name's Zach," he corrected. "And how was it mostly your fault? I don't mean to sound harsh, but the kid's nineteen. Don't you think he's a little old for you to be taking the blame and making excuses for his bad behavior?"

"Yes, way too old, which brings me back to what I told you last night. When I should have been strict and demanding, I cut him slack and did everything for him. When I should have disciplined him, I patted his head and pampered him. I was only a kid. I had no idea how to raise a little boy, especially not one with special needs."

"I know it must have been rough." Zach wanted to ask where the hell her father had been. Abusive or not, the man must have been present some of the time. "But the past is over. I only care about how Luke is now. I saw him take a swing at you. No matter how sad his personal story, I can't give Rosebud to someone who might mistreat her."

She rubbed her arms, making Zach regret his suggestion that they step outside. But this was a talk they needed to have, and it was better if Luke wasn't privy to it.

"I understand." In the yard lights, her eyes glistened up at him, large and pleading. "But, please, at least give him another chance. His behavior that first afternoon was deplorable, but it was mostly because he was afraid. At the time, he had it in his head that I wanted to get rid of him. He was fighting the college thing, thinking that I'd make him live elsewhere, then do a happy dance and go on a husband hunt. Now he understands that isn't my plan at all. I've assured him that he can go to college and still live at home. Knowing that, he's less apprehensive about getting a guide animal now."

Watching her face as she talked, Zach wondered if she'd ever secretly hoped to be rid of her brother. Apparently she'd been the kid's primary caregiver for years, and that was a heavy burden. How did she manage to have a social life? Maybe she didn't. That would account for the innocence he glimpsed in her eyes. The idea jolted him.

"Is your dad able to help out with Luke at all?" Zach asked. She stiffened, and her gaze went flat, but he plowed on anyhow. "I know you said he's . . . well, that there were problems. But surely he contributes financially."

"Our father is no longer a part of our lives."

Her tone didn't invite questions. Well, it was none of his business anyway. He barely knew her. "So, essentially, you've been responsible for Luke ever since your mother left?"

With a shiver, she said, "Let's go back in. I promised Luke some hot chocolate to go with his cookies, and I forgot to make it."

When they reentered the house, Zach stepped to the living room to check on his mini. Luke and Rosebud seemed to be getting along well. The kid laughed as he said, "No, Rosebud, only your treats for you. No cookies." And he was petting her. Eyes half-closed, Rosebud leaned against Luke's knee with every indication of contentment.

After delivering a mug of chocolate to Luke, Miranda served Zach more coffee in the kitchen and encouraged him to have more cookies. He took her up on the offer. She'd served a great dinner, but the portions had been small by his standards, and he still felt hungry.

He had just polished off cookie number five when Luke hollered from the living room, "Mandy, I'm done. Come get my cup and plate!"

Miranda leaped up to do her brother's bidding, which had not included a *please*. That rubbed Zach the wrong way. She wasn't Luke's servant. Surely the kid could bring his own plate and cup back to the kitchen.

Miranda had no sooner finished rinsing the cup and plate for the dishwasher than her brother yelled, "I need to use the bathroom!"

Zach watched in curious amazement as Miranda guided her brother through the house and then stood outside the bathroom, waiting for Luke to finish his business. Zach determined then and there that something was way off-kilter in this brother-sister relationship. Luke was pretending to be helpless, and Miranda was buying into it.

When Luke emerged from the bathroom, Miranda led him back to the sofa, where Rosebud awaited him. Zach's negative thoughts were mitigated slightly when he saw how eagerly the kid reached out for Rosebud. Miranda repositioned a cushion behind her brother and returned to the kitchen, gracing Zach with a hesitant smile.

"Mandy," he said. "That's your nickname?"

She nodded. "Hardly anyone calls me Miranda. You can continue to call me that, of course. It's what you're already used to."

"Mandy," Zach repeated slowly. "I like it, actually. It suits you somehow."

Searching her gaze, Zach decided he hadn't imagined the innocence in her eyes. All his instincts told him she was still wet behind the ears when it came to sexual experience. Zach would have gone to the bank on it.

He found that appealing, which made him wonder if he didn't need his head examined. He'd always preferred women who knew the score. Maybe that was why he'd never found anyone special. The gals who hung out in honky-tonks were looking for a good time, not a long-term commitment, and they seldom had a serious thought in their heads. Mandy was so different, shouldering the burden of a blind brother, working to earn the bread and butter, plus maintaining a home. Most of her thoughts were probably serious, and now that she was gearing up to send Luke to college, they'd only grow more serious. It would be a huge undertaking, both financially and emotionally. Right now she looked exhausted. Time for him to make a graceful exit.

"Well," Zach said, glancing at his watch. "How time does fly. It's already almost nine. The company needs to go home so you two can get some sleep."

"Oh, there's no need to rush off. Luke doesn't usually turn in until ten."

And when did she turn in? Zach suspected that she

stayed up late to work at whatever it was she did to make a living. He wanted to take her suggestion that he stay a bit longer as an indication that she was enjoying his company, but reality forced him to admit that she was probably only being polite. He had a feeling she'd be very busy over the next hour, getting her brother tucked in. *Weird.* If Carly Coulter could see this operation, she'd grab Luke by the ear and have him shaped up in two seconds flat.

"I get up well before dawn." Zach pretended to stifle a yawn. "It's time for Rosebud and me to make tracks."

She followed Zach to the living room, watching closely as he put the mini's harness back on. He realized she was trying to learn everything she could. That was nice, but it missed the real issue by a country mile. It was Luke who needed to learn this stuff. Zach had to admit that the kid had been much more pleasant this evening, but his apparent lack of desire to do anything without assistance was a huge concern. Even a small horse required care, and Luke wouldn't even take the initiative to care for himself.

When Zach and Rosebud were ready to leave, Mandy walked out onto the porch with them. In the dim glow of the yard light, she was so damned beautiful, her eyes shimmering, her soft mouth begging to be kissed. Zach was sorely tempted, but the innocence in her eyes held him back. If Zach kissed her, she might read more into it than he intended. So instead he shook her hand. Hers almost disappeared in his.

"Thanks a lot for dinner. It was quite a treat for a rancher who usually gets a microwave meal or something out of a can."

She looked down at their joined hands and smiled. "It was my pleasure. I'm glad you enjoyed it."

"Next time, why don't you and Luke come out to my place?" he suggested. "I'll crank up the barbecue. It's protected by the deck overhang, so even if it snows, I can still cook outside. I grill a great steak." He gave her a teasing wink. "It won't compare to your creamy sole fillets, but I can promise a decent meal."

She withdrew her hand. "We'd love to come. The third time is always a charm. If Luke is with Rosebud longer next time, maybe he'll forge a real bond with her. Can I bring something? A salad or dessert? Do you like chocolate cake?"

Zach's taste buds began doing push-ups. "Love it. You're on, if you're sure you don't mind. What evening would be good for you? I'm still open until Thursday."

"Are you free tomorrow night?" she asked.

In his wilder days, he'd always reserved weekend nights for raising hell in town, but those habits were far behind him now. A Saturday evening with Miranda Pajeck, even without chocolate cake, sounded great. "Sure, tomorrow night would be fine."

They both agreed that having some time to socialize prior to dinner would be good for both Luke and Rosebud, so they settled on a four-o'clock arrival time. Zach entered a reminder into his phone. Then he tipped his hat and turned to walk with Rosebud to the SUV. He'd gotten all of fifteen feet when her voice brought him to an abrupt halt.

"Mr. Harrigan? Zach?"

"Yeah?"

"Thank you. For letting there be a next time."

The soft tones made his heart jump. "That's okay. See you tomorrow."

Once behind the steering wheel, Zach realized his palms were sweaty. What was that all about? It wasn't as if the barbecue tomorrow evening would be a date. So why did he feel as nervous and keyed up as a green kid who'd just asked the high school homecoming queen to the senior prom?

Get a grip, Harrigan, he told himself sternly. *Okay, you're attracted to her. But chances are you won't end up giving Rosebud to that spoiled kid, and that will end any chance of romance, or even friendship, real quick. Get over it and go home.*

He started the truck. It was easy to make resolutions. But he couldn't kick the look in her eyes out of his mind.

Chapter Nine

The next day Zach made arrangements with Cookie to be absent that afternoon. The old foreman dropped a caustic remark about Zach fooling around like a city swell instead of working a full day, but he agreed to cover for him.

As Zach prepared for the barbecue, he felt far more nervous than the occasion warranted. About the only thing he wasn't concerned about was the present weather. They'd been gifted with a sunny day that was beautiful and shirtsleeve warm, featuring powder blue skies streaked with fluffy white clouds. He worried that a storm would roll in at any moment—the norm for February in central Oregon—to dump buckets of rain or, even worse, snow.

As four o'clock drew near, he fretted over the size of the spuds he planned to bake. He worried that he'd cut the salad tomatoes into too-large chunks. He set the table, and then he kept rearranging stuff, wanting the place settings to make a statement. Regular fork, check. Salad fork, check. Linen napkins, check. He'd borrowed the latter from his sister, pledging that he'd launder and press them before he returned them to her. Samantha had stared at him as if he had two heads, but she hadn't asked any questions. Small miracle.

When the table was set, he stood back to admire his work and decided it was all wrong. "I'm not fancy. This isn't me." He never pretended to be someone he wasn't. So why was he doing it for Mandy? She needed to like him for himself.

He snatched up the napkins and stuffed them in a drawer without a thought for potential wrinkles. The salad forks soon followed the napkins. This was a barbecue, not a state dinner. As a final touch, he plopped a roll of paper towels at the center of the table. Good enough. The lacy place mats, borrowed from his puzzled but cooperative stepmother, were a bit much, but he didn't have anything else. The table looked functional but not elaborate. Okay. He was ready.

Then he glanced down at himself. Instead of his usual blue jeans, he'd decided to wear his all-black honky-tonk duds, starched shirt, jeans with a crease, and church boots that shone like a mirror. Wrong look. Miranda might think he was trying to impress her. He was, but he didn't want to *look* like he was.

He raced upstairs, charged his bureau, yanked open drawers, and threw clothes until he found a go-to-town outfit: fairly new blue jeans, a white T-shirt, and a slightly wrinkled plaid shirt he pulled from the closet. He exchanged the shiny footgear for a pair of everyday boots. After dressing, he observed himself in the mirror, fussing with his collar, raking a hand through his hair, frowning at himself. *Shit*. He'd exchanged sophisticated for hayseed.

Before it was all over, Zach changed clothes twice, finally settling on the look he'd chosen in the first place. He was on the front deck scraping the barbecue grill with a wire brush when his sister Sam's voice came from behind him, startling him so badly he almost dropped the brush.

"I thought this was a business-type thing tonight. What's with the Goth look?"

Zach slammed the grill closed and spun to face his sister. She was a smaller, far more feminine version of the men in her family—slender and raven-haired with brown eyes, the Harrigan schnozzle, and a stubborn chin. She wore work clothes, dusty jeans, an oversize T-shirt, a ball cap, and well-worn riding boots.

"What's with the *what*?" he demanded.

"The Goth look." She gestured at her own clothing. "All the black. Are you socializing or holding a wake?"

Zach leaned his folded arms on the railing. "Samantha," he said with exaggerated patience, "I realize you're an old married woman now and no longer know what's hot, but puh-lease. Women go for black."

"Really?" Sam gave him another once-over. Her expression wasn't encouraging. "Is it some sort of 'watch out, babe' look?" She shrugged. "Miranda is really cute, but you didn't mention that this barbecue was going to be a date. No wonder you wanted my linen napkins." She peered through the screen door at the kitchen table. "Which, by the way, I see you aren't using."

Zach straightened away from the rail. *Shit*. Sam was right. He'd gone overboard with his dress. He glanced at his watch. It was three forty. He had twenty minutes or less to change clothes and finish up the last-minute things in the kitchen. "Sam, I need to run."

"Hold on a second. I've got a question I wanted—"

"Can it wait?"

His sister scowled up at him. "I suppose. But it really won't take—"

That was all Zach heard. He dashed back upstairs and in two short minutes of rummaging was once again wearing his town clothes—which equated to halfway new and clean without too many wrinkles. He was reaching for his boots when he heard a feminine voice calling from downstairs.

"Hello, Mr. Harrigan? Are you there?"

Zach shoved one foot into a boot, grabbed the second, and ran for the landing, hopping on one leg to finish donning the footwear as he went down the stairs. "Yo, right here."

Mandy stood on the front porch, her dainty nose pressed to the wire mesh of the screen door. She wore blue jeans, sneakers, and a green sweater, with the blue parka draped over one arm. As Zach moved toward her, he thanked God his sister had stopped by. Otherwise he wouldn't have changed clothes.

"Hey!" hc said, trying not to sound out of breath as he pushed open the screen door. "You're"—*early*—"right on time."

"A bit early, actually. I'm still learning how long it takes to get out here."

Miranda—Mandy, he preferred the nickname Mandy—stepped inside. Zach saw Luke sitting outside on the steps.

"Thirty minutes either way is considered on time in this family," Zach said, appropriating one of his father's sayings. "I'm the only exception to that rule. The rest of them will be late to their own funerals." Just then Zach glanced down. He'd snatched one brown boot and one black. *Damn.* Groping for presence of mind, he said, "Hey, Luke. Those steps can't be very comfortable. Why don't you grab a deck chair or come inside?" Directing his gaze at Mandy he said, "I have a couple of last-minute things to do upstairs. Soft drinks are in the fridge. Help yourself." *Look at the fridge, lady. Look anywhere but at my mismatched feet.*

Before she could say a word, Zach made a fast U-turn, his destination the master suite, now littered with discarded clothing. Black or brown? At this point he didn't give a shit which boots he wore. He just wanted two that matched.

Bemused, Mandy got Luke settled on a deck chair and took him an orange soda from the Sub-Zero refrigerator. Had her eyes played a trick on her, or had Zach been wearing mismatched boots? She'd seen men wear socks that weren't mates, but never mixed-up shoes. Strange.

Rosebud came to the screen and nudged the mesh, asking to be let outside. Mandy didn't know if the mini was allowed to leave the house without her master. Zach saved her from having to make that decision by appearing at the door. He pressed it open with the flat of his hand to let Rosebud out. The mini paused to let Mandy give her a quick pat on the head, then made a beeline for Luke. It warmed Mandy's heart to watch her brother and the horse make over each other. Within seconds, Luke was laughing and had one arm looped around Rosebud's neck.

Zach came to stand beside Mandy. He wore two brown boots now, but no hat. She'd seen him bareheaded, most recently last night in her kitchen, but it still seemed odd to see him that way now. His wavy hair glistened blue-black in the February sunlight that slanted in under the porch overhang. When he caught her studying him, he fiddled with the collar of his shirt, then checked his buttons.

"What?" he asked.

Mandy laughed. "Nothing. I'm just not used to seeing you without a hat. I thought cowboys wore them constantly."

His brown eyes warmed. "A gentleman cowboy removes his hat in certain situations: to greet a lady, to sit down for a meal, and sometimes briefly when he steps indoors. I've been going in and out, so my hat's on the coat tree for now."

"Ah, so you're a gentleman?"

A twinkle of mischief danced in his eyes. "Let's just say I aspire to be when the mood comes over me." He rubbed his hands together. "Hey, Luke, how would you like to take a spin around the yard with Rosebud? We've got plenty of time to fool around before dinner."

Luke looked startled by the invitation. "Oh, I don't know. I'm not sure—"

"Ah, come on," Zach insisted. "I'll be right there. I

promise not to leave you alone with her unless you ask me to."

Mandy stood aside to watch as Zach worked with Rosebud to get her down the steps. The mini kept trying to jump over several risers at a time.

"This is one thing she needs a lot of work on," Zach explained. "I called a trainer and talked with her. I guess stairs are difficult for most minis to master."

Mandy released a taut breath, relieved to have Zach's attention on the horse. Getting ready to come here today had set her nerves on edge. Zach was not only one of the handsomest men she'd ever met, but he was also nice and down-to-earth. She liked his easy manner, sense of humor, and lack of pretense. While getting Luke's soft drink, she had noticed the beautifully set table, with frilly place mats and everything just so. Yet smack-dab at the center he'd set a roll of paper towels, not even bothering to fold ripped-off sections and put them by the plates.

To Mandy, who'd been raised by a tyrant who insisted on pressed linen napkins at every meal, not to mention perfectly prepared and presented food, Zach's disregard of table embellishments was refreshing. He made her feel at case, the only exceptions being when he looked deeply into her eyes or when he asked questions she didn't wish to answer. But even when the latter occurred, he seemed to sense her reluctance and changed the subject.

Mandy had never felt quite this way about a man. Maybe it was foolish, but for the first time in her memory, she felt truly attracted and found herself yearning to explore the possibilities. Of course, realistically she knew there weren't any. She needed to focus on that.

After Zach led Luke down the front steps, Mandy perched on the top riser to watch as her brother took his first walk with Rosebud. Zach stayed close, not yet trusting Rosebud completely, but the little horse performed like the blue-ribbon champion she was. When she came to an obstacle, she veered around it. At the corner of a shed with low-hanging roof beams, she circled out so Luke wouldn't hit his head. It was all Mandy could do not to clap her hands.

Zach kept flashing Mandy broad grins and jabbing a thumb at the sky. She smiled back at him each time, as enamored of the horse as he was.

When Zach sensed that Luke was tiring, he invited the young man for a tour of the stable to meet the big horses. Luke immediately started shaking his head.

"I, um, don't think I want to do that. I haven't ever met a big horse."

Zach waved Mandy down from the steps. "Your sister will come. My big horses are wonderful. At least meet them before you decide you don't like them."

Mandy drew abreast of Zach. "What's up?"

Zach explained, and Mandy grasped her brother's arm. "It's fine, Luke. I'll be right there."

"Well." Luke tightened his hand on Rosebud's halter handle. "I guess. If I get nervous, we can leave, right?"

"Right," Zach assured the youth.

Luke touched Rosebud's ears with his free hand. "Okay, Rosebud, let's go."

As they drew near the arena, Tornado emerged from his stall and began to circle his paddock. The stallion let loose with a shrill whistle, clearly excited to see Mandy again. Zach was unprepared for what happened next. As the horse circled from the back of his paddock, he lengthened his lope, bunched at the rump, and went airborne, clearing the five-foot fence as if it weren't there.

"Oh, shit." Zach didn't know what to do. He had no way of protecting Mandy and Luke, and the stallion was bearing down on them at full speed, a glorious sight to see with his mane and tail lifting in the breeze, but a terrifying spectacle as well. "Head for the house!" he barked at Mandy and Luke.

Zach lunged into the horse's path, shouting and waving his arms, frantic to distract the stallion long enough to allow Mandy and Luke to escape. To his horror, Mandy ignored his instructions. Coming up behind him, she grabbed his arm and said, "Zach, it's okay. He's just coming to say hello."

Hello? That horse would pulverize all of them. "Get out of here! Now."

Miranda darted around him, straight into the stallion's path. "Don't be silly. He won't hurt me."

And, miracle of miracles, Tornado didn't. As Zach watched, frozen, the stallion braked at the last possible second, skidding to a stop a mere three feet away from Mandy. She laughed and moved right in. "Hello, Tornado. How's my big guy? Huh?" She tucked herself close to the stallion's shoulder, going up on her toes to loop an arm around his neck, her free hand fast at work to dole out rubs and scratches. "Ah, sweetie, you're shaking. It's okay."

Zach's muscles felt as if they had dissolved and run into his boots. Tornado whiffled and shoved his nose under Mandy's arm. It was as if the huge animal was trying to hide from the world, and her armpit was his only safe haven.

"What's happening?" Luke demanded, sounding panicked. "Is that a big horse? Where is it? Will it trample Rosebud and me?"

Making a mental note that the kid's first concern seemed to be Rosebud, Zach grasped Luke's elbow. "No worries, Luke. Let me get you and the mini back to the porch. I'll explain on the way."

Reluctantly, Zach left Miranda with the most dangerous horse he'd ever seen while he hustled her brother away. En route, he told Luke an abbreviated story of how Tornado, the stable nightmare, had taken a shine to his sister.

"I can't get near that beast half the time, and he's

never allowed me to pet him. But, I swear, your sister could climb on his back and he'd let her do it."

Luke chuckled. "Mandy's got a way with frightened things." The kid's smile faded. "I think it's because she's been afraid so many times herself."

Zach wanted to hear more about that, but right then, his one thought was to get Tornado back into his paddock. He'd holler for Cookie and Ethel, he guessed. Somehow they'd corral the horse and herd him back to where he belonged.

Zach carried Rosebud up the steps. No time to do battle with the stairs right now. Then he hurried back down for Luke. When the kid was safely sitting down, Zach started to tell him to stay put, but Luke interrupted him.

"She's fine, Mr. Harrigan. Hear that? They're coming this way."

Zach turned to look, and sure enough, there came Mandy, Tornado trailing behind her like a dog taught to heel. It was . . . incredible. No, damn it, it was impossible, and he would be a fool to believe the situation would remain status quo. Tornado had never been near the house, and strange things set him off. He could blow up at any second, and Mandy would be first in his line of attack.

Zach hurried back down the steps. The second his boots connected with the ground, the stallion snorted and stopped, head thrown up, ears back, eyes ringed with white. His lips drew back from his strong yellow teeth. Zach froze.

"I'm going to call for help. Stay where you are and keep him calm if you can. Reinforcements will be here within seconds." Zach grabbed for his cell. "Talk to him. Do the lovey-dovey thing. If he blows up, he'll take us both out."

Mandy placed a palm on the stallion's neck, gently stroking him. She fixed a questioning gaze on Zach as he dialed Cookie. "Reinforcements? For what?"

"To get him back in his paddock."

Cookie answered his cell and barked hello just then. Zach turned his attention to the foreman, but before he could get three words out, Miranda grabbed the phone and turned it off.

"A bunch of people will frighten him. If you want him in his pen, I'll take him."

Zach didn't want her within kicking distance of that stallion for another second. "Look, you've got to listen to me. I know he's taken a shine to you, but he's completely unpredictable. If the wind blows your hair wrong—if you move your hand too fast—" He broke off and pinned a worried glare on the horse. "He's quiet now, but if a worm pops its head out of the ground, he might go nuts. If he does, he could kill you. Even if he doesn't intend to. I mean it."

"He's a lot more predictable than most people." With a withering look at Zach, she turned on her heel. "Come on, Tornado. Let's go back to your pen."

Again, the stallion followed her like a well-trained dog. Zach fell in behind them, but kept his distance, terrified he'd spook the horse. He saw Cookie round the back corner of the arena building. The older man froze in his tracks when he saw Tornado. Zach shared the sentiment. It was an "oh, shit" moment.

Amazingly, Mandy led the stallion back to the fencing without incident. Once there, she crooked her neck to look back at Zach. "Which one is his yard?"

Zach cut a wide berth around her and the stallion to unlatch Tornado's gate. As it swung wide, Mandy led the horse inside. "Hurry out," Zach said.

"If I do, he'll only jump the fence again. Give me a few minutes with him. Let me assure him that it's okay."

Zach wanted to dash in there, grab her by the arm, and drag her out. But he didn't dare. "Mandy, don't push it with him. He's dangerous, I'm telling you."

"I know," she said softly, running light hands over the

stallion's regal head. "With enough reason, aren't we all, Zach?" She cooed softly to the sorrel, and the animal thrust his nose under her arm again, making her giggle. "More armpit sniffs? Tornado, ladies like their privacy."

Zach pushed the gate closed, rested his elbows on the top rung, and cupped a hand over his eyes. *Please, Jesus, keep her safe.* Zach sure as hell couldn't. He listened as she spoke to the horse. "I know, I know." Her voice trembled with understanding. "Someone was horribly mean to you, and you're still so afraid inside. But it's over now, sweetheart. Zach will never let anyone hurt you again."

Zach leaned closer, trying to catch each word. He knew the voice of experience when he heard it. She knew how it felt to be afraid, and the horse sensed that. They were kindred spirits, tempered by the same kinds of pain and betrayal. The tension eased from Zach's body. Even as tears stung his eyes—it made him sad to think Mandy had endured abuse—he smiled slightly. Once again, she'd nailed it on the head. Tornado didn't want to hurt anyone. He was just seeking love and comfort from the one person he sensed he could trust.

"Do you have any treats?" Mandy asked.

Zach jerked his mind to the question. "I, um, yeah."

"Can you get me some? I'll settle him in his stall and shut the doors so he can't jump the fence again while I'm here. Otherwise, he will, and for reasons that are beyond me, you don't seem to want him at our barbecue."

Zach pushed away from the fence. "Trust me, my reasons are many. If you can get him into his stall, that's where he needs to stay."

He hurried around the building to find Cookie standing outside the personnel door. The foreman doffed his hat to scratch behind his ear. "What the Sam Hill happened? He jump the fence?"

"He did. I saw my whole life flash before my eyes."

"I bet ya did. Where you goin'?" Cookie asked. When

Zach explained, Cookie said, "Why not let him attend the barbecue? The whole place is fenced. Ethel's the only hand still here. She can veer out when she leaves so as not to spook him. Let the little lady give him treats from the porch while he watches the fun."

Zach spun to stare at his foreman and wondered just how rapidly senility could manifest itself. "What? You're joking, right?"

Cookie chuckled and plopped his battered hat back on his head. "You're sleepin' outside that damned stallion's gate, tryin' to make friends with him. That's a great idea, but why miss another opportunity when it runs up and bites you on the ass? That crazy horse loves her. Won't hurt him a bit to stand by the porch, watchin' all of you makc happy. If he blows up, and I doubt he will with her there, your porch may take a few knocks, but other than that, what harm will be done? You already know he and Rosebud are friends. He wouldn't hurt her."

Leaving an unpredictable and potentially dangerous stallion loose in his yard near a lit barbecue and a blind teenager didn't strike Zach as a fabulous idea. But when he searched Cookie's gaze, he saw that the foreman was dead serious.

"Get the treats. Take them back to thc house. Before she leaves, have her put Tornado up for the night. Simple."

With that, Cookie sauntered past Zach into the arena.

Tornado handled the barbecue as if he'd attended dozens of them. He stood next to the elevated porch, gazing adoringly at Mandy. Occasionally Rosebud would tear herself from Luke's side to venture over to rub noses with her giant friend. The two equines whickered and chuffed, apparently communicating. *Unusual.* Large horses often detested smaller ones and picked on them, but Tornado was as gentle as a lamb. Maybe it was because Rosebud was a mare.

Zach was tense at first, but when Tornado continued to exhibit only calm acceptance of everything, including the repeated slap of the screen door, he started to relax. The horse seemed to cross over some invisible line when Mandy was present, going from crazy to sane.

While the potatoes baked—Zach liked to do them the old-fashioned way—Luke asked if he could take another walk with Rosebud, alone this time. Zach was about to say no. He didn't want Luke to leave the safety of the porch.

"It'll be fine," Miranda assured him. "I'll go out with Tornado."

Zach was dubious, but Miranda seemed so confident all would be well that he fell back on Cookie's advice—to let Tornado see life, up close and personal, with no abusive or fearful events. Over the time that the stallion had stood by the porch, Zach had started to buy into the idea that Miranda's presence somehow soothed the stallion, forestalling any maniacal outbursts from him. Zach could only shake his head and accept it.

Tornado didn't act up while Zach got Luke and Rosebud lined out for a walk alone. The stallion stood contentedly with his head hanging over Mandy's shoulder, watching with keen interest as Zach schooled Luke in the proper handling procedures. "If you feel her halt, pay attention. She'll tap with her hoof sometimes, so feel with your foot to see what she's telling you. It may be something in your path, a hole in the ground, a rock, or whatever. When you're holding this halter handle, Rosebud becomes your eyes. You understand? It's her job to guide you and warn you of danger. If you listen, you'll have a blast."

Luke nodded, his expression animated. "I can do it, I think."

Zach forced himself to back away. With more confidence than he actually felt, he said, "Sure you can. I'll watch. If you do something wrong, or if she does, I'll call out to you. Okay?"

Luke nodded and signaled Rosebud to move forward. Zach stepped back and folded his arms. It was gratifying, but also terrifying to observe Luke, a blind person, depending upon a horse that Zach had only halfway trained to guide.

"Loosen up on the grip, Luke!" Zach called. "You're confusing her. She thinks you want her to stop. Just relax. Trust her."

Luke relaxed his hold, stumbled after the horse, who quickened her pace, and then righted his balance. After he'd taken a dozen steps, a huge grin spread across his face.

Mandy watched for a moment and then turned her gaze toward Zach. Even from fifteen feet away, a distance Zach maintained because of Tornado's presence, he could see the gratitude in her eyes. "Whether or not this goes anywhere," she said, "thank you so much for this moment. Luke's never willingly walked outdoors alone. When I forced him, it ended in disaster. This is the very first time he's grabbed onto the idea and really enjoyed it."

Zach found it difficult to speak. Watching Luke and Rosebud together was the culmination of more than two years of dedication and hard work, the first stint with a dog trainer, and the last several weeks doing hands-on training with the mini. It was extremely rewarding, but for reasons beyond him, it was also earthshaking. He returned his gaze to Luke, taking in his glad smile. The kid hadn't relaxed yet, but with each passing moment, he seemed to gain more confidence.

"I hope this works," Zach heard himself say. "I hope Luke shapes up and proves to me that he deserves her."

He wanted to take the words back the instant he said them. This was Mandy's brother he was talking about.

To his relief, she didn't take offense. Instead, she smiled and said, "He has a lot of measuring up to do. But just look at him. He loves this. For the first time in years, he's free. That's such a gift for someone like Luke, who's fought so hard not to be free. Now that he's gotten a taste of it, he has something wonderful to work toward. Thank you."

Zach stiffened. "Yo, Luke! When she angles across your legs, listen up. There's a pipe on the ground a few feet ahead. You need to go around it or stop."

Luke jerked to a halt. "What do I do?"

Zach stepped forward a few paces so Luke could hear him clearly. It occurred to him that he'd just shouted and Tornado hadn't even flinched. "Steer her in one direction. See if she goes." Zach deliberately didn't tell Luke which way to go. "If she still angles in front of you, try the other way. She'll tell you when you're picking the right direction."

Luke aimed left, and Rosebud blocked him. Zach grinned as the kid switched directions. Rosebud happily went that way, and they were off again.

"That's amazing." Mandy curled a hand up over Tornado's neck as she flashed Zach a grateful smile. "Absolutely amazing."

What amazed Zach was that his head-shy stallion seemed to love having Mandy's hands on him, no matter where she decided to put them. Zach could get that. Oh, man, could he ever get that. Looking at her now, he knew he'd never clapped eyes on a more beautiful woman. The old oil stick went hard. He angled his body away from Mandy so she wouldn't see, silently lecturing that part of his body that had no brains to behave itself. Fat chance. He had to get out of here for a second.

"Hey, Luke, wait up!" he called. "I want to show you something else."

At least the kid wouldn't be able to see how embarrassed Zach was right now—or why.

Chapter Ten

Zach couldn't recall ever enjoying an afternoon quite so much. The weather was perfect, balmy for February, and kissed with sunlight. He worked hard to be a good host, engaging Luke in conversation, cracking jokes, and trying to set a relaxed mood. Except for the steaks, which would take only minutes to grill, the simple meal was ready once the potatoes had baked. Zach turned off the oven and left them inside to stay warm while he gave his guests a tour of the stable.

Tornado accompanied them to the arena. By this time, Zach had almost stopped worrying about the stallion. The horse stuck close to Mandy and seemed to take everything in stride. Still, Zach used a back entrance to avoid the stallion section at the front of the building. Cookie waved at them from across the arena. Ordinarily his smug expression would have irritated Zach, but today he decided the old codger was entitled to it.

Ethel, preparing to wrap it up for the day, emerged from the feed room, stopped dead, and gaped at Tornado in startled amazement. "Is that the same horse?"

Zach lifted his hands in bewilderment. He couldn't explain the transformation. Ethel waved and exited the barn through a side door well away from Tornado.

At first Luke was afraid to pet the horses. "I can hear them. That's enough."

"Don't be silly, Luke," Mandy said. "They're inside cages."

"Can't they bite?"

Mandy shot Zach a questioning look. He responded with, "Yes, horses can bite, but none of these have ever bitten anyone. You don't need to worry about that."

"They're just bigger versions of Rosebud," Mandy said. "You're not afraid of her."

To distract Luke, Zach began giving biographical sketches of every horse. When he mentioned that he'd bottle-fed Stormy when her dam rejected her, Luke stopped.

"She must be pretty used to people, then, right?"

"She is. For a long time she followed me around like a pup whenever she saw me. She thought I was her mother. I had an awful time living it down with the help."

Luke laughed. "Where is she? Are you sure she won't bite me?"

"Positive."

The boy held out his free hand and tentatively ran it over Stormy's lowered head.

"She's so *big*!" Luke marveled. "I never imagined they were so tall."

It struck Zach in that moment that Luke had never seen a full-size horse, or had forgotten if he had. What else had the kid forgotten or never seen? Looking around the arena, Zach realized it couldn't be easy to get around in a completely black world. No wonder Luke took the path of least risk, depending on Mandy for everything. By her own admission, she had made that easy for him to do.

Smiling, Miranda turned from the gate. "While Luke gets acquainted with Stormy, I'll take Tornado back to his stall. The other horses are eating. I think he missed dinner."

That was true. Cookie and Ethel had already fed the

animals. "They probably put hay in his feeder already. You want to give him his evening ration of grain?"

She smiled up at Zach, her eyes glowing with warmth. "I'd love to."

Zach glanced at Luke. "Hey, buddy, will you be okay for a few minutes?"

Tightening his hand over the mini's halter grip, Luke stopped petting the mare. "Can Rosebud stay with me?"

"Sure. The stallion section's only about sixty feet away." Zach wondered if Luke had a mental image of how long sixty feet was. The kid had undoubtedly learned measurements in school, but that didn't mean he could picture them. "Be right back."

Tornado didn't protest being returned to his stall. Zach remained outside the gate, allowing Mandy to shut the paddock doors and give the stallion his grain. Watching woman and stallion, Zach got an almost surreal feeling. He totally agreed with Ethel: With Mandy, Tornado was a different horse.

Minutes later, Mandy and Luke sat on the porch, snacking on corn chips and salsa—Zach's version of an appetizer. Mandy appreciated Zach's approach to entertaining. The simplicity allowed her to relax and enjoy the moment. And Mandy *was* enjoying it. The weather was perfect, with only a slight nip in the air as the afternoon gave way to evening. As the darkness deepened, Zach lit the gas fire pit, and Mandy helped Luke move his chair to sit by the dancing flames. She thought about getting Luke his jacket, but he seemed fine without it.

Mandy took a deep breath, appreciating the smells that surrounded her, the scent of pine trees mingling with the aroma of the searing meat that Zach had just put on the grill. Sitting beside her brother, she munched on chips and shared the salsa with him.

While the steaks cooked, Zach disappeared into the

house. Moments later, he shouldered his way back out the screen door, holding two wide-mouthed goblets, each half-filled with purplish red wine. Grinning, he offered one of the glasses to Mandy.

Her stomach knotted, and she actually felt the color drain from her face. "No, thank you." Even to her ears, her voice rang cold and sharp. "I don't drink."

Zach treated her to a long, penetrating look. "Okay. More wine for me, I guess. Can I get you and Luke a soda?"

"None for me, thank you," Mandy managed to push out.

Luke said, "I'm good for right now. Maybe I'll have some soda with dinner."

Get a grip, Mandy thought. *It's only a little wine.* But the silent lecture she gave herself didn't loosen the ball of tension in her middle, and to her dismay, she felt herself start to shake. She watched Zach set both wineglasses on the redwood barbecue shelf. Nausea crawled up her throat. Sweat filmed her face and the back of her neck.

"Stay calm," Luke whispered. "Lots of people drink wine at dinnertime, no big deal."

But to Mandy, it *was* a big deal. Her every childhood memory had been tainted by her father's drinking. Maybe it was irrational—no *maybe* to it; it *was* irrational—but to her, being around a man who drank was as chilling and frightening as having a loaded gun pointed at her head. And, oh, God, she felt betrayed, as if Zach had tricked her. Until now, she'd seen him touch no alcohol, and she'd started to think he never did.

Mandy struggled to calm down. This visit was for Luke, and she *couldn't* ruin it for him by saying or doing something stupid. How she felt didn't matter. Racing for her car and leaving wasn't an option. Somehow she'd get through dinner, smiling. She would not let on that being around alcohol made her feel panicky and claustrophobic.

Zach lifted the lid of the grill and glanced over his

shoulder toward the fire pit. "I like my steak rare. How would you two like yours?"

Luke put in an order for medium. Mandy's heart was pounding so hard it felt as if it might crack a rib. "I, um . . . Any old way is fine for me. I'm not fussy."

Zach pinned her with another of those thoughtful looks that seemed to pierce her skin like a laser. Then he turned the meat and lowered the lid.

A bit later, when they sat down for dinner at Zach's beautifully set kitchen table, Mandy's tension mounted. The remaining wineglass was set only three feet away from her, the deep red liquid inside it glinting in the overhead light. For her, it was like trying to eat with a coiled rattlesnake near her plate. She took a bite of meat and nearly choked as she swallowed. She pushed the food around, making little piles so it would appear that she'd consumed some of it. The untouched steak was a dead giveaway, so she cut off pieces that never went in her mouth.

Zach attempted to keep a conversation going, but Mandy was too distracted to offer anything more than monosyllabic rejoinders. When Luke dropped his fork, she jumped as if she'd been scalded. She tried not to watch Zach when he sipped the wine, but she couldn't stop herself. Once when he caught her gaping at him, the expression that crossed his dark face asked more clearly than words, *What the hell is* this *all about?*

Mandy couldn't have explained that to him if she tried. Luke was right: A lot of people enjoyed wine with dinner. It wasn't as if Zach were getting pie-eyed. Unfortunately, Mandy could tell herself that repeatedly and still couldn't control the mix of torrential emotions that kept crashing through her.

If it hadn't been for Luke, the meal would have been a nightmare. He talked excitedly about his walks with Rosebud and even asked questions about how she had been trained. Zach responded with appropriate noises.

Mandy could tell that he wished for the meal to be over, and she shared the sentiment. Even the German chocolate cake she'd brought didn't lighten the mood. She refused dessert, saying she was full.

Once the meal was over, Mandy offered to help with cleanup, but Zach declined. "I didn't think to pitch in last night when you fed me. Turnabout's fair play."

The relief Mandy felt must have shown on her face, because she saw a spark of anger flash in his eyes. She didn't blame him for that. He'd entertained them all afternoon. He'd been wonderful with Luke. Under any other circumstances, she would have savored every bite of her meal. Intellectually, she knew none of this was his fault, that her reaction to the wine had been and still was absurd.

Even so, she couldn't wait to leave. "Thank you for the lovely afternoon and dinner. It was fun. But if you won't let me help with the dishes, Luke and I really should be going." She glanced at her watch. "I'll have to work tonight to make up for goofing off today."

"Can I take one more walk with Rosebud?" her brother asked. "Just a short one?"

Mandy glanced out the window. "It's dark, Luke. Another time, perhaps."

"For me, it's always dark," Luke argued. "Come on, Mandy, please?"

"I said no, Luke. We need to get home."

Luke must have heard something in her voice, because he allowed her to hustle him to the car. Mandy's hands shook as she grasped the steering wheel.

"This is great," Luke said, his voice sharp with resentment. "Just frigging *great*. You yammered at me nonstop to make friends with Rosebud, and then when I do, you ruin everything by freaking out over a little wine."

"I didn't say a word!" Mandy cried as she backed up the car to turn around.

"You didn't need to. The tension at that table was

so thick I could have cut it with a knife! Do you think Zach's stupid? That he didn't realize you were upset? Get real."

"I tried my best, Luke. Now, please, just drop it. Give me a few minutes to pull myself back together."

"Would you listen to yourself? Why do you need to pull yourself back together over some stupid wine? He's not our father. Got it?"

Troubled by Mandy's behavior, Zach remained on the porch to wave them off. When the Honda disappeared, he gazed thoughtfully at Rosebud, who stood at his side. Luke had made great strides with her today. The ice had been broken, and the kid was starting to realize and relish the freedom the mini could offer him.

Unfortunately, Zach had lost ground with Mandy and he couldn't think why. He mentally rewound the evening. Had it been the wine? Up until he offered her a glass, she'd been laughing and talking, apparently having a good time. Then, bang, she'd gone as stiff as a frozen water hose. Zach didn't get it. It wasn't as if he'd gotten toasted. Most people couldn't on only two glasses.

Screw it. If she chose not to drink, fine. That didn't mean the rest of the world had to follow suit. If she didn't like it, that was her problem. He wasn't going to make it his.

After getting Luke tucked in, Mandy sat on the sofa in the dark living room, arms looped around her knees, head resting against the back cushion. The faint scent of barbecue smoke clung to her sweatshirt, making her want to change tops, but right then she didn't have the energy. Instead she listened to the creaks and groans of the old house settling, familiar sounds that normally soothed her. Not tonight.

She had work she needed to be doing, but she was too upset and frustrated with herself right then to concentrate. *Idiot*. She'd really started to like Zach Harrigan. Though she hadn't allowed herself to go anywhere with it in her fantasies, the possibilities had still tickled at the back of her mind. Did he like her as much as she liked him? Maybe something special could come of it. Zach would be so good for Luke. Her brother had never had a decent male role model, only an alcoholic father who got staggering drunk and flew into violent rages.

Zach had seemed so different—until he brought out the wine. Since childhood, Mandy had had a huge problem with alcohol consumption. With her dad, it had all started with a glass of wine, an infrequent and seemingly harmless indulgence, according to what Mandy's mother had told her. But then his drinking had escalated to a daily thing, he'd turned to hard liquor, and the amounts had increased. To this day, Mandy could remember watching him with a suffocating fear, waiting for that moment when he would go over the edge. And her father had *always* gone over the edge.

By age fifteen, Mandy had come to *detest* alcohol in any form. Wine, beer, whiskey—she hated them all. And she'd sworn never to touch them. She'd also sworn that she would never be like her mother, falling into a trap, married to a brutal alcoholic.

As irrational as Mandy knew it was, just the sight of someone drinking frightened her. That first night when she'd faked the car trouble, Zach had served Tucker and Cookie whiskey, but he hadn't poured any for himself, leading her to think he kept liquor on hand only for his guests. *Stupid me.* She'd been about to do something really dumb, like fall in love with him, and she was extremely lucky to have learned the truth about him tonight. But she didn't feel lucky. She felt empty. And alone.

Just the thought of falling in love with him made her wonder at herself. She'd sworn since her late teens never to give her heart to any man. Falling in love often led to marriage, and the very thought of that terrified her.

She'd seen what it was like for her mom, working from dawn to dark and long into the night, not to mention enduring physical abuse day in and day out. Granted, Mandy knew all marriages didn't turn out that way, but she was also aware that a woman never really got to know a man until it was too late. Zach clearly had money. His father was rich and had evidently shared the wealth. All those horses hadn't come cheap, and that fabulous ranch hadn't, either.

In so many ways, Zach was like Mandy's dad—well-heeled, handsome, charming, and influential in the community. And he drank as well. No how, no way. She never wanted to see him again. There was something about him that made her a little addle-brained, and that could be dangerous. She had the awful feeling he could sell her the Brooklyn Bridge if he set his mind to it.

Determined though Mandy was to stay clear of the man, she couldn't quite reason away the sharp pang of disappointment in her chest. He'd seemed so nice and wonderful. She'd been so close to throwing caution to the wind and taking the plunge. It could have been so perfect—if only he didn't drink.

Zach stood at his granite kitchen countertop, frowning at the half-empty wine bottle. It was definitely the wine that had set Mandy off. Had to have been. She had been all smiles until she saw the merlot. A sudden memory came to him—how Mandy had grown pale and moved away from the table that first night when he'd gotten the Jack Daniel's out of the cupboard for Tucker's Irish coffee. He'd known people who disapproved of alcohol, but she'd acted almost afraid of the stuff. *Weird*.

Bewildered, Zach dumped the rest of the wine down the sink. His drink of choice was beer. He drank wine only before or with meals, didn't cook all that much, and by morning, that was all the wine would be good for.

Normally most Catholics were pretty relaxed individuals, but Zach had encountered a few zealots over the years. Maybe Mandy was one of them, an ultrareligious extremist who didn't believe in drinking, dancing, going to the movies, or playing cards. If so, he was damned lucky to have found out tonight. Maybe that accounted for the Little Miss Innocent look in her eyes, because she'd spent her whole life avoiding everything fun.

Well, Zach was no puritan. He enjoyed a lot of things in moderation, and drinking was one of them. Yes, he overindulged sometimes, but he sure as hell didn't make a habit of it anymore. Hello, he'd finally grown up.

I'm not a bad guy, he assured himself as he opened the refrigerator to grab a beer. *And I'm sure as hell not an alcoholic.* Miranda Pajeck—right then he didn't want to think of her as Mandy—could take her judgmental attitude and shove it.

As the last of the ale slid down his throat, he lifted the empty longneck in an imaginary toast to her. "Put that in your puritanical pipe and smoke it, sweetheart."

Two weeks passed, and Mandy didn't call. Zach refused to be the first one to make a move. To hell with her. Rosebud was making huge progress. In a few more months, she would make some blind person a fabulous guide. *Too bad it won't be Luke.* It wasn't the kid's fault his sister had gotten her nose out of joint. If avoiding Zach was more important to Miranda than getting a guide horse for her brother, it was her deal. Zach had started to like Luke, difficult as he could be, and he'd begun to hope there was a chance that the young man might straighten up his act.

Zach continued to sleep in the arena every night outside Tornado's stall. At first the horse pushed his rump into a far corner, avoiding Zach as if he had the plague, venturing forward only to rub noses with Rosebud. Then, as the days passed, the stallion moved closer, sleeping dead center in his stall.

It was a fine morning when Zach was jerked awake long before dawn by a velvety nibble on his cheek. Thinking it was Rosebud, he pushed at the nose, registering its size only as he came more awake. *Tornado.* The stallion whickered and nudged Zach's shoulder, as if to say, *Wake up, you lazy sot.*

Zach smiled groggily. "Hey, big guy," he said softly, mimicking Mandy. Thinking of her made his heart catch, and that rankled. "How's it hanging this morning?"

A quick glance told Zach that everything was hanging just fine for Tornado, and the same held true for himself. Why was it that males always woke up with a hard-on? Zach needed to take a leak, and apparently so did the stallion, because just then he let loose. *Wake-up call.* Zach sat up, fast. When a horse pissed, the splatter effect was—well, far-reaching. He didn't want it in the face.

As Zach stood, Tornado turned his head sideways to nudge the treat pack on Zach's belt. Zach scooped out some pellets. As Tornado enjoyed the snack, Zach hesitantly rubbed the flat spot between the horse's eyes. The stallion didn't object. It was the first time Zach had ever been able to touch the animal without forcing the issue.

"Well, now, we're making some progress, aren't we?" Zach whispered. "You finally starting to think I'm okay?"

In response to that question, Tornado grabbed Zach's hand and bit down like a grain masher. *Pain.* Zach managed to jerk his fingers from the animal's mouth. Did a dance, the kind one executed when too breathless with agony to speak. And then, when his lungs could work again, he yelled, "You misbegotten, recalcitrant *bastard!*"

The arena lights came on, and Cookie appeared on the landing. "There's a bucket over yonder. Just don't bust your toe."

Zach flapped his hand and glared up at Cookie, who

was grinning from ear to ear. "That's real helpful. I almost lost all five digits, and you're directing me to a bucket?"

The old foreman shrugged. "That's your way, kickin' buckets." He settled a thoughtful gaze on the stallion, who was now pummeling the walls of his stall. "What's up with the little lady? Haven't seen her around lately. She worked magic with him."

"You won't be seeing her again," Zach shot back. "She's as crazy as the horse is!"

"That's too bad. I liked her." Cookie turned toward the door of his apartment. "Breakfast is on. I cooked for two. Denver omelets this mornin'. If you get over your grump, you're welcome to join me."

At twelve minutes past noon, Zach's cell phone chirped. When he glanced at the screen, a smug grin touched his lips. *Mandy.* She'd evidently searched her call records to retrieve his cell number. *Oh, yeah.* It was her turn to eat crow. Had the *little lady* decided that her abhorrence of alcohol wasn't quite as strong as her desire to get a free guide horse for Luke? *Hmm.* Well, he wouldn't let her off easy. *Hell, no.* Not that he wanted any part of her on a permanent basis, but sometimes revenge *was* sweet.

Zach opened his phone. "Yo, Zach Harrigan here."

He was geared up to hear Mandy's voice. Instead a hesitant male baritone came over the air. "Mr. Harrigan? Hi, this is Luke."

Zach regrouped. "Hey, Luke. How's it goin', buddy?"

"I, um . . . well, you're probably surprised it's me."

Damn straight. Zach still felt deflated. "I am. How'd you get my cell number?"

"It was on our caller list. Mandy got me special phones that talk."

"Ah. Well, it's great to hear from you. What's up?"

"I, um, just, you know, wanted to tell you I really had fun going for those walks with Rosebud at your ranch."

Zach was disappointed that it was Luke instead of Mandy on the phone, but he could tell from Luke's stammering that it had taken a lot of courage for him to call. Zach needed to hook in. Forget about Mandy and her irrational reaction to the wine. Forget about his personal feelings. The guide horse issue was about Luke. Period.

"I'm glad you enjoyed yourself."

"I did," Luke said. "And, I was wondering. . . . Well, I know you're really busy, but is there any way I could take a walk with Rosebud today, to the park maybe? It would only take an hour or two. I'd really like to be with her again, just for a little while."

Zach frowned. "Does Mandy know you're calling?"

"No, she's doing a burn. It's the booze thing. She's weird about it."

Zach tightened his hand over the phone and almost disconnected by keying a button he didn't intend to press. "The booze thing? I'd really like to understand that, Luke. What *is* the booze thing, exactly?"

"Long story. We've got a fucked-up family. You know? I'll tell you a little about it on the way to the park if you want."

Zach squeezed his eyes closed. He almost told Luke to watch his mouth, but given that he sometimes used the F-word around other men, that would've been hypocritical.

"You're kind of putting me on the spot, buddy. If your sister doesn't want you to go out, she may get pissed at me. I'd rather not step on any toes."

Luke groaned. "Hey, dude, I'm nineteen. Most guys my age are partying and screwing chicks. Do they ask permission? Why do I need my sister's to go for a walk?"

"I don't suppose you do. It's just . . ." Zach frowned. In Oregon, Luke was legally an adult. His being blind didn't alter that fact. "Mandy's gone, isn't she?"

"It's errand day," Luke admitted. "She hires a sitter

for me and takes one day every two weeks to go shopping and do other crap. She's usually gone about five hours."

"So you're wanting to sneak off while she's gone?"

"Okay, yeah. I want to sneak off. It's a first for me, man. Don't burst my bubble."

Zach grinned. For once, Luke sounded like a normal kid. At the same age, Zach had been doing a hell of a lot more than taking afternoon walks. He'd been in college at the time, and his father had essentially been paying out a small fortune in tuition so his son could be a party animal. Zach had definitely earned the handle *hellion of the family*. In retrospect, he wished he'd done many things different, but he also felt his wild years had made him a better person. Sometimes you had to make mistakes, deal with the ramifications, and live with the regrets before you changed your ways.

Zach had been a slow learner, and he didn't have any high ground to stand on with Luke. "Okay, you're a consenting adult. If you want to go to the park, you got it."

Luke released a blast of air that nearly punctured Zach's eardrum. "Thanks, man. I need a walk, not just with Rosebud, though. I, uh, kinda need to talk, if that's okay."

Zach knew better than to ask what about. A smart older person kept his lip zipped and let the kid pick the moment. "What time is good for you?"

"Mandy's already been gone about an hour. Can you come now?"

Zach glanced around the arena. Cookie and his employees could handle it for a few hours. He'd need to get Rosebud haltered up, but otherwise, there was nothing to hold him back. "I can be there in forty minutes. How much time will that give us?"

"Three hours unless she does one of her superwoman trips. She doesn't waste time. Sitters cost a lot."

And why, Luke, do you need a sitter? Zach refrained

from asking that question. "See you in forty. Have your walking shoes on."

Normally Mandy raced through Safeway, grabbing items and scratching them off her list with a speed born of necessity. Sitters for Luke were expensive, so she wasted no time comparing prices. Any amount she saved by being thrifty was canceled out by the charges she racked up at home. The tab today would be even worse than usual. The sitter that Mandy and Luke liked and normally used had undergone rotator-cuff surgery, and the only alternative, a coarse, rather unpleasant older woman, charged five dollars more an hour, didn't get along well with Luke, and ate Mandy out of house and home.

This afternoon Mandy couldn't seem to kick herself into high gear, though. Troubled and distracted by the thoughts that kept circling through her mind, she pushed the cart slowly and often found herself staring blindly at a product for seconds on end. When she came to the dog-food section, she stared sadly at the image of a golden retriever on one of the bags. Because of his fear of canines, Luke would never consent to getting a guide dog. A service horse was the only practical alternative.

And I'm ruining that for him.

Mandy released a sigh. She couldn't continue on this course. Zach Harrigan had been incredibly generous to consider offering Rosebud to Luke for free. Her brother and the mini had been forging a strong friendship. How could she allow her personal feelings about alcohol to stand in the way? Rosebud could open up a whole new world for her brother. *That* was the important thing, the *only* important thing.

She needed to call Zach and apologize. The very thought made her stomach clench. What would she say? *I'm sorry about my behavior at the barbecue. I have this fear of alcohol. In the future, would you mind not drink-*

ing around me and Luke? That would go over like rain at a picnic. She had no business telling Zach what he could or couldn't do at his own home. So how should she handle it?

Maybe, she decided, the solution was to mend her fences with Zach and henceforth arrange for all Luke's visits with Rosebud to occur at *her* place. That way she would be in control, she could monitor the situation, and she could also make sure Zach was never alone with Luke, with no opportunity to put bad ideas in her brother's head.

As soon as I get home and have all the groceries put away, I'll call the man. No excuses, no procrastinating. It wouldn't be easy, but she had to do it for Luke's sake.

En route to town, Zach barely noticed the passing landscape, washed with early March sunshine. Instead he did some soul searching and decided he didn't like himself very much sometimes. When his cell phone had rung and he'd seen Mandy's name, he'd been focused on making her squirm before he agreed to let Luke see Rosebud again. That had been horrible of him, and Zach felt ashamed of himself. This wasn't about Mandy's reaction to the wine or about Zach getting his feelings hurt.

It was about Luke. The kid had been kept in a protective bubble all his life. Rosebud offered him freedom that he'd never dreamed of having. Anyone who could forget the joyous grin that had lit up Luke's face the afternoon of the barbecue didn't have a heart. *That* was what Zach needed to keep front and center. Whatever happened between him and Mandy shouldn't factor into the equation.

As Zach drove up Maple Street to the Pajeck house, he pushed all negative thoughts from his mind, determined to make this a pleasurable outing for Luke. Because Mandy was out shopping, he parked on the street so the SUV wouldn't be blocking her driveway if she got back early. Rosebud, eager to unload because she recognized the house, hopped out onto the grass median. As Zach accompanied her up the walkway, he breathed deeply of the air, crisp with a bit of winter chill, but starting to smell like spring. It was nice enough not to wear a jacket, a perfect day for an outing.

A large woman wearing stretchy black slacks that were too small and a pink sweater that was too large answered the doorbell. When she saw Rosebud, her nose went up in the air. "I will not allow that *creature* inside the house," she informed Zach. "You'll have to leave it on the porch."

Well aware that Luke had difficulty navigating by himself, Zach said, "Luke is expecting us. We're going for a walk to the park. You can either bring him to the door, or we'll come inside to collect him. Your call."

Luke was slumped on the sofa. Zach wondered yet again if the kid spent his whole life there. The sitter huffed under her breath but allowed Zach and Rosebud to enter.

"He doesn't have his sister's permission to go," the woman said. "But he insists that he's going anyway. I'm being paid to watch him, and I'll not be party to this in any way."

The lady's attitude was starting to piss Zach off. "He's nineteen. Last time I checked, that makes him an adult. If he wants to go for a walk, I guess he can."

Luke didn't raise his head. He was wearing jeans, sneakers, and a blue fleece sweatshirt, which was as warm as most jackets. "Hi, Mr. Harrigan. Thanks for coming."

"I'm happy to be here," Zach assured him. "You about ready?"

"I need to use the restroom first."

"Your sister took you right before she left," the sitter objected. "Why do you need to go again so soon?"

"I just want to be sure I won't need to go on the

way to the park," Luke explained. "Can you help me, please?"

The woman turned toward the kitchen. "I want no part of this, I told you."

Luke sighed and said, "She's an old witch."

Zach chuckled. "Come on, Luke. I'll lead you to the bathroom."

Leaving Rosebud by the coffee table, Zach guided Luke through the house to the bathroom door, which opened off the kitchen. While he waited, the sitter said, "Ms. Pajeck has no cell phone with her, so I can't call to tell her about this. If she gets upset, it'll be on *your* head. I'm washing my hands of all responsibility."

Zach almost tried to mollify the woman by inviting her to go with them, but he agreed with Luke. She really was an old witch.

Seconds later, when Luke emerged, he said, "This is embarrassing. I have to be taken to the restroom like a baby."

Zach decided to let that remark pass until they were outside on the sidewalk. He got Luke situated with Rosebud, and then they moved into a walk, the shuffle of Luke's sneakers creating a rhythmic backdrop for the clop of the mini's hooves and the tap of Zach's boots. A breeze rustled through the denuded maple trees that lined the street.

Zach gave it a couple of minutes before he returned to the comment Luke had made outside the bathroom. "I know only one blind person, but she needs very little help to do anything. I can only wonder why you're so different."

Luke said nothing for almost half a block, his hand white-knuckled over Rosebud's halter handle. Finally, he blurted, "Why should I learn to do things by myself? It's Mandy's fault that I'm blind. If I become self-sufficient, she'll be totally off the hook."

The kid's response startled Zach. Zach knew, deep

in his heart, that Mandy would never purposely do anything to harm Luke. So why did the youth blame her for his blindness? Zach refrained from asking, and Luke didn't enlighten him.

"You think I'm a horrible person, don't you?"

That was a loaded question. Zach was glad they reached a crosswalk just then so he could collect his thoughts. In truth, Zach thought Luke was a spoiled brat, but he had also caught glimpses of a young man who yearned to change.

Rosebud signaled Luke that they had reached the curb. Looking on, Zach guided the kid through his first street crossing, explaining the cues the mini gave him.

"There's no streetlight here," Zach told him. "You need to listen for traffic and tell Rosebud when you feel it's safe to cross."

Luke tipped his head. "I don't hear any cars."

It was a quiet residential street. "You're right. There's no traffic."

Luke let Rosebud know it was okay to move forward. The young man faltered at first, but after handling the first curb, he gained confidence and lengthened his stride.

When they were safely across the street, Zach adjusted his pace to Luke's again. "In answer to your question, Luke, I don't think you're a horrible person. Shit happens. People get into ruts, and sometimes they can't set their feet on a new path. Even worse, sometimes they can't even see another path."

Luke laughed bitterly. "That's me. I can't see my own hand in front of my face." Moving along beside Rosebud, the kid got tears in his eyes. As they slipped onto his cheeks, which were peppered with tiny scars similar to pockmarks, he wiped them away with his free hand, clearly angry and embarrassed. "I love Mandy," he said fiercely, "but a part of me hates her, too. She made me blind. Even our dad said it was all her fault."

Red alert. Luke was obviously angry and hurting, and because of that, Mandy was paying a horrible price. Her devotion to Luke bordered on the abnormal. Clearly she felt guilty, blaming herself for the accident that had robbed Luke of his sight. Luke had flung out the accusation with an expression and tone that signaled he meant what he'd said. He hadn't spoken out of anger or pique. He believed it.

Zach considered asking how the accident had happened, but Luke was crying so hard he decided the timing was bad. When Luke wanted to tell Zach more, he would.

Instead of pushing, Zach chose to change the subject. "Mandy is really upset with me. I suspected the night of the barbecue that it was over the wine, and you confirmed that today on the phone. I don't want to pry for information, but I'd really like to know what the 'booze thing' you mentioned is all about."

Rosebud stopped suddenly and tapped the sidewalk ahead of them with her right front hoof. Without Zach saying a word, Luke felt the cement in front of him with the toe of his shoe, located a crack in the concrete that had lifted at one side to form a trip hazard, and stepped carefully over it.

He clicked the mini and gave her a treat. "Good girl, Rosebud," he said. "Good girl." Then to Zach, he said, "Mandy's way over-the-top about alcohol, and for someone outside our family, it's probably hard to understand. But she really does have every reason to detest the stuff. Our father was an alcoholic. When he drank, he ... he did really bad things. That was what made our mother take off, and then Mandy was left holding the bag. It wasn't easy for her. Our dad is a really mean person."

Zach itched to inquire about the "really bad things." Obviously that was a mild version of what Luke had intended to say before he caught himself. But he couldn't force the kid's confidence. "Mandy told me that he's no longer a part of your lives."

"Nope." Luke took a few more steps, then stopped and dragged in an unsteady breath. He turned to Zach with a swift movement that suggested a sudden decision.

"He's in prison for trying to kill her."

Chapter Eleven

"*What?*" Luke's revelation had roughly the same effect on Zach as an M-80 firecracker detonating behind him. "Can you run that by me again? I don't think I heard you right."

Just then, Rosebud warned Luke of another trip hazard. Instead of replying to Zach, the kid clicked the mini, gave her a treat, and doled out praise, making Zach wait to hear more. Maybe it was just as well. Zach had a few seconds to sort his thoughts.

"You heard right," Luke said as they resumed walking. "Our dad tried to kill her."

"*Why?*"

"Payback. Mandy kept quiet about the beatings until she was seventeen. Then I guess she had enough. Or maybe it was because he tried to hurt me the night before. I dunno. But she made a bunch of phone calls the next morning and turned him in."

Zach could only imagine how terrified Mandy must have been.

"The cops brought two ladies to our house. Caseworkers, I guess. Mandy told them everything. They took her to the bathroom to see her bruises. When they came out, the ladies talked with the cops, and the next thing I knew, Mandy and I were in the backseat of a police car. Not a regular car, because I heard a dispatcher on the radio."

"So your father was arrested?"

Luke nodded. "The cops went straight to his office. Cuffed and stuffed him in front of his important friends. He was in jail for a lot longer than anyone figured. Took a while for his fancy lawyer to get him out on bail. He was the mayor of Crystal Falls then, and the scandal ruined him. They made him resign as mayor, and all his fancy friends didn't want any more to do with him. He ended up selling our house and moving to another town. Mandy and I were stuck in foster care. Dad's parents wanted no part of us. We didn't hear from him after that and had no clue he was keeping tabs on us. But he was."

"And eventually he came back?" Zach asked.

Luke nodded. "When Mandy turned eighteen, they kicked her out of foster care. She wanted me with her, but the judge said no, not until she was twenty-one. She got a job and an apartment in Crystal Falls. Our dad found out where she lived. He broke into her place one night, beat the hell out of her, and left her for dead. When she came to, she managed to call for help. He'll be in the slammer for a lot of years this time."

Zach recalled his first phone conversation with Mandy and how the Pajeck name had seemed vaguely familiar. Now he knew why. *Tobin Pajeck*. He'd been the mayor of Crystal Falls for years. Zach barely remembered the scandal that had forced him to resign. He had just finished college and been starting up his own ranch. Newspaper headlines about the city mayor had been of no major importance to him. And at that point in his life, headlines were about all he read. His interests had been booze, women, and horses, the order of importance varying with his mood.

"Oh, man," he said softly. He thought of the dark look in Mandy's eyes and how she'd grown pale when he offered her the wine. He'd known then that she felt repulsed, but he hadn't understood why. He waited until Luke and Rosebud successfully negotiated another crosswalk. "Has your dad always been an alcoholic, Luke?"

The boy fed Rosebud a treat. "For as far back as Mandy can remember, yeah. He started drinking hard not long after he married our mom."

Zach's throat felt raw. He swallowed to steady his voice. "Did the bastard beat on Mandy all her life?"

"He always had to have someone to pound on, but when Mom was still around, he picked on her instead. She told Mandy to hide with me upstairs whenever our dad got pissed, which was almost every night. I was little, and Mandy kept me away from it, so I'm not sure what all happened back then. I just remember being in that closet and how scared I was. Mandy would tell me it was okay, but I could hear Mom screaming and feel Mandy shaking, and I knew it wasn't. Finally I guess Mom got fed up. One night, she just left, and none of us ever heard from her again."

"And that's when your father started in on Mandy."

"Yeah." Luke bent his head, his expression grim and pensive. "That's why she freaks about alcohol. He only went after her when he was drunk, and she thinks his rages were triggered by the booze. Sometimes I wonder if he wasn't just mean."

Luke fell silent for a moment. "I can remember sitting in front of the TV—that was when I could still see, so I was pretty young—watching cartoons while our dad guzzled booze before dinner. Pretty soon he'd be yelling, and Mandy would jab her thumb toward the stairs. That was my signal to run for the closet. It was the only safe place. For some reason he never thought to look for me there."

"Why didn't Mandy hide up there with you?" Zach couldn't resist asking.

"Because he would have come upstairs to find her, and when he did, she was afraid he'd start beating on me, too."

The pictures taking shape in Zach's mind were almost enough to make him swear off drinking. Who'd been more judgmental the evening of the barbecue, Mandy or him? Maybe, as Luke had put it, she was over-the-top about alcohol, but who could blame her? Anyone who had grown up in that kind of environment might detest the stuff and be very, very doubtful that others could use it judiciously.

There were two more streets to cross before they reached the park. Luke fell silent. Zach's mind was processing so much information that he went on autopilot, adjusting to the slow pace of boy and horse. He tried to focus on the scenery—well-tended yards splotched with snow, trees that were starting to develop tiny buds, the blue of the sky, and the yellow of blanched grass that had gained a foothold between cracks in the concrete. He found himself wishing Luke could see it all, and then he wondered what it must be like for the kid. The thought of being blind made Zach a little panicky.

Once at the park, Zach told Rosebud to find a chair. The mini led Luke to a park bench. Earning silent kudos from Zach, Luke clicked and gave the horse a treat before he sat down on the chipped green bench slats. Relaxing his shoulders against the curved backrest, Luke loosely curled one hand over Rosebud's halter handle, his head lolling backward, his mouth open to draw in deep gulps of fresh air.

"I love the smells here. What are they?"

Typical of most sighted people, Zach took so many things for granted. He had no clue what Luke smelled. He sat down, closed his eyes, and breathed in deeply, too.

"Pine trees, food," he said. "I also smell the stink of pond algae and duck poop."

Luke laughed. "Ah, yep, algae and duck poop. I don't get outside very much, especially not to a park. What're the food smells?"

Zach glanced across the rolling lawn to a concession

stand that faced a busier street. "Cotton candy, hot dogs, chili, and onions," he guessed. "You hungry?"

"I'm always hungry. Mandy says I've got hollow legs."

Zach pushed erect. "Me, too. Sit tight and I'll go buy us some lunch. You like Coney Island hot dogs?"

"I don't think I've had one. We don't eat out much. Can't afford it."

"A Coney is a hot dog on a bun with chili. If you go for the works, you get grated cheese, minced onions, relish, mayo, and mustard."

"I didn't bring any money."

"Got you covered. What's your poison?"

Luke wanted the works. Zach returned to the bench a few minutes later with a paper sack tucked under one arm, soft drinks in both hands, and two paper trays balanced on top, each brimming with hot dogs covered with chili and all the trimmings. Rosebud stood at Luke's side while he devoured the meal with surprising neatness.

"This is so good!" He grinned, not looking at Zach, but warming him with his smile anyway. "Do I have chili on my face?"

Zach chuckled. "A little, but so do I. That's the fun part, wearing half of it. We'll wipe up later. For now, chow down, bucko. Enjoy your first Coney Island experience."

Rosebud nosed Luke's plastic knife off the bench. When it fell to the grass, the mini retrieved it and nudged Luke to give it back to him.

"Hey, Rosebud, good girl," Luke said, reaching for the pellet pouch.

"No treats," Zach said. "She just conned you."

"Conned me?" Luke asked, bewildered.

Zach grinned. "She pushed the knife off the bench so she could pick it up for you and get rewarded. We're eating. She must feel left out."

"Shame on you, Rosebud," Luke said fondly. "You tried to trick me." He resumed eating. Pocketing a bite in his cheek, he said, "I hear kids."

"Little guys. They're behind us, playing on a merry-go-round, a slide, and a teeter-totter. The moms are sitting on benches at the other side of the playground. There's a busy street over that way. Positioned there, they can intercept an escapee before he runs out into traffic."

"I can remember playing on a teeter-totter," Luke said softly. "Mandy used to take me to a park. Not this one. We lived in another house then. She weighed more than me, so she'd push up with her feet to balance us out." His expression grew wistful. "She'd push me on a swing, too. It was fun."

"New smell," Zach said with a grin. "Rosebud just farted."

Luke laughed. "Nasty, Rosebud. We're eating here, you know." He took a pull from his soft-drink straw. "This is great, Mr. Harrigan."

"Zach. And I'm glad you're having a good time. Truth is, it's been way too long since I've done this. It's a nice break from routine for me, too."

"It's been forever for me," Luke confessed. "Mandy is so busy, we don't get out often. She tries to take me places, but sitting on a park bench doesn't happen much."

"Why don't you get good with a cane so you can go for walks by yourself?"

"It's Mandy's job to take me. Why should I go alone?"

Zach was beginning to get a bird's-eye view of Luke and Mandy's life, and it wasn't pretty. Luke refused to be self-sufficient because, in some twisted way, he wanted to punish his sister for blinding him. Why didn't he understand that, in the process, he was also punishing himself?

Wiping his mouth with a napkin, Zach asked, "How long will your dad be in prison?"

"I'm not sure. For a really long time, I hope. He still hates Mandy's guts, and if he's turned loose and gets tanked up, he'd be just crazy enough to come after her again."

The mere thought turned Zach's stomach. "So she lived alone when it happened?"

"Yeah. Because she'd been in foster care, she didn't have many friends, at least not any she knew well enough to have as a roommate."

"Being in foster care makes it difficult to have friends?"

"Well, for us it was difficult. I—um—acted up a lot, and people never wanted to keep us for long. The caseworkers try to keep you in the same school when they move you around, but that's not always possible. Mandy was bounced back and forth between three high schools. And before that, our dad didn't let her do much after school or on weekends. She's never had very many friends. I haven't, either."

"I see," Zach said to let Luke know he was listening.

"Anyway, Mandy got an apartment, like I told you, and for the next three years, she worked as a waitress at two different jobs, trying to save money to buy us a house. By the time she was old enough to petition the court for custody again, she'd gotten the place we live in now. An owner-carrying-the-contract deal. They let her make a smaller down payment and gave her lower interest rates than she could get at a bank."

Zach was impressed. A badly abused, seventeen-year-old girl had not only found the courage to report her father to the authorities, but then, at eighteen, had volunteered to assume responsibility for her brother. The lady had steel in her spine. He struggled to wrap his mind around the Pajeck family dynamics. A mother who had abandoned her children to a vicious, abusive drunk. A little boy who'd hidden in an upstairs closet nearly every night. A young woman, a very beautiful young woman, who now led the life of a saint, caring for a brother she'd blinded. It was like some frigging soap opera.

Zach had endured pain. He'd lost his mother to childbirth complications at a very early age, and it hadn't been easy for his dad to raise five little kids alone. But never had Zach been subjected to the twisted kind of crap Luke was revealing.

Luke finished his lunch. Zach took his tray and cup, then handed him a napkin. As the kid wiped his pitted face, he said, "It was a canning accident."

Zach crumpled the paper bag in his hands. "Pardon?"

"My blindness. I was six. Mandy was canning. I was standing beside her watching, and a jar exploded. It was hot in the kitchen from the pressure cooker, and our dad got pissed if we ran the air conditioner, so she opened a window. It was cool outside, September, I think. She was putting up the last of the garden produce. Our dad had this thing about saving money, so we always had a summer vegetable garden. When Mama left, it became Mandy's job to plant a garden and preserve the food for winter."

"And she was how old?"

"Thirteen when Mom walked. Fifteen when she blinded me."

Zach clenched his teeth to give himself a moment before he spoke. "Okay, so back to the accident. A jar exploded in your face?"

"Yes. I was in the hospital for a long time, and it was all because she did something stupid. When she opened the windows, it created a draft. Any idiot knows that those jars come out of a pressure cooker blasting hot. When she lifted one out and the air struck it, the thing went off like a bomb." Luke swallowed hard. "That was the last thing I saw, exploding glass. The shards hit me in the face, ruined my eyes, end of story."

Zach could remember a jar exploding once while Dee Dee was canning. "You know, Luke, it isn't uncommon for hot jars to shatter. My stepmom has had it happen to her. How can you blame Mandy for something that probably wasn't even her fault?"

Luke's head came up. His mouth thinned into an ugly curve. "It was her fault, all right. She should have known better than to open the windows."

"But *did* she know better? That's the question. How old was she when this happened? Fifteen? She was barely more than a child herself." Zach kept his voice low. "It was wrong of your father to place that much responsibility on her shoulders. Pressure cookers can be dangerous. The gauges need to be sent in every year to be checked. If your dad was a cheapskate, I'll bet he never paid to do that."

Luke's brows snapped together in a troubled scowl. "Probably not. He could squeeze a nickel until the buffalo hollered."

"When gauges aren't functioning right, the cooker can explode. Did you know that?"

"No."

"And jars—they just blow up sometimes. If Mandy had known, she'd have made you stand back as she lifted them out. Had she ever had one explode before?"

"Not that I know of."

"Then essentially, she was a kid given an adult's job, and she didn't know what the fuck she was doing." Zach caught the inside of his cheek between his teeth. He hadn't meant to use that word, but it was just so damned frustrating. He had his issues with Mandy. Well, make that before talking with Luke, he'd had issues with her. Now he had a far better understanding of why she'd gone off on him like she had.

"Here's the thing, and please understand I'm just a stranger, looking in. But I don't think it's fair to hold a young girl accountable for making a mistake when she was forced to do a job she shouldn't have been doing. Your *father* was the one responsible."

"He wasn't even home! Look, my dad was a jerk, no question, but he was also a really smart man. He was the mayor of Crystal Falls. He knew a lot of really important people. You don't get there unless you have a lot going for you."

"Like what, a gift for gab?" Zach walked over to put the remaining lunch garbage into a trash receptacle. "Your dad was an asshole. Sorry, but that's my take. He abused his daughter. He expected her to carry a load of responsibility that a woman twice her age might have found daunting. You want to blame Mandy for your blindness and make her pay for it? Hey, man, that's your deal. But if you do, it doesn't speak well of you. You're nineteen, and you can't find the bathroom by yourself. Yet you berate her for not being a bulletproof home-maker at fifteen? Give me a break."

Luke groped for Rosebud, who'd clearly become a comfort to him, slipping his fingers into her fore-lock. "If you're trying to make me feel like shit, you're succeeding."

"Good. I think it's about time you started to grow up." Zach realized how harsh he sounded and paced in a circle, taking deep breaths. "I'm sorry. I've got no business saying any of this to you. But one of my worst faults—and I've got a lot of them—is calling it like I see it. Your father was an asshole, and now you're following in his footsteps by punishing your sister for something that wasn't her fault. Sorry, partner, but that's my take. You need to shape up and cut her a little slack."

Luke's eyes went bright with tears again. His mouth trembled. "You really think it wasn't Mandy's fault?"

Zach tucked his thumbs under his belt and bent his head. Gifted with words he wasn't. No one would ever elect him as mayor. But at least he was honest, even when the truth hurt. "Some people are cruel in a lot of different ways. Your dad obviously enjoyed inflicting physical pain. But he didn't stop there, did he?"

"What do you mean?"

"Think about it. He also got off on causing injury with words. He turned you against Mandy, the one person who truly loved you. That's the worst kind of pain there is, not just for you, but for her as well. I've seen her with you. There's not much she wouldn't do for you. When accidents happen that hurt a loved one, we tend to blame ourselves, even if it wasn't our fault. Can you step away from your own feelings to imagine what hers must be like? Can you imagine living with that guilt every single day of your life?"

Shiny rivulets streamed down Luke's cheeks. "This is why I wanted to come here today, to talk to you about all this. Mandy and me—well, we got into a huge fight after we left your ranch that first day, and after it was over, we sort of—I don't know—understood each other better. Because of that, I've been thinking...." He gulped. "Well, I've just been thinking, is all. Mandy loves me. I know she does. And I keep taking jabs at her, trying to hurt her for what she did."

"And?" Zach asked.

"And nothing! I know I shouldn't do it, but ... but I can't stop. Sometimes I get to thinking maybe I'm just like my dad, mean to the core. And that ... that's the worst."

Zach plopped back down on the bench. A family counselor, he sure as hell wasn't. "Ah, Luke. You aren't mean to the core. You're a decent person. I've seen that in you."

"You have?" The kid sounded surprised.

"Little glimpses." Zach realized Luke couldn't see him grinning and gave the kid's knee a jostle to impart that he was teasing. "You're a mess. You know it?"

"I've been to counseling."

"And how did that go?"

"It was pretty much worthless." Luke wiped his face again. "I'm sorry. I'm crying like a baby. All of this shit has been eating at me for a long time."

"You think I never cry? Think again. I'm the biggest blubberer there is sometimes."

"You are?"

Zach considered the question. The man he most admired in the world, his father, had never been ashamed to shed tears. "A man who can't cry without feeling embarrassed isn't a real man."

Luke sniffed. "I guess I'm not a real man, then. I'm embarrassed."

"You're going to be a fine man someday. You've just got a little growing up to do. And please know I don't mean that as a slam. I was a jerk at nineteen. I'm surprised my father didn't give up on me. But he never did. He just gave me some time to grow up and get it all figured out. Eventually I did, and you will, too."

"I hope so. I've done such bad things to my sister. Since our fight, I've been better, but still, hardly a day goes by that I don't take jabs at her for blinding me. I pretend I can't do anything, just to make her pay. And—" He broke off and dragged in air through his nose, making a wet sound. "And I don't know how to stop. There's this awful feeling inside of me. Mandy's sent me to shrinks for years, but I'd never talk to them about it. I knew if I did that I'd have to try to fix it. Only it was too *big* for me to fix. You know? So I played the counselors like it was all a game. They tried to dig deep into me, but I never even let them scrape the surface. I was scared to."

Zach was in way over his head and knew it. "Luke, I'd like to be your friend. But I'm not qualified to help you with this."

"I think maybe you are."

Zach tensed. "I'm just a goat roper with degrees in agriculture and animal husbandry."

"Yeah, but I like you, and you're honest."

Zach didn't figure likability and honesty were all Luke needed. "If you've got bad feelings, you should talk with a professional."

"I'm scared," Luke whispered. "My mom—she just

left. You know? I was only four, and somehow that got all mixed up in my head, making me afraid Mandy would leave, too. All those times when my dad was beating on her? I was so afraid. This'll sound really bad, but I wasn't as afraid for her as I was for myself. I'd huddle in the closet, crying because I knew she couldn't take it forever. What if I woke up the next morning and she was gone, just like my mom? I'd be the only one left for him to pound on. You know? And I couldn't even see to try to get away from him."

"Sweet Christ." Zach put his hand on Luke's shoulder. "Don't blame yourself for that. It was just your survival instinct kicking in."

"But I cared more about me than I did her. I should have been praying she'd run away. Instead I prayed she'd stay and keep taking it. It was really bad shit he did to her, not just slapping her around, but using his fists and even kicking her sometimes."

Zach truly did feel sick now. The hot dog had settled in his stomach like a rock. "Ah, Luke. Think about what you're saying. She faced that, night after night, and *didn't* run. There's only one thing I can think of that stopped her. She couldn't run away and leave *you*. So what makes you afraid she'd consider doing that now?"

"We talked, and she promised she wouldn't leave. But she might. Even with my dad out of the picture, I'm still afraid to be all alone."

Zach took off his hat and rested it over his knee. Finger-combed his hair. Inhaled, exhaled. "All of us are afraid to be alone, I think. I've got a huge family, so it's not that big a worry for me. I can always count on somebody to be there when the chips are down. But all you have is Mandy. It's understandable that you panic sometimes."

"Exactly, and if she takes a powder, what'll I do?"

Zach considered. "The first thing I'd do is take action before that ever happens."

"What kind of action?"

"Try to become more self-sufficient. The stronger and more independent you are, the less afraid you'll feel. By doing that, you'll lighten her load so she won't *want* to take a powder. You get what I'm saying? Make yourself a more appealing package. She's stuck it out with you all this time when you weren't trying to do that. Do you really believe she'll leave if you take over some of the work?"

Luke tightened his hand over Rosebud's neck. "I don't know where to start."

"Start by finding the bathroom by yourself and take it from there. One little thing at a time. You can do it."

Luke nodded. "There are lots of things I pretend I can't do."

"Then stop pretending and do them. Sounds simple enough to me."

"Maybe it does to you. You can see. I'm just so scared."

"Yeah, well, life is scary for all of us sometimes, whether we can see or not. If you get in a pinch, you have my cell phone number. Give me a call." Zach wondered if he'd lost his mind, but he felt compelled to add, "I've got a big house, an even bigger ranch, and a mini to guide you. If you need a place to bunk, call me, and I'll come get you."

"Really?"

Zach reached over and patted Luke's shoulder. "Harrigan law. We never say anything we won't back up. If Mandy takes a powder, call me. You can room with me and Rosebud until you get it figured out." Zach let that sink in. "But I seriously doubt your sister could be pried away from you with a crowbar. She loves you. Give her some credit. Hell, if you shape up, she'll think it's a walk in the park compared to the way it is now. Why would she decide to dump you then?"

Luke released a shaky breath. "If I go home and start doing stuff by myself, she won't know what to think."

Zach chuckled. "I'm fairly certain it will come as a welcome surprise to her."

"Once I start, I won't be able to stop. She'll know then what a big fake I am."

"Once you start, will you want to stop?" Zach countered. "You have a life to live. There are so many things you haven't done. Don't you want to experience at least some of them?"

Luke sniffed and swallowed. "I'd like to have a girlfriend. What are my chances, though? No sighted girl will want anything to do with me."

"Why? You're a good-looking guy."

"I'm blind, man. Big turnoff."

"I don't think that's true. The biggest issue is that you're presently so limited in what you can do. A girl would *not* want to go on a date with you if your sister had to come, too."

Luke grinned, his eyes still bright with tears. "I really am a mess, aren't I?"

"You're fixable," Zach replied. "Problem is, only you can do the fixing."

"So what if I fix myself and Mandy decides to get married? She says she doesn't want a husband, but if she got one, he might not like me. Then I'd be all alone."

Zach knew he needed to stay focused on Luke's problems, but he couldn't help but ask, "Why doesn't she want a husband?"

"Hey, man. With a father like ours, would you ever want one?"

"No," Zach admitted. "I guess I wouldn't. Does she even have a social life?"

Luke shook his head. "I nixed that. She went out on dates a couple of times, but I—" He stopped talking and gulped. "You'll think I'm really awful if I tell you this."

"I won't think you're awful. Everyone does things they regret later. Spill it."

"I ruined her dates. On purpose, I mean. Stupid stuff,

like pretending I fell and hurt myself, or that I was sick. Another time, I sneaked into the kitchen when the sitter was in the bathroom and put a towel on the stove burner, turned it on, and almost made it back to the sofa before the lady came out. Nailed. She called Mandy and refused to watch me ever again. She said I was a pyromaniac."

"Well, I can sort of see her point. Did you set the kitchen on fire?"

"No, just the towel. The lady managed to put it out."

"That was a dangerous stunt to pull." Zach sensed there was more. "So what else did you do to ruin Mandy's dates?"

"When she went on the third one, I took a swing at the sitter. Mandy gave up after that. She never went out again."

Zach tugged hard on his ear. "You truly were a little shit, weren't you? It's not okay for a guy to smack women, Luke. You need to get that cemented in your brain."

Luke nodded. "I know."

Zach wanted to drive that point home even more but decided to save it for later. "So your sister has been on only three dates, and she's how old?"

"Twenty-eight."

"Damn, Luke. She's not a nun."

"Yeah, well, I'm not a monk, either, and it's *her* fault *I* don't have a life. Why should I let her have one?"

Zach said nothing. He let that hang in the air between them until Luke finally broke down and whispered, "I'm doing it again, aren't I? Blaming her for everything."

"Yes, and that's wrong. We all make mistakes. You've just admitted that you've made your fair share of them. A mark of maturity is when we realize that no one is perfect, including ourselves, and we're able to forgive others, not because we're noble, but because we know that, sooner or later, we'll screw up and need forgiveness, too."

Luke ran a hand through his hair, leaving rooster tails atop his head. "It's hard to change the way I've been thinking most of my life. It may take some practice."

"Probably so. Old habits can be hard to break. But it's not impossible."

"I'd really, *really* like to have a girlfriend."

Zach laughed. "Well, then, shape up and find one."

When Mandy got home, she saw Zach's SUV parked at the curb and wondered what he was doing there. She entered the house with one hand laden with heavy plastic bags to find the living room empty. "Luke? Mrs. Peabody? Yoo-hoo, I'm home!"

No one answered. She hurried to the kitchen, checking every surface for a note to explain why Luke and the sitter weren't there, but she found nothing. Her heart started to pound with fright. Abandoning her mission to get the groceries unloaded and put away, she put the bags on the counter and raced for the phone. Mrs. Peabody didn't answer until the eighth ring, and by then Mandy was in a full-blown panic.

"Hello," the older woman said.

"Mrs. Peabody, this is Miranda Pajeck. Where on earth is my brother?"

"At some park, best I know. A man with a little horse came and got him."

Mandy's pulse slowed a bit. "What park?" she asked tautly.

"How should I know? I was informed that Luke is legally an adult. I told both of them I wanted no part of it, that Luke didn't have your permission to leave. They paid me no mind. I hung around to finish out the hour, and then I came home."

"Couldn't you have at *least* left me a note?" Mandy cried. "When I came home to an empty house, I was scared half to death."

"If you had a cell phone like a normal person, I could

have called you when Luke told me he was leaving. You owe me for the whole five hours, by the way. I turned down another job to be at your place. It's only fair I get paid."

Mandy's temples throbbed with anger. She'd never liked Mrs. Peabody, but until now she hadn't realized the woman had an irresponsible streak a mile wide. "You'll be paid only for the time you were here and not a penny more."

"Fine. You just lost a sitter, missy."

"Like I care? You could have at least asked them what park they were going to and left me a note!" Mandy was so upset, she hung up on the woman.

Her anger mounted. There were three parks within walking distance of the house. Speaking of an irresponsible streak, why hadn't Zach or Luke left her a note? That was only common courtesy. She had no idea what time they'd left, no clue where they were. What if something happened—an accident or something?

Trying to calm down, Mandy paced in tight circles. Then she went to get the rest of her purchases out of the car, looking up and down the sidewalk, hoping to see her brother as she collected the bags. *Nothing.* Fury welled within her. When she returned to the house, she didn't bother to put away the food. Instead she tried Zach's cell and got no answer. Then she called St. Matthew's hospital to see if her brother had been taken in for emergency treatment.

Mandy was home by the time Luke and Zach returned. She stood on the front porch, arms tight around her waist, right foot tapping the concrete, eyes shooting daggers. How she managed to look beautiful when she obviously wanted to rip his head off, Zach didn't know. In the sunlight, her hair glistened like polished brass. Her tidy figure was shown off to perfection by dark blue slacks and a silky blouse the color of an orange. In the breeze, the supple cloth clung to her breasts.

"The shit's about to hit the fan," Zach murmured to Luke. "Your sister is on the porch, and if she had a gun, I think she'd shoot me."

Luke's head came up. "Why's she pissed at you? The walk was my idea."

Zach fell in behind Luke and the horse as the pair made their way up the narrow walk to the house.

"Where have you *been*?" Mandy cried when they were about fifteen feet from the steps. "I hire a sitter, and you just take off? She wants to charge me for the whole five hours. That's fifteen bucks an hour, Mr. Pajeck. After you left, she finished out the hour, and apparently all she did during that time was eat! The leftovers I hoped to serve for dinner are *gone*. Maybe you'd like to cook tonight, Luke. I'm behind on my work!"

To Zach's surprise, Luke straightened his shoulders. "Maybe I would. Like to cook, I mean. You'll have to teach me how first, so you're stuck for tonight. But I'll get there."

Mandy's lips parted as if she meant to say something else, but nothing came out. She stared incredulously at her brother for a long moment. Then, with crisp authority, she said, "Get into this house, *now*."

Luke thrust out the harness handle. "Here, Zach. Thanks a lot for the walk."

"You're more than welcome," Zach replied. "Call me anytime. It was good training for Rosebud."

"Hello?" Mandy descended the steps to grab her brother's arm. "There will be no more walks unless I give the okay, and I do *not* feel so inclined."

"I can go for a walk any damned time I want!" Luke objected. "You're not my boss!"

Mandy shot a cutting glare at Zach. "Two hours alone with you, and just listen to him! I was afraid this would happen—that you'd fill his head with crap."

"He didn't fill my head with crap! Damn it, Mands, calm down. It was just a *walk*."

"In the house. *Now!*" Mandy cried. "I'll deal with you later." She drew her brother toward the steps. Looking over her slender shoulder, she met Zach's gaze. "I'd like a word with you. Let me get him settled, and I'll come back out."

Zach didn't look forward to having a *word* with her, but he'd never been one to run from a confrontation. And in this particular instance, he had a few things to say himself.

Mandy was gone only a few seconds. When she stepped back onto the porch, she slammed the door so hard the window frames shuddered. Glorious hair drifting in the breeze, she marched past Zach toward his SUV. Then she turned and waited for him.

Zach put Rosebud in the vehicle. When he swung around, Mandy wagged a slender finger under his nose. "Don't you *ever* take my brother *anywhere* again without my permission. You're lucky I didn't call the police and file charges!"

"You'd have looked pretty silly trying to file charges. He called me, not the other way around. If he wants to take a walk, he's an adult, and that's his decision to make. He's not a baby, Miranda. Isn't it about time to let your brother grow up?"

Her lips went white. "I know my brother far better than you do, sir."

"Really? Are you aware that Luke blames you for blinding him and that he's been playing you for years, pretending to be helpless to punish you?"

Her eyes filled with tears, and her mouth began to quiver. "Yes," she admitted. "Luke blames me for the accident. Why shouldn't he? It was my fault."

Zach had been immersed in the Pajeck family dynamics for more than two hours, and his patience was wearing thin. "That is such a load of crap. You need to see a shrink almost as much as your brother does."

"*What?*"

"That canning accident wasn't your fault. You were only fifteen, barely old enough to be looking after yourself. Home canning is dangerous. Not only jars can explode. Pressure cookers can, too. Your father was wrong to blame you for Luke's accident. It was his fault, not yours."

She jutted her chin. "What do you know about it? You weren't there. And it's none of your business, anyway!"

"I'm making it my business."

"By whose invitation?"

"Luke's! He's not a child anymore, and he understands a lot more than you give him credit for. This afternoon, he talked to me about turning over a new leaf. Question is, will *you* allow it? Or do your feelings of guilt have you so messed up emotionally that you *want* Luke to depend on you for every damned thing? Great way to do penance, right, Mandy? Devote the rest of your life to him, give up everything for him. Well, news flash. You're not just screwing up your life. You're screwing up *his*."

She jerked as if Zach had slapped her, and he immediately wished he could call back the words.

"You don't know anything about us!" she cried. "I don't want my brother to be helpless! If that were the case, why would I have inquired about Rosebud? I want him to lead as normal a life as possible, but Luke has always refused to cooperate! Do you think this is *fun* for me? That I *enjoy* having no freedom? Every time I leave him, except to do grocery shopping and run errands, something horrific happens. It's true that my entire life revolves around Luke, but if you think I *choose* for it to be this way, you're out of your ever-loving mind!"

Zach felt as if he'd just stepped off into a hole, that awful, bottomless sensation that always came over him when he expected to find solid ground and met with empty air instead. He really, *really* wished he'd had the good sense to keep his mouth shut.

She whirled to return to the house. "To think I meant to phone you this afternoon and apologize for *my* bad behavior at the barbecue! Ha! On my worst day, I've never come close to being as obnoxious as you just were. I think we're even!"

"Mandy, wait. Please."

"Go to hell," she tossed over her shoulder.

"I'm sorry," he called after her. "I had no right to say those things to you. I'm sorry."

She stopped and spun to face him. Tears glistened on her cheeks. "Penance?"

Zach swept off his hat and slapped it against his leg. "That was a rotten thing to say. It's not your fault that Luke has insisted on being mollycoddled, and I can't blame you for giving in. When you love people, you're there for them. He needs you, probably more than we realize. He tried to talk with me about that, and I gave him the best advice I could. But I'm not qualified to counsel him. He needs to see a professional."

Her eyes blazed like firelight reflecting off water. "How *dare* you take him away from this house without even leaving me a note! He's nineteen. I'll give you that. But he's also my brother, my *blind* brother. I didn't know what park you went to—or if you even went to a park. I had no idea how long he'd be gone, if he was safe, *nothing*." She splayed a hand over her heart. "I was scared to death! I tried to ring your cell. No answer. I even called the hospital!"

Zach had turned off his phone during the walk, not wanting any calls to interrupt his time with Luke. "Surely the sitter explained to you where Luke and I had gone."

"She said she wasn't sure which park you'd gone to, and she was so angry about Luke leaving while he was in her care that all she wanted was her money."

Zach felt awful. Being of age didn't give anyone the right to make someone else worry. "Ah, Mandy, you're right. I'm sorry. I should have left a note."

If she heard his apology, she zoomed right past it. "As for taking him to a counselor? I've taken him to see professionals so many times I've lost count! Thousands of dollars down the drain. *Thousands*."

"I know. He mentioned that, too."

She wiped her cheeks with the back of her wrist. Zach saw some of the tension ease from her body. "I can't believe he talked to you about any of this. He never does with me."

"Sometimes it's easier to unload on someone you don't know very well. Less risky."

Her shimmering gaze sought his. With visible effort, she struggled to calm down and collect her composure. Zach guessed she'd registered his apologies, after all. They hadn't completely smoothed her feathers, but at least she no longer looked totally beside herself. "What all did he say?"

Zach sighed and thrust the hat back on. "I'm not at liberty to tell you everything, Mandy. I'm sure he trusted me to keep some of it confidential."

"In order to help him, I *need* to know."

"Then I suggest you ask Luke." Zach rubbed his jaw. "I apologize for sticking my nose where it doesn't belong, but the information came to me uninvited. And sometimes standing on the outside looking in gives a clearer view of a situation. My first instinct was to try to help."

"And your view of the situation is?"

Zach dug at the grass with his boot heel, thinking that he was so much like his father, it was scary— plainspoken, slow to collect his thoughts, and a habitual dirt kicker when he got upset. He glanced up. "Do you really want to hear my take?"

"I won't know until I hear it."

Zach stared past her at the house for a second. *What the hell*. He'd already stuck his foot in his mouth. "I think your father is a heartless bastard who played both

you and Luke like well-tuned fiddles. He made you believe you were to blame for the accident, and in turn, he
convinced Luke of the same. Step back from it, Mandy.
Look at it square-on. He drove a wedge between you
two. What's worse, he *intended* to do it. I think you *have*
sought absolution for the accident by catering to your
brother. Who wouldn't? He's blind, for God's sake, and
you feel responsible because your father *made* you feel
that way. You didn't know that pressure cooker would
get the jars so hot they could explode if cool air hit them,
did you? Well, did you?"

"I— No." He barely heard the reply.

"Well, there you are. You didn't know what could
happen. He told you it was your fault because he didn't
want to man up to the fact that he'd dumped adult re-
sponsibilities on a kid without ever making sure she
knew how to handle them. How can you make it up to
someone when you've robbed him of his vision? By sacrificing, by being there, by always going the extra mile,
that's how. Don't you see, Mandy? The man may be in
prison, but he's still inflicting pain, and you and Luke are
so caught up in it, you're both lost in the maze."

She blinked and looked away. Then she cupped a
hand over her eyes.

"That canning accident wasn't your fault. Jars just
explode sometimes. Your father should never have allowed a fifteen-year-old girl *near* a pressure cooker. It
was dangerous for you, too. And if anyone is to blame
for the loss of Luke's sight, he is."

Hand still over her eyes, she shook her head. The
slump of her slender shoulders filled Zach with an un-
reasoning yearning to close the distance between them
and catch her close in his arms. *Not a good plan.* He remained where he was.

"Before I finish mucking this up," he added, "let me
say one more thing. I'm sorry I opened the wine the
night of the barbecue. I didn't know your dad was an

alcoholic. Now that I do, I'll never drink around you two again. You've got my word on it."

She drew down her hand to gape at him in startled amazement. "I can't *believe* he told you about Dad. What other family skeletons did he drag out of the closet?"

"None that made me think less of you," Zach replied. "In fact, I came away from the conversation thinking you're one of the best sisters on record."

"You just said I was a sister who feeds on her brother's helplessness. Make up your mind, Mr. Harrigan."

Zach winced. "I never meant it to come out that way." He took another dig at the grass with his boot. "Can we back up and start over?"

She fixed a questioning gaze on him. "What do you mean?"

With a sigh, Zach tried to compose his thoughts before he spoke. "I'm just seeing such a change in Luke, is all. He's coming to love Rosebud, and it'll be a horrible shame if either of us stands in the way of that relationship. This isn't about me, and it isn't about you. It should be only about Luke. Can we both agree on that?"

Tears filled her eyes again. "That's why I was going to call you this afternoon, because I feel the same way. I can't allow my personal feelings to mess this up for my brother." She searched his eyes. "Do you mean it about not drinking? That's the biggest concern I have. I don't want my brother to be around it, and I can't stand to be."

Zach nodded. "My word is my promise."

She ran a hand over the buttons of her blouse. "Then I suppose Luke can see Rosebud again. They are forging a bond. We shouldn't stand in the way of that."

Zach touched the brim of his hat in farewell. "I'll call to set up a time for Luke to visit the ranch again, then. Rosebud is familiar with the layout there. I think it'll do Luke a world of good to go walking with her by himself."

With a hesitant edge in her voice, she said, "That sounds good."

Zach turned away and then spun back. "One more thing. Would you give me permission to take Luke on another outing soon?"

"Permission?" She arched a fine eyebrow. "I thought it wasn't needed."

"Well, I don't think it really is, but I'm trying to back up and start over, here."

She didn't exactly smile, but the dimple did flash in her cheek. "You're right. Sorry. Where would you like to take him?"

"My sister, Sam, has a sister-in-law named Bethany who runs a riding academy for the handicapped. Luke seemed to enjoy petting my big horses, and I think he might get a kick out of going for a ride. Bethany has special saddles, so Luke won't fall off, and she'll take every precaution to ensure his safety."

Mandy wanted to refuse. The thought of her brother on a horse made her heart freeze. But Zach was right. She did treat Luke like a baby. If he was ever going to lead a normal life, that had to stop. And, though her feelings were still bruised by what Zach had said, it appeared that he and Luke were becoming friends. If Zach kept his promise about not drinking around them again, the relationship might be good for her brother.

"If Luke would like to go, I won't object," she said. "It will have to be his decision, though. Petting a horse and being on one are two different things."

Zach nodded. "True. So feel him out about it. Bethany is great with young people. I think Luke will like her. But it's up to him."

Mandy loved that little gesture he made when he was about to leave, touching the edge of his hat with a bent finger. He did it again just as he turned the second time to walk away. How such a small act could be so sexy, she didn't know. She fixed her gaze on his backside, taking him in from head to toe. Had he practiced that strong, purposeful stride? And how on earth did he make dusty

Wranglers look so darned good? As she watched him swing into the SUV, she sincerely hoped he had no bridges to sell. She had a very bad feeling she'd be a sucker and invest.

He tooted the horn as he pulled away from the curb. Mandy watched the vehicle until it rounded the corner and disappeared. What, she asked herself, had just happened? She'd been so angry she wanted to snatch him bald-headed, and somehow he'd talked her down. It made absolutely no sense.

It also frightened her.

Chapter Twelve

Mandy's eyes nearly popped out of their sockets when she returned to the house and found her brother in the kitchen. She'd left him planted on the sofa, and once settled there he was usually good for the evening. As she drew up behind him where he stood at the counter, she peered around his elbow to see what he was doing. He was trying to make a sandwich, a PB and J, only it wasn't jelly he was about to spoon onto the smear of peanut butter.

"Whoa!" she said. "What are you doing?"

"Making a sandwich. Zach fed me, but I'm still a little hungry, maybe from the walk."

"Well, that isn't jelly. It's salsa, and it's the spicy kind."

Luke let go of the spoon handle. "Uh-oh."

Mandy screwed the lid back on the jar and returned it to the fridge, grabbing the strawberry preserves before she closed the clunky old door. "Here, let me."

"No." Luke said the word softly, but there was an underlying note of steely resolve in his voice. "I want to do it myself." He held out his hand. "Give."

Stunned, Mandy gave him the jar and watched in amazement as he groped in the drawer for a fresh spoon, finished making the sandwich, put it on a plate, and made his way to the table. He patted the air to find a chair, set the plate in front of it, and sat down. She doubted the evidence of her eyes.

Cheek bulging, Luke informed her, "I've decided to start doing more things for myself." When she said nothing, he cocked his head in question. "I'll need a little help. Can we reorganize the kitchen so I can find stuff?"

Mandy had the curious sensation that she'd been belted between the eyes with a fastball. Her legs felt weak as she went to the table and sat down. Luke had talked extensively to Zach Harrigan about his most private feelings and their personal business, and all she was getting out of him were a few cryptic sentences. She was the one who'd always been there for her brother. Yet he chose to share his deepest feelings with someone who barely knew him? Pain and anger merged and hardened into resentment. She took a deep breath.

Keeping her tone carefully neutral, she said, "I'm more than willing to help, Luke. I'm just not sure what brought this on."

"I've been thinking about it for a long time. Today was ... well, I guess a shrink would call it a turning point for me, deciding to do it instead of just thinking about it." He took another bite of the sandwich. "If I'm going to be able to do more for myself, we need to give this kitchen a major overhaul. Can we rearrange the shelves in the refrigerator and cupboards? If I know where things are, it'll be easier for me."

Mandy pushed out, "Just name it, you've got it."

"At my special school when I was in foster care, they had this labeler that punched raised lettering into heavy plastic tape. They're easier to find than the Braille ones, and cheaper, too. Do you think we could afford one of those?"

Mandy had seen the labelers and didn't think they were very expensive. If they'd been a hundred bucks, she'd still have found a way. "Sure. For the time being that might work, but I can order you a Braille one as well."

"The regular kind is all I need. If we labeled a lot of

the stuff in here, I could trace the letters, and know what it is."

Were they having this conversation, or was she hallucinating? Luke, who couldn't find the bathroom, suddenly wanted to reorganize the kitchen? What on earth had Zach said to him? A new person was walking around in Luke's body. Adjusting was going to take a while. Assuming the change was permanent, that was. *Don't get your hopes up*, she cautioned herself. But it was difficult not to. Luke seemed truly determined.

"Eat up," she said, glancing at her watch. "If we hustle, we can make it to an office supply store before it closes."

Luke grinned. "That would be *great*. Maybe we can start on the kitchen tonight."

By the time they found a labeler and Mandy drove home, it was nearly six. After getting Luke settled on the sofa and stashing their purchases in her office, she went to the refrigerator, trying to think what she might prepare for dinner that would be quick. If Luke wanted to reorganize the kitchen, she needed to strike while the iron was hot.

Intent on grabbing the makings for grilled cheese sandwiches, Mandy nearly jumped out of her skin when a chair scraped the floor behind her. She turned to see Luke lowering himself onto the seat. With his auburn hair standing up in peaks at the front, he looked so young, his face still in that teenage transition stage from boy to man. Occasionally, she glimpsed the hardening edges and planes of masculinity, but tonight in the soft golden glow of the ceiling light, a childlike softness dominated his features.

"You startled me. I'm not used to you moving around the house by yourself."

There was splotch of dried brown stuff on the front of Luke's fleece sweatshirt. Mandy guessed he'd spilled something during lunch at the park. Her throat went tight. It was wrong of her to resent her brother's budding friendship with Zach. She should be pleased that Luke was reaching out. Instead she felt hurt. She knew that wasn't right, but she couldn't help it. She felt . . . rejected, somehow.

"I'm going to try to become more mobile," Luke said. "Remember that afternoon when we got in the pissing match about the guide dog? You said you've still got my cane stashed somewhere. Would you mind getting it out for me now?"

"Uh, sure, right away." Mandy went to the closet. When *she* had suggested that Luke try using the cane again, he'd grown angry. Now, after one visit with Zach, her brother was all for it. How was she supposed to deal with that? "Here," she said when she returned to the kitchen with the cane. "Just take it slow. I don't want you to fall."

Standing at the counter, Mandy attempted to spread mayonnaise onto four slices of bread, but she could barely focus. Zach's accusations rang loudly in her mind. *It's a great way to do penance, right, Mandy?* In the heat of the moment, she'd discarded that charge as being groundless. But, oh, God, now that Zach had put the thought in her mind, she realized it was true. She *needed* Luke to depend on her. Doing everything for him and sacrificing her own happiness eased her feelings of guilt.

Mandy gave up on making sandwiches, hung her head, and held tight to the edge of the counter, her fingers aching at the force of her grip. Damn Zach Harrigan. His words reverberated in her mind, refusing to be dismissed. *You're not just screwing up your life. You're screwing up his.* What kind of person was she? She'd made all the right noises, trying to encourage Luke to get a guide animal and attend college, but when it came right down to it, had she done one single thing to *force* him to be self-sufficient?

No. She'd been right there, helping him to the toilet, helping him to shave and find his clothes. *Enabling.* She'd enabled her brother's helplessness. It wasn't pretty, but she'd done it, not because it had been best for Luke but because it had been best for her.

"Mands?" Luke said softly.

She swallowed hard, praying her voice would be steady. She opened her mouth and felt her throat clog. She settled for a grunt, which Luke took as an answer.

"Can dinner wait for a while? I've got some stuff I need to talk to you about."

Mandy managed to fake a cough that cleared her throat. "Can it keep, Luke? I have all the stuff out and—"

"No, I need to say it now before I lose the courage."

Mandy turned around and stared at him. "Courage?" she echoed.

Luke nodded. "Some of it is going to be rough to say. You know? And I'm scared you'll hate me after I tell you."

Mandy made her way to a chair. "I could never hate you."

"You think that now, but some of the stuff is really bad. Remember the times you tried to go out on dates? Well, I messed that up for you on purpose. It wasn't an accident when I fell, and the other time, I wasn't really sick. And that lady didn't lie about me trying to catch the towel on fire. I couldn't go out and have fun, so I didn't think it was fair that you could."

"Oh, Luke." Mandy had always known that Luke had ruined her dates on purpose. But hearing him admit it soothed a deep, unacknowledged ache within her. He was reaching out. He was trying.

"I told you it was bad." He made a fist in his hair, squeezed his eyes closed in a grimace that bared his teeth. "I know it was wrong of me, but at the time I didn't see it. I blamed you for blinding me, and I—" His voice cracked. "I was scared. You know? If you went on dates and met some guy you really liked, where would that leave me?"

"And Zach Harrigan said something to change your mind about all that?"

"He said some stuff, yeah, but it was more like he sort of confirmed what I was already starting to think myself. That's one of the reasons I asked him to take me walking today, so I could bounce a bunch of shit off of him. You know?"

"And you couldn't have talked to me?"

She'd tried to keep her voice impersonal, but Luke obviously picked up on something. He turned his head slightly to one side, as though listening for messages she hadn't spoken aloud. "You're upset because I chose him instead of you."

"I *am* your sister."

"Exactly. You're my sister, the person I've lied to and deliberately tried to hurt. Don't you get it? Zach's an outsider. He doesn't have a stake in this. He can listen and sift through the bullshit easier than you can."

Mandy bent her head, staring at the creases of her slacks. "What bullshit, Luke? I mean, I know we've had our problems, but have we gotten that far off track?"

Luke pushed at the tablecloth. "I think so. I've thought about this a lot. It isn't something that came up just today. I'm nineteen, and I spend my life on the sofa or in bed. How far offtrack is that? You're twenty-eight, you've been on only three dates, and I ruined all of them. You can't really think this is normal. You just can't. You think I can't find the bathroom by myself. I freak when you leave this house to do anything that might be fun, and I figure out a way to wreck it. Sometimes I even convince myself that I hate you. How far offtrack is that?"

Mandy heard the self-condemnation in her brother's tone. "Don't, Luke. So much of that is my fault."

Luke threw up a hand. "That's the same old bullshit, Mandy. Everything is *your* fault. You think that partly because of Dad, but mostly because of me. Well, everything *isn't* your fault. A lot of it is mine. I've accepted that, and you need to, too."

"I shouldn't have opened the windows. It was my fault the jar exploded." She was so upset she could barely hear her own voice, but Luke, with hearing more acute than normal, had no difficulty.

"You were a kid and the responsibility for what happened isn't yours; it's our dad's. Think about it. He used that accident like his fists, to hurt you *and* me. And, as always, he was successful. He's an expert at hurting people."

Mandy felt as if everything solid around her had turned liquid—the floor, the chair, even her life. When she looked at her brother, she didn't know him anymore. "I . . . Luke, this is a lot to take in. It's like you went for a walk and came home a different person."

Luke settled back on the chair. "It didn't suddenly happen today. I've been fighting with this for a long time, but I was scared to do anything about it. You don't really get that, not yet. But you need to try. There's this thing inside of me." He bunched a fist and pressed it to his sternum. "A fear. I know it sounds dumb but that's the only way I can describe it. It's been there for as long as I can remember, this huge *thing*, eating at me and making me do terrible things. If I were all the way crazy, maybe that wouldn't bother me, but the normal part of me knows it's nuts. I knew it was wrong, but the fear made me do it anyway. Does that make any sense?"

For Mandy, it *was* suddenly starting to make dreadful sense. "Luke, why did you go to Zach? Why couldn't you talk to me? I guess that's what I really don't understand."

"You were the last person I could have talked to. You're at the center of it. I was playing you, and I knew I shouldn't, but if I stopped, then what? Then the game would have been up. I would have lost all my power. So I kept doing it."

"Your power?"

"My power over you." He flung the words at her. "Keeping it was the only way I knew to make sure you wouldn't leave me."

She couldn't answer. Her throat felt constricted. Too much was coming at her too fast, uncovering emotions she'd thought safely locked away and forgotten. Luke turned his head. "Are you still there?" he asked sharply.

Leaning across the table, she took his hand, squeezed it, and found her voice. "So now you . . . you've come to realize you don't need the power and you've changed?"

"Not exactly, no. I just know I *need* to change. Big difference. I may wake up tomorrow and regret that I said any of this to you. But I had to. No matter how scared I am, I can't keep on this way."

"What exactly are you scared of?"

"Giving up the power."

Mandy tried to digest that. "What kind of power, exactly? I'm not clear on that."

"Making you feel guilty. And me acting like a jerk, letting you do stuff I can learn to do myself, never trying to make it easier for you. As long as I had all that going for me, I could keep you locked down here. I didn't need to worry so much that you'd leave."

"But, Luke, I *told* you—"

"I know what you've told me, but Mom said she'd never leave us, too. Remember? We're not talking rational stuff here. I'm mixed-up in my head, Mands."

"Then I'll take you for counseling."

"I've *been* to counseling. It might help if I cooperated for once and gave the doctors half a chance, but first I want to try it my way."

Her tone reflected her bewilderment. "What way?"

"Mands, aren't you listening? You're the best, okay? I mean, really, you're the best sister anybody ever had. You've been like a mom to me. I can't remember once ever needing you and you weren't there. The canning deal just happened. It wasn't your fault. That's why we call accidents *accidents*. Get it? No more guilt. If you hang in here with me, I need it to be because you want to, not because you have to."

"I've never felt that I had to hang in here, Luke."

"Yes, you have." He wiped his cheeks with his sleeve. "I made sure of that."

She couldn't speak. Her brother seemed to sense it, because he went on as if there hadn't been a pause.

"Both of us have to make some huge changes, not just me. I need to start taking care of myself, Mandy, and you have to *let* me. I'll need help at first, but not the kind of help you always give me. I need to learn how to stand on my own two feet."

Mandy rolled her lips in over her teeth. For years, all she'd heard from Luke were charges of blame. Now he was trying to set her free. She should have felt elated, but instead she felt like a tiny bird being shoved from its nest before it knew how to fly. It wasn't the time to say so, and there might never be a time when she should say so, but Luke wasn't the only one who was scared here.

"I'll give it my best, Luke," she said shakily. "To be honest, I think I need you to depend on me. It's my only way to make up for the accident."

"*There*, you see? You're as mixed-up as I am. You didn't deliberately hurt me. Turn loose of it. I'm going to. At least I'm going to try."

Mandy felt as if a thousand pounds were being lifted from her heart. Luke really meant it. He no longer blamed her for his blindness. She needed some time to roll that around inside her head before it could take root.

"I love you, Luke."

"I love you, too." He curled his hand over the grip of the cane and pushed to his feet. "We can talk some more while we make dinner." He tapped the linoleum in front of him. "How can I help?"

"You don't need to help. I've got it."

"*Mandy.*"

She laughed weakly. "Okay, okay. You did a fair job of smearing peanut butter on bread. We're having grilled cheese. You can try your hand at spreading mayonnaise."

"You ever had a Coney Island hot dog?" Luke asked.

"Not in a long time. You know Dad, gourmet all the way, and the habit stuck."

"All the more reason to break the habit," Luke said. "He's still running our lives. We need to fix that."

Mandy mulled that over. "You're right. When I go shopping, I'll buy some wieners."

"Make a special trip. And get canned chili. Making it from scratch isn't allowed. I don't want *gourmet* Coney Island dogs. I want the greasy, concession-stand kind that'll set me up for an early heart attack."

Mandy laughed. She let Luke grill the sandwiches. Under her watchful eye, he didn't burn himself, and the bread was only slightly too brown on one side.

One foot braced on the seat of a kitchen chair, her opposite knee planted on the countertop, Mandy twisted to secure a piece of red tape to the front edge of the bottom cupboard shelf. When the adhesive was secure, she ran a fingertip over the raised lettering. "You know, Luke, I honestly think this might work! I'm not as good at recognizing letters by touch as you are, but I can tell this says, 'chocolate drinks.' "

From behind her, Luke said, "Of course it'll work. Just make sure you mark the shelf where you keep the cookies. Okay? I *hate* having to go through all the plastic containers to find them."

"So the night I caught you eating cookies wasn't your first kitchen raid."

"Heck, no."

Mandy had suspected as much. Balancing her weight on her knee, she turned to look at her brother. He sat forward on a chair, knees spread to accommodate the cane, his hands curled over the crook of the handle. "You little sneak!" she cried.

Luke grinned. "I was sure you'd figure it out sooner or later."

Mandy laughed and turned back to her task. "I think the cereal should go on the second shelf. There's more height there. Will that work for you?"

"Sure. Can the cookies go on a lower shelf, though?"

Mandy smiled as she worked with the labeler. "No wonder the cookies disappear so fast. I thought I was eating them. You know how sometimes you just put stuff in your mouth without thinking? And all the time, it was *you*."

Luke said nothing. Mandy angled a glance at him over her shoulder. His grin had vanished. "What?" she asked.

He shrugged. "Just thinking."

"About what?"

"The night I pretended to fall on the kitchen floor and begged you to come help me get back to my room."

Mandy set aside the labeler and shifted to sit on the counter.

"I faked it all," he confessed in a hollow voice. "You'd caught me, and when you left me out here, I panicked. I had to convince you again that I was helpless. You know?"

Mandy closed her eyes, remembering how furious she'd been with Luke that night. She also recalled thinking—no, *knowing*—that Luke was putting on an act to bring her back to heel. Yet she'd gotten up anyway and returned to the kitchen to be his savior.

"Oh, God," she said softly. "Zach is right. You aren't the only one who's been playing games. I knew you were faking, and I let it slide. I *needed* you to need me."

"That time you made me walk in the backyard, I tripped over the shrub on purpose, too. I didn't mean to hit my head on the rock. I just wanted to get back at you." Luke puffed air into his cheeks. "I'll try hard never to pretend again. Okay? I'm sorry."

"It isn't that." Mandy ran her fingers into her hair and made a fist. "I'm just starting to grasp that I really do need counseling as much as you do."

Luke slumped back on the chair, resting the cane across his knees. "Counseling for both of us would cost a fortune. Why can't we just deal with most of this by ourselves?"

"I don't even know where to start."

Luke laughed, but there was no humor in the sound. "I said the same thing to Zach. You know what he told me? He said, 'You're nineteen and can't find the bathroom by yourself. Start with that.' It's only a tiny thing to change, but if I start with all the little things, pretty soon all of them together will be a huge change."

Mandy drew in a shaky breath. "Okay. So what little thing do I start with?"

"You've already tackled some stuff tonight." He swung a hand. "Reorganizing the kitchen is a start. And maybe, on top of that, you could pick one other thing to work on."

"Like what?"

Luke tipped his head, his sightless gaze pinned to her left. "The booze thing?"

Mandy stiffened and pushed off the counter. "It's getting late. We should wrap this up for tonight. I'll need to catch up on my work early in the morning."

"Alcohol in and of itself isn't evil, Mandy."

She began putting things back into the cupboard. "Do you have a good fix on this cupboard? Maybe you can make your own hot chocolate in the morning. I'll give you a crash course on how to punch the minute button on the microwave before we turn in."

"Dad wasn't mean because he drank," Luke persisted. "Stone-cold sober, he would have been vicious.

When Mom left, I got everything mixed-up in my head, and that's when this fear inside me started. Maybe Dad's drinking got everything all mixed-up inside *your* head, making you just as afraid of alcohol as I am of being left alone."

Mandy clenched her hand over a box of hot-chocolate mix. "Shut up, Luke. I'm not *afraid* of alcohol. I just detest the stuff."

"Bullshit." Mandy whirled to stare at her brother. Luke tipped his head in the other direction. "You *freak* over alcohol. It's a fright-and-flight reaction."

"That isn't—"

"Lie to yourself if you want," Luke broke in. "Keep running from the damned stuff for the rest of your life. But don't kid yourself into thinking it's normal, because it isn't. People who have a couple of drinks aren't alcoholics. They aren't bad people. And you know what, Mandy?"

"No, what?" she asked tremulously.

Luke leaned forward on the chair. "The world won't end if *you* have a drink. It's just a liquid that relaxes people. Yeah, some people go overboard with it, but Zach doesn't. Your behavior at his place was—how did you put it to me?—absolutely *inexcusable*."

Mandy cupped a hand over her mouth. She was shaking and couldn't stop.

"You asked where you could start. Face your fears." Luke grasped the cane and pushed to his feet. "I am, and let me tell you, it's not easy. I'm scared out of my skull."

She watched as he tapped his way toward his bedroom. "Where are you going?"

"To bed. And, *no*, I don't want your help. If I can't find my PJ's, I'll sleep in shorts."

Luke didn't slam the door behind him as he entered his room, but Mandy flinched as if he had.

Chapter Thirteen

Luke dropped a banana into the blender and groped to reposition the lid. Standing at his elbow, Mandy watched as he felt for the far right button to turn the appliance back on. Over the last three days, he had mastered many kitchen tasks, but his absolute favorite so far was his newfound ability to whip up his own smoothies. Mandy still needed to monitor him, but with each passing day, he became more adept.

Just as the blender roared back into action, Mandy heard the phone ring. "I'll be right back," she told her brother.

Mandy raced to the telephone stand. The base unit was announcing the name of the caller, but all the noise drowned out the words. She grabbed the portable. "Hello?"

"Hi, Mandy, it's Zach."

Mandy poked a finger in her ear and turned away so she could hear. "Hi." She searched for something else to say. "Are you, um, hating the rain?"

He chuckled. "Better than white stuff. They predict clear skies for tomorrow."

"Oh, I hope so." Mandy personally preferred snow to rain. It seemed less gloomy. "When it rains, I hole up in the house and grow moss."

"Sunshine is on its way, which is why I'm calling." The roar of the blender subsided, and suddenly his voice came through so defined Mandy felt as if he were in the same room. "I got in touch with Bethany Kendrick, the lady with the riding academy. She's got some free time tomorrow afternoon. Is Luke interested in going out for a ride?"

"I'll have to ask him. Can I call you back with an answer in a couple of hours?"

Just then Mandy heard the blender go back on with a strangled *ka-chunk*. Her brother yelled something that sounded more like *arghh* than an actual word. She whirled to see foamy stuff and ice cubes spewing from the blender. Luke was bent at the waist, holding his arms over his head.

"Oh, my *God*! Luke!"

Mandy dropped the phone and sprinted across the kitchen. Ice and foam coated the linoleum. When the smooth soles of her shoes connected with the slick stuff, her feet shot out from under her, and she landed on her rump. Staring up in horror, she saw an ice cube shoot from the churning appliance like a high-powered bullet.

Scrambling to gain her feet, Mandy managed to hit the "off" button. Then she turned to her brother, who was still hunkered down like a soldier under fire. "Are you okay?"

"Got hit by an ice cube on my forehead," he told her, "but I don't think I'm hurt."

Mandy had never seen such a mess. "What on earth happened?"

Her brother gave her a sheepish grin. "I forgot to put the lid back on."

At the other end of the line, Zach yelled, "Mandy, what's up? Are you all right?"

No answer. All Zach heard was a roaring sound and Mandy crying Luke's name. He was about to disconnect and call 911 when he heard laughter, both female and male. His shoulders relaxed, and as he listened to their giggles, he started to smile.

He heard Mandy say, "Oh, crap, I've got smoothie on the *ceiling*."

She and her brother started laughing again. Zach listened a moment; then he grinned broadly and broke the connection. A smoothie, huh? It sounded as if Luke truly was trying to turn over a new leaf—and possibly uprooting the entire tree in the process.

Zach had once forgotten to put the lid on the blender. The resultant mess had taken him hours to clean up. Mandy would be busy for a while. He glanced at his watch. If she didn't remember to call him by five, he'd give her a ring back.

Luke had a goose egg above his right eyebrow, but otherwise he was fine. After he and Mandy showered and changed clothes, Mandy spent two hours cleaning up the kitchen. It wasn't easy getting smoothie and chunks of banana off her ceiling and all the cupboards. She even had smoothie in her flower starts.

She didn't remember Zach's call until she happened upon the phone lying in the dining room. After returning the unit to its base, she asked Luke how he felt about going for a horseback ride. The very thought of her brother on the back of a full-size horse had Mandy's stomach tied in knots.

Luke, sipping another smoothie, which he'd insisted on making himself, broke off from sucking on the straw. "Tomorrow afternoon, you say?"

"Yes. The weather's supposed to be nice. I don't know what time yet. I'll have to call Zach to find out."

Luke took another sip of his drink, then sat back on the chair, the goose egg shiny pink as he drew his brows together in a thoughtful frown. "I don't think Zach would suggest I go if he thought I might get hurt."

Picking at a spot on the tablecloth, she replied, "No, I don't think he would, either."

Luke nodded. "Okay, then. Sure, why not? It might be a lot of fun."

Mandy keyed in Zach's cell phone number. He answered on the third ring. "How'd the smoothie wreck turn out?"

She smiled in spite of herself. "Messy, but we survived without serious injury."

"I did that once—forgot to put the lid back on, I mean. It was pretty bad."

Mandy, pacing by the phone stand, turned to study her brother. "I spoke with Luke. He thinks a horseback ride might be fun. What time will you pick him up?"

"Bethany is free around three. How does two fifteen sound?"

Mandy circled the dining room table. As she passed the living room archway, she noticed that no candy wrappers littered the carpet. Seeing the change, she felt her heart squeeze. "Two fifteen will be great," she replied, managing to inject some enthusiasm into her voice. "I'll have him ready."

Zach cleared his throat. "I, um, was sort of hoping you might come along."

Relief flooded through her. The thought of Luke on a horse frightened her, and if she stayed home, she'd be miserable. "I'd love that. Thank you for including me."

"Hey, it never crossed my mind that you wouldn't come. Two fifteen, then? Let's hope the weather forecast is right, and we have a nice day."

Zach rang the doorbell at exactly two fifteen the next afternoon. Luke and Mandy were dressed in jeans and sweatshirts, with coats for both of them over Mandy's arm in case a cold front moved in. In central Oregon, even a sunny spring day could turn chilly. Sweatshirts had struck Mandy as a smart choice, thick enough to provide warmth, but not too bulky.

When she opened the door, Zach stood on the porch, booted feet spaced wide apart, his clothes bearing signs that he'd been working. There was a smudge on his sleeve, and bits of straw clung to the crinkles of denim over the vamps of his boots. The ever-present Stetson, a brown one today that looked new, was tipped back to reveal his face. He flashed a smile, his white teeth a gleaming contrast to his sun-bronzed skin. Eyes as dark and clear as sweet sorghum syrup locked on hers. As Mandy broke the visual contact and stepped back to let him in, she noted the muscular contours of his thighs under his wash-worn jeans.

"You're right on time," she said.

He stepped over the threshold. "It's a rebellion of sorts, I guess. When you grow up on a ranch, people mosey everywhere. Drove me nuts as a kid." He swept off his hat just as Luke appeared. "Hey, man, I like the cane. You look distinguished."

"Really?" Luke smiled. "I hope all the girls think so."

Mandy gave Luke a puzzled look. He'd never expressed any interest in girls.

"I don't have any riding boots," Luke hurried to add. "Will running shoes work?"

"Like a charm."

Mandy moved over to the sofa for her purse. "You didn't bring Rosebud?"

Zach settled the hat back on his head. "No. We'll be busy with other horses today."

As the three of them stepped outside, Mandy drew out her keys to lock the door. She was nervous about Luke going down the steps, afraid he might fall. When she turned, she was glad to see Zach standing close at her brother's elbow, his hands poised to grab Luke's arm if he lost his footing. Luke made it down without mishap.

Mandy sat in back when they got into the SUV. Today was to have been an outing for Luke with Zach, and she wanted to interfere as little as possible. Luke fumbled with his seat belt. Zach waited for the buckle hasp to click home before starting the vehicle.

Mandy settled back for the ride, her plan being to let the guys talk, but Zach and Luke kept trying to draw her into the conversation. "So, Mandy?" Zach glanced into the rearview mirror. "You gonna saddle up and go for a ride with your brother?"

Mandy had never been on a horse, and she wasn't eager to change that. "I think I'll pass, thanks. Let Bethany focus on Luke. Maybe I'll go another time."

"It might be fun, Mands."

"We're both inexperienced riders." That didn't say it by half. "Bethany will need to teach you a lot. It'd be more distracting for her if she had two students."

"Well, you got your wish," Zach said. "It's a sunny day."

And so it went until they reached the Kendrick ranch, which overlooked Crystal Lake, a large body of water surrounded by pine forests. The surface sparkled like diamonds in the afternoon sunlight. The gravel road that led into the ranch proper curved around a knoll that sported a sprawling brick home. Across a paved parking area was an indoor arena similar to Zach's. Mandy peered out her window, noting that cement pathways crisscrossed the property, one of them leading down toward the lake.

Zach looked in the rearview mirror and caught her puzzled expression. "Bethany is paralyzed from the waist down," he explained. "She was injured in a riding accident at eighteen."

Just what Mandy wanted to hear when her brother was about to get on a horse.

"Anyway, her husband, Ryan Kendrick—one of *the* Kendricks—revamped the whole place so she can get around in her wheelchair."

Mandy had heard of the Kendrick family. They'd sold off some of their land during the construction boom and made a fortune. She turned her gaze back to the house, which was large, but nothing like the mansion she might have expected. It looked more middle-class America, with clean lines and an economy of roof angles.

"I thought they were unbelievably wealthy," she said.

Zach parked near the arena. "Trust me, they are. They just choose to live like normal folks. I think that's common with ranchers. It's kind of hard to wrap your mind around a lot of glitz and glamour when you wade through horseshit all day."

"How, exactly, is your family connected to them?" Mandy asked as she unfastened her seat belt. "Are you related somehow?"

"Not by blood. My sister, Sam, married Tucker Coulter, Bethany's brother, so it's an in-law thing." Zach pushed open his door. "They're great people."

Just then a petite brunette in a wheelchair emerged from the arena. The personnel door opened and closed automatically, saving her the trouble of struggling with it. She waved and flashed a warm smile. "Hey, Zach, right on time, as always."

Zach glanced at Mandy. "See? My reputation for being prompt follows me wherever I go." He swung out of the vehicle. "Unload, Luke." To their hostess, he called, "Hey, Bethany. How's it going?"

"Great." Bethany's blue eyes turned toward Luke as he crawled from the SUV. "Hi, Luke." She zoomed forward in her high-tech chair, one slender hand extended. "It's such a pleasure to meet you!" When Luke failed to grasp her fingers, Bethany leaned forward to grab his. "I'm Bethany." She pumped Luke's arm up and down. "I'm so *excited* about getting you on a horse. It'll be a *blast*. Have you ever ridden?"

"No. Good to meet you, too." Luke shifted the cane back into his right hand when Bethany released his fingers. "I, um, haven't been around big horses very much."

"Well, we'll fix that."

When Mandy exited the vehicle, she could appreciate the full impact of Bethany Kendrick's lovely, vivacious beauty. Her face was heart-shaped and framed by a wealth of shiny brown hair. Her eyes reminded Mandy of blue pansies. Her small, pointy chin sported a cleft. She wore Western-style clothing, a red fringed shirt, a pair of snug jeans, and plain, no-nonsense riding boots that looked brand-new. Accustomed to Zach's scuffed and dusty footwear, Mandy thought that was strange. But then it dawned on her that Bethany could only wear the boots, never actually walk in them.

How sad, Mandy thought, but before she could mentally explore the other woman's physical limitations and how they must affect her life, Bethany's laughter and warmth made Mandy forget she was in a wheelchair. As they shook hands, Bethany said, "Zach tells me you may be feeling apprehensive about all this." She released her hold on Mandy's fingers and gestured at the arena. "Relax," she said to Luke. "If you have a *single* reservation after you've met my horses, we'll just visit while I show you around."

That was good to know, Mandy thought. Luke wasn't locked in. If he chickened out at the last second, this lady would understand.

The next twenty minutes made Mandy's head spin. Bethany's wheelchair had all-terrain wheels that allowed her to zip around the arena. She gave them a tour, showing them the tack room and the special saddles, then taking them to meet her horses. She saved a reddish-colored mare for last.

"*This*," she informed them, "is the most wonderful horse alive. Her name is Wink. Normally I allow no one else to ride her. She's my baby." Bethany pushed up from her wheelchair to hug the horse's neck. When she saw Mandy's startled look, she said, "Oh. I can stand up now. Ryan got me braces and makes me work out every day. On my treadmill I even walk, after a fashion.

Not well enough to be useful in any practical way, but it forces my leg muscles to work, preventing atrophy and blood clots."

"Ah." Mandy could detect no braces under Bethany's jeans.

"I'm not wearing them now. They're beasts." She reached back to grasp the arms of the chair and lowered herself onto the seat again. "Without them, my only circus act is being able to stand for a few seconds." Her smile set her entire face aglow. "Go ahead, Luke. Get to know Wink. She'll be your steed this afternoon if you decide to go for a ride. I'll ride Margarita, a horse Rye picked up for me when he'd had a couple too many of the same. Fortunately, she turned out to be a fabulous mare. His instincts proved to be sound, even when he was three sheets to the wind."

Luke hooked the handle of his cane over his left arm and haltingly stepped forward, groping the air for the horse. Wink met him halfway, thrusting her nose under his searching hand. "Hi, Wink." Luke laughed. "I think she likes me."

"Wink is a big love. I've chosen her for you today because she's so hooked on me and will follow me anywhere. You won't need to worry about reining. You can just enjoy being on her back, and she'll do the rest." Bethany angled a questioning look at Mandy. "How are you feeling about this now? Still hesitant?"

Mandy dug deep for strength. "This is Luke's decision. If he wants to go for a ride, I'm fine with it."

Luke nodded. "I'd like to try. If I get scared, can I get off?"

Bethany laughed. "Of *course*. We'll ride in the arena for a while so you get a feel for it. Easy on, easy off." She drew a cell phone from a case clipped to her belt. Seconds later, she chirped, "Hey, Sly. It's a go. Can you come saddle the horses?"

A wiry cowboy appeared seconds later. Mandy's first

thought when she saw him was that his face looked like a brown paper sack that had gotten wet and then had dried all wrinkled up. He also had the most bowlegged stride she'd ever seen. Like Zach, he wore Wranglers, boots, a belt with a huge silver buckle, a dusty blue shirt, and a Stetson.

"Hey, Zach," he said cordially, with a thick Southern drawl. "Great day for ridin'. I've actually worked up a sweat!" Then he approached Mandy, touching a finger to his hat brim. Before offering her his hand, he brushed it clean on his pant leg. "Sylvester Galias, ma'am. Pleased as a speckled pup to make your acquaintance."

Mandy almost giggled. Stifling the urge, she grasped his hand. "Mandy Pajeck. I'm pleased to meet you, too, Mr. Galias."

He pumped her arm up and down, smiling warmly. "That's Galias, not *Galias*."

It sounded to Mandy as if he were saying the same last name.

He noted her confused expression. "That's G-L-A-S-S," he informed her. *"Galias."*

Mandy laughed in spite of herself. "Ah, Mr. *Glass*. Good to meet you."

"You can just call me Sly." He drew away and chafed his hands. "I'll get these critters saddled up. Won't take me more'n five minutes."

While Sly prepared the mares to be ridden, Bethany entertained her guests with stories about her riding academy.

"I've never heard of a riding academy for the handicapped," Mandy inserted. "What a fabulous idea!"

Bethany nodded. "The first time I heard about them, I knew I wanted to start one locally. Ryan was very supportive of the idea and backed me one hundred percent."

Sly moved toward them with the horses. Bethany thanked him as she took hold of Margarita's reins. "Luke, Sly will help you mount. You'll be strapped on, so don't be afraid of falling off. Okay?" She smiled at Mandy and Zach. "I have a special mounting sling. Excuse me for a moment. I'll be back in a jiffy."

Mandy gazed after their hostess as she led the mare across the arena. To Zach, she said, "Isn't she amazing?"

Zach nodded. "You gotta admire her attitude. She's in love with life and tries to enjoy every second of it."

"Hey, Mandy, look at me!" Luke cried. "I'm on a horse!"

A burn of tears washed over Mandy's eyes as she took in her brother's incredulous expression. "You sure are. How does it feel?"

"Great! Sly helped me up. It was easier than I thought." Luke extended his cane. "Can you hold this for me?"

Mandy hurried over to her brother's side, collected the cane, and then returned to where Zach stood.

Sly patted Wink's rump as he circled behind her to fasten Luke's leg straps on the other side. "You've got a knack for this, son. Some people do; some don't. We'll make a horseman out of you, lickety-split."

Bethany rode into the arena just then. Her saddle was similar to Luke's, sporting straps that anchored her to the seat. "Hey, Luke, you ready for our adventure?"

Luke grinned and shrugged his shoulders. "I think so."

Zach grasped Mandy's elbow and led her to Wink's unoccupied stall. With the ease and grace of a man who did hard physical labor, he swung up to sit on the top rung.

"Hop up," he said. "It's better than standing."

Mandy climbed the rungs to sit beside him. In silence, they watched Bethany and Luke make loops around the arena. Luke sat straight in the saddle. If Mandy hadn't known better, she would have thought he'd been riding for years. As Bethany had promised, Wink followed the other horse as if she were attached by an invisible lead rope. All Luke had to do was loosely hold the reins and enjoy the ride.

After about ten minutes, Bethany drew Margarita to a stop in front of Wink's stall. Twisting at the waist, she asked Luke, "Do you think you're ready for a real ride now? I thought we might go along the lakeshore for a while. We have some nice trails there."

"I'd love it!" Luke angled his head. "Do you care if I go, Mands?"

Over the course of the visit, Mandy had come to trust Bethany Kendrick and felt certain her brother should be safe. "You're nineteen, Luke. It's your decision to make."

Luke's smiled broadened. "Then let's do it, Bethany."

A tight knot formed in Mandy's throat as she watched her brother ride away.

"He'll be fine," Zach said. "Accidents happen, but Bethany takes every precaution."

"I know." Mandy drew in a bracing breath. "I've been meaning to call you, Zach." She forced herself to look at him. "I don't know what you said to Luke during that visit to the park, but he came home a changed young man. Thank you so much for that."

Zach took off his hat and thrust his fingers through his hair. "All I did was give him some straight talk. If he went home with a different attitude, it's his doing, not mine." He fell silent for a moment. "He's a good kid. He's just been a little confused, I think, and acting out in inappropriate ways."

"I'm still grateful. Whatever you said had a huge impact on my brother."

Zach settled the Stetson back on his head, tugging on the brim to adjust the angle. "I've been meaning to call you, too."

"You have?"

He nodded. "I stepped over the line that afternoon, saying all that crap to you. I've done a lot of thinking about it, and I owe you an apology. I butted my nose in where it didn't belong."

Mandy wanted to let it go at that, to simply accept his apology and say nothing more. But her sense of fairness wouldn't allow it. "Maybe I needed you to butt in."

He cast her a wondering look that eased the tension from her body and made her smile. "Raising a teenage boy isn't easy, especially for a single woman, and Luke's blindness has made it particularly difficult. I've made a lot of mistakes, but sometimes it's hard to see them until someone else points them out." Growing tense again, Mandy began swinging her feet back and forth, her gaze fixed on the toes of her sneakers. "I've done a lot of thinking, too. Much of what you said to me was true. I didn't want to believe it then. Truth is, I still don't. But lying to myself about it . . . well, that won't help Luke, and it won't help me. I have a lot of changing to do."

Zach was impressed by her candor. It was never easy to step back and take a long, hard look at yourself. "You're quite a lady. You know it?"

She gave him a startled look.

Zach chuckled. "Don't look so surprised. You're really something. I've made more than my fair share of mistakes. It took me a while to admit that, even to myself, and I still have a hard time admitting it to anyone else. It takes a lot of guts."

Her lips tipped up at the corners in a slight smile. "I've never thought of myself as being particularly courageous, but thank you for the compliment."

"It's well deserved." Zach searched her beautiful eyes. Then he dropped his gaze to her slender hands, which bore signs of ingrained dirt around the fingertips that he'd never noticed before. "Been gardening?" he asked.

Her cheeks went pink. She hid her fingers between her denim-clad legs. "It's way too early for that yet. I've just been working with starts."

"Starts?"

Her cheek dimpled with a suppressed smile. "Yes, starts, a term used by gardeners when they plant spring seeds in tiny pots to give the plants some indoor growing time before they're transplanted outdoors in the summer."

"Ah." Zach hadn't pegged her as a gardening type, but recalling her tidy, manicured yard, he guessed he should have. "What kind of plants are you starting?"

"Various flowers." She shrugged her elegant shoulders. "I like lots of color in my beds, so I grow a little of everything. It's fun to create a flowery blanket to complement my bulb plants when they begin to bloom."

What Zach knew about gardening would have fit in a thimble, but he found the subject fascinating because Mandy was obviously so interested in it. The conversation moved from flowers to weed varieties in the area, which she transplanted into her yard for a touch of the natural and wild. She especially liked mullein and wild blue phlox.

"Come out to my place," Zach said. "You can have a heyday. Mullein and phlox grow everywhere out there. You can even steal heaps of my clump grass."

She passed him a wondering look. "I get the feeling you aren't into flowers."

Zach suppressed a grin. "I'm into seeing them, just not into growing them. The only time you'll catch me weeding is when a poisonous species gets a foothold on my land."

She laughed, her expression laced with understanding. "It takes all different kinds to make the world go 'round."

Zach agreed with a sheepish smile. "I reckon so." He gave her a sidelong glance. "Are we okay now, Mandy?"

She hesitated a moment, then nodded. "Yes, I think we are."

* * *

"Wow!" Luke cried as he and Bethany rode back into the arena. "That was so much fun! I can't believe what a blast it was."

Mandy gazed fondly at her brother, trying to recall the last time she'd seen him so happy. Hair ruffled by the wind, he looked like a normal teenager, young, vigorous, and in love with life.

"I'm glad you enjoyed it," Bethany told him. "I'd love it if you'd come out often, Luke. No charge. You can ride for free."

"Can I, Mandy?" Luke asked.

Taken off guard, Mandy had to consider before answering. "I see no reason why you can't come out to ride again, Luke." She shifted her gaze to Bethany. "But we'll want to pay the usual fee. It wouldn't be right otherwise."

Bethany flapped a hand. "Now that I have kids, I don't hold as many events, and as a result, I don't ride as much as I should. Ryan is constantly offering to watch the children, but—" She broke off and shrugged. "It's just not as much fun to go riding alone. Luke would be doing me a favor. I need the exercise, and so do my horses."

Mandy glanced at her brother's beaming countenance and hated to protest any further. "I have my work, Luke. Coming here a few times a week would put me way behind. It's a long drive out this way."

"Couldn't you work out here on your laptop?" Luke suggested.

"I need the Internet to communicate with the—"

Bethany interrupted with, "We have high-speed wireless, Mandy. You could log in and use the stable office to work while Luke and I are riding. Would that help?"

Mandy could scarcely believe Bethany Kendrick's generosity. "Yes, that'd be . . . well, fabulous. But only if you're sure that—"

"I'm *positive.*" Bethany maneuvered Margarita close to Wink and leaned sideways to take Luke's hand. "It's been a pleasure, Luke. I hope we can do it again really soon."

"Me, too. It was incredible."

Sly appeared just then. He commandeered Wink's reins. Bethany smiled at Mandy and Zach. "I've got to go dismount. If you don't mind waiting, I'd love to have you come over to the house. Ryan would enjoy a visit, I know. He and Zach are good buds."

Zach looked questioningly at Mandy. She laughed and said, "I'm in no rush. For once, I'm actually caught up with my office work."

"It's settled, then," Bethany said. "I'll be right back."

"Those are two of the nicest people I think I've ever met," Mandy commented an hour later as they began the long drive home. "Talking with Ryan, you'd never guess that he's wealthy. He acts like an ordinary guy."

Zach grinned at Mandy in the rearview mirror. "All the Kendricks are like that. Maybe it comes from not always having been rich. They're pretty down-to-earth."

"Their children are darling and so well behaved."

"I really liked Little Sly," Luke observed. "He's not quite eight, but he sounds a lot older."

Mandy had fallen in love with Chastity, who would celebrate her fifth birthday in only a few days. She was a beautiful little girl with a wealth of sable curls and her mother's vivacious personality.

"I can't wait to come out again," Luke said. "It was so much fun, riding along the lakeshore! Bethany let the horses run. Except for in a car, I've never gone that fast. I loved feeling the wind in my face. The smells out there were indescribable!"

Smiling, Mandy settled back to listen as Luke went on and on about how much fun the ride had been. She definitely needed to bring him out again soon. She sneaked a glance at Zach, grateful to him for coming up with the idea. It was wonderful to hear Luke laugh and see his

cheeks flushed with excitement. Zach truly was good for
him, able to relate with him in a way Mandy could not.

True to his promise, Zach had turned down the beer
Ryan offered him, drinking coffee instead. Mandy appreciated that more than he could know. Being a good
host, Ryan had taken his cue from his guest, stashing the
beer back in the fridge and pouring himself a cup of coffee, too. She wasn't sure how she would have handled it
if Ryan had decided to drink in front of her. Just thinking about it made it difficult to breathe.

Crazy, so crazy. Staring at the back of her brother's
head, she recalled his words to her the other evening.
Alcohol wasn't evil, and her abhorrence of it was irrational. Maybe she should follow Luke's example and face
her fears instead of running from them. Easier said than
done. Luke was doing it, though.

Lost in the mire of her thoughts, Mandy jerked back
to the present when Zach parked in front of her house.
Still riding high on excitement, Luke was first to exit the
vehicle. He tapped the ground in front of him with the
cane until he found the sidewalk.

Zach, who'd just gotten out of the car and hadn't shut
the door yet, called over the roof, "The walkway is over
to your—"

"Don't tell me," Luke said, cutting him off. "I need to
find it by myself."

Mandy collected her purse and got out to stand on
the grass median, her gaze fixed on her brother. Zach
circled the SUV and joined her.

"No hints," Luke called over his shoulder. "I want to
get inside without help. Okay?"

Mandy eyed the steps with trepidation but gave her
brother the keys and stayed put, favoring him with a
feeble, "Okay."

As though Zach sensed how difficult this was for
her, he settled a hand on her shoulder. At his touch, she
jumped. He grinned when she looked up at him. "Even

if he falls, he's young and resilient. He'll survive a few bumps and bruises."

"I know. It's just difficult for me to stand aside and only watch when I've done just the opposite for so many years."

Luke whooped in triumph. "Found it!"

Mandy knew she should turn to watch her brother go up the walk, but Zach's gaze held hers, and she couldn't look away. With a sinking sensation deep in her belly, she realized she was starting to feel attracted to him again. *He drinks*, she reminded herself. But that knowledge no longer disturbed her as much as it had. Zach's fingertips shifted, and she felt the burn of his touch through her sweatshirt. *Oh, man.* She was in trouble. There was something about him that addled her senses.

She shifted the jackets they hadn't used to her left arm, putting the bulk between their bodies. "You don't happen to have a bridge you want to sell, do you?"

A bewildered frown drew his thick black brows together. "Bridge?"

Mandy laughed and shook her head. "Nothing. Just a silly thought that popped into my mind."

A slow grin moved over his firm lips. "A bridge? Ah, I get it." A twinkle of mischief warmed his dark eyes. "If I had one to sell, would you buy it?"

Heat inched up her neck. She stepped away from him to follow her brother into the house. "I'm afraid I might." She turned to walk backward. "Thanks for the outing. It was a great idea. I can't remember the last time Luke enjoyed himself so much."

"Five hundred, and I'll deliver it gift-wrapped to your doorstep," he called after her. "You interested in the Brooklyn or the Golden Gate?"

Mandy stuck out her tongue at him. He was still standing there, grinning, when she stepped inside and closed the door.

Chapter Fourteen

During the short drive to the market Mandy told herself that the sole purpose of her trip was to pick up the makings for Coney Island hot dogs. After tossing all the ingredients into the cart, she found herself standing at the store's wine display. Her fingers clenched over the cart handle so tightly they hurt. Looking at the bottles made sweat pop out on her forehead. Her stomach felt as if it weren't there, and her lungs hitched as if they might stop working. For an instant the display rotated sickeningly and she hauled in a steadying breath. Luke's voice whispered in her mind: *Run from it for the rest of your life if you like, but don't kid yourself into thinking it's normal.*

Oh, how she wanted to get away from all those bottles. Only shame and a sense of doom held her fast. *Alcohol isn't evil, in and of itself.* Luke was trying so hard to change. He'd even insisted he would be fine at the house alone while she went shopping. What changes had she tried to make?

Mandy grabbed the nearest bottle. She didn't know or care what kind it was, because she knew little about wine anymore. Handling the glass container as if it might detonate, she put it in the cart, then sped toward another section of the store where she could breathe. At the end of the aisle, she saw corkscrews hanging on a clip wire. She jerked one free and tossed it into the basket. *Sick, I'm going to be sick.*

In the bread section, she tried to talk herself down. *You're going to handle this. You can't chicken out.* In a moment of weakness—all right, *cowardice*—she set the bottle on a shelf beside a stack of bagels. No. She wouldn't let this beat her, not any longer. She put the wine back in the cart and gulped down the salty taste of nausea.

Once at home, Mandy set the wine on the counter, feeling as if an alien being had touched down in her kitchen. Trying to pretend everything was normal, she busied herself with the hot-dog preparation, which reeled Luke in like a starving trout.

"Yum," he said, sniffing appreciatively. "Can we do them with the works, chili, onions, relish, mayo, mustard, and grated cheese?"

"Of course," Mandy replied with forced brightness. "No point in going halfway. I even read the chili labels to get the very *worst* kind, guaranteed to clog our arteries."

Silence. With the intuitiveness he often displayed, Luke asked, "What's wrong?"

Mandy knew better than to pretend with her brother. "I bought some wine." Her voice quavered. "I feel like there's a tarantula sitting on the counter, waiting to bite me."

Another silence. And then Luke said, "Wow, Mands, I'm proud of you. We actually have *wine* in the house? What kind is it?"

Mandy tried to read the label but was so upset she couldn't. "Beats me. Pink stuff."

"If anyone on earth should know her wines, it ought to be you. Dad used to make you go down to the cellar to select the bottles. Remember? You were a vino expert."

Mandy could recall the spooky trips down the stairway into a section of the basement their father had converted into cellars. But she couldn't remember anything about the wines. It was as if that part of her memory bank had been obliterated.

She blinked and rubbed her eyes. When she could read the label, she said, "That's weird. It's pinkish, but it says it's white zinfandel."

"Are we gonna have some?"

That was the plan, to drink a glass, but now that the moment had come, she wasn't sure she could do it. "I—I don't know. Maybe it's a bad idea. I could just throw it out."

"Not." Luke tapped his way over to the counter. "Where is it? I'll open the sucker. Get us a couple of glasses."

Mandy stared at her brother in mounting dismay. "Luke, you're too young to drink, for starters, and second, I really don't want you touching alcohol."

"Why, because you're afraid I'll become a drunk, just like good old Dad?"

"I don't mean to offend you. It's just . . . well, what if alcoholism runs in his family?"

"If alcoholism runs in his family, it's unlikely to take hold of me if I have one glass of wine. And what if meanness runs in his family? What if being crazy as a loon runs in his family?" Luke whacked the cane on the floor in agitation. "We're *nothing* like him. We can't live our lives being scared that his bad traits are going to pop up in one of us."

Luke was right. Mandy closed her eyes. "I just can't help thinking, What if?"

"Well, stop. I do *not* want that jerk controlling me the rest of my life. You know what? I don't think he's truly an alcoholic. I think he was addicted to the rush he felt when he went on a rampage, and he needed booze to provide an excuse for going there. Maybe his parents abused him. Maybe his brain got injured at birth. Who knows? The only absolute is that neither of us is *anything* like him." He groped for the wine bottle. "I'm not going to turn into a monster if I have a glass of wine, and you aren't, either." He fingered the mouth of the bottle. "There's no lid. How does this open?"

With trembling hands, Mandy took it away from him. "You need a corkscrew."

Luke rested his hip against the cupboards. "This may be fun. I've never had wine. Do people ever drink it with Coney Island hot dogs?"

Trying to get into the spirit, Mandy said, "*We're* going to. Does that count?"

With several quick twists, she buried the screw into the cork and pushed down on the levers. Memories flashed. How many times had she done this at her father's fancy dinners? A cold sweat filmed her body. Her pulse picked up, and between every beat, electricity seemed to snap through her bloodstream.

Mandy drew two tall tumblers from a shelf. She had no wineglasses. Her hand shook so badly as she poured that she nearly sloshed white zinfandel all over the counter. The smell—oh, *God*, that smell. Her gorge rose. The room seemed to pivot slowly on a wobbly axis. She grabbed hold of the counter to steady herself.

"I can't do this," she whispered.

Luke felt along the worn Formica surface until his fingertips touched the base of one glass. He curled his hand around it. "Oh, yes, you can. It's all in your head." He took a sip of the wine and went still. "Mmm, it's *good*, Mands. Sort of sweet. Try it."

He made his way back to the table. Mandy, frozen in place, engaged in a stare-down with her glass. Finally she reached for it. A chill washed over her as she lifted it to her lips. *Just one tiny sip*. She had to do this. If she freaked out and didn't, Luke would accuse her of running from what she feared most.

And, like it or not, she knew he'd be right.

The sweetness filled her mouth. She struggled to swallow, couldn't. It was physically impossible to ingest fluid when your throat was convulsing to purge your stomach. Holding the glass out to one side, she rushed to the sink and spit.

From behind her, Luke said, "Ah, Mandy. If it were juice, you could drink it. This is no different. Come sit at the table with me. We'll do it together."

Mandy walked jerkily to a chair. Her knees nearly buckled as she lowered herself onto the seat. She set the wine in front of her and stared at it until her eyes burned. "For me, it's like knowingly drinking poison."

Luke laughed, but there was no humor in the sound. "It isn't poison."

"To me it is. Do you know how many times Dad knocked me around for making some stupid mistake with the wines?" Her lip curled, a reflexive sneer. "He'd *die* if he saw us drinking junk that costs less than five bucks a bottle."

"Good. Let's rebel." Luke held up his glass and waited. "You with me?"

Mandy grabbed her tumbler and lifted it. "I'm with you."

In tandem with Luke, Mandy took another sip of wine. This time the taste was less of a shock, and she was able to swallow. Tense as a well-tuned piano wire, she waited. She wasn't sure what she thought might happen. When several seconds passed and all she felt was pleasant warmth moving through her, she relaxed slightly.

"You still alive over there?"

"Yes. Lightning didn't strike. The roof didn't cave in. I can't believe it."

Luke grinned. "I never thought I'd have a glass of wine with my sister. I mean, it's more likely that we'd buddy-jump from an airplane. You know?"

Mandy giggled. "You're right. Me and wine? Highly unlikely."

"Another sip," Luke urged. "And no trying to cheat. I can hear when you swallow."

Mandy lifted her glass again. "It's actually kind of good."

"Kind of? I think it's great, sort of like juice, but with a kick."

They remained at the table to finish that first glass of wine, revisiting unpleasant memories from their childhoods, but creating a lovely new one in the process. Mandy poured them each a little more wine to drink while they made dinner. When they sat down to eat, they were both a tiny bit tipsy.

It was a wonderful dinner. Luke grew more talkative, but otherwise he was the same, only a little more relaxed and inclined to laugh. At moments, she wondered at the wisdom of letting him have alcohol. But if young men his age were being sent off to die for their country, then in her opinion they were old enough to have a glass or two of wine over dinner at home.

As they did the dishes—Mandy rinsed while Luke fumbled to put them in the racks—Luke lectured her once more about alcohol and their father.

"It wasn't the drink that made him mean, Mands."

Mandy had to admit that she felt mellow, not agitated, and Luke appeared to be experiencing the same reaction. "What do you think made Dad the way he is?"

Luke felt for the silverware holder. "I have no idea." He braced a hand on the counter. "I only know I'm really proud of you for what you did tonight."

He held up his hand. She laughed and gave him a high five. "I was scared."

"Yeah." Grabbing another plate, Luke stuck it in the dishwasher, missed the wire uprights, and had to feel with his other hand to position it. "We both have our demons. I'm finding that the more often I face them, the less they frighten me." He smiled. "This morning when I woke up, I wasn't scared. I knew you were in the house even though I couldn't hear you. We're going to get through this, and come out on the other side."

She had to think about that. Alcohol. Her dad. All of

the changes. But Luke was working with her now instead of against her, and that was a gigantic improvement. "You're right," she agreed. "I honestly think we will."

An hour later, the phone rang. The recorded voice butchered the pronunciation of Zach's name. Maybe Mandy was still feeling the effects of the wine, because instead of picking up with her usual hello, she said, "Is this a Greek pasta dish calling?"

"A Greek what?"

His voice, rich and deep, came over the airways and wrapped around her like warm tendrils of smoke. "My phone. The way it says your name, you sound like something I'd see on the menu in a Greek restaurant."

"Oh." He laughed. "You tempted to have a taste?"

Mandy grinned and leaned a shoulder against the wall. "I'm not into Greek cuisine."

"How about Irish?"

He's flirting with me. She'd had men flirt with her, but it had been so long ago that she'd forgotten all her canned responses. "You're Irish?"

"What, you haven't noticed my Irish charm?"

"I've heard rumors of your Irish temper."

He groaned. "Cookie is going to pay for telling you all that crap."

"It wasn't true?"

"Am I under oath?"

"No, but if you're really a man of your word, you'll be honest anyway."

"It was true. I kick buckets, and if I see someone mistreating an animal, I go ballistic. I do not, however, pick my nose. Not in public, anyway, and I *never* consume the proceeds."

Mandy laughed. "That's good to know." She switched the phone to her other ear. "So . . . to what do I owe the pleasure of this call?"

Long silence. "Damned if I know. I had a reason for calling. Now I've forgotten."

"Back up. Think. When you dialed my number, you had something on your mind."

"Ah!" It sounded as if he snapped his fingers. "My place, Luke, another visit with Rosebud. I've got Friday free. I can quit early. I was thinking we might do another barbecue, sans wine this time."

She smiled at the remark. "We'd love to come. Is there anything we can bring?"

"Just yourselves. I've got everything else covered. Unless, of course, you can find time to whip up another fabulous chocolate cake from scratch."

"A cake it will be," Mandy assured him. "Do I have your word that you won't try to sell me any bridges?"

He chuckled. "Ah, come on. Let a guy have a *little* fun. Actually, I've got a special on one right now. It's painted bright orange and spans a rather well-known body of water in northern California. If you act quickly, I think I can get you a great deal." He paused. "You sound different. More relaxed or something."

Mandy did feel more relaxed. She'd just done battle with a fire-breathing dragon and trounced it. "It's been a nice evening. We had Coney Island hot dogs for dinner."

"Ah, those will mellow anybody out. Wish I'd been there. I love those puppies."

"Next time we make them, I'll give you a call."

"I'll hold you to it."

Mandy was still grinning when they disconnected.

On Friday afternoon, Mandy whipped her car into a Safeway parking spot before leaving town for the Crooked H. Luke, in the passenger seat, did the head-tipping thing, a habit of his when he had a question or felt bewildered.

"Why are we stopping so soon?" he asked.

Mandy grabbed her purse. "I need to run into the store for something."

"What?"

"Wine." The word came out as little more than a whisper.

Luke cocked his head even more. "Did you say *wine*?"

In a stronger voice, she said, "Yes, wine. You're right. I was awful at the other barbecue. I need to let Zach know I realize I was wrong, and this is the only way I can think of to do that."

Luke nodded. "Get more of that stuff we had the other night. It's pretty good."

"You aren't having any."

"Oh, Mands!"

"At home, it's one thing. In public, it's another. You aren't twenty-one yet."

"Zach's ranch isn't exactly what I'd call 'public.' "

Mandy was finished arguing. She exited the car and closed the door, cutting her brother off midsentence.

A half hour later, when she handed Zach her contributions to the meal, a chocolate cake and the recently purchased wine, he got a startled look on his face. He wore all black this afternoon, his jeans creased, his shirt crisply pressed. With his jet hair, burnished skin, and dark eyes, the overall effect was stunning, especially when he searched her gaze as if trying to read her mind.

She inclined her head at the bottle in his hand. "It's my way of apologizing for being so rude and unreasonable the last time. Would you mind pouring me a glass?"

He looked uncertain, but he stepped to a cupboard to extract one wineglass and then set about opening the bottle. Mandy took a seat at the table, which had already been set. Linen napkins, artfully crimped into standing fans, adorned the center of each plate, she noticed, and salad forks had made an appearance. She bit back a smile as she watched Zach use the corkscrew with an expertise born of long practice. He was putting on the dog for her, she realized. That made her a little nervous, but it was a giddy, delicious kind of nervous. She pictured those big hands coaxing the napkins into fan shapes and suppressed a giggle.

When he turned toward her with a half-filled goblet, she said, "Won't you join me?"

He froze in his tracks. "I promised not to drink around you or Luke anymore."

Luke was out on the porch with Rosebud. Mandy glanced in that direction. Then she met Zach's gaze again. "I'm releasing you from that promise. My brother isn't the only one who has issues. I have a few, too, and my irrational fear of alcohol is one of them. If you stick to that promise, I'm going to feel like more of an idiot than I do already. I'd really appreciate it if you'd join me."

Zach had been trying to make some changes of his own recently. Mandy's reaction to the merlot at the last barbecue had started him thinking, and Luke's revelations about their father's alcoholism had made him think even more. When it came to alcohol, he could take it or leave it. But maybe, just maybe, he had been drinking a little too often. How long did it take for frequent alcohol consumption to get its hooks into a man? The very thought had prompted Zach to back off on the drinking.

Hell, he no longer even missed visiting the honky-tonks. Over the last two years, he'd sometimes stopped in at one of his former haunts and hooked up with a lady to scratch his itch, but since meeting Mandy he didn't even get the urge. The women in those places didn't interest him now. Glancing at Mandy, he suspected she was the reason that blondes had lost their appeal. She wore a soft-looking green sweater and snug jeans that showed off her figure, only in a tasteful, understated way. He liked that. A man didn't get the contents of the package shoved in his face. She came gift-wrapped, and he had to use his imagination to guess what was under the layers. And his imagination had been running up a lot of overtime ever since he'd first met her.

He liked the way she wore her hair today, clipped in a sleek twist at the back of her head. Little tendrils had escaped to lie like ribbons of silk on the pale nape of her neck. The upsweep accentuated the delicate line of her jaw. *Damn.* The closer he looked, the more he wanted to touch and taste.

He could think of a few other things he wanted, too, but this wasn't the time to dwell on them. He'd have to spend half the evening turned away from her.

Instead he granted her request and poured himself some wine. Together they went out onto the porch. Zach saw Mandy glance toward the paddocks in search of Tornado. "I closed the paddock doors," he told her. "There are more hands working in the stable than last time. I don't want Tornado to get loose again."

Zach got Luke lined out to go walking with Rosebud; then he joined Mandy on the top step to watch the pair explore the ranch proper. Being with Mandy relaxed him. She was okay with silence and didn't try to fill it up with ceaseless chatter.

"Ah," she said softly, her smile radiant. "Would you look at that?"

Zach found it difficult to drag his gaze away from her profile, but as he settled his attention on Luke and Rosebud, he grinned. The young man and the little horse were forging a fast friendship. When Rosebud veered around an overhead obstacle, she nudged her handler's leg for a treat.

"Be right back," Zach said, setting his glass aside.

He scaled the steps. When he reached Luke, he said, "You're missing some of her cues. When you feel her swing out, she's going around things. You need to concentrate, and when you feel her do that, always click and give her a treat. Later, when she's all trained, it won't be so important, but for now, she needs reinforcement."

Luke nodded and fell into a walk again. Zach stayed close, softly telling Luke when Rosebud had given him a cue. Within minutes, Luke began to pick up on the subtle changes in the mini's gait, the shifts and gentle turns. Satisfied that the kid would reward Rosebud when appropriate, Zach returned to the porch.

"At the risk of being repetitious, I want to thank you for all the wondrous changes I'm seeing in my brother," Mandy said softly. "He's becoming more self-sufficient with each passing day."

Zach laughed when she told him about the peanut-butter-and-salsa sandwich. "Thank God you found a labeler."

"Oh, yes." The dimple flashed in her cheek. "My kitchen is now so organized, Luke can find everything, and I'm lost."

"Ah, well, you'll get oriented." Zach hesitated. "I'm really proud of him. In the beginning, I doubted he'd step up to the plate. This is one time I'm glad to be proved wrong. What he's doing . . . Well, he's making a lot of changes at once. That can't be easy." Zach watched as she took a small sip of white zin. "I'm proud of you, too." He inclined his head at her goblet. "That's not an easy change for you to make, either."

"I'll never be a frequent drinker. But it feels good to be able to have a glass of wine and not feel panicky." Her cheeks went pink. She fixed her gaze on her brother. "Last night, I showed Luke how to form hamburger patties. He did really well. He's also learned how to heat soup in the microwave and make his own hot chocolate."

"Wow." Zach realized she wanted to change the subject. "Luke's progress is amazing. But you need to stop thanking me." Zach felt uncomfortable with her gratitude. "The effort he's putting into this tells me a lot about him." He took a sip of wine, then turned the goblet stem between his fingers. "For one, it says how much he loves you. It also says a lot about his character. He's a fine young man with a caring heart and a good head on his shoulders." He met Mandy's shimmering gaze. "That's *your* doing. I didn't raise him. You did."

She looked quickly away. "Sometimes I feel as if all I did was goof up."

Zach smiled. "Hey, if you're going to take the blame for his screwups, you also have to take credit for his fine points. Get used to it."

"I will if you will."

Zach sent her a questioning look.

"I'll always believe you were the force that set Luke on another path. He and I are actually becoming friends. That was never possible before. I'm grateful for that." When Zach started to say something, she held up a hand. "No argument."

With a chuckle, Zach set aside his goblet. "Okay, I'm a miracle worker. On that note, do you mind if I butt my nose in where it doesn't belong again?"

She arched her brows. "No. Butt in all you like."

"I know this lady who works with the sight impaired. Her name's Carly Coulter. She's another of Sam's sisters-in-law." Zach handed her a slip of paper. "That's her contact info. I'd love to see Luke hook up with her. She could do wonders for him."

Mandy nodded. "Thank you, Zach. I'll give her a call."

Keeping an eye on Luke, Zach pushed to his feet and went to light the grill. Glancing at Mandy over his shoulder, he asked, "You going to bite my head off if I offer you more wine?"

She grinned and held up her glass. "Only a little. I'll have to drive home later."

Zach poured each of them another small measure of white zinfandel, which wasn't his favorite. Then he joined Mandy on the steps again.

"So," he said, "tell me about your work."

She groaned. "I'm a medical transcriptionist, it bores

me to death, and I refuse to spend my downtime talking about it."

Zach chuckled. "Ouch. That smacks of a lady who hates her job. How does it work, anyway? Being a medical transcriptionist, I mean. Do you have to physically go to the offices?"

She sighed, her expression resigned. "Sometimes I do, but most clinics are set up now to send material to me online, even the audio versions of a doctor's dictation. When they can't, I stuff Luke in the car and make a quick run into town."

"Not a very stimulating job, I take it."

"Not for me. But it allows me to work at home, thanks to the Internet, and I can set my own hours. I contract out to clinics and private practices. It brings in enough income to make ends meet. For now, I have to be thankful for that and not complain."

"And if the sky were the limit, what line of work would you be in?" he asked, genuinely interested in hearing her answer.

She rolled her eyes, and that adorable dimple flashed at him again, making him want to touch a fingertip to the spot. "You'll laugh."

"No, I won't."

She cupped her elbows and propped her folded arms on her knees. "I'd love to own a plant nursery that caters to people who do their own landscaping. I like working in the dirt. Seeing things grow. It excites me when a flower blooms, especially if I started the plant from a seed or a cutting."

Zach digested that. He could see the yearning in her expression when she spoke of plants. "Hmm. Like I said before, gardening isn't my deal, but I sort of understand where you're coming from. For me, it's starting horses from scratch. There's no thrill to match the one I get when I raise a foal from birth, training it, loving it, working with it every day, and then getting to see the end result, a champion cutting horse. That's when my flower blooms."

She nodded. "It is sort of the same, I guess."

Zach talked for a while about his horses, and she seemed to hang on his every word. He enjoyed that. Normally women got a dazed look on their faces and almost fell asleep. *Damn.* He'd heard men claim that when they met the right woman, they felt as if they could drown in her eyes. Zach had even heard his brothers talk that way. Until now, he'd always thought it was hogwash.

He did a quick visual check on Luke and Rosebud, who were over by the paddock fencing. Then he cupped Mandy's chin in his hand. Her eyes widened, and he felt her stiffen. He didn't let that stop him. He moved in.

As their lips met, his first thought was that she kissed like a schoolgirl, teeth clamped closed, arms still locked in a fold. But then—*oh, man*—her mouth was so sweet, soft and silken, with lingering traces of wine to intoxicate him. He remembered his reaction the first time he ever saw her, and it was the same again. Just a chaste touch of their lips, and she managed to inflame him as no other woman ever had.

Zach didn't want to rush her. When a woman clenched her teeth during a kiss, any sane man knew it was a warning. He gently broke the contact, straightened, and watched with fascination and no small measure of bewilderment as her cheeks turned red. Her embarrassment made him want to smile. He bit it back. He yearned to kiss her again, but he held that urge in check as well. This was too important—*she* was too important—for him to risk moving in on her too quickly.

Chapter Fifteen

Since kissing Mandy again clearly wasn't a smart move, Zach decided to concentrate on getting to know her better. Both she and Luke had mentioned that their mother had flown the coop, but neither of them had been forthcoming with any details. He figured getting her to tell him that story might be a great way to begin an exchange of personal information. He glanced across the parking area to make sure Luke and Rosebud were okay. On familiar ground, the little horse was performing beautifully, and Luke had lengthened his strides and was looking more confident.

"So, tell me, what exactly led up to your mother doing a disappearing act?"

She blinked at the sudden change of subject, but then her mouth tightened, and the shimmer in her eyes gave way to shadows. For a second he thought she might tell him to mind his own business, but then the tension went out of her. Rubbing her palms on the knees of her jeans, she took a long breath and slowly released it. "There was nothing really different that happened. My father started beating on her. That was pretty much a nightly occurrence at our house. I carried Luke upstairs to hide with him in the closet. Those were Mama's orders. I was to always grab Luke and get him safely away. She was terrified that Dad would finish with her and turn on us."

"So that was it? He beat her up, like always, only that time she decided to leave?"

Mandy gazed off across the pastures, her eyes getting a distant look in them. Her brows drew together in a slight frown. "Actually, one thing was different the last night. Mama always begged him to stop hitting her, but that time, when he didn't stop, I heard her scream that she'd had enough and was going to leave him."

"What happened then?"

"It really scared me. I heard Dad yell, 'So you want to leave me, do you? Over my dead body!' I was so afraid for my mom. You didn't say things like that to him and get away with it. I thought he'd go clear over the edge. Only he didn't."

Zach studied her delicate profile. "He didn't?"

"No. Right after that, it went quiet downstairs. I think he passed out. When I felt it was safe, I picked up Luke—he'd fallen asleep in my arms—and took him to bed."

"You didn't go back downstairs to check on your mom?"

"No. I was forbidden. When Dad got like that, he was crazy. Mom wanted me nowhere near him. So I just went to sleep." Her slender shoulders lifted in a fatalistic shrug. "The next morning when we woke up, she was gone. Her suitcase, most of her clothes, her personal effects, all gone. She didn't even leave us a note."

Zach searched her expression for any sign that she was about to cry, but all he saw was hollow resignation. She was either the strongest woman he'd ever met, or she'd separated herself from all emotion when it came to the subject of her mother. He rested his arms on his knees, letting his hands dangle at the wrists. To his way of thinking, it was understandable why the woman had fled from such an abusive relationship, but it sucked that she'd left her kids behind. "That must have been really rough."

Mandy nodded. "I always believed she loved us more

than anything. I used to beg her to leave him, but I never dreamed she'd go and not take us. I trusted her as I've never trusted anyone. She taught me a valuable lesson, I suppose. Now I know better than to count on anyone but myself."

Zach listened in silence, uncertain how to respond. He could scarcely imagine how much it must have hurt Mandy to realize that her mom had run away, leaving her behind to take the heat. Losing your mother was pure hell. Zach knew that firsthand. But at least he'd always known his hadn't left him by choice.

"You know what hurt the most?" she whispered.

"No, what?" Zach's voice had gone thick.

"I figured she'd call—or that she'd send us money to join her somewhere. For nearly a year, my heart soared every time our phone rang, and I checked the mailbox every single day, not just hoping but *knowing* she'd get in touch. But she never did. I can only assume she started a new life somewhere, and there wasn't room in it for me and Luke. If I live to be a hundred, I'll never forgive her for that."

What kind of mother did such a thing? "And after she left, you took the brunt of your father's rages."

"Yes. Until I was seventeen, anyway, and called the authorities."

"That took a lot of courage."

"I didn't have a choice." She pushed at a curl that had come loose from her hair clip. "The night before I made the call, Dad went after Luke. Luke was blind by then, and when our father started in on me, Luke grew frightened and disoriented. When he couldn't find the stairs, he huddled in a corner, crying. Then he wet his pants. When my dad saw pee on his precious hardwood floors, he grabbed Luke by an arm. Shook him like a rag doll and started slapping him. I was afraid he'd seriously injure my brother, so I grabbed a skillet off the stove and clocked Dad on the head."

"Oh, my God," Zach whispered. "That can't have ended well for you."

"It was bad," she agreed. "But Luke got away. He finally found the stairs. He was safe, and that was the important thing."

"What about you, Mandy? You couldn't get away, and you weren't safe."

"I was bigger. Besides, I was used to it."

Again, Zach looked for telltale signs of intense emotion, but her expression remained stoic. He'd always admired her, but never more than in that moment.

She turned her hands palms up and studied the creases as if she were trying to read her own future. "The next morning, we pretended to leave for school, but instead we hid in the toolshed until Dad left. I had to do something. Sooner or later, I knew Luke would get in the line of fire again." She sent Zach a haunted look that chilled him clear to his center. "I didn't know who to call. I phoned Dad's parents. I thought they might take us in. Grandma refused to interfere and hung up on me. She was afraid Dad would get mad at them, and she didn't want to jeopardize their relationship with him.

"Next, I called my school counselor. She got in touch with people who would help us." A distant look came into her eyes again. "Two ladies came with a police escort. The cops were reluctant—a loyalty issue, because my father was the mayor, a big shot in Crystal Falls. The women took me in the bathroom, looked at my torso, and when they told the cops how badly beaten up I was, they came around. Neither of them said as much, but I think they were furious with my dad. Our clothing was packed, we were put into the police car, and by nightfall we were in a temporary foster home. Dad was in jail."

"Did that bother you? Knowing you'd gotten your father thrown in jail, I mean."

She shook her head. "I hoped they'd keep him locked

up forever. I hated him, and I was terrified that sooner or later I wouldn't be able to stop him from hurting Luke." She began studying her palms again. "He was ... There's something *wrong* with him. On the outside, he's charming, well educated, funny, and warm. But on the inside, all you find is ice. Even when he beat me, there was something cold and calculated about it."

"Meaning?"

She lifted a slender shoulder in a halfhearted shrug. "There's no point in revisiting all of that. Suffice it to say he made sure no one outside our family ever saw the bruises. There's something— I don't know how to explain it, but something's missing inside him. He doesn't know how to love anyone. He didn't even love my mother. She was pretty, and I think he thought of her as an ornament, something to have on his arm in public to make him look like the perfect family man. But he didn't love her."

Hearing Mandy talk, Zach realized how very lucky he'd been to have such wonderful parents. "On some level, he must have cared for her, Mandy. Maybe not—"

"No," she interrupted emphatically. "After she left, he pretended in front of all his friends that he was devastated. But he wasn't. You know what he did one week later?"

"What?"

"He revamped our whole backyard to be the entertainment showplace of Crystal Falls. It was a huge yard, probably twice the size of mine. And in the far left corner, he paid to have an elaborate outdoor kitchen area built, a gigantic cement pad trimmed with brick benches and a brick barbecue." She shook her head as if she still couldn't believe he'd done that. "My mother had been gone only a week, and he revamped the yard? If he'd loved my mom—her name is Sharyn—he would have been devastated. Instead, all he could think about was the fabulous garden parties he was going to throw for all his important friends. And he had the first one two weeks after she left."

Zach thumbed a flyaway curl from her cheek. He wished he knew something wise to say, something that might heal the wounds that he sensed festered so deeply within her. Sadly, all that came to mind was, "If you ever need to talk, you've got my numbers. Early morning, way late at night, you can call me anytime."

She curled her fingers over his wrist, the tips reaching only a little over halfway, reminding him how fragile her bone structure was. Though she chose to be reticent about the beatings she'd received from her father, Luke hadn't been, so Zach knew more of what had gone on than she realized. The thought of some man pounding on her with his fists and kicking her made his blood boil. He would have emptied his bank accounts and liquidated all his assets for ten satisfying minutes alone with Tobin Pajeck.

The realization stymied Zach. He'd never before felt so protective of a woman outside his family. *Mandy.* When he looked at her, warmth sluiced through him. He was coming to care for her, perhaps far more than was wise. But how in the hell could a man stanch the flow of feeling?

Luke and Rosebud returned. Zach pushed to his feet, belatedly remembering that dinner was his show. He had to get the spuds in the oven and take a wire brush to the grill. He kicked it into gear, helping Rosebud up the steps while Mandy guided Luke to a deck chair. Then he hit the kitchen. Mandy followed him inside.

She stepped to the sink to wash her hands. "What can I do to help?"

"I haven't made the salad yet."

She dimpled a cheek at him. "One of my specialties. Do you like Caesar?"

It was one of Zach's favorites. "I don't have any Caesar dressing or croutons."

"You don't need any. I make everything from scratch. If you have all the ingredients, it'll be awesome."

The Caesar salad *was* awesome, and so was the rest of the evening. Zach hated to see it end. Luke and Rosebud were getting along famously, and so were Zach and Mandy. As they worked together to clean up the kitchen, with Luke in charge of loading the dishwasher because he'd insisted on helping, they told silly knock-knock jokes.

"Knock, knock," Luke said.

"Not another one!" Mandy protested.

Playing along, Zach asked, "Who's there?"

"Me, you idiot," Luke shot back. "Are you blind or something?"

When they ran out of knock-knock jokes, Zach asked, "What do you call a gorilla with a banana stuck in both ears?"

"Developmentally challenged," Mandy tried.

"A banana fiend," Luke suggested.

Zach laughed. "You can call him anything you want. He can't hear you."

Luke laughed. Mandy groaned. When the dishes were done, Zach brewed coffee, and the three of them sat at the table to enjoy Mandy's chocolate cake. In Zach's estimation, it was delicious. He had three pieces. After putting their plates and cups into the machine, Mandy glanced at her watch and smiled regretfully at him.

"That time already?" he asked.

"It's almost ten. We need to get home."

Zach sighed. "I wish you didn't have to go."

Her gaze searched his. "Me, too. It's been fun. Thank you so much for inviting us."

Luke went down on his knees to tell Rosebud goodbye. The two had been inseparable all evening. "I hate to leave her," he said.

Zach winked at Mandy. "You'll see her again."

"When?"

Zach lifted an eyebrow at Mandy. She smiled as she collected her purse. "I'll call you to set up a time."

"Sounds good," Zach agreed.

As Zach walked them to their car, he took Mandy's hand. For a moment she looked startled, but then she smiled uncertainly and didn't pull away. At the driver's door, he stepped in close, bent his head, and kissed her cheek as he told her good night. She pressed her fingertips to the spot where his lips had touched her skin.

"Good night," she whispered. "See you soon."

Tomorrow wouldn't be soon enough to suit Zach, but all his instincts told him not to push her. He watched her car until it was swallowed by darkness; then he went back into the house. Rosebud looked forlornly up at him.

"You're starting to love him, aren't you, girl?" Zach patted the little horse's head. "He's shaping up to be a pretty nice young man. Maybe it'll work out for the two of you."

Zach stepped over to open the fridge and grab a beer. Then he changed his mind. If he wanted to start a serious relationship with Mandy, and he had come to realize he did, he needed to curb the amount of alcohol he consumed.

After setting the coffeepot up for the morning, Zach put the harness on Rosebud and they went to the arena. Tornado met them at the gate. Zach was pleased by the changes he was seeing in the stallion. The horse was learning to trust again. Soon, Zach would stop sleeping in the arena. Tornado no longer really needed that, and it was time to move on to the next step, which would be to love on him with no expectations riding drag.

Zach gave the stallion some pellet treats. Then he removed Rosebud's gear, got her feeder and water pail, shook out his bedding, and went to turn out the lights. Instant blackness. After a second, his eyes adjusted.

Faint shafts of moonlight came in through the skylights, providing just enough illumination for him to see. He rejoined Rosebud in front of Tornado's stall, climbed into the sleeping bag, and tipped his Stetson down over his eyes.

In the habit of getting up long before dawn, Zach was weary, and he expected to fall asleep almost instantly. Instead he lay there listening to Rosebud munch on her hay, his thoughts circling back to Mandy's story about her mother. Zach couldn't believe Tobin Pajeck had bounced back from losing his wife within a week and started redoing his backyard. What kind of man could be so heartless? Even worse, what kind of father could distance himself so completely from his children's pain and sense of loss?

Zach's eyes drifted closed and then popped back open. According to Mandy, Sharyn had seemed to love her children with her whole heart and protected them at every turn. How, then, could she have abandoned Mandy and Luke, leaving them with a man she knew would abuse them? It made no sense to Zach. Hell, it would have been easier for him to believe Tobin had murdered her that night and hidden the body.

Zach jackknifed to a sitting position. *After that, everything went quiet*, Mandy had told him. And she hadn't gone downstairs to check on her mother. *I was forbidden*. Zach stared into the shadows of the arena. It was late. He was tired. The evening had been emotional. That was why his imagination was taking such a morbid turn.

Maybe. But he couldn't convince himself of it. Tobin Pajeck, the mayor, a prominent citizen, had been deserted by his wife, and instead of exploding in rage, he'd constructed an outdoor entertainment area that took up much of the yard. Then he'd thrown a party. No sense of humiliation had touched him. Mandy had made that clear. And angry humiliation would be the natural reaction for a man like him. Zach's mind raced. What better way was there to hide a body than to cover it with concrete?

Nah, Zach told himself firmly. His imagination was running wild. That kind of crap rarely happened in real life. This was Crystal Falls, Oregon, not a crime-ridden metropolis. Maybe Pajeck was a violent alcoholic, but that didn't make him a killer.

Forcing himself to lie back down, Zach tipped the Stetson over his eyes again, but sleep eluded him. *I'm losing it.* Sharyn Pajeck had had every reason to run scared, and there might be a perfectly rational explanation for her failure to send for her kids. Maybe she'd never contacted them because she was terrified her husband would find her. Or perhaps she'd had no education or training, which forced her to take a menial job that didn't bring in enough income to support two children. That made more sense than the murder plot he was cooking up in his sleep-deprived brain.

The next morning as Zach strode up the arena hallway to the tack room, he stopped to stare at the concrete flooring. Four inches thick, impervious to wear, it had held solid for more than ten years and would probably hang tough for another thirty. He'd built it to last, reinforcing the cement with rebar. Over time, fissures had developed in the surface, but the only way the walkway would ever fall apart was if he took a jackhammer to it. If a man wanted to hide a terrible secret, covering it with cement would certainly do the trick.

Zach's attempts to focus on work were invaded by visions of murder, grave digging, and the silent gloating of a man who knew he was beyond the law. He couldn't push the thoughts from his mind. *Who do I think I am, Sherlock Holmes?* Murder scenarios weren't part of his usual thought processes.

After putting in several hours with the horses, he

broke for lunch at the house. While eating a turkey sandwich in his office, he called his uncle Hugh, a state cop who'd been based in Crystal Falls for most of his career. Hugh sounded surprised to hear from his nephew, which made Zach feel guilty for not calling or going to see him more often. The two men exchanged pleasantries, and then Zach got around to his reason for phoning.

"Do you remember back fifteen years ago when Mayor Pajeck's wife disappeared?"

"*Disappear* is a strong word," Hugh replied. "Sharyn Pajeck left her husband."

Zach frowned. "Are you sure of that?"

"Pretty damn sure. According to Tobin, they got into a horrible fight the night before, and she said she was going to leave him. The little girl, I can't recall her name now, verified that she'd heard her mother say that."

"So the authorities took it at face value and never searched for Sharyn?"

"We had no reason," Hugh said. "She was a grown woman. There's no law against skipping out on your husband and kids. Tobin called to report her missing, but he wasn't really interested in filing a missing-person report. The marriage was rocky; he didn't want her back. No signs of violence were seen inside the house, end of story."

Zach sighed. "Did you see the house yourself, Uncle Hugh?"

"I did, actually. I was on duty when he called. Tobin acted as if he had nothing to hide. Her closet was empty, her suitcase was gone, along with all her personal things."

"Did you happen to notice any freshly turned earth in the backyard?" Zach inquired.

Hugh laughed. "No, son, I didn't. What are you suggesting, that Tobin knocked her off and buried her out there?"

That was precisely what Zach was suggesting, but he

could understand how outrageous it might seem to his uncle.

"Why are you asking about this?" Hugh queried.

"I've met his daughter. Tobin is now in prison for trying to kill her. The story of Sharyn's disappearance doesn't add up for me. I was just curious to learn what kind of investigation ensued after she vanished."

"There was no real investigation." Hugh sounded troubled by the admission. "At the time, we weren't aware of Pajeck's abusive patterns; his story made sense, and the daughter backed him up on it. We figured Sharyn had just left him."

After chatting for a few more minutes, Zach ended the call, feeling completely unsatisfied with the answers he'd gotten. No investigation? Now that Pajeck's vicious nature had come to light, Zach believed that had been a huge oversight on the part of the police. Determined to rectify that, Zach got on his computer to search old public records. Tobin Pajeck's former celebrity status as mayor made him an easy fellow to find. Within only minutes, Zach located the address of the home where Mandy had grown up. He didn't need to jot it down. One look and it was burned into his brain.

After working with Rosebud and spending some time whittling outside Tornado's stall that afternoon, Zach hunted down Cookie. He found the old fart in the arena office.

"I need the rest of the evening off. Can you button it up around here for me?"

The foreman had doffed his hat. He looked like a mad scientist when he glanced up from the paperwork, his flyaway gray hair poking out in all directions. "Sure. What's up, a date with Tornado's lady friend?"

Zach propped a shoulder against the doorjamb. "Not tonight. I just have a hunch I want to check out, and I'd like to do it before dark."

"Anything special you need taken care of here?"

"Nope, just the usual."

Zach lifted a hand in farewell. Once outside the arena, he opted to drive his Ford diesel truck. The engine, left to sit for days on end, sputtered and coughed before it started to rumble. The drive into town passed swiftly, Zach's mind spinning faster than the truck tires. Was he nuts to be doing this? *No.* Sharyn Pajeck had taken countless beatings over the years and had always, without fail, protected her children. To Zach, that spoke volumes, creating an image in his mind of a devoted mother who would have made any sacrifice for her kids. Why would she suddenly decide to take a hike, leaving them behind? Zach couldn't shake the gruesome suspicion that she hadn't. He wanted to see that entertainment area. How he meant to get into the backyard, he didn't know. Sneak, maybe? The residents of the home would think it a little strange if he knocked on the door and asked for a guided tour.

Fourteen fifty-six Montrose Place was located in an older area of town. As Zach drove along the street, he noted that most of the large houses were still elegant and well maintained, but Mandy's childhood home, a once impressive two-story with gable ends and dormer attic windows, had gone to seed, the exterior in need of paint, the yard weed infested and overgrown. Zach parked at the curb, his gaze drawn to a warped For Rent sign on the front grass, which was yellow and almost a foot tall. The house, once white with green trim, now looked almost gray, with chips and peels in the paint. Some of the shingles on the roof had curled at the edges.

For several minutes, Zach sat in the truck, the chug of the diesel engine a drone in the background as he tried to envision Mandy skipping up the front walkway to the double front doors. Had a jack-o'-lantern ever sat on that porch? Had Christmas icicles ever been taped to the windows? He doubted it. Even now, all these years later, the house emanated a cold, formal aura.

Zach cut the engine and swung out of the truck. The place looked uninhabited. Just in case the present occupants had given notice to the landlord but were still in residence, Zach made a beeline for the front door. The hard rap of his knuckles on the wood roused no one. He approached a dirty front window. Cupping his hands at the corners of his eyes, he held his breath so as not to fog the glass and peered into an empty living room. No furniture. Tobin Pajeck's precious hardwood floors were scratched, worn, and littered with debris, the kind of stuff tenants didn't bother to pick up when they moved out. No one was living here.

Okay. Coast clear. If a snoopy neighbor asked Zach what he was up to, he'd just say he'd seen the For Rent sign and might be interested. Wading through the tangle of tall grass, he circled the house. The backyard was enclosed by a six-foot-tall cedar fence that had long since lost its moorings. When Zach opened the arched back gate, the adjacent posts wobbled. No matter. He was willing to bet Tobin Pajeck's elaborate outdoor entertainment area had weathered the neglect far better.

As Zach entered the enclosure, he heard Mandy's voice playing like a recording inside his head. She hadn't lied. It was at least twice the size of the backyard she had now, maybe even three times larger. Zach's gaze shot to the left corner, where a large cement pad had been poured and then trimmed with a massive brick barbecue and perimeter benches. *Damn.* The center area was big enough to accommodate a ten-foot-long picnic table and still leave room for thirty people to line-dance.

A chill prickled over Zach's scalp as he walked closer. Was it only his imagination, or did the air feel colder? He'd never been a fanciful guy, and he didn't believe in ghosts, but this place gave him the heebie-jeebies. The patio slab was extra thick, exceeding the usual four inches by two more. Zach was willing to bet the concrete had also been generously reinforced to prevent cracking. Tobin Pajeck had built this sucker to endure over time, not to mention that he'd sunk so much money into it that anyone who owned the house would be reluctant to get rid of it. Zach wondered if that had been Tobin's intent. By the time the patio needed to be replaced, Tobin would be dead. A deceased individual couldn't do time for murder unless he served the sentence in hell.

Zach tested the concrete with a whack of his boot. *You under there, Sharyn?* He went still, listening, breathing slowly. He wasn't sure he wanted to hear anything, and he was even less sure what he'd do if he did. He didn't believe the dead could communicate with the living—never had. But he had the creepy feeling that Mandy's mother was close and wanted to be found. *I'm losing it. This is nuts.* But even as Zach told himself to leave it alone, he knew he wouldn't. Tobin Pajeck had done plenty to damage Mandy and Luke emotionally, but the most serious injury to them had resulted from their mother's defection. What if Sharyn hadn't left them by choice? Tobin could have carefully lifted the sod and then replaced it over the grave so the police wouldn't see freshly turned earth. What if Sharyn rested here in a shallow grave under this concrete? If Zach found her body, wouldn't it go a long way toward healing both Mandy and Luke? At least then they'd know their mom hadn't willingly abandoned them.

Zach stood there for at least five minutes, absorbing the ambience of this place. It felt like a frigging cemetery to him, and he reached a hard decision: He was going to rent this house, and before the ink had dried on the contract, he'd be out here with a pick and jackhammer. If he found nothing, fine. He'd just cough up the bucks to have the entertainment area reconstructed. It wasn't as if he couldn't afford the expenditure.

And if he found a body? Well, then, Sharyn Pajeck would be vindicated. Mandy and Luke would be set free.

And Tobin Pajeck would rot in prison for the rest of his life.

As he returned to his truck, Zach stopped at the For Rent sign and entered the contact number into his cell phone. He no sooner got into his vehicle than he called the landlord. The thought of leaving the house up for grabs until morning didn't sit well with him. He wanted to secure the place tonight.

An old guy with a gruff voice answered the phone. While talking with him, Zach learned that he'd had a minor stroke a few years ago, had moved to a high-end retirement community with assisted-living services, and hadn't been able to sell the house because the market had gone sour. He'd been renting the place out ever since.

Two hours later, Zach had leased the house, paying a large damage deposit as well as the first and last months' rent. He'd hated to sign on for an entire six months, but the old fart who owned the place had been adamant. Apparently prior tenants had been inconstant, and the landlord wanted a guarantee that he'd have a monthly stipend rolling in for at least half a year. *No big.* Zach would never miss the thousand he'd have to cough up each month. In fact, for that area, the rent was actually far less than he expected.

As Zach drove back to his ranch, he mentally circled the situation. Should he inform Mandy of his suspicions? Granted, learning that her mother might have been murdered wouldn't be one of her happier moments. But what if his hunch was correct? She'd gone all these years with a broken heart, and she had confessed to Zach that her mom's betrayal had left her unwilling to trust anyone but herself ever again. Learning that her mother hadn't abandoned her might help her put the past to rest.

On the other hand, what if Zach was wrong and

put Mandy through that kind of trauma for nothing? Wouldn't it be better to follow through on his suspicion without her knowledge? If he found only dirt under that slab, he could just rebuild, and Mandy would never be the wiser.

Zach tried to imagine how he would want it to play out, and he decided he'd want to be in on it from the start. Mandy had been so young when her mother vanished that she probably hadn't been able to conceive of her father doing something so horrible. Zach wasn't young, and he wasn't innocent. He believed Pajeck had offed his wife.

Zach spotted a wide spot off the shoulder of the two-lane road and whipped the truck into a fast U-turn. Mandy might think he'd lost his frigging mind if he showed up on her doorstep at this hour, babbling about murder and treachery, but this wasn't something he could keep from her.

It was half past eight when Zach parked the diesel truck in Mandy's driveway. He strode up the steps and rapped his knuckles on the door before he could change his mind. Inside he heard the soft pad of bare feet on carpet. The porch light flared to life. Then came the rattle and click of the doorknob being turned. A chain guard snapped taut as the portal opened a scant six inches. Mandy's delicate countenance appeared behind the breach.

"Zach?" Surprise flitted across her face. Then her soft mouth curved in a pleased smile as she fumbled to disengage the chain. "I didn't expect you. I'm in my PJ's."

"Sorry. I should have called. It was a spur-of-the-moment thing."

The door swung open, and Mandy stepped back to let him in. The living room was dark, the only light coming from the television, which washed the walls and furniture with flashes of muted color. Mandy wore a Mickey

Mouse nightshirt over a pair of black sweatpants. Her hair was clipped at the top of her head, clumps of reddish brown poking up every which way. She looked adorable.

Luke sat at the far end of the sofa. He drew off his headphones and grinned. "Hey. That you, Zach?"

"It's me," Zach replied.

"Did you bring Rosebud?"

"No. Sorry, buddy." Luke's crestfallen expression prompted Zach to add, "I'll bring her by tomorrow. Okay? Maybe we can take another walk to the park."

"Right on! Maybe Mandy can come. We can go Dutch for a Coney Island experience." Luke sat forward on the cushion. "Guess what!"

Zach tried to smile, but his lips felt like rotten rubber bands that might snap in two if he stretched them. "What?"

"I went to see your blind friend, Carly Coulter, today. She can see right now, but even so, she knows what it's like to be blind, and she's totally awesome!"

Zach listened with genuine interest as Luke talked about all he'd learned during the first session. "Hey, man, that's great. When will you see her again?"

"Next week. She hardly charges anything, so we can afford it. I'm really excited."

Zach touched his palm to the small of Mandy's back. "Can I talk to you for a few minutes?" he asked. "Privately?"

She glanced at Luke. "Sure. Headphones back on, brother dear, and no fair turning the volume way down so you can eavesdrop."

Luke grinned, shoved the headphones on, and fiddled with the volume control. The muted blast of rap was audible. "That loud enough for you?"

Zach guided Mandy to the kitchen with every intention of telling her of his suspicions about her father. But when they were settled across from each other at the table and he looked into her eyes, the words jammed in his throat. She had already endured so much. How could he bring himself to layer on even more pain?

"Is something wrong?" she asked. "Is Rosebud okay?"

Reaching a quick decision, Zach replied, "She's great, and it just happens that she and Luke are what I want to talk to you about. Rosebud looked so sad when Luke left last night, and I thought for a minute I'd have to pry him away from her with a crowbar. They've really formed a strong bond."

Mandy glowed with happiness. "Isn't it awesome? Luke talks about her constantly. It isn't only that he's fallen crazy in love with her, but he's starting to believe in the life she'll be able to help him have. He's getting excited about going to college, but even more important, he's looking forward to going out into the world and enjoying all the things he's never experienced."

That had been Zach's dream all along—what had driven him to embark on this journey—and now it was happening.

"I'm so thankful, Zach. I'll never be able to express it with words."

Zach waved a hand. "Hey, I'm a horse trainer. Working with Rosebud hasn't been a huge leap for me."

"Let me get my shoes on," she said, her voice laced with excitement. "I want to show you something."

Zach trailed her with his gaze as she rushed to her bedroom. She reappeared a second later with tennis shoes, bouncing on one foot and then the other to slip them on.

When he realized she meant to go outside with the laces dangling, he turned sideways on the chair and patted his knee. "No way. You'll trip and break your neck."

"Don't be silly," she protested, but as she spoke, she plopped a foot on his knee.

After tying her shoes, Zach followed her out into the

backyard. The glow of the porch light barely reached the far left corner, but Zach had excellent night vision and saw that she'd driven some stakes into the ground and strung red tape to outline the shape of the shed she hoped to build.

"Will that be big enough?" she asked.

Zach nodded in approval. "Plenty big enough." Sensing her excitement, Zach turned to reassess the yard. He'd been unenthusiastic the last time she'd shown it to him, but Luke's determination to change had eliminated most of his concerns. The kid clearly loved Rosebud and would provide her with a good home. "She's going to love it out here, Mandy. Just look at all the space she'll have to run and play. That's vital for a mini that is indoors so much of the time." Toeing a clump of grass, Zach angled a querying glance at her. "You do realize that Rosebud will take dumps on the lawn."

Mandy laughed. "I did some surfing on the Net and found a poop scooper I'll order. It'll make cleanup a snap, and I honestly don't give a hang about the grass."

"What about your flower beds?"

She shrugged. "I'll have the front yard for gardening. This area is for Rosebud."

Zach moved toward her. At first, she smiled up at him, and then, as if she sensed what he meant to do, a look of uncertainty settled over her beautiful face. Zach cupped her chin in his hand. "Don't be nervous," he whispered, his voice gone husky with desire that surged through him, making his blood feel thick and molten. "I'll never harm a hair on your head. You've got my word on it."

Moving slowly, Zach settled his mouth over hers. When she failed to part her lips, he gently encouraged them open with the press of his fingertips and thumb on her cheeks. The instant he gained access and tasted the sweet recesses of her mouth, his desire for her became more intense—a yearning so powerful that his body tightened and his pulse started to slam in his temples.

He couldn't hear, could barely think. *Sweet, so sweet.* She melted against him like a pat of butter on a hot biscuit. Opened for him. Moaned into his mouth.

Need and longing obliterated Zach's common sense. He forgot where they were, slipped his hands under her nightshirt, and moved his palms up to cup her bare breasts. She jerked when he grazed one turgid nipple with his thumb. Then she twisted her face to one side, ending the kiss.

"Stop, Zach, please."

Nothing had ever been quite so difficult for him to do. He wanted her so much that he ached. Only the trepidation he glimpsed in her eyes enabled him to let go of her. She planted a trembling hand at the center of his chest as if to hold him at bay.

"I'm *very* attracted to you," she whispered tremulously.

Ditto, he thought.

"I just don't see how a relationship between us can go anywhere. I mean . . . well, I'd be a liar if I said I haven't thought about it—but I always end up at the same place."

"Where's that?" he managed to ask, the words gravelly.

"A dead end," she whispered. "I'll never get married, *never*, and when it comes to physical intimacy, anything short of that isn't my style."

Normally Zach would have run like a scalded dog if a woman had said the M-word after only two kisses. But with Mandy, he felt different. It had been that way from the start, an instinctive knowledge deep within him that she was special, the woman he'd been waiting all his adult life to meet. She was so affectionate with Rosebud, so devoted to Luke, so courageous, and so unfailingly kind. How could any man get to know her and not dream of slipping a ring on her finger?

"Sweetheart, why is marriage out of the question for you?"

She shivered and rubbed her arms. "After what I've already told you, you need to ask? It just is. After my dad ... well, I can't imagine *ever* giving another man that kind of power over me. I know you don't understand."

Zach did understand, and it made him feel half-sick.

Face draining of color, she struggled to explain, her kiss-swollen lips quivering. "One time at a dinner party, I forgot to tip the goblets as I poured a vintage merlot for his guests. When everyone left, he beat the hell out of me, and after I went down, he started kicking me in the stomach."

Nausea mixed with a burn of rage pushed up Zach's throat. "You don't have to tell me, honey. I know talking about it ... well, it can't be easy."

She shook her head. "Normally I avoid talking about any of it, but I need you to understand." She splayed a hand between her breasts. "He kicked me and kicked me. And you know what he said each time? 'I'll teach you not to bruise the wine, you little bitch.'" In the moonlight, the tears that filled her eyes sparkled like diamonds. "There I was, huddled on the floor, wondering, 'What about *me*, Dad? You're bruising *me*.' But he didn't care. His precious wine mattered more to him than his own daughter did."

Zach scuffed the toe of his boot through the grass. He'd seen her childhood home this evening. He'd pictured her there as a kid. Now she'd put a new vision in his head, that of a helpless thirteen-year-old girl curled into a fetal position on the floor while her father worked her over. The image filled him with such anger that he trembled.

"That was just one instance," she whispered. "If I scorched one of his shirts, it was punching-bag time. If I pressed a wrinkle into a napkin, punching-bag time. If he saw a dust bunny, punching-bag time. I never knew what might set him off next. I only knew something would. He didn't need much of an excuse."

"Ah, Mandy." In that moment, Zach knew, without a doubt, that he had fallen wildly, madly, Stetson-over-boot-heels in love with her. Done deal, no turning back. He wasn't sure when it had happened—or even *how* it had happened—but his feelings for her ran so deep now that a surgeon couldn't have excised them with a scalpel. "I'm so sorry."

Zach wished he could tell her that Harrigan men never lifted a violent hand to a woman and somehow make her believe him. But Mandy had to learn that over time.

"I know it sounds weak of me," she went on, "but I don't have it in me to love or trust anyone, Zach. My dad . . . well, he left me feeling broken inside." She lifted her shoulders in a helpless shrug. "I like you a lot, truly I do, but that's as far as I'm able to take it."

Chapter Sixteen

Mesmerized by the twin beams of his truck's head-lights, Zach stewed all the way home about Mandy's inability to trust again. *I'm not a wife beater, damn it.* But he could probably tell her that a million times and never get her to believe him. He also had it in him to be steadfast and true to only one woman. It was the way his father had raised him to be. But how could he convince Mandy to set her fears aside—all of which were understandable—and get her to take a gamble on him?

Usually Rosebud's excited whinnies of greeting made Zach smile, but tonight when he entered the arena, all he could do was scowl. He got the mini set up for the night outside Tornado's stall, shook out his sleeping bag, and then went to cut the lights. Cookie startled him half out of his wits when he called down from the landing.

"What's got your tail tied in a knot?" the older man asked.

Zach sighed and put his hands on his hips, gazing solemnly up at his foreman. "I'm in love with her, Cookie. Crazy in love, and she can't love me back."

"Well, shit." Cookie rubbed the crown of his head, then gestured Zach upstairs. "Only one thing to do in a situation like that—have a counselin' session with good ol' Jim Beam."

Zach nearly refused. He was in no mood to get drunk. But then he decided it wasn't a bad idea. He would find no answers at the bottom of the jug, but with enough booze in his system, he might get some sleep. He had a long day planned for tomorrow. He mounted the steps with quick, angry taps of his boots. When he entered the apartment, Cookie was already sloshing Jim Beam into two tumblers. He motioned at a bar stool. "Hang your hat and have a seat. Tell me all about it."

Zach needed a good belt of bourbon before he could sort his thoughts and say anything that made sense. "I need all day tomorrow off." He held up a hand. "And, *please*, no lectures. It won't be a play day. I'll be working my ass off."

Cookie listened as Zach briefed him on his suspicions about the disappearance of Sharyn Pajeck. "Sweet Lord have mercy," he whispered. "You really think he killed her and buried her in the backyard?"

Zach raked his fingers through his hair, not caring if he made it stand on end. "Yes." He spat the word, then met Cookie's gaze. "Sharyn loved those kids. She always made Mandy grab Luke and hide upstairs when Tobin flew into a rage. She took beating after beating after beating, and she never left. What else could have happened that night to suddenly make her do a vanishing act?"

Cookie's ruddy complexion had turned almost as ashen as his frizzy hair. "It's just hard for me to think of it. What kinda man does stuff like that, son?"

"The Tobin Pajeck kind. He didn't give a damn about his wife or kids. All he cared about was himself." Zach took another slug of whiskey and whistled air through his teeth. "Here's the dilemma. Do I tell Mandy, or should I tear up that slab first?"

"If it was me, I'd wanna be there."

"But, Cookie, what if I don't find a body? Then I'll have put her through hell for nothing."

The foreman passed a gnarly hand over his eyes and blinked. "I don't think that'll happen. A mother's love . . . well, it's mighty powerful stuff. Don't get me wrong. There's women who don't give a rip. They can walk off and leave their kids without a second thought. But those that love their babies?" He shook his head. "They'll fight like she-bears to protect 'em. I'm with you. I don't think Sharyn Pajeck ran off."

Zach couldn't argue the point. "So you think I should tell Mandy? Cookie, what if I *do* find her mother's body with her standing right there beside me?"

"Tell her, Zach. Make it her call if she's there with you or not. But tell her. She deserves the chance to decide for herself."

The following morning, Zach awoke with a headache and a rotten taste in his mouth, but he wasn't about to let a hangover alter his plans for the day. After a quick shower, he gathered some tools and tossed them into the bed of his truck, then headed for town, his first stop a rental supply outfit that carried jackhammers. Once he'd gotten the equipment, he took it over to Montrose Place to drop it off before going to Mandy's.

In broad daylight, the house and yard looked even seedier than they had late yesterday. Clearly the old fellow who owned it had experienced difficulty finding good renters, or possibly any renters at all, for a good long while. Zach carried the jackhammer out to the patio, then used the wheelbarrow to haul the picks and other tools he'd brought from the ranch. Pausing to catch his breath, he almost hoped he wouldn't get the heebie-jeebies again. Digging up a decayed corpse wasn't high on his list, and he would have happily passed. But when he went still, his skin went cold. She was down there. He couldn't explain why he felt so certain. He only knew it was so.

Drawing his small digital camera from his shirt pocket, Zach took snapshots of the entertainment area so he could reconstruct it later. Then he fetched a tape from the wheelbarrow to take measurements. He used his BlackBerry to e-mail the dimensions to himself for future reference. If the landlord found out what was happening over here, Zach could plead a convincing case that he intended to replace everything.

In no hurry to tell Mandy of his plans for the day, Zach decided to take a short tour of the house. He unlocked the back door and entered through a utility room. Recalling Mandy's story about scorching her father's shirt and pressing a wrinkle into a napkin, he opened a tall, narrow door set into the wall and stared at the drop-down ironing board. Maybe it was dumb, but he ran his fingertips along its bottom edge, picturing Mandy letting it down. It made him feel connected to the child she'd once been.

His boot heels clunked on the hardwood floor as he moved through the house. The echoes filled him with melancholy. He envisioned Mandy in every room—on her knees scrubbing floors, rushing about to polish furniture, and wrinkling her cute little nose as she cleaned the toilets. How could her father have expected her to keep this huge place clean while she attended school full-time and cared for her little brother? It blew Zach's mind. But, bless her heart, she'd done it. That was Mandy, with more grit in her little finger than most people had in their entire bodies.

He wished—*what?*—that he could rewrite the story of her life? That wasn't possible, but when he thought of all she had endured within these walls, he wished he could do it anyway. No little girl should ever go through all the horrors that she had.

Upstairs, he found the closet where she'd probably hidden with Luke while her father pummeled her mother. It angled back under the attic stairs, one of those long, deep closets with a sharply pitched ceiling. Crouching down inside the doorway, Zach stared into the shadowy recesses until his eyes smarted. *This is definitely the place where they hid.* He could have sworn he tasted the metallic tang of her fear on the back of his tongue. He remembered Luke's tale of how scared he'd been when he came here, and how Mandy had always told him it was okay. She'd held her brother close and tried to comfort him even as terror filmed her small body with sweat.

Tears burned at the back of Zach's eyes. He didn't try to blink them away, wouldn't have even if someone else had been present. He believed what he'd told Luke that day at the park: A real man wasn't embarrassed to cry. Frank Harrigan said it best: *A real man has nothin' to prove to anybody but himself.*

As Zach made his way back downstairs, he looked out the kitchen window and saw what a bright, sunny morning it was, a perfect day for patio demolition. As the thought slipped through his mind, he belatedly remembered his promise to Luke last night about taking Rosebud over to his house for a visit. *Damn.* A promise was a promise, and Zach took that seriously. If his hunch was correct and Sharyn's corpse lay under that slab, it had been there for fifteen years and would keep for another twenty-four hours.

Zach returned to the ranch to switch vehicles and collect Rosebud before going to Mandy's house. Luke met Zach and Rosebud at the door and barely let them cross the threshold before dropping to his knees to hug the horse. Rosebud snorted and whinnied, clearly as delighted as Luke to be reunited. Mandy appeared in the archway. Circles of exhaustion underscored her eyes, a sign that she hadn't slept well. She'd probably lain awake worrying herself sick over her feelings for him.

Oh, yes, he felt certain she *did* have feelings for him. He wasn't the only one who'd fallen in love. Mandy was just having a good deal more trouble accepting it.

"Hi." She rubbed her palms on her jeans. "I didn't expect you until around noon."

"I thought we might fool around at the park for an hour or so before eating lunch." Zach glanced at his watch, saw it was only half past nine, and regrouped. "It is kind of early, I guess." He swallowed, glanced down at Luke. "The truth is, I made other plans for today, some important ones, and almost forgot I promised to bring Rosebud over."

"Oh." Mandy plucked at an imaginary piece of lint on the sleeve of her sweatshirt. "We can go to the park another day. Right, Luke?"

Luke's face fell. He straightened away from Rosebud. "Sure, I guess so."

"Actually, the plans I'd made for today involve both of you, and I've put them on hold until tomorrow," Zach said carefully. "I thought I might fill you in at the park." *And ruin your appetites for Coney Island hot dogs.* "I . . . Well, it's something important. I almost kept it to myself, but after thinking it over, I've decided both of you have a right to know."

Mandy's brows drew together in a bewildered scowl, but she refrained from pressing him for information. Instead she helped Luke find a fleece sweatshirt, grabbed her keys and some money, and trailed out the door behind Zach, her brother, and the horse.

As had occurred during the last walk to the park, Rosebud performed her job beautifully. Soon Zach would be able to begin her training in a couple of large cities. This time Luke was far more confident and attuned to her signals. The kid crossed each street without help. Zach was pleased to note that Luke also clicked and treated the mini without any reminders. The young man and horse had become a team.

Zach almost wished he'd said nothing to forewarn Mandy. She was pale and quiet this morning, walking mostly with her head bent. He kept remembering that damned closet and picturing her there, how he'd wished he might rewrite the story of her life. Now he was about to tell her something that could rock her whole world off its axis.

Once at the park, they sat on the same chipped green bench, Zach at one end, Luke and Rosebud at the other, Mandy sandwiched between them. Zach was acutely conscious of her shoulder pressed against his upper arm, of how much taller he was—which was saying something, because he wasn't a tall man, measuring in at only five feet, eleven inches in his stocking feet. Next to her, he felt like a giant.

Luke went into chatter mode, reminiscing about the times he and Mandy had played on a teeter-totter. He talked about the scents he caught on the air, about the little tricks for navigating the world that Carly Coulter was teaching him, and about how much he was starting to look forward to college.

About the time Zach was gearing up to dash Luke's cheerful mood, a girl he recognized from St. Catherine's spotted him. Pretty with streaked blond hair, she waved and smiled as she walked toward the bench. "Hey, Mr. Harrigan! You recognize me, I hope. Laurie from church, Jim Patterson's daughter?"

Zach stood and tipped his hat to her. "Of course I remember you. How are you?"

"Good."

Her blue eyes sparkled in the morning sunlight. She angled a curious glance at Luke, reminding Zach of his manners. "Laurie, this is Mandy Pajeck, a friend of mine, and that's Luke, her brother. Luke, Mandy, this is Laurie from my church. Her dad serves on the council."

"Hello." Mandy extended her hand and smiled. "It's good to meet you."

Chatty Luke had gone suddenly quiet. Zach realized the kid wasn't sure what to say. Laurie saved the day. "I saw Rosebud on the news, Luke. Is she going to be your guide horse?"

Luke nodded. "I hope so. I have a lot to learn before I can take proper care of her."

"How does she help you?" the girl asked.

"She, um . . ." Luke got a blank look on his face. "She just guides me." He stroked Rosebud's neck. "She's totally awesome." He cocked his head. "Is it all right if I show Laurie how Rosebud guides me, Zach?"

Zach bit back a grin and relaxed against the bench. "Of course it's all right. Just don't go too far. Okay? Rosebud isn't bulletproof yet. I need to keep you in sight."

Luke shot up from the bench as if someone had lit a match under his butt. As the trio walked away along the park path, Mandy glanced at Zach and dimpled her cheek. "It appears that Rosebud is a pretty-girl attractant."

Zach chuckled. "Yep. Luke may net himself a girl-friend without half trying." He angled a questioning look at Mandy. "How will you feel about him dating?"

"I, um, don't really know. Until now, he's never shown any interest in girls."

Zach sighed and folded his arms. "Brace yourself. He's plenty interested now." He paused. "Laurie's a nice kid. Maybe they'll hit it off."

When Luke and Laurie returned, Zach invited the girl to join them for lunch. Laurie called her mom on her cell phone to ask permission, and then said, "I'd love to."

Zach drew his money clip from his pants pocket and peeled off two twenties. He leaned forward to slip them into Luke's hand. "You and Laurie can do the honors today. I want a Coney with the works and a giant root beer." He glanced at Mandy. "How about you?"

"That sounds fine." She looked worriedly at Luke. "Can you handle this, Luke?"

Luke straightened his shoulders, a picture of stung masculine pride. "Of course."

"I'll be with him," Laurie inserted.

"When you get there, tell Rosebud to find the checkout counter," Zach instructed. "It'll look a little different to her from the ones in a store, but I think she'll figure it out."

While the kids were gone to get the food, Mandy turned sideways on the bench to face Zach. "What are the plans you made for today that involve me and Luke?"

Zach met her gaze. "That conversation will keep. Let Luke enjoy lunch with Laurie. Then we'll talk after she leaves. Okay?"

"Why do I get the feeling you're going to tell me something awful?"

Zach didn't want to lie to her. "You're fishing," he accused with a grin. "Let it go, Mandy. I'll tell you all about it later."

Laurie and Luke ate lunch on another bench farther along the pathway. The sound of their voices and intermittent laughter rang in the spring sunlight, warming Zach's heart. Luke was obviously smitten. Zach just hoped Laurie realized that and didn't lead him on unless the interest was requited.

As if Mandy read his thoughts, she whispered, "If she hurts him, I'll wring her neck."

Zach gazed at the younger couple. They had chili ringing their lips and were talking with their mouths full. "Like I said, she's a nice girl." He took a pull on his drink straw. "As for hurting him, maybe. Luke will kiss a lot of female frogs before he finds his princess, and he'll get his heart broken a few times along the way. That's life."

Mandy wiped her mouth with a napkin. "Have you ever gotten your heart broken?"

Zach nodded. "I've been lucky. It's only happened once."

"When was that?"

He thought carefully before replying. "Last night."

Her pale cheek bulging with a bite of hot dog, she stopped chewing to shoot a startled look at him. For an awful moment, Zach thought she might choke, but she collected herself, took a sip of root beer, and swallowed the food without mishap.

"Last night?" She gazed at him with a question in her lovely eyes. "Are you implying that I broke your heart?"

"I'm not implying it. I'm straight-out saying it. I'm in love with you."

Her eyes went bright. "Don't say that, Zach. I like you as a friend, but I—"

"Bullshit." Zach set aside his hot-dog tray and drink, no longer hungry. "You have feelings for me, Mandy. I can understand how that must frighten you, given your past, but please don't lie to me about it."

She dabbed at her lips again, then stared at the tray balanced on her knees. "All right, I admit it. I have feelings for you." She brought her head up. "I've never felt this way about anyone. But, as I tried to explain last night, the situation is impossible."

"Difficult, but not impossible." Zach got up to dispose of his lunch. The trash can flap made a clicking sound as it swung back and forth. "We'll take it one step at a time."

She parted her lips to reply, but Luke and Laurie returned just then. "Thanks for lunch, Mr. Harrigan," the girl said. "It's been fun. I wish I didn't have to go, but my mom has a hair appointment, and I promised to babysit my little brother." She bent to pat Rosebud's head. Then she touched Luke's arm. "Bye, Luke. I'll call, okay?" She patted her cell phone, clipped to the pocket of her jeans. "I've got your number."

Luke smiled. "I'll look forward to hearing from you. Bye, Laurie."

As the girl walked away, Zach studied the expression

of hope and trepidation on Luke's face. "She wants to go to a movie. Hello? I'm blind as a bat."

Zach couldn't help but laugh. "Luke, you have a lot to learn. When you take a girl to the movies, you aren't necessarily there to watch the show."

"*Zach!*" Mandy scolded. "Don't tell him stuff like that."

Zach grinned at Mandy. "He's nineteen."

"So you think she's hoping I'll kiss her?" Luke asked, as eager as a puppy.

Zach rolled his eyes at Mandy. To Luke, he said, "I think she'll probably be pretty disappointed if you don't."

Mandy sat back and closed her eyes, clearly disapproving of the conversation. As far as Zach was concerned, that was her deal. In every way but one, her brother was physically normal, and it was high time the kid started acting like it.

Mandy felt as if she'd stepped over the edge of a cliff and was plunging, end over end, in a crazy free fall. She'd barely slept a wink last night, lecturing herself on the follies of loving Zach Harrigan, but it hadn't done a bit of good. She was totally bonkers over him, even when he was telling Luke stuff she would have preferred he not know. Mandy had never gone to the movies with a boy when she was a teenager. Her father hadn't allowed her to date, and after she went into foster care, she had never gotten to stay at one school long enough to have a boyfriend. Did kids really go to the theater and kiss?

Her mind turned traitorous. What would it be like to go to a movie with Zach? Did adults kiss during a movie, too? Her feelings for him scared her half to death. He was so handsome and so nice and just so . . . *everything*. When he'd kissed her last night . . . Well, she'd never dreamed in a million years that anyone could make her feel like that. Her knees had felt as if they turned to water, her heart had pounded, and for a horrible second, she'd felt so light-headed she was afraid she might faint.

She'd been honest with Zach. Marriage was taboo for her. She could never go there. And it was also true that having an intimate relationship with a man outside of marriage wasn't really her style. But, oh, man, he tempted her to change her mind. She was twenty-eight years old. Until last night, she'd never been properly kissed. Was it so wrong of her to entertain the notion of saying to heck with her morals and just going for it? She wouldn't be making any permanent commitment that way. When it was over, she could just walk, no strings attached. Zach would have no hold over her. Besides, she was probably the only twenty-eight-year-old virgin on the face of the planet. If she told the Smithsonian, they'd put her on exhibit.

Sweat broke out on her forehead. She opened her eyes to stare stupidly at the food perched on her lap, only vaguely aware of Zach and Luke's conversation. Was she actually considering having an affair? *Yes.* Was it so wrong of her to want what other women took for granted? Just once, Mandy wanted to be held in strong arms and pretend for a while that the sweet lies whispered in her ear were true. If she was ever going to experience that, she wanted Zach to be the man holding her.

"Earth to Mandy."

Zach's voice jerked her back to the moment. She stood to toss her trash into the receptacle. "Sorry. I was woolgathering."

As she turned back toward the bench, Zach patted the spot between him and Luke. "It's time for that little talk now," he said, his tone serious, almost glum. "I have something I need to tell both of you."

When she sat again, Zach didn't immediately speak. He turned his watch on his wrist, scratched beside his nose, repositioned his hat, and then tugged on his earlobe. "I'm not sure how to say this." Expelling air, he slumped on the bench and cursed under his breath. "It's really, *really* difficult for me to get out."

Mandy's heart caught. Was he about to tell them that someone else had offered a huge amount of money for Rosebud? Then an even worse thought came to her: What if the little horse was sick with leukemia or something that wasn't presently obvious?

"You're scaring me, Zach. Whatever it is, just say it and put me out of my misery."

He pinched the bridge of his nose, coughed, then stared off across the park. "Night before last, you told me about the evening your mom disappeared."

"Yes. What about it?"

He turned to settle a coffee-dark gaze on her. "It doesn't add up for me, Mandy. None of it. It doesn't make sense."

Her heart started to beat faster. "What do you mean?"

"How many times, rough estimate, would you say that your mom sent you to hide in the closet while she stayed downstairs and let your father beat the hell out of her?"

Mandy tried to think. "It happened night after night. A lot of times. I'm not following where you're going with this."

"Here's where I'm going. She loved you and Luke so much that she sacrificed herself on a daily basis to protect you." He gestured with one hand. "I'll never understand why she didn't seek help. Even back then, they had women's shelters. But that's beside the point, and I can only assume she must have had her reasons."

"Money was part of it," Mandy said faintly. "She had no training. She told me more than once that she'd leave him in a heartbeat if she thought she could support us. And Dad also threatened to take us away from her if she dared to divorce him. He had buckets of cash from his grandparents, a fancy lawyer always on retainer, and he was an important man in Crystal Falls. She was afraid a judge would rule in his favor."

Zach waved his hand again. "Whatever. The fact is, she *didn't* leave. She stayed, and she was as good a mother as she could be under the circumstances. She definitely did her best to keep you and Luke safe. That tells me a lot. It doesn't paint a picture of a woman who would ever willingly abandon her children. So what happened that night to alter her character so greatly that she suddenly decided to leave?"

Mandy tried to take a deep breath, but her lungs hitched. "Nothing," she murmured.

Zach held up a finger. "Oh, but one thing did happen that night, Mandy. She finally gathered the courage to stand up for herself. She threatened to leave the bastard. And right after that, everything went quiet downstairs. Right?"

Mandy felt as if she were suffocating. She stared stupidly at Zach, wanting to clamp her hands over her ears.

"The next morning, she was gone. Suitcase, clothing, personal effects, gone, and"—he held up a finger again— "she left no note. Doesn't that strike you as being a little strange? Even stranger, before a week passed, your father poured a thick slab of concrete in the backyard and weighted it down with several thousand pounds of brick."

Mandy was on her feet before she even realized she'd moved. "No," she whispered. *"No."* She felt as if all the blood in her veins had drained out through the bottoms of her feet. "That's enough, Zach." She reached out to grab something, *anything*, for balance, but her hand met with air. "That's not how it went. She just left. He pushed her too far, and something inside of her snapped. She just ran away."

He drew off his hat and stared into the bowl. As he set the Stetson back on his head, he met and held her gaze. "Is that the deal here, Mandy? You didn't go down to check on her after the fracas, so you're afraid to think about any other possibility?"

"What are you saying?" Luke asked. "That our dad might've *killed* our mother?"

Mandy made fists in her hair. There was a searing pain in her belly, as if claws were ripping at her internal organs. Little black spots danced before her eyes. She felt Zach's big hands lock like manacles over her shoulders.

"Deep breaths, sweetheart. Come on. Deep breaths. Don't pass out on me."

Mandy couldn't have taken a deep breath to save her soul. "Stop!" she flung at him. "Shut up, Zach. Just shut up! *Stop!*"

"I can't," he whispered. "If it went down the way I believe it did, honey, it wasn't your fault, it wasn't Luke's fault, and it wasn't your mother's fault. The blame rests on one individual."

Mandy shook her head, her vision so distorted by tears and spots that she couldn't see his face. "No. Please, Zach, no. That can't be what happened. I stayed upstairs with Luke. I didn't go down to see if she was all right. I loved her so much! Don't you see? That isn't how it happened."

"You were forbidden to go downstairs, and thank God you didn't," Zach said softly. "Mandy, he killed her. I'm almost positive of it. And if you'd gone down to check on her, he might have killed you, too."

Chapter Seventeen

Mandy stared stupidly at Zach, trying to stop shaking and wrap her mind around what he was saying. Then, like a bone-chilling fog, the reality of it crept into her brain. In all these years it hadn't occurred to her, not once. Why? She'd always known her father had few limits when he went into a rage. Now that she'd heard the words spoken, she could easily imagine him killing his wife. He'd come close so many times that Mandy had begged her mom to leave before it was too late, and years later, when Tobin had broken into Mandy's apartment, she'd been lucky to escape with her life.

"But, Zach, if he killed her, what did he do with her body?" Luke asked. "Bodies are usually discovered sooner or later. Surely Mom's would have turned up by now."

Zach firmed his grip on Mandy's shoulders. "I think he buried her in the backyard and then brought in a cement truck to cover up the evidence."

It was a good thing Zach had hold of Mandy, because this time she truly did almost faint. "No. Dear God, no. Not even Dad would do something that despicable. Not *there*. He made me bury Dog out there, right at the edge of the patio in the flower bed."

"Dog?" Zach echoed.

"Dog was a Doberman our father bought," Luke inserted. "He'd been raised in a kennel and trained to be a guard dog. Dad was all hot on him at first, but then he ignored him and never even gave him a name. Mandy was afraid to name him herself for fear Dad would get pissed, so we just called him Dog."

"And Dog is buried out there near that slab?"

Mandy nodded. Her voice rang tinny in her ears as she explained. "Dog had never been indoors until we got him, and all the strange noises made him go berserk. For Luke's seventh birthday, I bought him a fire engine that had moving parts and a siren. When Luke pressed the button to make the siren wail, Dog went nuts and attacked the toy. In the process, he bit Luke's hand. When our father got home that night, he took Dog outside and shot him." She weaved on her feet. Zach tightened his hold on her shoulders. "I begged him not to do it. I begged him. But he wouldn't listen. Luke is terrified of dogs to this day."

"No wonder that entertainment area feels like a cemetery to me," Zach said softly. "It actually *is*."

Mandy frowned up at him. "You've been there?"

Zach led her back to the bench. "You need to sit before you topple like a ninepin."

Mandy did as he suggested and waited for him to take a seat beside her before pressing him to go on. "When were you in our backyard?"

"Last night and this morning." He looked deeply into her eyes. "I leased the place. I'm going to rip up that slab and do some digging. If I'm right, and your mother's remains are there, it's only fair that I give you both the option of being there."

"Holy shit, dude." Luke's voice rang shrill. "I can buy that Dad might have killed our mom, but why would he bury her in our own backyard? Who'd be that stupid? What if the cops had gotten suspicious? He'd have been better off burying her miles from our house out in the woods somewhere."

Zach shook his head. "The cops weren't suspicious,

and bodies in wilderness areas are usually unearthed by animals. The skeletal remains are stumbled upon later by unsuspecting hikers or hunters. Remember the Green River Killer? They're still finding bones. Burying her in the yard under thick cement was the smarter choice."

Mandy rubbed her arms. Her heart labored as if there were nothing left in her veins to pump. A cold sweat filmed her body, making her sweatshirt and jeans stick to her skin. "And later, he ordered me to bury Dog only a few feet away. What kind of man would have so little respect for another human being? His own *wife*, the mother of his children." Even as she spat the words, she knew the answer to her own question. Her father was exactly that kind of man. Zach echoed her thoughts.

"I don't think Tobin Pajeck understands the meaning of the word *respect*. Particularly not when it came to his wife and kids."

Mandy remembered how angry she'd been with her father for revamping the backyard so soon after her mother left. No tears, no apparent sorrow. Her dad had just moved on with his life. At the time, Mandy had been so young and her grief so all-consuming that she'd been unable to see past it. Now she could look back with more clarity. She didn't want to believe her dad might have done something so despicable, but she knew, deep in her heart, that he might have.

"I almost started the demolition without telling you," Zach confessed. "But I decided that would be wrong. So here I am, issuing an invitation, if you can call it that. Do you want to be there? I know it'll be difficult for both of you, especially if I find your mother's . . . well . . . if she's there. But in my opinion, never knowing for certain what happened that night would be even worse. Maybe I'm wrong and Sharyn Pajeck is alive and well somewhere. But what if she isn't?"

Mandy thought back to that night, the memories hitting her hard and fast. Her father had been yelling, and she'd been able to hear the sound of his fists connecting with flesh. Her mother had sobbed, begging him to stop. Then, after she threatened to leave, there had come a sudden and eerie silence. Mandy had almost disobeyed Sharyn by going downstairs to check on her, but she'd had Luke to think about. What if her brother had followed her? If Luke had gotten hurt, Mandy would never have forgiven herself. So she'd stayed in the closet as she'd been told to do.

"Oh, God," she whispered. "I don't want to believe you, Zach, but it all makes sense." She sent him a stricken look. "You're actually going to tear up the slab?"

"Yes. I've already rented the jackhammer and have my tools over there. I'm starting tomorrow morning. If you and Luke want to be there, I'll drop by and pick you up."

Mandy didn't know what she wanted. "I need some time to think about it."

Luke spoke up. "I'd only get in the way if I went. I couldn't help much, and I don't have any desire to go there. All I have are bad memories of that place." He tipped his head. "If Mandy decides to go, can Rosebud spend the day with me?"

"Sure," Zach replied. "I see no reason why she can't."

After Zach walked them home and departed, Mandy lay down for a couple of hours. She'd hoped to sleep, but her brain kept fast-forwarding to tomorrow and reversing into the past like a tape player gone mad. Memories of her mother's last night churned in her mind, and no matter how many times she tried to tell herself differently, her gut told her Zach was right. Her father had killed her mother. Maybe her mother wasn't buried under the concrete slab in the backyard. But even so, her father had murdered her. The horrible fight, the screaming, and then that sudden, absolute silence. Why, oh, why hadn't she gone downstairs? Maybe she could have saved her mom.

When she finally gave up on resting, Mandy went to the kitchen. Luke sat at the table, wolfing down a PB and J sandwich, his mouth ringed with white from the glass of milk at his elbow. Mandy wondered how he could possibly eat.

As if he guessed her thoughts, he said, "Sorry, Mands. I don't mean to seem callous. It's just . . . well, I can't remember Mom real well anymore. I loved her. I loved her a lot. And I can still remember how good it felt when she hugged me. But in my mind, she's more like a character in a bedtime story now than a real person."

Mandy sank down onto a chair. "I remember her very well."

Luke pushed aside his plate. "Sure, you would. You're older. I know this is tough for you. Do you think Zach's right, and the old man murdered her?"

Mandy smoothed the tablecloth, thinking as she did that it would be nice if life's wrinkles could be dealt with as easily. "Yes," she finally answered. "It tears me up, but I think he did, Luke. What really gets to me is that I did nothing to help her."

"You heard Zach. If you'd gone downstairs, the bastard might have killed you, too." He slumped on the chair. "I can't believe we're talking about this. It's like discussing a plot in a book. Shit like this doesn't happen to normal people."

"When has our family ever been normal?"

Luke considered the question. "We're getting close to normal now, aren't we?"

Mandy released a tremulous breath. "We're getting there. At least, we were."

"You're going tomorrow, aren't you?"

Mandy forced herself to stop rubbing her hands

over the tablecloth. "Yes. It's something I need to do. If she's—" Her voice caught and went squeaky. "If she's under that slab, I feel obligated to be there."

"This has really hit you hard."

"Like a train," Mandy admitted. Her eyes burned, and so did her throat. "Do you know how many times I've told myself I hated her? How many times I refused to forgive her for leaving us? Up until the night she left, she was the best mom ever. She loved us. She cared for us. And in the end, all of that counted for nothing with me. I should have known she would never leave us if she could help it."

"Don't be too hard on yourself, Mandy. I've had all the same feelings. If he killed her, we didn't know it. Dad led us to think she just up and left, and you did hear her say she was going to leave him. It was natural for us to feel angry and hate her a little."

Mandy nodded, but her brother's words failed to ease the ache of guilt deep inside her. Wearily she pushed to her feet and went to the phone stand. She rang Zach's cell. He answered so quickly she wondered if he'd been waiting for her call.

"Hey," he said, his voice husky and filled with warmth. "How you doing?"

Mandy saw no point in pretending that his suspicions hadn't left her reeling. "Better. I, um . . . well, I've thought about it, Zach, and I would like to be there tomorrow."

"I've been thinking, too," he replied. "Chances are I'll mostly be tearing down the brick stuff. I won't get to the slab until the following day. You could stay home until—"

"No. When the first brick is knocked loose, I want to be there." Mandy couldn't articulate her feelings. She just knew she needed to be on-site the entire while. "What time will you pick me up?"

"You okay with seven thirty? Most of the neighbors will be up and about by eight. The noise shouldn't bother them too much then, and I'd like to get a fairly early start."

Mandy tightened her hold on the phone. "I'll be ready."

Silence. She could hear only his breathing. As irrational as it was, she wished he were there beside her, that she could reach out and grab hold of his hand.

"You okay?" he asked softly.

"Come on, Zach, what do you think? I've never been less okay in my life. I think she could be under that slab, and I can't help but ask myself why it never once occurred to me. I just never dreamed that he'd do something so horrible, I guess."

"You were a child, Mandy. Give yourself a break."

She closed her eyes. "I need to go. I'll see you in the morning."

"Wait! Don't hang up. You sound pretty rocky. If you need me tonight, just call, all right? I can be there in thirty minutes, twenty-five if I push it."

Mandy was tempted to tell him she needed him right now. Instead, she said, "I've got your numbers programmed in. Thanks for offering."

They said good-bye. After Zach hung up, Mandy stood with the phone still pressed to her ear, reluctant to break the connection at her end. What was happening to her? She was twenty-eight and had been on her own for more than a decade. In all that time, she'd never needed anyone, and now, suddenly, she had an almost desperate yearning for Zach. She wanted to feel the warmth of his hand, hear the rumble of his voice, and have his strong arms around her.

"Mandy?" Luke said. "Talk to me. Don't hold it all in."

Mandy returned the phone to its recharging base. "I'm wondering if this is how Alice felt after going down the rabbit hole. Nothing seems real."

*   *   *

The next morning, Zach dropped Rosebud off at precisely seven thirty. He and Mandy arrived at Montrose Place well before eight. She hadn't stepped foot on the property in eleven years, and a shiver of dread moved through her when Zach parked at the curb. She forced herself to look at the house. She'd left it behind so long ago. Now she had cause to wonder if her mother hadn't remained there all this time.

"No hurry," Zach said. "I know this has to be a hard moment for you."

Mandy had always prided herself on burying her emotions deep and showing a brave face to the world, but ever since Zach had dropped that bomb on her yesterday, maintaining control was more difficult. It felt as if spiders were skittering under her skin.

"I'm fine," she told him, but as hard as she tried to keep her voice steady, it wobbled treacherously. "It's only boards and plaster, a place where I grew up. I've moved on."

"Do we ever really move on, Mandy?"

At the question, she turned to look at him. His burnished face was solemn and cast into shadow by his hat, but she could still see the ache of sympathy in his dark eyes. She wanted so badly to grab hold of his hand, to cling to him like a frightened child. *Madness*. She was a full-grown woman.

He reached out to trail a work-hardened fingertip along her cheekbone. "I don't think we can ever move on until we lay the past to rest."

She ached to turn her cheek into his palm, but something within her, stupid pride or possibly fear of loving him, made her draw away. "I'm ready," she said. "We can't accomplish anything here in the car, and there's a lot of work to do."

She opened her door and forced herself to climb out onto the untended grass median between the street and the now-cracked sidewalk. Staring at the double front doors of the house, she tried to remember a single time during her childhood when she'd felt truly happy to come home from school. Even before her mother left, she'd always stopped at the steps, dreading what the night would bring.

The sound of Zach's door closing made her jerk. He came to stand beside her. "Would you like to go inside?"

That was the last thing she wanted to do. "Yes, I think I should."

He shut her door and placed a supporting hand on her arm. The warmth of his touch seeped through the sleeve of her sweatshirt. "All right, let's take a quick tour."

Mandy forced herself to keep pace with him as they traversed the walkway to the porch. When he slid the key into the lock, her heart began to slog in her chest like a rubber ball bouncing over tacky flypaper. She felt as if she might vomit.

As the door swung inward, Zach locked a hard arm around her shoulders. "You don't have to do this."

"Yes. According to Luke, we have to face our demons. This house is one of mine."

She was relieved when Zach kept his arm around her as they stepped into the foyer. "Don't close the door," she whispered. As irrational as it was, she needed it left open for escape. "It's musty," she said, grabbing at the first excuse she could think of.

He moved his hand over her arm, stroking and squeezing, as he guided her through the archway to their right into the living room. It stood empty. She'd remembered it all these years as it had once been, perfectly appointed with expensive furniture and Oriental rugs on the gleaming hardwood floors. Now the floors bore scuff marks, and stains on one wall showed evidence of past leakage from the bathroom above. For some reason, seeing it this way, abandoned and in disrepair, released the vise that had been squeezing her stomach. She dragged in a bracing breath.

"It's so different. The same, but not the same."

"A lot of people have probably lived here since your father sold the place."

All Mandy picked up on were her memories, few of them pleasant. On the lower level, they went from room to room and then made their way upstairs. Zach never withdrew his arm from around her until they came upon the closet where she'd once hidden with Luke. She pulled away from him then, drawn toward the dark shadows within, memories ricocheting inside her mind like pebbles shot from a scattergun.

She placed a hand on the doorframe and leaned around to look inside. "Oh, God," she whispered. "Being here brings it back as if it all happened only yesterday."

"It didn't, though. It happened a long time ago, and your father will never harm anyone again."

At the certainty in his voice, Mandy turned to look at him. "If he gets out of prison, he will. I don't think he's capable of restraining himself."

"He won't get out of prison," Zach replied. "If we find what I think we will under that cement slab, he'll be locked up until his dying day, or he'll have an up-close-and-personal experience with a lethal-injection needle."

Mandy was starting to feel better. Less shaken, stronger. It was as if Zach radiated some kind of energy that soothed all her raw nerve endings. "A lethal injection would be too easy. I'd rather see him stay in prison. Let him think about it for the rest of his life."

Zach grinned, but the gesture didn't warm his eyes. "There you go. I don't believe in capital punishment, but for him, I could make an exception. Either way, he'll pay."

Mandy was ready to go outside. Back downstairs, she paused by the kitchen range, remembering that afternoon when the jar exploded. Thanks to Zach, Luke had absolved her, and because he had, she'd finally been able to forgive herself.

Once out in the backyard, Mandy went to stand at the edge of the patio. She couldn't bring herself to walk on its surface. At the moment, she couldn't remember why it was supposedly a bad thing to step on someone's grave. She knew only that she didn't want to commit the offense. Zach left to go get the cooler out of the car. He'd brought bagels, cream cheese, and orange juice for breakfast; sandwiches, chips, and soft drinks for lunch. While he was gone, she closed her eyes and cleared her mind, trying to sense her mother's presence. *Nothing.* Surely she would feel something.

Turning, she wandered around the yard and came upon the garden area, which had been turned into lawn. Even so, this section of the yard calmed her. As hard as she'd worked there every year, tending the plants, she'd found a measure of peace as well.

Zach returned, plopped the cooler on the overgrown grass, and grabbed a pick from the wheelbarrow. "May as well get started." He doffed his hat and arched a brow at her. "You want to take the first swing?"

Mandy did and reached for the pick handle. He held up a finger to forestall her and tugged a pair of gloves from where they'd been tucked over his belt. "Sam's. I figured you might want to help. The leather will protect your hands."

Mandy slipped them on. They fit her perfectly. "Thanks, Zach. I do want to help." She took the pick and forced herself to step onto the concrete slab. "Where do I start?"

"Wherever the hell you want."

Mandy had always detested that damned barbecue. Stepping over to the massive structure, she turned sideways to the pit, braced her feet wide apart, and swung with all her strength. The pick bounced back and almost nailed her on the head.

"Whoa!" Zach wrested the tool from her hands. "Let me get it started for you." When he swung, the pick

wedged deep into the mortar, and the top brick broke loose. Smiling grimly, he returned the tool to her. "There. Now you can finish it off."

Mandy did so, and the release of anger that had festered for so long within her felt magnificent. The brick fell to the cement at her feet. She bent to pick it up.

"Thank you," she said. "I don't have the strength to knock all of them loose, but it was important to me to take out the first one."

Zach nodded and accepted the pick. "If you really want to help, you can put the bricks in the wheelbarrow. We'll start a pile somewhere away from the demolition area."

Mandy set herself to that task while he concentrated on breaking the bricks apart. Maybe she needed a distraction, but she found herself watching the play of muscle under his shirt and jeans as he worked. He moved with precise, masculine power that was oddly graceful, making the job look easy. She'd felt the jolt upon impact clear up her arms, so she knew better. He was hitting that structure with incredible force.

By noon, the barbecue was flattened, Mandy's back had started to ache from all the lifting, and she was more than ready to break for lunch. They sat on the back porch off the laundry room to eat. Mandy had no appetite, but the orange soda tasted wonderful.

"You need to get something down besides that," Zach told her. "That's hard work you're doing, and the day is only half-over."

She stared at the cement slab. "I'm just not hungry."

"Could you eat if we went to a restaurant?"

"I don't know. Maybe."

He tossed his sandwich back in the cooler. "Let's go and find out."

The remainder of that day and the one that followed were among the most difficult of Mandy's life and passed in a blur. Being at her childhood home brought back so many memories. It was like slipping into the dark, shadowy horror of a nightmare.

Late the second day, Zach finished breaking apart the cement slab with the jackhammer. He helped her load the remaining chunks of concrete into the wheelbarrow and then wheeled it over to the dump pile, which had grown massive. Minutes later, when he grabbed the shovel that had been lying unused in the grass, he settled a questioning gaze on her.

"Sweetheart, it might be better if you wait in the car while I do this part."

Probably so, but when she looked at the damp, disturbed dirt, littered now with bits of broken concrete, she couldn't leave. If her mom was buried there, it seemed only right that one of her children should be present when her remains were exhumed. "I'm good," she said. "Just do it, Zach."

As he began digging, Mandy flinched every time the shovel blade rasped in the soil. When thirty minutes had passed, she started to relax, believing Zach might find nothing, and the coward in her sincerely hoped he didn't.

"Damn." He paused to wipe sweat from his brow with the sleeve of his shirt. "Maybe I was smoking crack. I'm not finding anything." Bareheaded, his hair glistening in the fading sunlight, he gave her a hangdog look. "I'm sorry, Mandy. I've put you through sheer hell, and it may have been for nothing."

"That's okay," she said as he resumed digging. "I'm relieved, actually. Maybe Dad didn't lie, and she just left us. Or maybe he buried her somewhere else. I—"

Zach's shovel blade struck something hard. He went still and then crouched to brush away the soil. When he'd cleared a foot-wide area and could see the surface of what he'd found, he said, "It looks like an old suitcase."

Mandy's legs went watery. She could remember standing in front of her mom's empty closet that long-ago morning. She clamped her arms around her ribs, watching as Zach straightened and began taking shallow bites with the shovel. When he had completely unearthed the suitcase, she squeezed her eyes closed, knowing what he would find next. The realization nearly took her to her knees.

The remainder of the excavation seemed to take forever. Zach lifted away only bits of dirt at a time. Mandy knew why he exercised such caution. He didn't want to disturb any evidence. Suddenly he stopped and stepped back, wiping his mouth with his shirtsleeve.

His voice shook. "Sweetheart, I think you should go sit on the front porch."

Mandy felt as if her feet had been glued to the ground. "Why?" she asked.

A muscle ticked in his lean cheek. "There's a faint odor coming up through the soil. I think I've found her."

Her stomach lurched.

"Please," he said. "There's no need for you to see this."

Mandy couldn't move. "I want to be here. I owe her that."

He sighed, tossed away the shovel, and crouched to brush away dirt with his gloved hands. Soon he unearthed something yellowish brown. It looked like a small piece of wood. Beside it lay a corroded ring. Mandy stared at it and then jerked as if someone had struck her. As encrusted as the piece of jewelry was, she recognized it. She'd saved her allowance to buy it for her mom's birthday. Sharyn Pajeck had never taken it off. Mandy's gaze went back to the small piece of wood. Only it wasn't wood, she realized now.

It was a finger bone.

Chapter Eighteen

Unprepared for Mandy's reaction, Zach had to lunge after her, snatch her into his arms, and hold her back as she ran toward the grave. Never had he seen anyone so pale. Her face had gone as white as a motel room towel. Her eyes, wide and unfocused with what he recognized as shock, implored him to turn loose of her.

"You can't, honey. If you touch anything, you might destroy evidence. You don't want your father to get away with this, do you?"

Her response was a high-pitched wail. Her legs buckled, and she went limp in his embrace. Zach clutched her firmly against him to keep her from falling.

"Mama!" The sobs that racked her slender body frightened Zach. They came from deep within her, sharp, tearing sounds born of grief and horror. "He *k-killed* her!" she cried. "That *m-monster*! He k-killed my m-mother!"

In that moment, Zach wished his hunch had been wrong. He'd hoped that finding Sharyn Pajeck would be hcaling for Mandy. How could he have been so stupid? He should never have given her the option of being here while he dug up the rotting corpse of the person she'd loved most in the world.

"She never stopped loving you and Luke," Zach whispered when she quieted a little. "And she didn't abandon you. Your father just lied about that to cover up what he'd done. She loved you, Mandy. With her dying breath, she loved you."

She went up on her tiptoes and hooked both arms around Zach's neck. He tightened his embrace, trying to absorb the spasms that still racked her slight frame. Her fingers dug into the back of his neck so hard he was sure her nails drew blood. In a tortured voice, she asked, "Oh, God, w-why didn't I go downstairs that night? I could have helped her, Zach. Instead I hid in a closet." She moaned and pounded a fist against his shoulder. He barely felt the blows, which were more a release of emotion than an attempt to inflict pain. "I hid in a closet!"

Zach ran his hands over her trembling back, up and down, up and down, trying to soothe her with his touch because words so often failed him. He had to give it a shot, though. Mandy needed answers—not the ones she was inventing in her guilt-ridden mind, but rational ones that would ease her pain.

"Sweetheart, it's a miracle you *didn't* go downstairs. He might have killed you, too. Why do you think your mother forbade you from being around him when he got like that? She knew what he was capable of."

"But ..." She sobbed, the sounds breaking Zach's heart. "She *needed* me."

"She may have needed help," Zach replied, groping frantically for the right words, "but she would never have wanted you to interfere, Mandy. She tried too hard to protect you and Luke. She knew why you didn't come down. You did what she wanted."

It was a moment before she could reply. "B-but he was killing her!" It was a half scream, and he heard the hysteria rising again. *Please, God, let me find the right words for once in my life*, he begged silently.

"That wasn't your fault," he told her firmly. "Your mother made her own choices, and your father made his. You and Luke had no say in any of it. We can only imagine what she went through or why she made the de-

cisions she did. The only absolute is that she loved you
and did the best she could at the time. She knew that
what was happening wasn't your fault."

Mandy pressed closer against him. With a jerk of her
shoulders, she said, "Mama was such a sw-sweet person.
She didn't deserve to be tr-treated that way."

"No one does." Zach realized he'd started sway-
ing back and forth. As a youth, he'd held his sister,
Sam, in his arms while she cried a few times, but never
had she wept over something this horrible. Mandy's
anguish—oh, God, his chest hurt as if he'd swallowed a
half dozen razor blades, and it was all he could do not
to sob himself. She spoke of how sweet her mother had
been? Mandy was the dear one, in Zach's opinion, and
he would have happily killed Tobin Pajeck for doing this
to her. "I'm sorry your mom had to go through something so awful." He searched for something more that
he might say. "It wasn't her fault, sweetheart, and it definitely wasn't yours. Your father is the one responsible.
Are you following what I'm saying?"

"I'm trying," she said shakily. "And I know you're
right. She would n-never have blamed me. It's just . . ."
Her voice trailed off.

He hugged her hard and let his lips graze the top of
her head lightly, so she wouldn't notice. "I know, honey.
I know."

When Mandy calmed down a bit more and regained
some of her composure, Zach led her around the house
to the front porch. Keeping one arm around her, he sat
with her on the steps and grabbed his cell phone. "I need
to call the cops," he told her.

She nodded, her expression dazed, her tear-swollen
eyes bleary and unfocused.

Zach made the call. It felt weird to be telling a dispatcher that he'd just exhumed the remains of a woman
who'd been murdered by her husband fifteen years ago.
At first the lady at the other end thought it was a prank

call. She was about to disconnect when Zach gave her his full name.

"Zach Harrigan, the horse trainer?"

"Yes," he replied. "And I'm not joking about the body. Don't send a bunch of blue shirts. We need some detectives who know what they're doing."

The woman's tone became brisk and businesslike. She asked for the address and told him she'd have someone there in five minutes. Zach was about to remind her that he didn't want rookie cops near the crime scene, but she ended the call before he could get the words out. He frowned at his phone.

"What?" Mandy asked in a dull, muted voice.

"I'm just worried she'll send yahoos who don't know what the hell they're doing."

Mandy bent forward to rest her forehead on her knees. "I can't believe it," she whispered. "My father made me bury Dog only a few feet away from my mother. Was it his idea of a sick joke? His way of showing how little respect he had for her?"

"I don't know, honey." It was all Zach could think to say.

"My mother worked like a slave for him. He never appreciated anything she did. That's why I'll never get married. I know how horrible it can turn out for the woman."

Zach said nothing. He just let her vent. His only hope was that learning the truth would eventually give her a sense of closure and set her free. Maybe in time, she would begin to realize that all marriages weren't made in hell.

Until then, Zach's life would be on hold. Mandy was the only woman in the world for him. He knew that for certain now. He would never feel this way about anyone else.

As promised, the police arrived in only a few minutes. *Blue shirts*. Zach didn't want to leave Mandy alone on the porch, but he felt compelled to accompany the officers to the backyard to make sure they destroyed no evidence. The cops surprised him. They stood back from the shallow grave, perused the fleshless bones Zach had unearthed, unmistakably those of a human hand, and then cordoned off the area.

Confident that the crime scene would remain intact, Zach retraced his steps to the front of the house. Two more men in uniform had arrived and stood at the steps, questioning Mandy. One, a redhead who looked to be in his early twenties, took notes while the older officer, a stocky fellow of about forty, conducted the interrogation. One look at Mandy's drawn expression had Zach shifting into fast gear. When he reached the porch, he sat beside her and looped an arm around her trembling shoulders.

"Go easy on her, Officer. That's her mother out back. This has been hard for her."

The older man acknowledged Zach's request with a slight inclination of his head. Just then, a green sedan pulled into the driveway. Two guys in gray suits climbed out. They had *homicide* written all over them. Before they reached the steps, the coroner's van pulled up at the curb behind Zach's SUV and the two bubble-tops. Zach got a sick, sinking sensation in his stomach. He hadn't envisioned all of this hoopla. It was going to turn into a media circus, and that was the last thing Mandy needed. Here came the mobile news unit of the local TV station, and he knew others would arrive shortly. A helicopter whirred overhead, zooming in low. Neighbors were starting to come out of their fancy homes, attracted by the commotion. Mandy was in no shape to field a bunch of questions, and he had a very bad feeling the police would probably grill her for hours. He almost wished he'd left this alone. Almost.

Before Zach knew it, Mandy was escorted to a police car for further questioning at the station. Zach wanted to go with her, but the redhead blocked his path.

"Sorry, sir. You can drive to the station and wait out front for her if you like, but you can't be with her while she's being questioned."

"Why?" Zach couldn't keep the edge of frustration out of his voice. "She's hanging on by a thread. Can you imagine how shaken up she is? All this will be easier for her if I'm there."

"Are you a relative?"

"I . . . No," Zach admitted. "But I'm a good friend."

"Not possible." The young man's blue eyes took on a determined glint. "Don't push it, Mr. Harrigan. We have to follow procedure."

Zach took that to mean he'd be cuffed and stuffed if he tried to get in the car. He'd been arrested a few times, and for Mandy he was willing to go through it again. But what good would that do? He'd end up cooling his heels in a cell, and she'd still have to go through the questioning alone.

"I don't get it," he told the cop. "It's not as if *she* killed her mother. Why put her through all this?"

"We aren't certain of that," the redhead replied.

"You aren't certain of what?" Zach snapped.

"That she's innocent of any wrongdoing. She lived in the house at the time. Her story is that her father did it, but she wouldn't be the first juvenile to kill a parent."

Zach couldn't believe his ears. What the frigging hell had this jerk been smoking? Shock coursed through him. As the redhead got into the police car, Zach stood there and stared in stunned disbelief as Mandy was driven away. His pulse started to slam. Those jackasses thought a thirteen-year-old girl had possibly killed her mother?

He swore under his breath and grabbed his cell phone. His dad answered on the second ring. Zach by-passed *hello*. "Dad, I need a lawyer, fast."

Frank never missed a beat. "What kind of lawyer?"

"A criminal lawyer." Zach spewed out the whole story, quickly bringing his dad up-to-date. "Those stupid cops think Mandy may have killed her mom. *Jesus, help me*. This is my fault. I'm afraid they're going to charge her with murder. Can you believe it?"

"They have to look at every possibility, son. They can't just take her word for it. It'll all come out in the wash."

Zach raked a hand through his hair. "I never should have touched that slab."

"Don't panic," Frank said firmly. "She's innocent. They'll find no evidence to prove otherwise. Her father is in prison for trying to kill her. It stands to reason that he'll be the prime suspect. As for a lawyer, I'll have to make a couple of calls."

Despite what his father said, Zach did feel panicky. "How long will it take you to find a top-notch attorney?"

"Well, son, that's a good question. Let me get back to you."

"I'll be at the station."

Frank replied, "As soon as I can, I'll meet you there."

Zach cut the connection and dialed Luke, who picked it up on the fifth ring.

"Luke? Listen up; we don't have much time. We found your mom. Mandy's at the police station for questioning, and they'll probably come get you, too, so be ready. Bring Rosebud; she'll be fine. I'm heading to the station right now."

Once he reached the station, Zach paced before a bank of metal-framed, green plastic chairs for more than an hour before he saw Luke and Rosebud, escorted by two cops, come in through the revolving front door. He got up at once and went over to Luke, who was pale and sweating but composed. "Hey, Luke."

"Oh . . . hi, Zach. They just want to ask me some questions. And they say it's okay for Rosebud to stay with me."

Zach patted him on the shoulder. "Okay. I'll be right here."

Zach paced and stewed and second-guessed himself for another forty-five minutes before his father finally arrived. Even dressed in ranch-issue chambray and denim with a dusty Stetson tipped low over his eyes, Frank Harrigan emanated power and authority as he strode across the gleaming tile floor.

"Thanks for coming, Dad," Zach said as he hugged his father. "I'm worried sick. Nobody'll tell me anything, and they won't let me see her. They hauled Luke in, too."

"Of course I came, and stop worrying. I won't let them lock up my future daughter-in-law or her brother."

"I never said—"

"You didn't need to. I heard it in your voice on the phone, and it's written all over your face now. You're in love with her."

Zach sank onto a chair, feeling as if all the starch had drained from his legs. Frank sat beside him. "The attorney is on his way. Fellow named Payne."

"Pain? What kind of name is that for a criminal lawyer?"

"Not that kind of pain." Frank's weathered brown face crinkled in a grin. "Calm down. He's the best. He'll have her out of here lickety-split."

Zach could only hope. His heart sank when the blond lawyer showed up in a red polo shirt, wrinkled Dockers, and mud-streaked golf shoes. As the man shook hands with Frank and Zach, he said, "Sorry. First round of the season. I was at the nineteenth hole having a couple of beers with my buddies when I got your call."

Frank clapped the man on the shoulder. "We appreciate your showin' up so fast. No apology necessary."

The attorney hefted his briefcase and smiled. "I'm not wearing my power suit, but I'll give it my best shot." He turned and headed for the front desk.

"The clothes don't make the man," Frank observed.

Zach wanted the guy to go home and suit up. Didn't his father understand the seriousness of the situation?

"Dad, that guy may be good but he looks more like a golf instructor than a criminal attorney," he said. "You sure he's the best?"

"Son," said Frank, the corners of his keen eyes creasing the way they always did when he was amused and trying not to show it, "you're a frigging mess. You're covered with dirt and you need a shower bad. Right now I'd say you look more like a construction laborer than a world-class horse trainer. Point made."

Frank sat down and tugged on Zach's shirtsleeve. "Take a load off. This is his bivouac. Let him do his stuff."

Zach flopped back down onto a chair. "I wish now that I'd left Sharyn Pajeck under that damned slab."

"You don't wish that. The woman was murdered. Someone has to pay for that."

"What if that someone is Mandy?"

"It won't be. Have a little faith."

By the time Mandy was released, she was so exhausted she could barely walk. Her legs had fallen asleep from sitting so long, and it was all she could do to move in a straight line. When she reached the front of the station, she saw Zach and Luke sitting side by side, with Rosebud pressed against Luke's knees. Zach leaped up from the chair and strode toward her. She'd never been so glad to see anyone in her life. She yearned to throw herself into his arms and beg him never to let go.

"They think I did it," she told him. "Nobody came right out and said so, but I could tell they suspect me."

Zach's father materialized, seemingly from out of nowhere. He rested a strong hand on Mandy's shoulder. "Don't worry about it. The attorney says that's par for the course in any murder investigation. They suspect everybody." Frank smiled at her. "He's a good lawyer. Your father's past record stands to implicate him. Payne will handle it."

"How much does he charge? I can't afford a lawyer."

She felt Zach's arm encircle her shoulders. "I've got you covered."

"But—"

"No buts. Consider it a loan. You can pay me back in installments." He gave her a jostle. "Come on, let's get out of here. Police stations give me the creeps."

Mandy hated the idea of depending on Zach to get her through the evening, but he didn't give her a choice, and she couldn't help but be glad. It had been a trying day that had gone from really bad to horrible. The police suspected her of murder. Every time she thought about it, her stomach clenched and she broke out in a sweat. The evidence at the grave site had been compromised over time. What if forensic science couldn't prove her father had committed the crime? She was just thankful that Detective Randolph had made it clear that they didn't suspect her brother.

"Don't even go there," Zach said as he drove her and Luke home. "The evidence may be old, but they should still be able to determine the cause of death, and I'm guessing it was violent in nature. Chances are, once they determine the cause, they'll conclude that a small thirteen-year-old girl wouldn't have had the strength to do it."

That comforted Mandy. Darkness had descended, and only brief flashes of light from street lamps and other vehicles illuminated the interior of the car. Luke sat in back, shoulders forward so he could attend the conversation. Mandy worried that he wasn't wearing a seat belt, but before the thought could take root, others bounced in. She settled a grateful gaze on Zach's sharp profile, which was washed with a green glow from the dash. She wasn't sure when it had happened, but he had become her rock.

"I'm terrible. Mama was murdered, and all I can think about is what may happen to me."

"You aren't terrible. Your mom's been gone for fifteen years. You still have a life to live. When the cops start asking questions, leading you to think you're a suspect, it's normal to feel alarmed. It's all just routine, though. It's their job to suspect everyone."

Mandy sighed. "I am so tired, but my brain won't shut down."

Zach squeezed her hand. "I'm here. No worries. Let me handle everything. Okay?"

Mandy groaned. She felt too exhausted to move. All she wanted was to get home and rest. Luke answered for both of them. "Okay, Zach. Thanks."

Once at Mandy's place, Zach sat with them at the kitchen table. Mandy looked ready to fall off her chair and do a face-plant on the floor. In the yellowish glow of the ceiling light, Luke looked young and vulnerable, his expression going from incredulous to stricken. But he was a tough kid, and he rallied quickly.

"It doesn't surprise me that he killed her," Luke said. "He almost killed you once, Mandy." He groped for his sister's hand. "I'm so sorry, sis. This has to be rough for you. I can't really remember Mom very well. You can look at pictures of her and stuff. I think that probably helps to keep her fresh in your mind. For me, it isn't that way."

"I have precious few pictures of her," Mandy informed him. "I had time to grab only one family album when they removed us from the house that day."

Zach glanced worriedly at Rosebud. He'd brought her only enough food for the morning and afternoon, and she'd been at the station for hours. He needed to take her home. *Problem.* He wasn't about to leave Mandy. She'd weathered the first storm, but now the reality of it was going to start sinking in. Unless he missed his guess, she'd fall apart again before the night was over, and if she did, he wanted to be with her.

"He's going to pay," Luke said angrily. "I hope the old bastard rots in prison for the rest of his life."

Zach could well understand Luke's rage, but before the young man went off on a long rant, Zach wanted to campaign for a change of venue. "We have the rest of the evening to talk," he said. "I'm thinking we should all go to my place. Mandy hasn't eaten a bite today, and Rosebud has no more food here. I'll throw together some dinner. You two can crash at the ranch tonight."

"Oh, I don't think that's necessary," Mandy protested. "I'm really not that hungry, and—"

"Mands," Luke broke in, "for once in your life, shut up and go with the flow. You're upset. Zach is nervous about leaving you. Right, Zach?"

Zach could have hugged the kid. "I just don't think this is a good night for the two of you to be alone. At times like this, it's good to have friends around."

"I vote that we go to the ranch," Luke told his sister. "Zach can bring us home tomorrow. What harm can it do?"

"We'd have to pack overnight cases. I'm exhausted. I'd rather just stay here."

"Mandy," Zach inserted, "you've eaten absolutely nothing all day and very little yesterday. If I leave you here, you won't make a sandwich. You'll just do without and possibly make yourself sick."

"I'll be fine."

Luke pushed up from his chair and made for his bedroom. "I'm packing." At the door, he stopped. Not turning around to address his sister, he said, "If you don't gather some stuff, I'll do it for you. If you want to go out there with holey underwear, liniment instead of toothpaste, and the wrong nightclothes, fine, but we're going with Zach."

"That isn't for you to decide," Mandy objected.

"Yeah, well, I'm making the decision anyway," Luke

retorted. "Neither of us should be alone tonight, especially not you."

Rosebud followed Luke into the bedroom. At any other time, the mini's unswerving devotion to her new human friend would have made Zach smile. He settled a concerned gaze on Mandy's pale face instead.

"If you're bent on staying here, I'll take Rosebud home and come back," he told her.

"I'm not helpless. Today has been rough. I admit it. But I'll be fine here with Luke."

"Luke wants to go with me."

She huffed under her breath and pushed to her feet, weaving like a drunk until she caught her balance. Zach almost shot up from his chair to grab her arm.

"All right, fine. I'll pack some things," she said over her shoulder. "But I think it's silly for us to go out there when we'd be perfectly okay staying right here."

She was about to collapse. If she wanted to call that "perfectly okay," he wouldn't argue as long as she went with him to the ranch so he could keep an eye on her. Zach knew a breakdown was coming. As strong as she was, she'd been through hell, and a dozen different emotions were going to start pummeling her. Grief, guilt, and what-ifs always reared their ugly heads after the first shock wore off. And did she really think tomorrow would be easier?

As Mandy tossed stuff into a satchel she'd set on the bed, she struggled to keep her thoughts straight. She ended up with two nightshirts, had to return to the bathroom for her toothbrush and moisturizer, which she'd set out on the vanity, and then stood over the bag, trying to think what she should take to wear in the morning.

Zach appeared and rifled through the bag. "You'll need fresh underwear."

He began opening her drawers. Mandy didn't have

the energy to object. He returned with a pair of her panties in one fist and a pair of jeans and a knit top tucked under his other arm. "You want a fresh bra? You worked up a sweat today."

A bra? Were they really having this conversation? She'd never discussed her undergarments with a man, and she didn't want to start now. Zach tossed what he'd collected into the satchel and began fishing through her underwear again. She kept everything in neat piles. He was scooping and dropping garments like a man sorting through beans to find rocks.

He turned, dangling a lacy bra from his forefinger. "You like this one?"

Mandy tried to focus. What was to like or not like about a bra?

"Sam has favorites and standbys. You want this one or another one?"

"That one will be fine."

He returned to the bed and shoved the bra inside her satchel. Mandy noticed that her knees came even with the top edge of the mattress and his were several inches higher. Why her brain got stuck on that, she didn't know, but suddenly his knees became her only focus.

He caught her staring. "What?" He glanced down and checked to make sure his fly was zipped. "Is something wrong?"

Everything was wrong. She'd just found out her mom had been brutally murdered, and all she could think about were Zach's knees. "It's nothing." She forced her gaze up and found herself staring with the same intensity at a button on his shirt. Her brain felt as if someone had zapped it with a hot wire. "I just don't seem to be tracking very well."

He closed the bag, lifted it in one hand, and grasped her arm. "That's why I'm here, honey, to do the tracking for you."

Luke was waiting for them in the kitchen. A bag similar to Mandy's sat on the floor near his feet. Rosebud stood at his side. "I'm ready," he said.

The next thing Mandy knew, Zach was helping her into her parka. Her arms felt like overcooked fettuccini, limp and unresponsive. She tried to stick one into a jacket sleeve, missed the hole, and aimed again. Zach finally took over, got her into the coat, and zipped it up. Then she was in the SUV with no memory of having walked there. Luke sat in back so he could reach over the seat to pet Rosebud, who rode in the cargo area.

Mandy tried to relax during the drive, but as exhausted as she was, her nerve endings seemed to be electrified, a hum of tension zinging through her body. The thirty-minute ride passed quickly. As bleary as her vision was, she knew they'd reached the ranch when the SUV started jolting over the rutted road.

"I need to grade this damned thing," Zach said. "These potholes are getting deep enough to swallow a Volkswagen."

Zach was growing truly concerned about Mandy. He'd never seen her like this. Come to think of it, he couldn't recall ever having seen anyone in this shape. Was it shock? She seemed to be off somewhere in another dimension, not hearing half of what was said to her, staring blankly at stuff, and looking ... hell, the best way he could describe it was bloodless and limp. He needed to get some food into her. And maybe he should call a doctor. She'd been through a lot today. A sedative might level her out.

When they'd all exited the car, Luke asked if he could take Rosebud for her potty run. Zach considered the request and vetoed it. "Sorry, partner, it's dark."

"Can't Rosebud see well in the dark?"

"Well, yes, she has reflective retinas that give her great night vision, but—" Zach broke off, getting Luke's point before he made it. "Okay. Go for it," he said reluctantly.

It was very dark in the countryside after the sun went down. It was difficult for Zach to wrap his mind around the fact that Luke could navigate the ranch proper just as easily now as he did in broad daylight. "I'll get Mandy settled and then help Rosebud up the steps."

Zach got Mandy into the house. *Literally*. She moved like a robot that needed a recharge. He deposited her on a chair, gazed down at her white face, and then whipped out his cell phone to call the Harrigan family physician. He got the answering service. Doc was out of town and another doctor was standing in. Mandy wasn't one of Doc's regular patients, and the guy on call refused to see her, an infuriating turn of events Zach would address later. Next he called the ER and got a nurse with a voice so nasal, she sounded as if she had a clothespin clipped over her nose. She was no help. If Zach felt his friend was in shock, she recommended that he bring her in.

Sighing, Zach broke the connection. After studying the exhausted slump of Mandy's shoulders, he decided a three-hour stint in the ER waiting room and God only knew how long in a treatment cubicle was *not* what she needed right now. Zach speed-dialed Sam's house.

Tucker, often on call, answered on the second ring. "Hey, Zach, I hear you had quite an unusual day."

Zach stepped into the living room so Mandy wouldn't overhear the conversation—not that he believed she was connecting with the world around her at the moment. He quickly explained his reason for calling.

Tucker groaned. "I don't treat people, Zach. I understand that she's been through a terrible ordeal, and I'd love to help, but there's not really anything I can do."

"I just hate to make her sit in the ER waiting room for hours. She's been through enough for one day. Do you have any sedatives that are safe for humans?"

"I do, but I'm not going to risk my license by giving her any. I'm sorry, but if she had a reaction, it'd be my ass on the line. We're talking a controlled substance."

Zach made a fist in his hair. "What can I do for her, then?"

Tucker huffed softly. "Well, if it were Sam, I'd give her a couple of stiff drinks and screw her brains out. No matter how upset she is, that always puts her out like a light."

Zach rested his shoulder blades against the wall. "I hear you, but the second part won't fly. Mandy and I haven't taken our relationship to that level yet."

"Damn, man, you're slipping. I thought you took every relationship to that level."

"Not anymore, and even if I did, I wouldn't with Mandy. She's different."

Tucker fell silent for a moment. "Uh-oh. Sounds serious."

"It is—for me, at least."

"Don't get your heart broken, partner."

The warning came too late. Zach was already in too deep to wade back out. He thanked his brother-in-law for the advice and broke the connection. When he turned to go back to the kitchen, he stiffened in surprise to see Luke and Rosebud standing in the archway.

"How did you get back in the house?" he asked.

Luke grinned broadly. "I just let her bring me in. She did awesome."

Zach settled a bewildered gaze on his horse. "She went up the steps?"

"And cued me to go up them," Luke informed him.

"I'll be." Zach crouched in front of the mini. "Have you been playing me, girlfriend?"

Rosebud met his gaze with innocent bewilderment, but Zach wasn't fooled. When had the little stinker mastered steps? Maybe she liked the extra attention Zach gave her whenever they went up and down a flight.

Luke signaled the mini to return to the kitchen. He stood near Mandy, his head angled, his expression concerned. "Mands?"

"What?" she asked hollowly.

Luke said to Zach, "She doesn't sound so good."

Zach agreed and stepped to his liquor cupboard to get the bottle of Jack Daniel's. Exhausting Mandy with lovemaking might be out of the question, but he could definitely relax her with a couple of drinks. *Decaffeinated Irish coffee, coming right up.* While he added water to the reservoir and ground the decaf beans, Luke fumbled with Rosebud's guiding gear to get it off. Zach almost went to help but then decided against it. Luke might take longer to accomplish the task, but he'd get it done, and Zach sensed it might be time to start backing off. The young man and the little horse were nearly inseparable now. Rosebud still wasn't completely trained, but she was getting close. She and Luke had to start figuring it out by themselves.

Mandy wanted nothing to do with the eggs, bacon, and toast that Zach set in front of her. She felt separated from everything by a foggy wall, and on her side, thoughts and feelings were slamming through her like fists.

"If you can't eat, at least drink the coffee."

Mandy lifted the cup, got a whiff, and set it back down. "There's whiskey in it."

"For purely medicinal purposes," he replied. "At least try to drink it."

It was the strangest thing. She could hear Zach's voice, but she had to search through the blur to find him. When she did, his face swam out of focus.

"How do you think she died?" she whispered. The question had been tormenting her, slipping in and out of her head like a knife. "Did she suffer? Was it quick? I heard no gunshot. Did Dad stab her? Strangle or suffocate her?" Dimly, she was aware of tears streaming down her cheeks. "Why didn't I go downstairs and try to help her?"

Zach's hard, warm hands curled over hers. "Mandy, don't do this to yourself."

"But she died down there. She *died*, Zach. While I hid in a closet, my mother *died*."

He tightened his hold on her fingers. "Sweetheart, I know that can't be easy to accept, but you were a kid, doing what your mom told you. Can't you turn loose of it?"

"No." And Mandy couldn't. Her mom had loved her and Luke so much. She would have walked barefoot through fire to keep them safe. Zach was right: Their mother wouldn't blame her daughter, but that didn't absolve Mandy from her own thoughts. It half killed her to think that she had cowered at the far end of that closet while her mother was murdered. "I don't know if I'll *ever* be able to turn loose of it."

Zach released her hands and pushed the coffee mug toward her. "Just a sip or two. It'll help, Mandy. Do it for me, please?"

Luke came to sit across from his sister. "Drink it, Mands. If you don't, I will."

Mandy blinked and tried to focus on her brother's face. "Over my dead body."

The minute she spoke, her father's voice ricocheted through her head. *Oh, God, oh, God.* Those had been the last words her mother had ever heard. Had her father been strangling her even then? Or had he been gripping the handle of a knife that he'd just driven into her heart?

Sick. Mandy leaped up from the chair, her throat convulsing. Where was the bathroom? She'd used it once and tried to move in that direction, but the contents of her stomach erupted before she took two steps. She spewed bile into her cupped hands. Little came up, but still her body convulsed, her stomach twisting to purge itself. Then Zach was there, mopping her hands with a wad of damp paper towels, his deep voice curling around her.

"It's okay, sweetheart. Just get it up."

There was nothing more to bring up, but even so, Mandy couldn't stop gagging. Pain ripped through her. She'd hidden in a closet while her mother was murdered. How would she ever forgive herself?

Chapter Nineteen

Zach got Mandy cleaned up and safely sitting in a chair again. Spine curved, hands limp on her lap, she let her head fall forward, her shoulders jerking with sobs.

"What's happening?" Luke asked with a frantic edge, his hands white-knuckled on the crook of the cane. "Is she still vomiting?"

Zach checked his watch. "She's just having a hard time. If I get Rosebud harnessed, can you handle getting ready for bed by yourself and bunk on the living room sofa? That'll be easier than trying to get you upstairs. Right now I need to focus on Mandy."

"Sure." Luke angled his head sharply to one side. In a voice pitched barely above a whisper, he said, "I wish I could beat the hell out of him for doing this to her."

Zach shared the feeling. He couldn't fathom how he might feel if his mom had been murdered while he'd hidden in a closet. Much like Mandy did, he guessed, going over the things he should have done and beating up on himself for failing to do them. He wished he knew something to say that would wipe thoughts like that from her mind.

Zach got Rosebud haltered and handed Luke his satchel. "Just tell her to find the bathroom. When you're ready for bed, tell her to find the living room and then the sofa. Take her gear back off before you hit the sack."

Leaving Mandy while he found bedding and a pillow and made up the sofa for Luke was one of the hardest things Zach had ever done. But later, her first worry would be for her brother. Like mother, like daughter. Zach wanted to be able to tell her that Luke had been fed and was already in bed, fast asleep.

When Zach returned to the kitchen, Mandy was sitting with her head in her hands. He crouched in front of her, grasped her arms, and pressed her erect. "Better now?"

Face swollen from crying, she nodded. "I can't go back and change any of it. And even if I could, would I want to? You're probably right. If I'd gone downstairs and Dad had killed me, what would have become of Luke?"

"Your father would have led him to believe that both you and his mother had abandoned him," Zach answered without hesitation, "and he would have mistreated him."

"Yes," she whispered. "That would have been so horrible. Luke was only four and would've been completely helpless." Tears sparkled in her eyes. "It's easy for me to think I should have done this or that, but for Luke's sake, maybe it happened the way it was supposed to and, without a doubt, the way Mama wanted it to."

Zach had never admired Mandy more than he did then. He had expected to be busy for hours, holding her, mopping up her tears. But she was pulling herself back from the edge without his help, reasoning her way past the guilt to focus on the realities.

"You're one hell of a lady, Mandy Pajeck."

She wiped under her eyes and tried to smile. "I don't know about that. But it's definitely time for me to stop with all the theatrics. I'll only make myself sick."

"Maybe you could try to eat," he suggested.

She gazed dully at the food he'd prepared for her. Zach stepped around her to grab the plate. "Let me give this a zap to warm it back up."

"I'm really not hungry."

"I know, but you need to eat. You worked your tail off yesterday and today with very little nourishment. Once you take a bite, your stomach may wake up with a vengeance."

"Where's Luke?"

"In the living room, asleep on the sofa," Zach told her.

"Did he eat?"

"Like a horse." *Talk, Zach. Keep her distracted.* "It must cost you a small fortune to keep food in the cupboards."

"He does have a healthy appetite."

Her voice sounded steadier. Zach turned to study her and was pleased to see a hint of color returning to her lips. When he set her plate back on the table, she nibbled on a piece of crisp bacon, took a few swallows of the milk, and then reached for the mug.

"I hate the smell of whiskey," she said as she took a sip. Her eyes widened at the taste. "My stars, this is actually good."

"Irish coffee, one of my father's specialties." Zach sat across from her and tipped his chair onto its back legs. "It's his remedy for nearly everything: a bad cold, frazzled nerves, insomnia, chills—you name it, and he fixes you Irish coffee."

He smiled to himself as she tried the eggs, and then bit into her toast. "Well, his recipe is delicious." She drank from the mug again. "Maybe it will help me sleep." She forked eggs into her mouth, chewed, and swallowed. "You're right. Now that I'm eating, my stomach is waking up."

When she'd cleaned her plate, finished the milk, and emptied the mug, Zach made her another Irish coffee. She didn't protest when he set the second round in front of her. He talked with her while she drank it—about the weather, his horses, Rosebud and Luke, and any other damned thing he could think of to keep a conversation rolling. With any luck, the small amounts of whiskey would help her to get a good night's rest.

After Mandy finished the coffee, Zach collected her overnight satchel and led her upstairs to a guest room. The bed furnishings and curtains fairly screamed "expensive," and the adjoining bathroom was the largest Mandy had ever seen. The walk-in shower would have accommodated a full-grown horse, and the bathtub looked deep and wide enough to swim in. Zach indicated a switch in the tub with a jerk of his thumb.

"Chromotherapy," he said. "You might want to use it." Seeing her blank look, he continued, "It's underwater mood lighting. If you punch the button twice, it changes colors. Light the candles, turn out the ceiling lights, and enjoy. There's an in-line heater that keeps the water at any temperature you choose. You can lie back, close your eyes if you like, and let the whirlpool jets massage all the tension right out of you."

That sounded divine to Mandy. Zach showed her where the butane lighter was to ignite all the candles placed strategically around the tub, kissed her lightly on the forehead, and said, "Good night, Mandy. My room is two doors down on the right. If you need anything, just knock. I'm a pretty light sleeper."

She followed him to the door. After he let himself out, she turned the lock. Reflex action, she realized, and unlocked it again. She didn't need to worry about Zach acting on any inconvenient impulses. Hand still closed over the knob, she thought for a moment, then turned the lock again, not sure if she was locking Zach out or herself in.

A few minutes later, chin-deep in hot water, with the jets and lights adjusted to her liking, she fantasized about having a tub like this available every night. She'd never experienced such luxury. It was so soothing and relaxing that she hated to get out.

She enjoyed the delicious sensations for several minutes. But then thoughts of her mother returned. Pictures of that horrible grave and her mom's bones eddied in her mind like dry leaves on the surface of turbulent water. And, oh, God, to see that ring had been such a shock. She would always shiver when she recalled that moment.

She ducked her head, came up sputtering, and shampooed her hair. After exiting the tub, she wrapped herself in a thick terry bath sheet the color of Zach's merlot, wound a smaller towel around her head like a turban, and rinsed out the Jacuzzi.

The bathroom came equipped with a hair blower and a magnifying mirror on a pull-out bronze frame, both wall mounts. Mandy wondered if this was similar to the setups in expensive hotels. It would be easy to get used to such luxuries. She blew her hair dry, brushed her teeth, moisturized her face, and slipped into a nightshirt covered with whimsical butterflies. Gray sweats completed her bedtime ensemble.

When she entered the bedroom, she couldn't imagine going to sleep. Bypassing the bed, she knelt at the window and gazed out into the darkness. Here on Zach's ranch, the stars seemed brighter, a sprinkle of brilliant diamonds on blue-black velvet. At any other time, Mandy would have found it breathtakingly beautiful, but tonight it only made her sad. Her mother had loved the stars. She said they gave people hope.

Zach had been right earlier, Mandy realized. This wasn't a time for her to be alone. She wanted to be with him—a yearning that ran so deep it was almost an ache. His arms always soothed her, and oh, how she needed to feel them around her now.

Zach was almost asleep when he heard his door latch click. He squinted through the moonlit shadows and saw Mandy slipping into his room. As she carefully closed the door, he pushed up to turn on the nightstand lamp. She jumped and whirled.

"I'm sorry. I hoped not to wake you."

"You didn't. I hadn't dozed off yet." Zach pulled the sheet and blankets tight across his lap. After showering and shaving, he'd slipped on only a fresh pair of briefs. "Are you having a rough time?"

She stopped midway across the carpet, looking nervous and too beautiful for words in a corny butterfly nightshirt and baggy sweats. "I, um, just wanted to be with you. I mean, I thought . . ." She lifted a hand, a helpless gesture that went straight to his heart. "Well, I was hoping you were asleep and I'd be able to just, you know, lie beside you."

Zach had tossed his soiled clothing in the hamper. He gestured at his dresser across the room. "Would you grab me some jeans? Third drawer down, on the right."

She flapped her hand. "No, no. It was silly of me." She backed toward the door. "I'll just go back to my own room. I, um, shouldn't have come."

Zach allowed her to leave. The moment the door closed, he swung out of bed, walked to the dresser, and slipped into a fresh pair of Wranglers. Then he grabbed a clean shirt. He didn't bother with boots and stepped barefoot into the hall. When he reached Mandy's door, he discovered it was locked. He tapped lightly and heard her fumble with the latch. She cracked the door open to peer out at him.

"I really shouldn't have bothered—"

Zach planted a palm against the wood, applying enough pressure to make her back up. "It's not about should or shouldn't. If you need company, it's understandable, and I don't mind."

She made a smothered sound and whirled away, pushing at her hair. Her nightstand lamp was on, the bed still made up. Zach pushed the door closed with his back and leaned against it, folding his arms and crossing his feet. Then he realized she might feel trapped. He practically jumped away from the door and positioned himself against the bureau, propping an elbow on it to assume a casual stance.

"It's not just company I need," she confessed shakily. "I know this will sound idiotic, but I . . ." She floundered to a halt and shot him a desperate look. Her gaze dropped to his bare chest. Zach realized he hadn't buttoned his shirt and immediately rectified that. When he was decently covered, he followed her to where she stood at the window. She jerked when he stepped up behind her and grasped her shoulders.

"I'm sorry, Zach," she whispered shakily. "I know I'm not making sense. I just feel . . . I can't explain it—like all the glue that holds me together is dissolving, and the only thing that makes it better is when your arms are around me."

"It makes perfect sense. We all need a hug sometimes."

"I . . ." He heard her gulp. "I think I might need more than just a hug."

Zach stared at the back of her head. Was she saying she wanted him to make love to her? At any other time he would have done a happy dance and granted the request. But she was on very rocky ground tonight, and he'd given her two drinks. She wasn't used to the stuff. Only a low-down skunk would take advantage of that.

She leaned her weight against him, making him acutely conscious of her softness and warmth. *Oh, shit*, he thought, *I'm a low-down skunk*. "Mandy, you're upset right now. Let's not do anything rash, okay? I'll happily sit up with you. We can talk. If you like, I'll make you a couple more Irish coffees. Maybe they'll help you fall asleep."

She stiffened and stepped away with a decisive movement that caught him off guard. "No, never mind. I'm sorry. I shouldn't have gone to your room. I'll handle it."

Zach tracked her with his gaze as she paced back and

forth at the foot of the bed. Though still pale, she had a red flush creeping up her slender neck, and when she looked at him, there was no mistaking the bruised expression in her eyes.

He raked a hand through his hair. "I have a really bad feeling I just stuck my foot in my mouth." *Clear up to the knee, Harrigan,* he added silently.

She waved him off. "Don't worry about it. I just misread your signals, I guess." The fiery blush now pooled in her cheeks. "You, um . . . I think you'd better go now."

Zach wasn't about to leave on that note. "I will if you'd like me to, but, Mandy, if you're thinking that I don't want you, you're dead wrong. I've never—and I do mean *never*—wanted anyone as much as I want you."

"Then why—"

She caught her lower lip between her teeth and stared at him with a shimmering, injured expression in her eyes that had him cursing under his breath. Zach closed the distance between them with three strides, grabbed her by the upper arms, and claimed her lips with his, not waiting this time for her to open for him before thrusting with his tongue to taste the sweetness of her mouth. She moaned and melted against him. Zach struggled for control. His aim was to show her how much he desired her, not make love to her. Only Mandy was screwing up his game plan, hooking one arm around his neck and fisting her other hand in his hair. She kissed him back inexpertly, but what she lacked in finesse, she made up for with enthusiasm.

When he ended the kiss to tell her that he couldn't in good conscience take this any further, she cut him off with a shaky, "I'm twenty-*eight*, Zach, not a child who doesn't know her own mind."

Grabbing for breath as if he'd just sprinted a mile, Zach rested his forehead against hers. Neither of them closed their eyes, and he felt as if he were drowning in a blur of hazel. Even worse, he didn't care if he ever surfaced.

"Mandy," he said hoarsely, "be damned sure this is really what you want. No regrets tomorrow, no recriminations. I'm trying like hell to be a gentleman, but you're not making it easy."

"Maybe I don't want you to be a gentleman. Maybe I want you to make me feel like you did when you kissed me in my backyard, only I don't want you to stop this time. Just hold me, Zach. Make me forget everything and let me just be with you."

"Are you feeling tipsy?" he asked. "From the alcohol, I mean?"

"No."

That was all Zach needed to hear. He stepped away from her. "Hold the thought. I'll be right back."

He rushed to his room, located the case of condoms in his bathroom drawer, and drew out three foil packets, praying the contents weren't rotten. How long had it been since he'd gone out for a planned night on the town? He honestly couldn't remember. He'd had a few impromptu encounters with women over the last two years. He wasn't a monk, after all, but he'd purchased protection each of those times from a restroom dispenser because he hadn't been prepared. How long did a prophylactic remain uncompromised by time? The high desert climate was dry and might deteriorate a rubber more quickly than a moist climate did. In his wild days, the question had never come up, because he'd gone through a fifty-count case every few months. He kissed the foil, said a quick Hail Mary, and then shoved the packages in his pocket, wondering if he'd just condemned himself to hell for asking thc Holy Mother for intervention when his aim was to commit a mortal sin. *Probably*.

When had his life gotten so complicated? He wanted to walk the straight and narrow, but Mandy had an abhorrence of marriage. Somehow he needed to fix that.

Zach returned to the guest room. Mandy still stood at

the foot of the bed, looking bewildered and forlorn. He swept her up into his arms and carried her to the bed.

Mandy didn't know what was happening to her, but right now she needed Zach's arms around her nearly as much as she needed air to breathe. As he laid her gently on the mattress, she felt no apprehension, only eager anticipation, and when he bent his dark head to kiss her again, she ran her fingers into his hair, urging him down on top of her. His weight, his hardness and warmth—ah, yes, *this* was what she needed—to be surrounded by his heat and strength. And it felt right. Wildly, gloriously right.

With light nips on her bottom lip to end the kiss, he rose up to look at her. In the lamplight, his black hair, still damp from his shower, glistened like polished jet, falling in lazy waves over his high forehead. Looking up at his burnished face, Mandy decided she'd never seen a handsomer countenance, all hard planes and sharp angles, his brows arching like thick black wings over his coffee brown eyes.

"We have a little ground to cover before we take this any further," he told her. "I'm crazy, Stetson-over-boot-heels in love with you, Mandy Pajeck. The last time I told you that, you tried to feed me a line of bullshit about caring for me as a friend." He gently pushed an errant lock of hair from her cheek. "There was a time when I would have settled for friendship—or maybe only a come-on smile. But not with you. You're special to me. I don't want to dirty that up with meaningless sex. Are you following me?"

Mandy's heart caught. Zach was the kind of man who'd want the whole nine yards if he loved a woman—commitment, marriage, and a family. She could love him with all her heart, but she could never marry him. "I'm following."

He acknowledged her response with a kiss on the end

of her nose. "Have I ever told you that I think your nose is sexy as hell, and that I love your eyes?"

Mandy smiled slightly and shook her head.

"Well, I'm telling you now. I love everything about you. I won't push you right now for marriage. I know the very thought sends you over the edge. But can you at least give me a long-term promise of commitment with the word *love* tossed in somewhere? I need this to be special. If you can't give me that, I've got an unopened bottle of Jack Daniel's downstairs, and I'll talk your ears off all night, but I won't make love to you."

Mandy's throat went tight. "I'm not sure what love feels like, Zach. I mean, I love Luke, no question, but my feelings for you are so different."

"Tell me about them."

Mandy groped for words, swallowed hard, and curled her hand over his upper arm, trailing fingertips over the bulge of his biceps. "Well, I . . . I think about you all the time, and I try to remember how you looked and what you said. I miss you when we're not together. When I'm upset, I feel like I can't breathe unless you're with me. I need to hear your voice, and I want you close, and I want to feel your hand holding mine. But mostly I want your arms around me." She gulped and stared at him. "It scares me, needing someone. For so long I never did. Is that love? It's nothing like what I feel for Luke. He needs me, not the other way around. Is needing someone . . . well, is that love?"

His firm mouth tipped into a crooked grin. "It's definitely part of it. I feel the same way, needing to be with you. When I'm not, it feels like the sun went behind a cloud."

"Me, too," she whispered. "And when we talk on the phone, it's hard to hang up because then I won't be able to hear your voice." A hundred different feelings welled within Mandy at that moment, and she had words to describe none of them. "You make my world seem right.

When you're close to me, I know everything is going to be okay."

He lightly dragged his thumb over her lower lip. "Love is only a word. It's the feelings that count, not the sounds we utter to describe them."

"So have I passed your test?"

He chuckled and bent to nip lightly at her chin. "It wasn't really a test, but yes, if you feel that way about me, I'll accept that as love with a capital L."

Mandy's body went limp. She'd been so afraid he might leave her, and right then, she felt as if she might fall apart if he did.

"Last chance," he whispered. "We don't have to do this. With you, my willpower sucks, but I'm pretty sure I can just hold you until you fall asleep."

Mandy wanted more than that. She wanted to melt and be absorbed through the pores of his skin. She wanted—no, *needed*—to feel him all around her and all through her. Just being near him made her body ache and feel hot inside. She sensed that he had the power to make her forget the sight of her mother's corroded ring and finger bone lying in the dirt. But it was more than that. She wanted him because he was Zach, and somehow he'd sneaked past her defenses to become the center of her world.

Of course, she wouldn't tell him that. She wasn't going to marry him—or anyone. Ever. But she had to have tonight with him.

"I want to be with you," she whispered. "Tonight, I *need* to be with you. Just having your arms around me won't be enough, Zach. I want you."

His body tightened, and he yanked in a ragged breath. "God, don't say things like that unless you're sure. Do you have any idea in hell what you're getting yourself into?"

Mandy's throat had gone so tight she could barely speak. For the first time, she was experiencing the power of being female, and the feeling made her dizzy. She brushed a fingertip over his lower lip and felt him shudder. Oh, she loved being able to make him feel like this. She arched her back and gloried in the smothered groan he couldn't suppress.

"Zach, I'm a big girl, remember? I know about the birds and the bees, and I've watched a lot of movies and done a lot of reading."

A twinkle of amusement warmed his eyes. "Mandy, love, I don't think your vicarious experiences have prepared you for my version of lovemaking. How about this? I'll aim for middle-of-the-road. If I do anything you don't like, say so and I'll stop. Deal?" He braced his weight on his left arm to shift and lie beside her. "Let's establish a signal, all right? If I go over the line, just tap me on the shoulder."

That sounded easy enough. Mandy nodded. She expected him to get right down to business, but instead he lifted her hand and pressed light, whispery kisses to her palm before suckling each of her fingertips. The soft, silken pull of his mouth felt incredible. Then he nibbled at the sensitive inside of her wrist. By the time he reached the bend of her arm, Mandy's heart was skittering, her breasts ached, and a molten, shivery sensation had taken up residence at the apex of her thighs. It radiated outward, sending urgent messages all through her.

Zach. He tasted her skin like a man savoring a rare delicacy, titillating her senses, making her head swim, and filling her with needs she'd never dreamed of, let alone felt. She expected to feel embarrassed when he tugged her nightshirt off over her head, but by then she was too far gone to care and only went after the buttons of his shirt so she could see that muscular chest and striated abdomen again.

She'd just pushed the shirt down off his shoulders when his mouth laid claim to her left nipple. Mandy gasped at the jolt of sensation. Sensory overload. Alarms went off in her brain. What was that "stop" signal? She couldn't remember. And before she could think of it, she decided she didn't care. She couldn't bear it if he stopped.

In the end, she just arched her spine to accommodate him. He responded to the silent request with hard pulls and light tugs of his teeth, filling her with such longing she felt completely disoriented and could only cling tight. When he slipped his hand inside her sweatpants and found the wet center of her, she parted her knees and lifted her hips. He stroked her lightly, tenderly, until her flesh throbbed with the need for more. He seemed to know when she was ready, increasing the pressure of his fingers a little at a time until she felt her nerve endings bunch, her arousal so compelling that it was almost frightening. Was this supposed to be happening? She felt like she was going to explode. She opened her lips to ask him, only nothing came out but a tiny moan.

He seemed to understand her wordless cry, because he buried his face in the lee of her neck and whispered to her, his voice so close to her ear that its husky timbre seemed to roll clear through her. "Just let go, Mandy. Trust me and just let go."

So it was okay. He knew. She shuddered as the pressure within her mounted, pushing her higher and higher, until finally her body convulsed with shivers of pleasure that eclipsed her vision with spirals of color and left her muscles quivering. Cries she vaguely associated with herself beat in her ears, but the only solid reality was the hard, secure grip of Zach's arms. The loss of control might have alarmed her, but he was there, kissing her throat, whispering reassurances, the heat of him cocooning around her. He held her until the spasms subsided and she could breathe normally again.

He rose to his knees, stripping his shirt the rest of the way off and casting it aside, then unfastening his jeans. In the glow of the lamplight, his rippling flesh looked like seasoned oak rubbed to a high sheen. After some shifting and tugging, his jeans and briefs were discarded. He slicked a condom onto his erect manhood with an ease born of long practice. Bracing his weight on his well-muscled arms, he moved over her, his gaze locked on hers.

"This first time may hurt," he whispered. "I'm not sure how much."

Mandy realized he was reluctant to cause her pain, and that touched her as nothing else could. Pleasure. He'd given her so much. Now it was her turn. What did a little pain matter? In the past, she'd been kicked in the ribs repeatedly and survived. She smiled at him in invitation and saw his eyes darken with passion. He rubbed himself back and forth in her slick, wet cleavage of flesh for a moment, and then she felt the tip of his shaft nudge into her. He hesitated, and she tugged at his shoulders, urging him forward. She bit down on her lower lip at the sharp stab of discomfort, but he had prepared her well, her passage slick to ease his way, and with one smooth thrust, he was deep within her. He went still.

"Do it," she whispered urgently. "Do it, Zach. I want you. I need you. Please."

He groaned and began to move. With each thrust, Mandy felt an explosion of tingling delight deep within her. She caught and matched his rhythm, tightening herself around him until he cried out and lifted her hips toward him. He drove her on until together they climaxed. He bucked and stiffened in her arms, his face contorted as she gasped his name and dug her fingers into him.

Incredible. It was the most incredible experience of her life and he'd given it to her.

Afterward they rested, arms wrapped around each other, her pelvis riding his hips. Mandy drifted in a cloud of contentment, feeling safe, happy, and utterly satiated. As long as Zach remained beside her, she didn't care if she ever moved again.

"Hey," he murmured. "How about taking a shower with me?"

Mandy smiled sleepily, her lips curving against his neck. "Do we have to? I'm happy right here."

He trailed kisses along her eyebrows. His voice, louder this time, was husky and thick. "You'll be even happier in the shower with me," he promised.

"Not possible."

A hint of laughter edged his reply. "Oh, yes, it is. Come on."

She crawled off the bed and grabbed her nightshirt, holding it to her breasts. Narrowing an eye at her, Zach bent to get something out of a pocket of his Wranglers. He seemed to feel absolutely at ease with his nudity, and Mandy could understand why. His body was so sculpted and perfect it could have been a work of art.

"Drop the shirt," he told her. "Covering that body with anything should be a criminal offense. Besides, I've already seen everything."

Mandy didn't think her body was all that great, but if the gleam in his dark eyes was any indication, he seemed to think differently. Reluctantly, she tossed the nightshirt on the foot of the bed. "I have small breasts."

His gaze dropped. "You have beautiful breasts."

"And my thighs are fat."

He grinned, his teeth flashing white in the lamplight. "I'm a leg man. Trust me when I say your thighs are gorgeous." He came around the foot of the bed and grabbed her hand. "Come on. It's time you experienced a shower Zach Harrigan style."

Within three minutes, Mandy's body was slick with soap and water, and Zach's hands were coursing all over her, teasing, caressing, and possessing her in a way that made her head spin. So much to learn, so much she didn't know. She'd never dreamed he could use his fingers to bring her to another climax while the hot, soothing water beat down over them. Her knees jellied, and his powerful arms locked her tight against his hard torso. He held her erect until the last quake subsided and then eased her onto a built-in slate bench while he put on some protection. Then he gathered her into his arms, lifted her against the shower wall, drew her legs around his hips, and thrust deep inside her. The shock and pleasure were so great she gasped, arched her back, and whacked her head against the wall. It didn't matter. Nothing mattered but the sensations. With each push, he sent a thrill of feeling spiraling through her. She cried out, unable to believe this time with him was even more wonderful than the last. She rode the waves, so lost in the electrical swirl of delight that the only word she could remember was his name. *Zach*. Over and over, that word trailed from her lips, sometimes a whisper, other times a high, keening wail of need.

Before he satisfied himself, he made her climax again and again, taking her to heights she'd never dreamed existed. Dimly she felt him stiffen. The hot surge of his release ignited her at the center and pushed her toward another crest. They tumbled over the edge together. Mandy felt as if she were free-falling without a para-chute, but with Zach's arms around her, she didn't care. He'd catch her. He always would.

He supported her against the wall with the press of his hips until their breathing returned to normal. Then he gently bathed her, his big hands moving tenderly over intimate places that were now sore. He wrapped her in a bath sheet and carried her back to bed. Mandy wanted to protest that her hair was wet and would soak the pil-low, but she was so limp with exhaustion she couldn't speak. Instead she just closed her eyes, wishing for his arms to be around her again.

He left her there. She heard the shower come on again. A weary smile curved her lips. As soon as he got cleaned up and dried off, he would return to her. She'd be okay without him for only a few minutes.

*   *   *

Zach adjusted the water temperature and stepped over to the wastebasket to tug the condom from his still-erect member. What he saw made him freeze and sent his heart into overdrive. The prophylactic was torn clear to the rim.

He groaned and planted a hand against the wall. Several expletives exploded inside his mind. He gave voice to none of them, afraid Mandy might hear him cursing. *Oh, God.* He'd spilled his seed directly into her. He remembered how fabulous her slick heat had felt around him, and now he knew why. He'd been making love to her with no protection, and he'd been too caught up in the incredible sensations to stop, to check, to think at all.

A dizzying rush of panic sent a chill down his spine. What the hell would he tell Mandy? *Sorry, sweetheart. I may have just knocked you up.* She grew frantic at the very thought of marriage. To her, it was tantamount to a lifetime sentence in the downtown business section of hell. She'd made it clear from the start that their relationship had to be a no-strings deal. She was already financially strapped, trying to support herself and Luke. A baby would be an additional expense she couldn't afford. And he wasn't at all sure she'd allow him to help . . . or even be involved. Oh, he'd screwed up royally this time. *Great job, Harrigan.*

Zach pulled off the condom and let it fall into the receptacle. He stared at it with loathing. If he'd made her pregnant, he'd step up to the plate; no worries on that count. And if he were totally honest with himself, he had to admit that having a baby with her would make him the happiest man alive. What worried him was what Mandy might think when he told her. Would she see it as a trap and freak out, thinking that he was trying to trick her into marrying him? Probably. She was already plenty wary of men.

Zach didn't know what to do. As he stepped into the

shower, he seriously considered just buying a new case of condoms and praying she wasn't pregnant. That way, he'd never have to tell her this had happened. *Not.* His father had raised him better than that. Not telling Mandy would be the coward's way out, and dishonest, to boot.

Mandy felt a tug on the towel that Zach had wrapped around her. She blinked awake to see him leaning over her. She rolled off the damp terry without opening her eyes again and reached for him. He wrapped his arms around her. She sighed and snuggled close, loving his hard strength and wishing the night would never end. She was tired, but she felt more secure and at peace than ever before.

Peace. Safety. They were things she didn't know much about, but she was learning. And Zach was helping. Vaguely she became aware that his body was tense, and she made a small inquiring sound. He rose up on one elbow.

"Mandy."

"Mm?" She kissed his arm and tried to pull him back down beside her.

"Mandy, look at me."

She opened her eyes a crack, saw his expression, and started to sit up. "Zach? What is it? What's wrong?"

"I need to tell you something," he whispered. "If I wait until morning, I'm afraid I'll chicken out."

Stark misery lurked in his eyes. A chill swept through her. What in the world could have gone wrong? "Zach, what is it? Can I help?"

"The condom tore. In the shower. It tore clear to the rim."

"What . . . ?" It took a second for the words to connect. Her lips parted in wordless shock.

"When I came inside you, I didn't have any protection. It'll probably be fine. But there's a possibility I could have made you pregnant."

Mandy jerked bolt upright and shoved him away from her. Her eyes snapped all the way open.

"What?" Even through her emotional turmoil she felt astounded at the condemnation that rang through the single word she flung at him. *"What?"*

Chapter Twenty

Panic coursed through Mandy. Still groggy, she stared at Zach, who lay on his back, arms folded under his pillow. In the lamplight, he looked incredibly sexy, his body hard, his skin glistening from his recent shower. There was a wary darkness in his eyes.

He couldn't have said what she thought he'd said. No way. No, she'd heard wrong. "Did you say the condom tore?"

He dipped his chin in what she took to be a nod. "It's my fault. I've had the box for ages, and I should have replaced it. I just didn't expect—" He broke off and swallowed. "Well, until tonight, you never hinted that you were ready to become intimate, so I wasn't prepared."

Mandy did some rapid mental calculations and felt the tension ease off. "Well, I don't think I'm ovulating right now. I could be wrong but I don't think so."

He expelled a breath so carefully that she realized he must have been holding it. He drew a hand from under the pillow, cupped it around the back of her neck, and whispered, "Come here."

As she gave in to the tug of pressure and rested her head on his shoulder, she said, "Only to cuddle, right? I can't risk getting pregnant. It would be a disaster."

"If you're pregnant, and I stress the *if*, it won't be a disaster. I'll step up to the plate. I'd never let you face it alone."

Mandy closed her eyes. She didn't want to say it aloud, but Zach's stepping up to the plate was neither in question nor was it the point. Having Zach's baby would place her in an awful position. He would not want his child to be born out of wedlock, and she could never marry him. For her, that was impossible. She couldn't even think about it without feeling breathless. And it wasn't a good breathless.

"Fortunately I don't think it's that time of the month for me, so the mishap tonight shouldn't be a problem. I just don't want to push our luck." Mandy pressed closer to him, craving his warmth even though she wasn't cold. "Hold me, Zach. Please?"

He shifted and drew her into his arms. Kissing her forehead, he whispered, "You need to rest, sweetheart. Close your eyes, think happy thoughts, and go to sleep."

Think happy thoughts? Today she'd seen irrefutable evidence that her father had killed her mother, and now there was a chance, however remote, that she might be pregnant. For the first time, she felt a sense of sisterhood with the many women she'd heard utter, "*Men!*" She doubted she could fall asleep. The events of the day lurked like black shadows in her mind, and on top of all that, the possibility of an unwanted pregnancy was now front and center. She couldn't be pregnant. She just *couldn't* be.

That was her last conscious thought.

Zach lay awake long after Mandy drifted off. As beautiful as their lovemaking had been, he worried that she would have regrets in the morning. He'd broken one of his own rules: never to make love to a woman when she was upset and vulnerable. He should have waited until Mandy had recovered from the shock of finding her mother's remains. It didn't matter that she'd essentially pleaded with him to do it. He should have found other ways to comfort her and held fast to his resolve.

He pressed his face against her hair, breathing deeply of her scent—clean feminine skin, traces of soap, and an essence that was apparently all her own, a light, airy fragrance that reminded him of roses even though he knew she wore no perfume. Oh, how he loved her. He thought back, trying to recall the precise moment when he'd taken the plunge, but there had been so many special times he couldn't pinpoint only one. The first time he met her, a strange feeling had come over him, and he guessed he'd known, even then, that she was the one. He smiled, remembering the night he'd found her with Tornado and how she'd reamed him out for mistreating the horse. Zach admired anyone who threw caution to the wind in defense of an animal. Maybe that had been the moment when he'd lost his heart to her.

It didn't really matter. He loved her, and God help him, somehow he had to make this work. She was so wary, his Mandy. That shallow grave in the backyard of her childhood home pretty much summarized her life experience, and it had ingrained in her a fear of being dominated by a man.

Zach didn't see marriage that way. To him, it was a partnership. But she wasn't buying his version, and he couldn't blame her. Over time, he hoped Mandy would come to trust him enough to become his wife. If and when she did, he'd do everything in his power to make her happy. All he needed was the chance to prove that to her.

Sunlight slanted through the guest room windows, dappling the gold walls and ivory coverlet with splashes of bright yellow. Mandy's lips curved in an appreciative smile. She didn't want to budge. She wanted to stay right where she was, in Zach's arms. He stirred and groaned softly, running his hand into her hair.

"Mmm, I like waking up this way," he whispered. "I could become addicted."

Mandy shared the sentiment and shifted her head back to study his face. Wrinkles in the pillowcase had left creases on his jaw. His eyes had a sleepy, unfocused look. In the morning light, his lips shimmered like polished satin.

He arched a dark eyebrow. "How're you feeling this morning? Any regrets?"

Mandy considered the question and decided that nothing would ever make her regret their lovemaking. It had been sweet and wondrous, the most incredible experience of her life. If she was pregnant, which she seriously doubted, she'd deal with it somehow. Granted, she preferred not to be put in that position, but she wouldn't be the first unmarried woman to have a child, and she had every confidence that Zach would help her out financially.

"My only regret," she told him, "is that we couldn't go back for thirds."

He gave a startled laugh, kissed her forehead, and then rubbed noses with her. "How about going back for thirds this morning?"

"We can't. We have no reliable protection."

He trailed light kisses over her cheek. "There are ways around that."

"There are?"

He tickled her ear with the tip of his tongue. "Oh, yeah. I didn't take it there last night, but I will this morning if you're feeling frisky."

Mandy felt like a child in a candy shop with only a pebble in her pocket. "I don't think I'm ovulating, Zach, but I can't be certain."

"Trust me. What I have in mind won't put you at risk."

She believed him. Weird. He'd told her once that he would never harm her, and she believed that as well. Already aroused by the things he was doing to her ear, she said, "Take us there, then." His teasing grin made her shiver in anticipation.

He rolled her onto her back and trailed his lips from her ear down her neck. The caress made her breath catch. Her skin grew so warm and sensitive that even the touch of the sheets sent tingles up her spine. He bent his head to her breast, his lips searching for the peak. She gasped when his hot mouth closed over her throbbing nipple. The teasing drift of his tongue brought the already turgid tip to a pulsating erectness, and it felt to her as if every nerve ending in her body convened there. He caught it between his teeth, torturing her with light tugs. Every flick and pull sent a jolt of pleasure streaking to the pit of her stomach. She dug her heels into the mattress, arching toward him. She clutched his shoulders, never wanting him to stop.

"Zach," she whispered. "Oh, Zach."

Her thoughts streamed in a dizzying swirl. Last night had been wonderful, but *this* . . . She felt as if her body had suddenly come alive after a long sleep, instinctively wanting things from him that she couldn't even name. Intoxicated, she lifted her hips, yearning for his hand at the apex of her thighs. Instead he stopped teasing her breast and moved down to pleasure her there with his mouth.

Startled, Mandy cried out and tried to push him away, but he'd wedged his broad shoulders between her legs, grasped her hips, and settled in for a long stay. With only two passes of his tongue, he put an end to her protests. With three, he pushed her beyond all thought. She felt like a stringed instrument being played by a master. Every pull of his mouth sent vibrations of delight through her. She opened her legs, rocked up with her hips, and allowed him to possess that part of her completely. Her body went into spasms, and still he worked her, suckling, flicking with his tongue, pushing her higher, giving no quarter. After she climaxed the last time, he gentled the assault, soothing her swollen flesh with soft caresses.

Mandy was too exhausted to move and could barely

think, but even so, she realized the inequity of this kind of lovemaking. As he kissed his way back up her body, she whispered, "What about you?"

He shifted to lie beside her, his upper body supported on the bend of one arm. She felt his erection against her thigh. The gentleness and warmth in his expression made her heart hurt. "Come have a shower with me, and we'll take care of that."

She giggled.

Twenty minutes later, Mandy decided that taking showers with Zach had become her favorite pastime. Well, one of them, anyway.

Luke was awake and sitting at the kitchen table when Mandy and Zach went downstairs. Zach felt bad about that. The kid usually got up at six; it was now half past nine, and he was in an unfamiliar kitchen. Zach went right to work fixing some breakfast, smiling to himself because Mandy blushed every time he glanced at her. He made a mental note to stop by the drugstore after taking her and Luke home, because he wanted to give her more to blush about tonight. The thought that he'd been her first, that he'd given her such pleasure, had him grinning like a burro eating cactus.

She peeled potatoes and diced them up for a skillet fry. Luke wanted to help, so Zach assigned him the toaster detail. When the potatoes were on, Mandy asked if she could use his phone to check her messages at home. Zach had always thought it strange that she didn't have a cell phone. Was it because she couldn't afford one?

She returned from the living room a couple of minutes later, phone still in hand. The instant he saw her face, he knew something was wrong. He turned down the flames under the food and went to her. "What is it?"

Eyes huge and filled with worry, she said, "Apart from the fact that every reporter in Crystal Falls apparently wants to interview me, nothing much. Detective Randolph called to say he's going to the Warner Creek Correctional Facility today to question our father. I think that's good news. Maybe it means they've decided to suspect him instead of me."

Luke swiveled his head around. "Finally they're thinking straight."

Zach took the phone from her hand and hooked an arm around her shoulders to draw her close. "So why are you upset?"

"The reporters," she said thinly. "My neighbor called and said they're parked all along the street, waiting like vultures for me to go home."

Zach wanted to knock some heads together. The color that had been in her cheeks a short while ago was gone. Her soft mouth was drawn into a taut line. She'd been rallying from the ordeal yesterday, and now the reporters were shaking her up again.

"You don't have to talk with them, you know."

The tight clutch of her fingers on Zach's shoulders told him how tense she was. "I just want to forget. Why can't they leave me alone so I can try to forget?"

Zach had no answers. What really concerned him, though, was how *long* the news media might continue to hound her. A murdered woman buried under a slab of cement had all the elements of a sensational story.

The next three weeks seemed like one long nightmare. Mandy couldn't go out on her porch, let alone to the grocery store, without cameras flashing and reporters shouting questions at her. The media was camped at the edge of her yard, and she'd had so many calls about the purchase of her rights and offers to tell her story to tabloids that she'd quit answering the phone.

Her attorney, Mr. Payne, had given her strict instructions to say, "No comment." What he'd failed to tell her was that reporters weren't that easily discouraged. Their harassment of her was topped off by several phone calls from Detective Randolph to verify or negate information he'd gotten while interrogating her father. He was also keenly interested in Tobin Pajeck's patterns of abuse. Revisiting the past was difficult for Mandy, sharpening her memories of events that she wanted only to forget. Despite the strain on her nerves, she was advised by Payne to cooperate with the police in any way she could. In light of her mother's murder, it was imperative that her father never walk the streets again.

Mandy agreed and didn't object to the detective's questions, no matter how much answering them upset her. Her appetite vanished. She slept in fits and starts, and had horrible nightmares, even with Zach beside her. As a result, she fell behind in her work and lost two accounts.

The only bright spot for Mandy during this time was Zach. He arrived at her house every night at seven sharp and never left her side until just before dawn, when he had to return to the ranch. When she was frightened, he held her in his arms. When she was tired, he and Luke cooked and cleaned the kitchen afterward. When the laundry piled up, Zach did the wash. Mandy didn't know what she would have done without him, but what really saved her sanity was the frequent, mind-boggling sex. Afterward all the tension was drained from her body, and she was able to sleep, if only for a short while.

Luke seemed to take Zach's all-night visits in stride. The first few times, Zach pretended that he would sleep on the sofa, only to sneak in to be with Mandy after Luke went to bed. That lasted almost a week, until Luke made it clear he wasn't that easily fooled.

On the way to his room, he stopped at the door. "Don't bother to put bedding on the couch, Zach. It's a silly waste of time when you aren't using it."

Zach shot a startled look at Mandy. "What makes you say that?"

"I knew you and Mandy were sleeping together the very first night. And, hey, dude, I'm fine with it. You guys don't have to pretend nothing's going on. We're all adults. It's not like I'm going to pass judgment, and I'm definitely not an impressionable young kid."

Even with Luke's blessing, his presence in the small house forced Mandy and Zach to make love on the sly. Her box spring squeaked with the slightest shift of weight, so a horizontal position was a rare treat for them. Fortunately Zach was flexible and creative. More than once he drew Mandy into her bedroom, pushed her against the back wall, and made love to her standing up. He also fell into the habit of putting a load of laundry into the washer late in the evening. When the machine went into its spin cycle, it danced on the old, uneven floor, making such a horrible racket that Mandy could moan with delirious delight all she wanted without worrying that Luke might hear.

Sex with Zach was, in a word, wonderful. No, *fabulous*. Mandy had always been half-afraid that physical intimacy would be unpleasant. As a child, she'd heard her mother weeping behind the closed bedroom door too many times to believe in romance, fireworks, or fairy-tale endings. But Zach proved her wrong about that on all counts. Making love with him became more enjoyable each time, and being with him felt right and absolutely perfect. In between encounters, she couldn't wait to be with him again.

One night after Luke was asleep, Mandy turned to Zach in bed and kissed him with frantic urgency. He was taken back to the first time they'd ever made love. She'd needed him to make her forget that night, and now she needed him to do it again. He was more than happy to oblige, but as he drove her beyond thought to that place where she could only feel, his heart broke a little. She was so dear to him. She was the last person on earth who deserved to go through pain. *Damn Tobin Pajeck to eternal hell.*

Mandy was still quivering from the aftershocks of her last orgasm when Zach collapsed beside her and enfolded her in his embrace. "I love you," he whispered. "If I could rewrite the story of your life, you know what I'd do?"

"No, what?" she asked.

"I'd write it all happy," he told her. "You'd have a dad like mine, who worshipped your mom. At least once a week, he'd bring her flowers, and then he'd cook dinner for her and clean up the kitchen. You'd look down from your bedroom window and see them dancing in the moonlight, and you'd go back to bed feeling loved and safe."

"Oh, Zach. What was it like, having a dad like yours?"

"I'm trying to give him to you," he whispered. "So shut up and listen."

He felt her mouth curve in a sad smile against his shoulder. "I'm listening."

"Every night when he came home from work, you had this ritual. He'd hunker down and open his arms, and you'd run as fast as you could, jumping at him with absolute confidence that he would catch you. And then he'd toss you so high in the air you'd feel like you were flying. You loved it, and so did he."

"Oh, yes," she said with a sigh.

"On your fifth birthday—hmm, living in town, he couldn't have given you a horse. Nope, a puppy—a really cute little mongrel, white with black spots, one over its right eye. You named him—"

"Spot?" she guessed.

Zach grinned and kissed her forehead. "No, you silly girl. How uninventive is that? You named him Happy, because that's how he made you feel. He'd lick your face and make you laugh. And when he pooped and pissed on the hardwood floor, your dad just laughed and said you needed to get him housebroken."

"Your dad didn't get mad when a dog messed on his floor?"

"We only ever had one dog when I was a kid. It was Clint's, a birthday present from my folks. Then my mom died, and Clint gave it away. He's never been able to talk about that with me, so I'm not real sure why, but I've always had this feeling he blamed himself for her death, and somehow the pup factored in." Zach realized he was off topic. "Anyway, no, when that pup messed on the floor, Dad just took it outside, and someone cleaned up the mess. He never got mad."

"I would have given anything to have a father like that."

Zach smiled. "Someday you will. I'm going to convince you to take that walk to the altar someday, doll face, and when I do, my dad will be as much your dad as mine."

He felt her tense and realized, even now, that the thought of marrying him made her nervous. It was difficult for him to wrap his mind around that. The setup they had right now was about as perfect as it could get. He loved her, and he'd even come to love her brother. They had become a family. She needed to start thinking about making that official.

He kept his thoughts about that to himself and held her until she drifted off into a restive sleep, talking out loud, thrashing, and fighting against the covers as if they were launching a physical attack on her. Was she dreaming about her father beating her, or was she dreaming about her mother's death? Six of one, half a dozen of the other. Either way, she was having a bad nightmare, and Zach was powerless to help. If he woke her up, he knew from experience that she'd just fall back to sleep and return to the dream. As much as he wished it were different, he couldn't protect her from her memories.

The next morning, when Mandy's phone rang, she cringed, half expecting it to be another reporter. She was relieved when the caller ID announced that it was a local mattress warehouse calling.

"We're scheduled to deliver your order today, Ms. Pajeck," a woman said, "and I was wondering if sometime between two and four might work for you."

Mandy frowned. "Um . . . what order?"

Paper rustled at the other end. "Last Friday, a mattress and box spring were purchased, and your name and address are on the invoice."

From where Mandy stood at the phone table, she could see through the open doorway of her bedroom. She stared at her dilapidated bed, her mouth curving in a knowing grin. "Ah, I see. If I'm not here between two and four, my brother will be. That will work fine."

The moment the call ended, Mandy speed-dialed Zach's cell. He answered with, "Hello, gorgeous. You missing me already?"

Mandy sank onto a chair. "Did you buy me a new mattress and box spring last Friday?"

"Guilty."

"But, Zach, I can't afford to pay you back."

"Squeak, squeak, *squeak*. Does that ring a bell? I'd *really* like to make love to you in a horizontal position more often. Even with the washing machine making like a German tank last night, I know damned well Luke heard us doing the bedroom tango."

"Shhh. Where *are* you? Someone might overhear."

She heard him chuckle. "Hey, Cookie, you didn't hear that, did you? Nope. He says he didn't hear a word."

Mandy rolled her eyes. "You're impossible."

"I've been told that a few times. I let it slide like water off a hog's back."

"It's water off a duck's back, and I can't accept expensive gifts like that."

"I didn't buy it for you. I bought it for *me*. If you insist that I return it, then you and Luke can move out to the ranch. Better setup all the way around. You can work in my office. Luke would have his own bedroom. And, hello, every wall in the house is soundproofed. I won't have to clamp a hand over your mouth anymore to keep you from shrieking when you have an orgasm."

"If anyone can hear you, Zach Harrigan, I swear, I'll make you pay."

"That sounds interesting."

"And you have *not* moved in here."

"I haven't? Hmm. It's where I hang my Wranglers over the bedpost, and the last time I checked, my shaving gear and toothbrush were in the bathroom cabinet. I've also got a couple of changes of clothes there. If that's not moving in, what do you call it?"

"Indoor camping." She heard him chuckle as she broke the connection.

When the conversation ended, Mandy went into her bedroom. Sure enough, Zach had commandeered a drawer of her bureau for his jeans, socks, and briefs. Two of his shirts were hanging in her closet. For an instant, Mandy battled against an irrational wave of panic. Then she managed to talk herself down. Living with a man didn't give him any real power over her. Considering her abhorrence of marriage, this arrangement was the next-best thing. She enjoyed Zach's company. He did more than his share of the chores. The sex was amazing. She had absolutely no complaints.

She was smiling when she returned to the front of the house.

Every night when Zach got home—he'd come to think of Mandy's place as home—he asked if any reporters had phoned that day, and each time, her answer was no. After an entire week passed without any more calls, Mandy dimpled her cheek at him and said, "I think I'm finally off the hook."

Zach leaned around the bedroom doorframe to toss his Stetson on the top of her bureau. "Good. Now you can have some peace and quiet."

She walked into his arms and pressed her cheek against his chest. "I'm so glad to have them off my back, I just can't tell you. A juicier story must have come along. Now maybe I can move on and try to forget."

Zach buried his face in the coppery silk of her hair and breathed in deeply. "No *maybe* to it, Mandy. From this point forward, the past is behind you. It's time to start making some beautiful new memories."

She leaned back in the circle of his embrace and smiled up at him. "I like the sound of that. What kind of memory shall we make tonight?"

Zach bent his head to settle his mouth over hers. She melted into the kiss with an eagerness that instantly aroused him. "Let me surprise you," he whispered.

When another week passed with no calls from reporters, some color returned to Mandy's cheeks. Zach was also pleased to note that she was sleeping more soundly, no longer jerking awake several times a night. The circles under her eyes went away. She laughed more readily. Her appetite improved. She seemed more like her old self.

Over the weeks that followed, they slipped into a comfortable pattern. Mandy continued to work out of her home as a medical transcriptionist while Zach was at his ranch, training his big horses and Rosebud. Each evening, he knocked off at six thirty, loaded up the mini, and drove to town to spend the night with Mandy and Luke. After dinner, which the three of them cooked together, they watched movies and ate popcorn, or they listened to novels on CD. Sometimes Mandy read aloud.

During this time, Zach hopped online one night and ordered a bunch of games for the blind. He found dominoes, Braille letters on clear tape that fit on wooden

Scrabble squares, a game of Battleship, a talking USA jigsaw puzzle, Braille Monopoly, dice, and playing cards. He even found a Braille bingo board. This gave Zach the brilliant idea of enlisting Carly Coulter's aid in altering some regular game boards and the pieces so Luke could play them. Carly used dots of resin to accomplish that.

Luke took to gaming with enthusiasm. He loved playing checkers, Monopoly, and Scrabble. At first he was a bit slow, but with practice he got faster. He also became quite a good poker player and enjoyed canasta. Of an evening, they often gathered around the table, and the kitchen rang with laughter.

Zach felt as if they were becoming a true family, and he told Luke that. "When Mandy and I get married, you'll always have a home with us, so no worrying, okay?"

Zach was, without question, madly in love with Mandy. The musical lilt of her voice warmed him. He couldn't hear her laugh without chuckling. Over time, he discovered she had a zany sense of humor that complemented his own, and a competitive spirit. When they played games, she was always bent on winning. When Luke or Zach happened to trounce her, she teasingly vowed to get even, and the next night, she usually did. Zach could easily imagine himself spending the rest of his life with her. In fact, he couldn't imagine being without her. He never mentioned marriage to her, but the possibility was constantly on his mind. Surely, he convinced himself, she would eventually realize they were meant to be together and would agree to become his wife.

The alternative, to him, was unthinkable.

Chapter Twenty-one

The morning of June 2, Zach decided to go to the ranch later in the day so he could help Mandy with the Tuesday cleaning. At his house, he had a housekeeper, but Mandy had refused his offer to hire someone to come in at her place to do all the menial chores. That bothered Zach, mainly because he suspected Mandy wanted to avoid becoming any more indebted to him than she already was. In her mind, if she got in so deep she couldn't pay him back, he might feel it gave him a hold on her.

They had been involved in an intimate relationship now since late March, and during that time, Zach had done everything in his power to prove he was nothing like her father. Yet she still didn't trust him, not in the deep, unconditional way he yearned for, anyway. He didn't understand that. The last two months had been the happiest of his life, and every signal from Mandy told Zach she felt the same way. Luke liked him, too, and had made his approval plain. Despite the fact that they kept two households, the arrangement they had was almost perfect. Why was she so reluctant to take the next natural step and make the bond between them sacred and unbreakable?

Zach had just folded a load of clothes and was putting a stack of Mandy's panties in her drawer when he accidentally uncovered a plastic disk. Birth-control pills? If she'd been taking them before meeting him, she wouldn't have been worried that first night when the condom tore, so Zach felt it was safe to assume she'd gotten the pills afterward and had chosen not to tell him. He opened the case and saw that she'd almost completed a cycle; she'd been on the pill for at least a month, if not longer.

Zach's stomach knotted as he slipped the disk back into her drawer. Leaving the rest of the laundry on the foot of the bed, he went in search of Mandy. He found her at the kitchen sink, scrubbing the stove burner plates. He rested his hips against the edge of the counter and leaned back slightly so he could see her face.

"Hey," he said, trying to keep any note of accusation out of his tone. "I was just putting clothes away and found some birth-control pills in your drawer."

She nodded. "I went to the clinic right after we first made love."

Zach searched her face. "Why, Mandy? I always use protection."

She rinsed a plate and set it on a towel to dry. "Yes, but as we both know, prophylactics aren't always effective. I can't risk getting pregnant." She lifted her slender shoulders in a shrug. "It's not that I doubt my ability to raise a child alone. I'd love to have a baby and think I'd be a great mom. But caring for Luke is already almost more than I can handle. So it's best if I play it safe—for now, anyway."

Zach couldn't feel his feet. He crossed to the table and sank onto a kitchen chair, staring at her back in bewilderment. "Do you honestly think I'd get you pregnant and leave you in the lurch?" he asked. "No way, Mandy. I'd marry you. You wouldn't be a single mom with a blind brother to look after. I'd be there to help out. I like Luke and truly enjoy having him around. As for a baby, I can't claim to be an old hand at changing diapers, but I'm a quick study. We'd raise our child together."

Mandy turned from the sink, her face losing color as she emphatically shook her head. "I've been up front with you from the start, Zach. I will *never* get married, not to you or anyone else. I just can't go there."

Zach tried to stay calm. "I understand you have more reason than most women to feel uneasy about marriage, but I figured you'd get past that with time. Now that you've come to know me, surely you realize I'd never hurt you or be a dictatorial husband."

"You definitely won't, because I'll never give you a chance."

Zach felt as if a horse had just kicked him in the solar plexus. Looking at her beloved face, every line of which had been engraved on his heart, he suddenly felt as if he were facing a stranger. Dimly he was aware that Luke had emerged from his bedroom and stood frozen in the doorway.

"We have a great thing going between us, Zach. Why can't you be content with that? I love you." She pressed a fist to her chest. "I truly do. But loving you doesn't mean I want to marry you."

As a small child, Zach had liked to peer into his mother's curio cabinet at all her knickknacks. His favorite piece had been a beautiful little hummingbird made of blown glass. At certain times of day when the light had struck it just right, it sent out a rainbow of color. One afternoon, the temptation to touch it became so strong that he lifted the hummingbird from the shelf with his clumsy little fingers and lost his hold on it. The figurine shattered into tiny fragments. To this day, he remembered staring at the shimmering pieces, wishing he could glue them back together.

He felt exactly that same way now. Unbeknownst to him until this moment, his relationship with Mandy was made of blown glass, beautiful on the surface, but too fragile to hold together over time.

"I love you, too," he said hoarsely, "but for me, love

and marriage go hand in hand. What do you expect of me, Mandy, to just keep things as they are indefinitely with no thought of our future? I want to have babies with you. I want to grow old with you and sit on the veranda someday to watch our grandchildren play in the yard. I can't sneak around to have sex with you for the rest of my life." He glanced uneasily at Luke. "I want and need more, and damn it, I think I deserve more."

Mandy's eyes went round and filled with tears. Her mouth trembled as she said, "You undoubtedly do, Zach, but I have nothing more to offer."

Zach pushed to his feet and went to the bathroom to collect his toiletry items. Next he went to the bedroom to get his changes of clothes. Mandy trailed behind him. From the doorway, she asked, "What are you doing?"

Zach couldn't believe it had come to this. "I think that's obvious. I'm leaving."

She gripped the doorframe as if she needed the support. "For good?"

"That will depend on you," he told her. "You are in serious need of some counseling. Your father is a heartless bastard, and I totally understand why you have trust issues. But if you really love me, Mandy, you'll get some help and move forward. "

Zach pushed past her, briefly touched Luke's shoulder as he stepped around him to collect Rosebud, and then left the house.

Mandy couldn't move. The slam of the front door resounded in her ears. She was shaking so badly that she could barely stand up.

Luke went to the table and slumped on a chair. "Well, Mands, you did a bang-up job of getting rid of him. I hope that was what you wanted."

"Shut up, Luke," she said in a thin, quavering voice. "This is none of your business."

"Damn right it's my business. He's sharing my sister's

bed and living at our house. I heard the whole thing. How could you talk to him that way?"

Tears streamed down Mandy's cheeks. "Is it so wrong to be honest? What would you suggest, that I lie to him?"

Luke shook his head. "I suggest that you take Zach's advice and get some counseling. A really great guy just did everything but beg you to marry him, and you turned him down, not because you don't love him, but because our father is such a jerk." In agitation, he tapped the floor with his cane. "How do you think Zach felt when you told him you'd never give him a chance to hurt you or be a dictatorial husband? You as much as said, straight out, that you believe he *would* hurt you and be a bastard if you gave him an opportunity. He didn't deserve that from you, Mandy. It was a horrible thing to say to him. He's never done one damn thing that wasn't in our best interests and you know it."

"Don't swear," she said. Autopilot. She needed to think.

"Then don't be a stupid idiot."

Mandy needed to be alone. She went to her office and tried to work, but she could barely see through her tears. Zach Harrigan was a proud man. She knew he wouldn't come crawling back. And, oh, God, she already missed him, and he'd been gone for only an hour. How was she going to feel after a week or a month?

Counseling. Mandy didn't believe talking to someone about her deepest fears would make a difference. Why couldn't she be like other women? Zach would marry her in a blink. He was handsome and fun to be with and kind. In short, he was a dream come true. Why, then, did the thought of marrying him make her feel as if she couldn't breathe? She'd overcome her aversion to alcohol by taking a drink. Why couldn't she overcome her aversion to marriage by simply saying, "I do"?

Mandy buried her face in the fold of her arm and wept until her temples throbbed. She loved Zach with all her heart, but marrying him would be her worst nightmare. And he was right: He did deserve more. He deserved everything, and she just didn't have it to give him. He'd find someone, someday, who was good enough for him.

No. He wouldn't. Because no one was good enough for him, including her.

Zach had never considered himself obsessive, but he caught himself checking his cell phone and answering machine fifty times a day. At first he'd been fairly sure that Mandy would break down and call him, but when a week passed, he had to accept that she might never do so. The long and short of it was that she was too messed up, and even with counseling, that might never change. *It's over*. Knowing that nearly broke Zach's heart, but he needed to get the concept through his thick skull. She refused to marry him, and Zach couldn't remain in a relationship that could never go anywhere. He'd been raised with strong values. If he shacked up with a woman indefinitely, his father would have a coronary. Zach loved Mandy, but he needed more from her than just sex.

A week became two, and two became three. Zach continued training Rosebud, determined to get the little horse ready for Luke. Zach and Mandy had crashed and burned, but that wasn't Luke's doing. Zach wanted the young man to have Rosebud. He'd made that clear when Luke called one day, so the young man knew that Rosebud was a certainty in his future.

When a month had passed without a word from Mandy, Zach told himself that the ache in his chest was fading and that he rarely thought about her now. He was moving on with his life, putting his memories of her away in a deep, hidden place inside of him.

Most of these thoughts came to Zach when he was sloshed. In the evenings, he couldn't stand the silence of the house or the silence of the phone or the emptiness in every room. God, he missed her—the lilt of her voice, her zany sense of humor, and her infectious laughter. He wondered sometimes if he would ever laugh again. He found solace in a bottle, which he knew was foolish, but a part of him felt a sense of satisfaction with every swallow. For Mandy, he'd stopped drinking almost entirely, and she still hadn't wanted to build a life with him. So what difference did it make if he drank? He was hurting no one but himself.

One evening the phone rang. Mandy's name popped up in the display window. Zach's heart leaped with joy. Then he told himself to get a grip. There were a hundred different reasons why she could be calling. It was highly unlikely that she'd changed her mind about allowing him to put a wedding ring on her finger.

"Yo, this is Zach."

"Hey, Zach, it's Luke."

Zach dropped onto a chair and squeezed his eyes closed. *Idiot.* Of course it wasn't Mandy calling. He'd been crazy to let himself hope it was. "Hi, Luke. How's it going?"

"I just called to give you an update. Detective Randolph called to tell us the forensics report came back today. In addition to some other evidence I'm not clear on, Mom's hyoid bone was broken, and the medical examiner's office has ruled it as death by manual strangulation. Mandy wouldn't have had the strength in her hands to break that bone, and other stuff rules her out and implicates our father. He's been formally charged with murder. He's screaming to high heaven that he isn't guilty, but no one believes him. It'll probably be months before he goes to trial, but it'll happen eventually. I'm hoping the bastard gets a life sentence."

Zach wondered how Mandy was handling the news. Her worst fear had been that her mother had endured a torturous demise, and Zach didn't think strangulation was a painless way to go. "How's Mandy doing?"

"Not good," Luke replied. "She's lost heaps of weight since you left. I know that because she bought some smaller belts to hold her slacks and jeans up. Then this afternoon after Randolph called, she got on the computer to look up manual strangulation and learned that it can take several minutes for the victim to die. She went totally over the edge, man."

Zach felt as if a knife has been plunged into his heart. He'd never meant for things to turn out this way. "I'm really sorry to hear that, buddy."

Luke sighed. "Not your fault. I heard what she said to you that morning. I would've walked out, too."

"Where is she now?" Zach couldn't resist asking.

"Lying down. I think she cried herself to sleep."

Zach wished ... Oh, hell, he didn't know what he wished. "Well, it's a small offering, but I got some news today, too. Maybe it'll cheer her up. Steve Ristol, the guy who abused Tornado, was convicted this morning on forty-three separate counts of animal cruelty, and in Oregon each offense is a felony. He's being sent up for twenty-five years, and he won't be eligible for parole for fifteen. If he gets out early, he'll never be allowed to work with horses again without jeopardizing his freedom."

When Zach and Luke ended the call, Zach sat in the deepening shadows of the kitchen, staring at nothing. Maybe he should take Rosebud over for a visit with Luke. Or he might call Mandy to express his condolences. Better yet, why didn't he just show up on her doorstep and sweep her into his arms? To hell with worrying about their future.

In the end, though, all Zach did was crack open a new jug of whiskey. He and Mandy were poles apart on the subject of marriage. If there was any one thing that Frank Harrigan had taught Zach during his growing-up years, it was to always be true to himself. Zach had had sex with women outside of marriage. What single man who reached his thirties hadn't? But he could never be in a long-term relationship without making it right in the eyes of God. It just wasn't how he was wired.

If he went back to Mandy on her terms and she accidentally got pregnant, Zach would want to marry her and give the child his name. Mandy would never agree to that. Frank Harrigan truly would have a heart attack if a grandchild of his was raised as a bastard. Old-fashioned term, but Frank was an old-fashioned man, and that was how he would see it: that Zach's kid wasn't getting a fair shake. Zach agreed. Maybe he was as hopelessly old-fashioned as his father, but he didn't know how to change.

He'd made it for more than a month without her. Seeing her now would only prolong the torture. She'd drawn the line in the dirt. He couldn't step over it and be the man she wanted him to be. It just wasn't in him.

Another two weeks dragged by. Late one evening, Zach was well into a bottle of tequila, his new poison of choice, when a knock came at the door. He swore under his breath. His family was concerned about him, and lately they'd been taking turns coming over. The nightly visits, though well-intentioned, were starting to wear on Zach's nerves. It wasn't as if he were suicidal or anything. A man had a right to drink if he wanted. Why couldn't they just leave him the hell alone?

He shoved to his feet and strode over to the door. By his calculations, it was Quincy's turn to come tonight. As Zach drew the door open, he said, "If you brought another green smoothie, you're going to be wearing it when you leave."

Shock coursed through him when he saw Mandy standing on his porch. She was alarmingly frail. Her face was so pale that her hazel eyes looked gigantic. Zach stared at her stupidly for several seconds before he found the presence of mind to invite her in.

She stepped over the threshold and moved aside so he could shut the door.

He gestured at the table. "Have a seat."

She wore a lightweight summer blouse the color of a watermelon rind without the streaks, and a pair of white capris. Both garments swallowed her. Luke hadn't exaggerated: She'd lost a shitload of weight.

She took a chair. Zach saw her gaze shift to the bottle of tequila. Then she flicked a questioning look at him.

He shrugged. "I'm three sheets to the wind. So shoot me. I lost the love of my life a month and a half ago, and I'm drowning my sorrow in booze." When she said nothing, he joined her at the table and refilled his tumbler, bypassing ice. He would have shot the damned stuff straight into his vein if that had been an option. "I pretty much gave up drinking for you," he told her as he took a slug. "You tossed me aside like so much garbage anyway. So what's the frigging point? Abstaining sucks."

She leaned across the table and took the glass from his hand. "You haven't lost me," she told him, her voice tremulous. "I took your advice and started seeing a counselor."

Zach's heart jerked. "And?"

"The sessions haven't brought about a magical cure, but I am working through my problems."

"That's nice." Great answer. *Careful, Zach. She's broken your heart once. Don't open yourself up to it again.* "So where does that leave us, Mandy, still on hold?"

Her eyes clung to his. "I came here tonight to ask a favor. It'll probably sound stupid."

"What kind of favor?"

"To please not give up on me." Her eyes went bright with tears. "I've been so worried that you'll find someone else that I can't sleep at night. I'm still not ready to get married yet, but I think I will be eventually. I just need to know you're willing to wait."

Zach sank back in the chair. She was worried that he'd find someone else? If it hadn't been so sad, he would have laughed. He'd looked high and low for the right lady, and Mandy was it for him. "Mandy, please don't take this wrong, but where the hell were you when I told you how much I love you? There'll never be anyone else."

"Truly?"

Zach's stomach was in knots and his hands had started to shake. He grabbed the tequila bottle and took three big swallows. Wiping his mouth, he whacked the jug back down on the table. "I seldom say things I don't mean." He passed a hand over his eyes. "I love you. So much I can't think of a way to describe it. I'll happily wait if you're going to counseling and seriously trying to get your act together."

"Oh, yes, I am seriously trying. It—" She broke off and smoothed the palm of her hand over the tabletop. "It isn't easy. I can't tell you how many times I've gone to a session and wished you were there. I'm discovering—and this isn't easy to admit—that I'm a lot more mixed-up than I realized." She tapped her nails against the waxed walnut surface. "I've almost called you so many times. Just to talk, you know. To tell you about the day's session and what I got out of it. Sometimes I'd get your number almost dialed and then lose my nerve at the last second."

Zach swallowed hard. That last line sounded all too familiar. He'd been doing the same thing. "I wish you had kept dialing. I didn't know you were going to counseling. These last few weeks would have been a lot easier if I'd known that."

"I . . . I went today, too. It was . . . I think . . . sort of a turning point. So I had to come and tell you about it."

"I'm listening." Zach propped his crossed his arms on the tabletop. "Shoot."

She looked him directly in the eye. "I wanted to tell you that I realized I've been a total fool. That without your support, I don't think I can do this. That I need you as a sounding board. That I need to hear your take on my feelings. And I needed to come here tonight and tell you personally, not over the phone, but straight to your face, that I'm sorry for what I said to you that last morning. It was a horrible thing to say, and you didn't—" She gulped. "You didn't deserve that. I wish I could take it back, but I can't. Just please know I didn't mean it to hurt you. I didn't even mean it at all. It just popped out. I was feeling trapped and scared to death that I'd ... that I'd lose you if I didn't agree to your terms, and I said it without thinking. I don't believe you'd ever do *anything* to hurt me, and I know you'd never be dictatorial. It was a stupid thing to say, and I hope ... well, someday I hope you'll find it in your heart to forgive me."

Zach stood up and opened his arms. "Come here, sweetheart."

She leaped up, circled the table, and launched herself at him with such force that she knocked him straight back into the wall. He didn't care. Tightening his embrace, he buried his face in her hair. "Over the years when we quarrel, both of us are going to say things occasionally that we'll wish later we hadn't said. I'll forgive you for what you said to me that morning if you'll promise to give me a pass in the future when I stick my foot in my mouth. I have an unfortunate talent for it. Do we have a deal?"

She laughed softly, the sound wet and smothered. "That strikes me as being a great deal."

"I didn't think I'd ever hold you like this again," he whispered. "It feels so damned good to have you in my arms."

She hugged his neck. "It feels good to be here. Right, Zach, perfectly and absolutely right."

He swayed with her, wondering as he did if he wasn't a little more toasted than he'd thought. "If you really need my support to get through this, Mandy, how would you feel about it if I went to the counseling sessions with you?"

She leaned back to search his expression. "You'd do that for me?"

Zach couldn't help but smile. "Mandy, I'd cut off my right arm for you."

"The sessions are boring. The counselor goes over and over stuff with me. You'd probably go brain-dead."

"I doubt it. Nothing about you bores me. And being there, hearing how you feel and why you feel that way, might help me to understand you better. I think that might be a very good thing. Counseling can take you only so far. Then you'll have to do the rest. It only makes sense for us to tackle your problems as a couple. Don't you agree?"

She smiled. "I'd love to have you go with me. That would be awesome."

Zach didn't want to let go of her, but he felt her try to pull away and forced his arms to his sides.

"Well," she said softly. "I, um . . . As soon as I get my next appointment scheduled, I'll give you a call. Maybe we can meet at the clinic. Would that work?"

Zach realized she meant to leave. "No, that won't work."

She looked startled. "It won't?"

"No. If we're going to tackle your problems as a couple, then we should *be* a couple. You've got two choices. I can move back to your place, or you and Luke can move in here. I vote for the latter. This house is larger. Luke can be with Rosebud almost full-time. My home office will be a better working environment for you, and I'll leave less of a carbon imprint if I'm not driving back and forth."

"But I'm not ready for marriage yet, and you said—"

"I know what I said, but that was when you'd ruled out the possibility of marriage. Now you're working on that. It's a whole different kettle of fish. So, you choose, your place or mine?"

She ran back into his arms. "I don't care where I live,

Zach. All I care about is being with you. You could pitch a tent and I'd be happy."

He chuckled. "I think I can do a little better than that." He held her close, reveling in the feel of her against him. "There is one thing. My dad is old-fashioned. For the sake of Harrigan family harmony, would it bother you to wear an engagement ring? It can be a real engagement—or not. I won't push you on that. But it will be easier for my dad to accept us living together if he believes our intent is to get married soon."

She slipped her slender arms around his neck and leaned back to smile up at him. "I'd love to have an engagement ring. And it won't be a fake engagement, Zach. My intent truly is to marry you. I'm just taking the long way around. But I love you, I want you, and I want terribly to spend my life with you."

Those were, without question, the most wonderful words Zach had ever heard. She truly did mean to marry him. He didn't care how long it took them to get there. Mandy was worth the wait.

"Ring shopping tomorrow. We'll celebrate over lunch. Sound good?"

"It sounds divine."

Zach kissed her then. The instant their mouths met, desire flared through his veins. He bent to catch her behind the knees, lifted her into his arms, and carried her up the stairs to the master suite. Clothes, boots, and shoes went flying. They fell on the bed, so hungry for each other that their lovemaking was almost frantic. Zach tried to hold himself in check and wait, but it had been too long. His body screamed for release.

"I'm sorry," he told her.

"Need you," she whispered. "Need you, need you, need you."

Zach thrust deeply into her. She arched to meet him. As her wet heat enveloped him, he felt as if he'd been lost and had finally found his way home.

"Don't *ever* leave me again," she murmured against his shoulder. "Don't ever, Zach. I don't think I could bear it."

Zach struggled to slow his pace, wanting to make this as pleasurable for her as it was for him. But when she said that and he heard the sincerity in her voice, he lost it. His body clenched. He pushed in deep. She cried out and met him with an eager tilt of her hips. They clung to each other as a galvanic climax rocked them to the core.

Afterward when they lay wrapped in each other's arms and Zach had caught his breath, he pressed a kiss to her forehead and told her, "Never worry that I'll leave you again, Mandy mine. This time around I'm here to stay."

Epilogue

Six months later

Mandy stood in the vestibule of St. Catherine's, so nervous her knees were knocking. She plucked at her wedding gown, readjusted her veil, and turned frantically to Luke, who was going to give her away. "Please tell me I didn't just mess up my hair."

The moment she spoke, Mandy realized how stupid that was. Her brother couldn't see her, but he was managing so well on his own now that she occasionally forgot. He smiled slightly. "You didn't. Your hair looks perfect, and so do you. When I smell beautiful, I know it, and you're beautiful today, Mands. Absolutely beautiful."

Mandy giggled. "You're looking pretty darned good yourself." Zach had chosen to wear a Western-style tux, insisting that all males in the wedding party follow suit. She straightened Luke's bolo tie, a gift from Zach that sported a chunk of amber that glinted in the light coming through the windows. "You make a very handsome cowboy."

Her brother grinned. "I hope Laurie thinks so."

Luke and Laurie had been dating hot and heavy. She had her own car and was out at the ranch so often that Mandy was coming to think of her as a member of the family. Because Luke and Laurie were so young, Mandy doubted the relationship would last, but Frank Harrigan, whom she now called Dad, assured her that twenty-year-old kids could and did fall in love and stay together. He and his first wife, Emily, had married young. He claimed that first loves were the truest and ran the deepest.

Mandy took that to be a good omen for her and Zach. He was her very first true love, and he often told her that she was his.

"You okay?" Luke asked. "Don't do a runaway-bride thing on me. I can't see to chase you down."

Mandy hooked arms with him. "I am perfectly fine. I'm ready for this, Luke. I truly am. The last thing I want to do is run."

And she meant that from the bottom of her heart. As promised, Zach had gone to counseling with her, never missing a single session, and afterward they'd spent hours talking about her feelings. Zach had also spent a lot of hours wanting to break into the prison and bludgeon her father, but for Mandy, even Zach's anger had been healing. She knew now, deep within, that Zach would never be like her dad. He was funny, sexy, sweet, and always her rock, no matter how crazily her emotions oscillated.

Mandy couldn't remember ever being so happy. Zach had built her a gorgeous greenhouse at the ranch where she could dabble with her plants, and he insisted that she start college as soon as possible to get a degree in horticulture so she could open her own nursery in town. Mandy had already quit her job and hoped to enroll at the university for the spring quarter.

Her life had become exciting, wonderful, and filled with promise.

She leaned over in front of Luke to pat Rosebud on the head. "Are you ready, sweetheart? Don't let all those people in there make you feel nervous."

"They won't make her nervous," Luke said. "She likes crowds. Her only problem today will be that you're suddenly getting all the attention. She's used to the spotlight."

Mandy laughed. "Too bad, Rosebud. This is *my* day to shine."

The mini had completed her training and, as Zach had predicted months before, she was an amazing guide animal. She had become Luke's constant companion. Recently Zach had received notification that the agency in charge of the Americans with Disabilities Act had voted to ban many species as service animals, and horses of all sizes were on the list. Fortunately, the ruling hadn't yet come into effect, and Zach had the financial support of his entire family to launch a campaign to get the ruling reversed. He vowed to take it clear to the Supreme Court, if necessary.

Mandy could only pray that the decision would be overturned. Rosebud would be with Luke until he was almost fifty, unless something unexpected happened. With Carly Coulter's help, Luke now managed to get around quite well with a cane, but Rosebud gave him increased confidence, allowing him access to places where he might have hesitated to go without her. And she was such a little lady, perfectly mannered and calm, regardless of what went on around her. If she was banned as an assistance animal, Luke would keep her, utilizing her services in places where her status didn't matter. But ideally, he should be able to have Rosebud accompany him to college. He was enrolled for the winter term, and the mini would make it a lot easier for him to find his way around.

Animals generally weren't allowed in a Roman Catholic church proper, but Rosebud was welcome because she was a service animal. Father Mike, who'd given Mandy and Zach their marriage preparation classes, was choosing to ignore the rumors about horses being banned. He'd gotten to know Rosebud well over the last few months. An Irishman with a thick brogue, he'd said during the rehearsal last night that anyone who thought a mini guide horse like Rosebud was unfit to perform the task had a blindfold over his eyes.

Mandy heard the first strains of organ music and nervously clutched Luke's arm. "She's warming up. She's going to play a couple of numbers before the wedding march. We need to listen for her cue. I don't want to be late for my own wedding."

As if Luke sensed her mounting anxiety, he bumped his arm against her shoulder. "So when are you and Zach planning to leave for your honeymoon?"

"After the reception. Cookie will have Tornado and Whirlwind in the trailer, ready to go, and we already packed our supplies." Mandy and Zach planned a week in a California wilderness area. She couldn't imagine anything more romantic, just the two of them and the horses, enjoying pristine lakes, fishing, and swimming, taking hikes to scenic spots, and making love whenever the mood came over them. Tornado had become Mandy's horse. When she rode him, he was a perfect gentleman. Last week, he'd even allowed Zach to get on his back and he hadn't acted up. Like Mandy, the stallion was finding his way back to sanity and leaving the past behind him. "Zach wants to be on the road before dark. We'll spend tonight at the trailhead and head up in the morning."

"I wish I could go."

"No way, Luke. It's our honeymoon." Zach had gotten Luke a saddle similar to those that Bethany Kendrick used, and now Mandy's brother went riding on the ranch practically every day. He loved it. "This spring we'll go again, and you can go with us. But this time, you're staying with Frank and Dee Dee."

The opening thrum of the wedding march vibrated through the church. "That's our cue," Mandy whispered.

"Calm down. You look fabulous. I can smell beautiful, remember."

Mandy lowered her veil and held fast to her brother's arm. Together they stepped forward, Rosebud steadfast at Luke's side. Mandy thought of all the people who would be staring at her as she walked up the aisle. The church was packed. The Harrigans, their many friends, and Sam's in-laws were present. Even the filthy-rich Kendricks had accepted the invitation. In fact, Bethany and Ryan's daughter, Chastity, was the flower girl. Clint's son, Trevor, now ten, had been chosen as the ring bearer.

"Oh, God, maybe I'll run after all."

"Don't you dare," Luke whispered. "Just find Zach, Mands. Keep your eyes on him, and nothing else will matter."

Luke was right. As Mandy stepped inside the church proper with her brother, she sought out Zach. He stood with his back to the altar to watch her walk toward him. The moment their gazes locked, all her anxiety drained away. It didn't matter if her hair was mussed, or whether her train was trailing straight behind her. Zach loved her. And he was waiting, his expression solemn yet aglow with happiness.

The nuptial Mass was beautiful. Mandy anticipated making her vows with no sense of dread. With Zach's support, she'd benefited greatly from the counseling sessions. She had come to understand herself and had learned to deal with her fears instead of always trying to run from them. She felt confident now, and she knew, deep in her heart, that Zach would be a wonderful, loving husband.

When it was her turn to say "I do," Mandy looked into Zach's eyes and said the words loudly, clearly, and with absolute certainty. Marriage truly was a life sentence, but it wasn't in hell. It was going to be the closest thing to heaven that Mandy would ever find here on earth.

She loved this man. She wanted to fall asleep in his

arms every single night and awaken beside him in the morning. She wanted to laugh with him, play with him, cry with him, and face the trials of life with him. How could any woman wish for more?

Zach Harrigan was her everything.

Special Note to My Readers

In the autumn of 2009, the U.S. Department of Justice, in charge of overseeing and enforcing the Americans with Disabilities Act, removed many species from the list of sanctioned assistance animals. With a heavy heart I must inform you that horses of all kinds have been banned. In my opinion, this is a shame, and I hope to see this ruling reversed soon. Please get on the Internet to inform yourself about mini guide horses, and if you would like to see this ruling reversed, please flood the Department of Justice with letters asking for more hearings to reconsider this law. Well-trained mini horses of an appropriate size are incredible service animals. Please join me in asking for horses to be returned to the list of sanctioned assistant animals, with strict regulations to govern their size and the quality of their training. Some sight-impaired individuals cannot have a guide dog, for one reason or another, and well-trained mini horses provide them with a viable alternative.